TOM GA

Tom Gallacher was best known as a playwright until the publication of his short stories, APPRENTICE, which won a 1983 Scottish Arts Council award. His greatest achievements in the theatre were the three plays MR JOYCE IS LEAVING PARIS, SCHELLENBRACK and REVIVAL! The three books APPRENTICE, JOURNEYMAN and SUR-VIVOR form a trilogy. THE JEWEL MAKER won a Scottish Arts Council award.

Apart from London, Tom Gallacher has worked in Denmark, Germany, New York, Montreal, Edinburgh and Dublin. He has now returned to Scotland and lives in Glasgow.

sceptre

Tom Gallacher

THE WIND ON THE HEATH

First published in Great Britain in
1987 by Hamish Hamilton Ltd.

Sceptre edition 1989

Sceptre is an imprint of Hodder and
Stoughton Paperbacks, a division of
Hodder and Stoughton Ltd.

British Library C.I.P.

Gallacher, Tom
    The wind on the heath.
    I. Title
    823'.914 [F]

    ISBN 0-340-50801-9

Printed and bound in Great Britain
for Hodder and Stoughton Paper-
backs, a division of Hodder and
Stoughton Ltd., Mill Road, Dunton
Green, Sevenoaks, Kent TN13
2YA. (Editorial Office: 47 Bedford
Square, London WC1B 3DP) by
Richard Clay Ltd., Bungay, Suffolk.

CONTENTS

'There's the wind on the heath, brother;
if I could only feel that, I would gladly
live for ever.'

George Borrow, *Lavengro*

THE WIND ON THE HEATH

DAME ANNIE JEYNOR

I would not be in a position to tell Annie Jeynor's story were it not for the fact that my wife, too, is an actress. A few years ago she signed on for a season with the Citizens Theatre in Glasgow. As I have a great fondness for Scotland, and Barbara, I went north with her. There was nothing to detain me in London anyway. I'd just completed a trilogy of books about my experiences as a marine engineer and was beginning to think there would not be anything else for me to write about which compelled enough of my interest. The fear persisted when we rented a flat above Sauchiehall Street, but there, at least, I could persuade myself I was really on holiday.

Although I'd grown up knowing the name Annie Jeynor, I'd never seen her on stage. Indeed, I'd never seen her at all until she appeared in a television interview which purported to celebrate her life and achievements.

I watched it, sitting alone in the Glasgow flat, waiting for Barbara to get back from the latest extravaganza in Gorbals.

The interviewer was respectful of the legendary stage lady. There she was – poised and witty on a brocade-covered chair; a small dainty woman who'd long ago learned the great virtue of sitting at ease and perfectly still; willing to answer whatever she was asked, but just as willing to confess what she didn't know, or that she couldn't understand the question. I turned the volume control higher and began to pay close attention.

She was being asked why she had never permitted a biography to be published. Apparently she had even gone to court and obtained an injunction against Dr Angela Sleavin who'd written an unofficial biography. 'Why did you do that?' the interviewer asked.

'Because Dr Sleavin was only interested in what I'd done insofar as it confirmed *her* reasons for why I'd done it.'

I felt myself grinning at the disdainful face on the screen. I'd never heard of Dr Sleavin, but I was absolutely sure the actress had hit a nail squarely on the head.

'You read her book, then?'

'Certainly.' The lady smiled an implacable smile. 'There was always the chance that Dr Sleavin had discovered a little truth among all the facts.' She shrugged despairingly. 'Or even a little of me.'

I wanted to know there and then what she meant by that. But the questioner steered quickly back to safe ground. His guest's remarkable debut in *Twelfth Night* was mentioned, and she was asked if she could remember any lines from her role as Viola.

The lady smiled. 'Why, yes. Of course. I can remember all of it.'

'Really?' The interviewer just managed to conceal his incredulity. 'That was fifty years ago!'

'Yes. But it's a well-known play . . . and the words haven't changed.'

I smiled but the interviewer did not respond to her bantering tone. Sternly he suggested, 'Perhaps you'd do one of Viola's speeches for us now.'

'If you like. Remember, though, that Viola is a young girl.' She leaned forward and tapped the interviewer's knee. 'So, close your eyes.' Then she turned directly to camera and asked the viewers, 'Will you close your eyes, too?'

I closed mine. And, what I heard was not a seventy-five-year-old woman reciting, but the voice of a girl, achingly sincere and vulnerable, confessing a love which could not be requited. It was a speech we'd been taught at school but I was caught unprepared for the freshness and painful reality of the moment. I experienced a feeling of guilt that I should eavesdrop on such an intimate revelation.

Then, suddenly, the woman in her chair was Dame Annie Jeynor again, smiling at the reaction she'd produced. The interviewer bubbled with astonishment and praise then, somewhat incautiously, remarked, 'It was very brave of you to attempt that.'

The old woman's blue, vital eyes glittered slightly and she repeated the word: '"Attempt"?' She shook her head with polite impatience. 'Not at all brave. If I hadn't been perfectly sure I could do it well, I wouldn't have done it at all.' Her hand described a graceful, modest gesture. 'Making a hash of it would have been so embarrassing . . . for *you*.'

Again, I was grinning, but the young man was embarrassed. He preferred subjects who stuck to the pre-arranged outline, or who ad-libbed only predictable things. To compensate for his unease, his smile became even more expansive.

'It really is amazing that you can still remember the lines of your first role.'

'No. Viola was not my first role. Before that I was in a Sunday tryout at the Royal Court. I can't remember anything of the play.' For a moment a look of pain hovered on her face. She brushed the thought away and added, 'Even the author wanted to forget it.'

'Really? And now the author's forgotten, I suppose.'

'No. He was J. M. Barrie.'

The interviewer sat a little straighter. 'Oh! What did you think of Barrie?'

'I liked him,' she said firmly. Then – surely with no intention of mischief – she added, 'He had no patience with foolish questions.' The old lady tilted her head slightly, and to me it looked as though she was inviting the next foolish question.

The interviewer avoided the trap by merely making an observation which would get them back to the next item on his list. 'I suppose you've met a lot of famous people.'

I groaned. It was like asking a jackpot pools winner how it feels to be rich. (It feels fine. Naturally, it feels just fine. God! Who *hires* these television interviewers?)

Annie Jeynor was used to such inanities. She nodded, 'Oh, yes. Many famous people. And some of them were interesting as well. Marie of Romania, for example. She was a fascinating woman. She gave me this brooch.' Dame Annie fingered the sapphire and diamond rosette on the lapel of her suit. As arranged, the profile camera closed in on the brooch which was in the form of a rose; a blue rose. The curved petals of sapphire were separated and enhanced by the strings of tiny diamonds. But the young man failed to ask why the Queen of Romania had made such a gift. I wriggled in my chair. How could anyone be so incompetent? It transpired that he had on his clipboard a good quote which he was anxious to get at. First the lead-in. 'The only thing I know about Marie of Romania was written by Dorothy Parker.' He glanced just past Dame Annie's chair so that he could read the cue card and give the impression he knew the lines by heart.

> '"Oh, life is a glorious cycle of song,
> A medley of extemporanea;
> And love is a thing that can never go wrong;
> And I am Marie of Romania."'

'Poor Dorothy,' the old lady recalled, 'she was such a *moaner!*' The interviewer did not pursue that either, and his subject, who had gone through this routine many, many times before, obligingly named the names with which an Arts programme television audience would be familiar.

This fascination with famous names was something which puzzled me. The public took pleasure, apparently, in just seeing someone who'd been on friendly terms with celebrated persons, regardless of what they were celebrated *for*. And interviewers never wanted to know what lay behind the well-documented façade of those who'd filled the headlines and the newsreels. All they really wanted was more façade. As Annie Jeynor rattled through her stock of brief, amusing anecdotes, it obviously did not occur to her that she too was party to evading the truth.

Only when the programme was nearly over did it become evident that there would be no coverage of the subject's early life. Strict agreement had obviously been reached before Dame Annie would come anywhere near the studio as to which sort of questions were allowed and, more specifically, which would not even be alluded to. The enraptured audience, therefore, could be left to assume that the actress had simply materialised as a beautiful young woman in her early twenties, accomplished and ready to be adored by James Agate.

But even that young woman was worlds away from this rich eccentric. For the interview did establish that she was rich. Apparently her wealth had been made, and was sustained, by the half-dozen films she'd made during the 1940s in Hollywood. Contrary to established practice at the time, she had taken a small salary and a substantial percentage of gross, and those films had been earning increasing sums for her over forty years. Little wonder, then, that she could afford a permanent suite at the Dorchester. The interviewer asked if she intended to go on living there.

'No. I'm moving away from London,' she said. 'I've bought a house in Scotland.'

'Scotland!' He could not prevent amusement as well as surprise getting into the word.

The lady raised her eyebrows at his tone but offered no further information on this bizarre decision. She was giving nothing away. And yet, a little later, something did slip through. And it was that something which, however undefined, persuaded me there was more to this celebrated actress than her profession or celebrity. It was as though two people occupied that brocade-covered chair, and they did not like one another. The exchange started innocuously enough.

With gallant disregard for her age the young man asked, 'What are your plans for the future?'

'The future what?'

'I mean your future roles.'

'Ah. My future role will be the hardest one of all.' The soft, well-modulated voice suddenly armed itself with an edge of spite. That is the absolutely accurate word to describe what was in her voice as she went on, 'I'm hoping, eventually, that I'll manage to be myself.'

The camera did not blink as it held the close-up and the television lights blazed down on the pause.

The interviewer gave an embarrassed chuckle. 'Haven't you always been that?'

'No. Not since I was a girl.' To my relief, the man did know when to keep his mouth shut. The old woman went on with fierce regret, 'And I hope to God I haven't killed her. That would be too much of a sacrifice . . . even for entertainment.'

When Barbara got back from the theatre I was still thinking about Annie Jeynor. I reported on the interview I'd seen, and at once she was concerned. 'That was a repeat.'

'Are you sure?'

'Yes. I saw that a few years ago.'

The thought which immediately struck both of us was that the actress must have died. It seemed the only apt reason for repeating the programme. My wife's expression was sombre. She poured more whisky in her glass and sat uneasily on the edge of the sofa.

'But surely it would have been on the news,' I said.

'Did you watch the news?'

'No.'

Barbara got up. 'I'll call Doreen. She'll know.'

'Now? It's almost midnight!'

'I've got to find out. I won't be able to sleep until I know for sure.' She went out into the long cold hall where the telephone was.

From my wife's reaction I assumed she must have known Annie Jeynor quite well, though I'd never heard her mention the friendship. Apparently there was no reply to the call. I heard Barbara dialling another number. Only then did the obvious solution occur to me: checking whether or not the interview was a scheduled programme. It was. The newspaper listing mentioned the repeat was to mark the actress's eightieth birthday.

Barbara's relief was as marked as her concern had been. She is not a woman who suppresses anything. And she told me of her association with Annie Jeynor. They'd worked together in the late 'sixties and early 'seventies when the star had returned to London after touring the world with a one-woman show. Barbara had appeared with her at the Haymarket in a series of classical revivals. Miss Jeynor was still the star, of course, and Barbara was playing supporting roles.

'I've never heard you talk about her before,' I said.

'Habit. Self-protection, really. Annie has trampled on too many important toes to use her name as any sort of recommendation. But she's a great old girl, no matter what they say about her.'

'What do they say about her?'

'Oh, the usual sort of thing, I suppose. They say it about anybody who's been wildly successful. That she's a selfish egotistical tyrant and a heartless perfectionist. That she uses her supporting players as a trampoline . . . and cuts their billing.'

'Cuts their *billing*!' I repeated in mock horror.

Barbara nodded, too concerned to be amused. 'But with Annie Jeynor they have a lot of heavier ammunition. They say she insisted on getting the principals sacked before her first big success transferred to the West End. That was in the 'twenties.' Barbara sighed at the familiar list which was probably known to everyone in the profession. 'Later, that she was too pally with the Nazis. That she deserted her only child so she could make it in Hollywood. That she ruined a cabinet minister; destroyed quite a few competing careers; and was – maybe still is – an alcoholic. Also, that she couldn't leave any man alone. All in all, a thorough-going monster.'

'And is it all true?'

'No!' Barbara protested vehemently. But almost immediately, and much less certainly, added, 'I don't know. Some of it, maybe. Most of it was before my time. All I know for sure is that she was one hell of a performer and she was very kind to me. And I'm glad she's still alive.'

In the following days the reshowing of the interview coincided with a number of feature pieces in the newspapers, which kept Annie Jeynor's name near the surface of my attention. And I could not rid myself of a fascination with those odd replies in the programme. What Barbara had told me did not fit either the image in my mind or the quite different image the television producer had tried to construct.

A few days later I idly remarked to Barbara, 'I wonder where Annie Jeynor is living now.'

'The Dorchester. She has a suite at the Dorchester.'

'No. That was four or five years ago. Remember? It was a repeat. And she said she was moving to Scotland.'

'Really?'

'Yes. She made quite a point of it.'

'In that case we must pay her a visit.'

'If we could find out where she lives,' I said.

Barbara took a thick little book out of the desk drawer and went to call one of her many contacts.

Ever since I had known Barbara it had surprised me how efficient theatre people are at finding each other. No doubt it comes of the necessity to stay in circulation in order to get work, but they all maintain the habit of constantly updating their list of secret telephone numbers. After only a couple of tries Barbara found somebody who had the information. She came back grinning broadly and waving her book. 'She bought a house in Dumbarton. That's only . . .'

'I *know* where Dumbarton is. I used to stare across at it every morning.'

'Oh, yes. I keep forgetting you're a crypto-Scotsman.'

And so there would be no difficulty about visiting Annie Jeynor – if she'd agree to see us. Dumbarton is no more than twelve miles west of Glasgow, an old county town which was the ancient capital of Strathclyde. As we continued eating breakfast I visualised the huge castle rock jutting out into the Clyde, which is about a mile wide at that point. The rock had been the upriver marker for me on many cold misty mornings as I went to work, an apprentice, across the river in Greenock. Later I'd passed through the town briefly and had not been impressed, though wide new roads had been laid over the remnants of its long-gone industrial past. It certainly was a very odd place for a famous international actress to choose for her retirement. Unless, of course, it was her home town.

'Is that where she came from?' I asked my wife.

'No. She's English.' But then again the doubt. 'I think.'

Recalling the careful evasion of her early life in the television interview it seemed clear there was a great deal which nobody knew about Annie Jeynor.

When my wife called her there was, apparently, some doubt in the old lady's mind as to which 'Barbara' she might be. For some reason – and in spite of the accent – Barbara Bel Geddes seemed to be the front runner. It wasn't until identities had been translated into theatrical terms that everything became clear. 'I was Gwendolen to your Lady Bracknell at the Aldwych,' my wife said. And from her smile it was clear she'd scored a direct hit. Several other productions were mentioned before they got down to giving and receiving instructions on how to find the house.

We found it without difficulty – a large stone-built villa standing high on the bank of the Clyde. We drove there on Wednesday afternoon late in September. Dame Annie came out on the raised porch to greet us as the car drew up. As she embraced Barbara I was astonished to see how small and thin our hostess was. But her voice was as strong and compelling as it must always have been and, as she showed us into a huge bare reception room, it was encouraging to note her energy.

She was saying, 'I can't expect you'll feel comfortable in here, but I do.' The room was very high and long. Perhaps it had been the billiards room originally, but now, though beautifully decorated, it contained no ornaments or pictures or bric-à-brac and very little furniture. There was a great acreage of open carpet, two armchairs guarding a small coffee table halfway down the room at the fireplace and two high-backed Windsor chairs some distance beyond that, drawn up at the enormous window. That was all. It seemed obvious that Dame Annie was not in the habit of entertaining more than one person at a time.

She must have noticed my inventory for she explained, 'There's no point in buying this amount of space then cluttering it up so you can't *move*.'

I smiled and nodded. You could certainly move in that room. In fact you could have fielded an athletics team without cramping anyone's style. But it was not conducive to a close and friendly conversation. Barbara and I were pressed into the armchairs and our hostess fetched one of the Windsors for herself. Not that she settled in it for very long. In the first long bout of theatre talk, from which I was largely excluded, she kept springing up and striding about to illustrate a point or jolt her memory. It brought to mind something my wife had once told me. 'The audience watches anything that moves.' We were very much the audience and, even at eighty, Dame Annie Jeynor moved with a grace and precision which was quite captivating.

The tea things were carried in by a cheerful middle-aged woman, and when she left the room again we learned something of how the house was run. The woman was Mrs MacKenzie, housekeeper and cook, whose husband was employed as gardener and general handyman. There was also a secretary-companion, Elspeth, who was having a day off. Then, over tea, I had the opportunity to ask the question I'd had in mind since we arrived. 'Why did the Queen of Romania give you the brooch?'

The old woman gave a whoop of laughter, then looked earnestly into my eyes to declare, 'For revenge, really.'

Barbara leaned forward. 'Revenge? Annie, how could that be?'

'Oh, not revenge against me.' She laughed. 'I mean, there isn't a Carpathian curse on it or anything. But it had been given to the Queen by that Lupescu woman and I was about to meet Madame Lupescu.'

She could see from our expression that the name meant nothing to us, and explained. 'It was all part of a great scandal at the time. The talk of Europe for years. You see, Marie's son had given up his right to the throne and deserted his family to go and live with his mistress, Magda Lupescu, in Paris. The country was in uproar and Magda was burned in effigy all over Bucharest. A couple of years later the king – Marie's husband – died. So it was her grandson who came to the throne. But he was only six years old! The situation was chaotic and Marie had to bear the brunt of it. All because of the Lupescu woman.

'However, in Paris things looked different. The runaway couple thought that with a new king on the throne the whole dispute was settled. Certainly Lupescu thought all the trouble was over and sent Marie a valuable sapphire and diamond brooch as a sort of peace offering.' Annie shook her head amusedly and laid down her teacup. 'Of course, I didn't know that at the time.

I was in Berlin then and Queen Marie came with a group of friends to see the performance.

'I'd met her once or twice before that, but on this occasion she gave me a gift as token of her appreciation. The brooch. That's what *she* thought of the peace offering. She gave it away to a strolling actress. In fact, she insisted that I should wear the brooch as part of my stage costume in that part.' Annie laughed. 'The point was, I was playing a famous harlot and the Queen knew we'd be taking the production to Paris where, no doubt, her son Carol and his mistress would attend. And they did. There was the usual party directly afterwards on the stage and Magda Lupescu saw exactly what Marie of Romania thought of her and her gift. Just the gaudy decoration of a whore.'

'Did Madam Lupescu say anything about it?' Barbara wanted to know.

'Not really.' Annie got to her feet and acted out this meeting – alternately playing herself, then the other woman, moving short-sightedly along the line. 'Carol was behind her. A charming man, but weak. When Magda got to me she did peer pretty close. And I looked close at her. She was a strange neurotic woman. And she had red hair . . . just like mine. Probably that's what gave Marie the idea in the first place. It was not just an actress playing a whore, but a red-headed whore too. Anyway, Madam Lupescu stared at me, then at the brooch before she stood back and remarked, "How charming you look, Miss Jeynor".'

I said, 'But that was a dirty trick to play on *you*. How did you find out about it?'

'Oh, the Queen and I became quite friendly in later years.' Annie resumed her seat. 'She told me about it herself. In fact, at the time of the English abdication crisis she suggested I might offer my services to Queen Mary.'

'What a pity you didn't,' Barbara said.

Annie shook her head vehemently. 'Oh no! That was a different situation altogether. Edward and Wallis Simpson didn't come *back*, you see. Carol and Magda Lupescu did. It could never have happened in England but, after three years exile, Carol and his mistress went back to Romania – and they gave him

21

back the crown.' She paused, then added with some indignation, 'I wouldn't give back the brooch, though.'

Barbara gasped. 'The Queen didn't ask for it back, did she?'

'No, no, no. This was much later when I was asked to return the gift. During the war. Marie was dead then, but I was still in Berlin. King Carol was just about to give in to the Nazis when Madam Lupescu wrote to me. I think she must have heard – God knows how . . . there were spies everywhere – anyway, she seemed to have heard that I wanted to get out of Germany. She thought she could help . . . at a price. The price was the brooch. Marie's insult must have had quite a sting for the effect to last that long.'

Barbara asked, 'What reason did she give?'

'Oh, she said the piece had great sentimental value – a family heirloom. Ha!' Annie tossed her head contemptuously.

'But she did offer to get you out of Germany. Why did you not take that chance?'

'Because my own escape was already planned. I was just about to make the first move. And I didn't trust the woman.'

'Maybe it *was* a family heirloom,' I said. 'She could have been attached to it.'

'If so, she took plenty to console her,' Annie said tartly. 'When Carol and Lupescu made their getaway they took a whole trainload of loot over the border into Yugoslavia, then on into Switzerland. Those boxcars were packed to the roof with other people's heirlooms, jewellery, paintings, furs, tapestries, furniture – everything valuable they could lay their hands on.' The old woman shook her head cynically. 'For years afterwards in the castles and mansions around Bucharest there was just one message scrawled over all the blank spaces on the walls: "Lupescu was here."'

I leaned back in the chair and stared at the ornate ceiling high above me. The story of the brooch had raised more questions than it answered. What was an English actress doing in Germany all that time? In particular what was she doing in Berlin during the war? And how *did* she escape? Following close on these thoughts was the realisation that this vivacious, neat little woman must have met or have known practically everybody of note during a large part of the twentieth century; and had seen them clearly from behind her own protective mask of make-believe. No doubt that was the main incentive of the biographers who'd pursued her. She was a rewarding subject. But she'd no intention of becoming an object for anybody. In the Queen of Romania story she'd told us, and several other stories she recalled that afternoon, there was always some specific point and she kept to it with admirable economy. That was why, as we were preparing to leave, I suggested, 'Why don't you write your own memoirs?'

She stopped abruptly in the middle of the hallway. 'I have thought about it. And I've tried.' She shrugged. 'But I can't write. I get nothing back from writing. It's like playing to an empty house. There's no response.'

'You could dictate it to a secretary.'

'I tried that too. That's what Elspeth was for. I took her on as a secretary-companion and now I can't stand the sight of her. But I can't very well get rid of her.'

'Why not?'

'Because it's not her fault.'

That seemed a weak reason for a tyrant. 'Perhaps you could work with another secretary,' I suggested.

Barbara immediately saw the objection to that idea. 'No, Bill. A secretary isn't an *audience*.'

The old lady nodded quick agreement. 'I believe the modern expression is "feedback". A secretary wouldn't feed back. Elspeth certainly doesn't. Though she feeds forward, abundantly. And there's no secretary who would *care*. Like Dr Sleavin. She didn't care either. Do you know, the stupid woman even seemed to think she had to *approve* of my life.'

It was then that my wife – with what forethought I did not know – stated, 'Bill cares. And I can vouch for the fact that he's a marvellous audience.'

My laugh could not conceal my embarrassment. 'I get a lot of practice.'

There was a long pause, then Annie turned on her heel and beckoned us, calling over her shoulder, 'Let's talk about that.'

Now I really was embarrassed. Surely it must seem to the famous actress underhand of Barbara to use their past association in order to weaken the long-held defence of her privacy. As we followed her back into the room we'd just left, I squeezed Barbara's arm angrily but she shook off the grip and pursued the advantage it seemed she had gained. Not for the first time did I ruefully acknowledge that I have a very pushy wife.

We stood in the centre of the bare plain of carpet and Annie Jeynor took a new look at me. Then she turned to my wife. 'He reminds me of Jamie Northcott. Did you ever meet him, Barbara?'

'No, I don't think so.'

Annie sighed. 'He was the one man I *should* have married.' She looked at me again. 'You don't dance, I suppose?'

'I'm afraid not.'

'But you can *write*?'

'There are many people who can write,' I said.

'Oh yes, I know.' She sniffed and paced carefully in a small arc in front of us. 'Perhaps you could send me something you've written.' A slight pause. 'Unless you have brought something with you.'

I said I hadn't but instinctively sensed that if I had, the matter would not have progressed beyond that polite enquiry.

She smiled as though I had passed a small test and went on, 'Meanwhile, you might like to consider whether or not you would want to write about my life.'

Barbara was about to jump at my chance but, by sheer effort of will, I stopped her. This was the second part of the test. My reply was as carefully matter-of-fact as the question. 'Yes. I'll think about it.'

'Whether you approve of it or not.'

'I can scarcely disapprove when I know so little about it.' Unfortunately that sounded as though my ignorance was due to her obscurity. She laughed and I resisted the impulse to correct the error.

'Let's have a drink,' she said, and strode to the window. There she revealed a cupboard under the window-seat stacked with enough glasses, wine and liquor to stock a bar.

Had I been a little sharper, I would have realised at the first meeting that Annie Jeynor was eager – even anxious – to go back into her past; if only she could find the right person to make the journey with her. For I'm sure it was not examples of my previous work which made up her mind in my favour. The important thing was that I reminded her of Jamie Northcott. Very often, later, when she was talking to me it might have seemed to her that she was talking to him. It was just my good fortune that I was linked so closely with someone in whom she had always confided. There was also an advantage I held over Elspeth and Angela Sleavin – in being a man.

Certainly, things moved fast after the first meeting and, with very little discussion, Barbara and I abandoned the rented Glasgow flat and went to live in Dumbarton as Annie's guests. Not before we'd checked that the guest rooms were admirably furnished and not of a daunting size. In fact, it was only that huge ground-floor reception room which was in the least spartan. But *that* was the one room in which Annie felt comfortable.

For Barbara there were many advantages, and the only disadvantage was an additional twenty minutes to and from the theatre. For me, there were no disadvantages at all.

Initially I worried about poor Elspeth. She was a tall, rather sorrowful young woman of remarkably equable temperament. Annie decided, 'She can be *your* secretary. God knows, she'll be glad of something to do; and I'll be spared the job of thinking up things to make her feel needed.'

'Do you think she'll agree?'

'Of course she'll agree. She's being well paid to agree. And that's the work she came to do in the first place.'

We fell into a leisurely routine. Both Barbara and Annie slept very late – my wife because she was at work most of the night and the old woman because it was hard to break the habit of a lifetime. So, during the morning, I was able to give close study to all the papers, programmes, photographs and memorabilia which our hostess had accumulated and which she made available to me.

The earliest photograph was one which I did not at first

recognise as my subject. It showed a cheerful but scruffy-looking urchin in well-worn breeches and jaunty flat cap. Then there was a beautiful, large-eyed girl caught in a blaze of stage lighting which made a diaphanous cloud of her wispy dress. And betrayed her excellent slim figure. Later, a whole stack of stage prints illustrating every aspect of Viola: eager, laughing, hurt, sad and triumphant. And there were many press and magazine photographs, too. Annie, svelte and thirtyish, chatting with Josef and Magda Goebbels; surprised outside the Haymarket theatre with Marie Tempest; on a back-lot peak with Tyrone Power; arriving at a premiere with Ben Tierney; having tea with Lady Dorothy Macmillan and Clarissa Eden; at a banquet with President Kennedy and Frank Sinatra; looking pale and woebegone in San Francisco; haggard in Las Vegas; old and tired at St Jean-Cap Ferrat . . . there were boxes of photographs. What remained constant, as the hoyden matured, bloomed and aged was the vitality in her eyes. Always, they had a challenging, direct look which saw beyond the occasion and the photographer and the time.

There was also the unpublished manuscript of the derided but, to me, invaluable biography written by Dr Sleavin. And it was difficult not to admire the sheer organisation and range of factual detail she had compiled.

I made notes and stocked up on the questions which would dictate the scope of the day's effort. The four of us had lunch together, then Barbara drove to Glasgow in the afternoon for rehearsals or readings or fittings and remained there for the performance. Elspeth withdrew to type up whatever had been accomplished the previous day. Meanwhile, Annie and I – whatever the weather – took a long walk; usually along the Havoc shore but often through the town as well. Wherever it was, we talked all the time. And that conversation was the basis for the long, recorded, working session which occupied the evening.

I soon realised that whatever form my book might eventually take I'd be foolish not to concentrate on the men in Annie's life. To them, I gathered, she had entrusted aspects of her real self. And that was quite different from the ironclad monster which

26

her profession had forced her to become. The person behind the monster was what she hoped to find again. That was her own priority. All the other events followed from her desire for, and love of, men.

ALBERT LANE

Annie's first job when she came to London was on the floor of Covent Garden. The opera house had been converted to a public ballroom during the war and still had not been restored to its former use several years later. There she earned sixpence a dance and was allowed to keep fourpence of it. She'd always been a good dancer and, up north in the munitions factory, she'd taught the other girls the latest steps. She found it much easier to dance with men, even though there was a constant need to dance *away* from them.

While all the pitfalls and hazards were still new to her, she was taken under the wing of a more experienced hostess: an Irish girl called Eileen Docherty. Eileen was tough and cynical and she saw to it that Annie's ticket stubs were correctly accounted for. She also found her cheap lodgings with a relative in an alley off Houndsditch. It was a tiring journey from the centre of the city out to the overcrowded slums of the East End but it was cheap and the new girl felt at home there.

In fact, she was delighted with the bustle and noise of London which was just starting to let itself go. All the restrictions of war had finally been lifted and the first numbing shock at the number of dead had eased. But although it was possible to come to terms with the loss of life, it was not possible to forget the wounded. They hobbled along the streets supporting each other, and formed a variable but always pitiable tableau on the steps of the Underground. Many who could not face the hopelessness or humiliation killed themselves and became unacknowledged casualties, deprived even of a place on the carved memorials. It seemed there were suicides in the paper nearly every day. Those who were whole and in good health had therefore to

29

make a determined effort to overcome the sadness and regret. Maybe that was one reason why the ability to dance well became a kind of duty.

Annie spent very little time in the hostess pen during the afternoon sessions and no time at all in the evenings. But it was hard work. And the regulation black dress she'd spent so much of her savings to buy soon had to be augmented with a second and then a third to prevent the sweaty patch in the back of each one becoming permanent during the hot summer of 1920. It seemed to her unfair that whereas she was obliged to wear gloves, her partners were not.

Mainly, they were working-class ex-servicemen who couldn't afford a whore and thought sixpence should cover everything they could get away with on their feet. They also thought the individual hostess cubicles apt enough for what they could manage sitting down. But the Garden was efficiently policed – especially in the afternoons. Stewards patrolled constantly around the edge of what had been the stalls and there were one or two management lookouts where the theatre boxes had been.

The evenings were much more relaxed. Then wives or girl-friends kept a more stringent, if laughing, surveillance and the atmosphere was lightened by a generally better class of cus-tomer. Then, too, there were 'regulars'. Good dancers sought good dancers for no other pleasure than executing the steps with precision and grace.

There were several girls among the hostesses who were excellent dancers. But most of them were tall, and customers preferred their partners shorter than themselves. So Jamie Northcott chose Annie. Over several weeks he came to the Garden on Monday and Wednesday evenings. Usually he came with his sister and her girlfriend, but he danced almost exclus-ively with Annie. And he was so taken with her that he insisted she should join him at their table between dances. This surprised the ladies. But they were not surprised at the young man's enthusiasm for his partner as they watched the perfectly matched couple glide around the floor.

His sister said, 'Miss Jeynor really is very good.'

Emily nodded, 'Yes. But then she gets so much practice.'

Celia was aware of the slight edge in her friend's voice and felt a little guilty. It had been her idea to bring Emily along so that Jamie would get to know her better. It was no secret that Emily had a crush on her young brother. In Celia's opinion it was about time Jamie married and he couldn't do much better than marry Emily Sartain whose family was very well-connected and quite rich. The security wouldn't come amiss, since he showed no inclination for the family shipping business – and he needed someone to steady him, too.

Emily leaned forward as the dancing couple came close under the balcony. Though necessarily in each other's arms there was no sign of familiarity. But the girl was very attractive in the fashionable urchin style. Her short auburn hair was cut like a sleek Juliet cap, her face was round and glowed with health even in the subdued lighting at the edge of the dance floor. And she certainly could dance. As the couple whirled away down the far side of the floor Emily glanced across the table to her friend. 'Do you think she gives lessons? I mean, apart from being a paid hostess, I wonder if she could improve *my* dancing?'

Celia was fitting another cigarette into the holder. 'Why don't you ask her? They'll be coming up after this dance.'

'I certainly can't ask with Jamie listening.'

'In the 'tiring room, then.'

Emily shook her head. 'The hostesses mayn't use ours, and I've no idea if they have one.' Celia lit her cigarette and gave some thought to the problem. 'Suppose I ask her, then? As though for myself.'

'Would you, Celia?'

'Of course. I daresay it would do no harm to improve my own technique.'

When the question was put to her, Annie immediately agreed. But she made one condition. 'I will not expect to be paid for the lessons.'

Celia raised her eyebrows. 'But, Miss Jeynor, I wouldn't think of taking up your time without payment.'

'I should think not,' Jamie said.

Annie held her ground. She already knew what could be gained

31

from this opportunity. The difficulty was phrasing it in a manner acceptable to the young widow. 'My time would be well spent, Mrs Grenville, if I could learn from you while I am teaching.'

'Learn what?' Emily wanted to know.

The snub-nosed girl smiled so that none of them would guess how uncertain she felt. Her humiliation and embarrassment could be immediate if she told them plainly that she wanted above all to learn how to behave like a lady. That would be presumptuous and they would be offended. Instead she made use of a chance remark of Jamie's a few weeks earlier. He'd mentioned that his sister could drive a motor car. 'Well,' she said, 'if it's not too much trouble I would like to learn how to drive a car.'

Celia was amused. 'Do you have a car, Miss Jeynor?'

Annie shook her head.

Emily suppressed a giggle and Celia enquired, 'Then what possible use would it be?'

Annie blushed but felt an unblushing resentment at the question. The embarrassing moment was bridged by a loud and triumphant chord from the orchestra. Out to the centre of the cleared dance floor strode the professional exhibition couple. Annie switched all her attention on them. There was a job worth having. They got two pounds a night and she was sure she herself was expert enough to be an exhibition dancer – if only she could find a competent partner.

When the performance ended Annie applauded loudly while glancing covertly at Jamie Northcott. He was good enough to be her partner. But he was not interested enough even to watch the professionals. Instead he was having a whispered conversation with Miss Sartain.

The end of the music prompted a return to the previous subject. Celia realised that she'd given offence to the young hostess and made amends by the enthusiasm with which she now pursued the offer of dance lessons in exchange for driving lessons. Secretly, though, she was displeased at the likely encroachment on her time. After all, the idea had been to improve Emily's chances.

Soon after eleven, when the dance hall closed, Annie went

back alone to her room in Houndsditch. As she passed through the market area to catch the Aldgate tram, she always encountered the first of the barrows being trundled early to secure a good pitch. Their steel-shod wheels struck little sparks from the cobbles in the dark. And as they passed, their tarpaulins gave off the scent of yesterday's fruit. The girl was always very hungry by that time, yet, when she'd climbed to the third floor at her digs, she was always too tired to prepare more than a sandwich and a cup of tea.

It was in the autumn of 1920 that she became involved in the affair which had such disastrous consequences. And it happened by chance. Annie noticed the burly, handsome young man long before he reached the enclosure where she sat with the other girls. It seemed as though he was looking for someone in particular. He moved with awkward care, as though the polished, sprung floor was a newly planted field and he was anxious not to damage the seedlings. And there was an open-air freshness about his complexion and his expression. He might have been a young farmer up to the city for the day. But he carried himself with more assurance than that. He stopped and looked admiringly at each of the girls, and gave each one the same friendly grin. Really, he'd already made up his mind. He chose the small slim girl with the reddish hair. Annie smiled up at him then got to her feet with that eagerness they'd all been taught to display. This time it was genuine.

He proffered a handful of tokens. Annie laughed and took one of them which she tucked into the small purse attached to her belt.

'Take the lot,' he said.

'No. You might change your mind after the first one.'

'No. I won't.'

'We'll see,' Annie said and took his arm to be led onto the floor.

He held her much too tight and for a few moments the girl assumed it was because he was uncertain of the steps. Quite a few men did it when they were anxious to impress and lacked proficiency. She tried to ease away a little.

'What's wrong? Don't you like me?'

'I'm just trying to help,' Annie explained. 'If we're too close our feet get tangled up.'

He chuckled, 'Oh, I don't want our *feet* to get tangled up.'

Annie said, 'I'm glad I didn't take all your tickets.'

'You will, though,' the young man assured her.

And she did. They danced together for most of that evening. He also bought her ices and cakes and tea.

His name was Albert Lane and he mentioned that he'd recently taken on a job that gave him great satisfaction. He wouldn't say exactly what the job was, beyond hinting that he was 'a soldier of fortune'. Considering how attentive to her he had been all evening, Annie felt sure he'd insist on seeing her home. She rehearsed the manner in which she would decline the offer. But it never came. They danced the last waltz together, then he bade her good night and left. The girl found it disconcerting and immediately concluded that Bert Lane was married.

It was exactly a month before Annie saw him again. At the Garden on a Friday night he waited at the pen as she danced by in the arms of a naval officer. He grinned and gave an exaggerated salute. He was very smartly dressed and his black hair swept away from the centre parting was like finely stitched patent leather. The naval officer took the next two dances as well but Bert didn't want to dance with anyone else and waited until she was free.

In one hand he held several dance tokens and in the other a small package inexpertly tied up like a miniature brown paper parcel. The hostesses were not allowed to accept gifts. At least, they were not allowed to be *seen* accepting gifts. Annie tucked it quickly into the purse at her waist before they took to the floor.

At the first opportunity she undid the little parcel. It was an expensive cameo brooch wrapped in a fine lace handkerchief. Annie held the brooch closer to the gas mantle in the female staff restroom. At first she thought Bert had had it inscribed for her, but she could not make out the blurred markings on the back. Probably it was just the hallmark stamp which had not been properly applied. As she stood on the chair close to the light, one of the other girls came in. She nodded appreciatively when she saw what Annie held. 'Oh!' she said. 'Nice bit o' Cavendish bait, eh?'

Annie jumped down and shook her head. 'No such luck.' She knew that her colleague had stashed away quite a few items of 'Cavendish bait'. Most of the girls shared an ambition to be invited by a gentleman to that exclusive but raffish hotel in Jermyn Street. More than one Gaiety girl had spent a night there as earnest of her aptitude for marrying into the nobility. Albert Lane was very far from nobility.

But on this evening, and without asking, he did walk her home. He put his arm round her waist and they strolled through the quiet streets as though they'd been doing the same thing for years. Annie was struck by the ease with which he did everything and the friendly confidence with which he treated her. She was also very much attracted to him and planned to offer only token resistance when he asked to come up to her room for a few minutes. But again he surprised her. They stopped at the street entrance, she thanked him again for the beautiful brooch, then he doffed his hat, gave her a light kiss and watched her start ascending the stairs to her room, alone.

Annie reached the first landing and decided he was being *too* much of a gentleman. And there was her own growing feeling of frustration to consider. She ran downstairs again, determined to call him back. It was unnecessary. He was still waiting there on the pavement. He smiled broadly as though they were both engaged in a tantalising game. They climbed the stairs together.

In the over-furnished room he looked around brightly and asked, 'What's for supper?'

'I don't usually eat much at this time of night,' Annie said.

'But you must be hungry. I am.'

'What would you like me to . . .'

'No. I'll do it.' He took her by the shoulders and urged her to move backwards to the bed. 'You rest. I'll see what's here and make the most of it.'

Somewhat bemused, Annie kicked of her shoes, eased the stockings away from her toes and lay back on the bed. She asked, 'Where did you learn to cook?'

'Where I learned everything else – in the Army.'

And really, considering how little he had to work with, Bert concocted a very enjoyable meal. When it was almost ready, Annie stirred herself to take off her formal working dress and put on a dressing gown before setting up the folding card-table on the hearthrug.

When they'd eaten, Bert also allowed a rest for digestion before he plunged into his role as a lover. Again Annie was struck by the ease of his whole approach. He behaved as though they both knew that, naturally, sex was the next item on the menu. The girl could not quarrel with the assumption – even if she'd wanted to. It was she who'd invited him up to her room and that was the only initiative required of her. Bert took it from there with a verve and a boldness which quite captivated her. And yet he took his time. While it was plain that his own eagerness was barely held in check he pandered endlessly to her feelings. Time and again what seemed imperative and inevitable was delayed. And every new delay increased the girl's emotional and physical abandonment. Finally, when they were perfectly tuned to each other, the climax was reached. And before long, the whole delightful preamble was begun again.

Next morning it was Bert's turn to rest while the girl prepared breakfast for them. Then they strolled down through the bustling streets towards the river. It was a bright clear day and the air was sharpened by the first real frost of the year. Noticing a newsvendor's placard, Bert bought a paper. Annie, who gave her attention only to the society notes in newspapers, now read the words, 'SIX POLICEMEN MURDERED'. Bert immediately started reading the story and she released her hold on his arm. She suggested diffidently, 'That's a terrible thing, eh?' She glanced up into Bert's face. 'Where were they killed?'

'Ireland,' he grunted. 'Where else?'

'I wonder why they do such things?'

'I know why they've done *this*,' said the man grimly. 'Kevin Barry was hanged yesterday.' He turned his attention fully upon the paper once more and added, 'The bastards.'

They walked westward along the waterfront promenade of the Tower. They were diverted by the activity on the Thames and Annie thought no more about the newspaper report. If Bert gave it any further consideration he didn't mention it.

On the Clyde shore at Dumbarton, Annie halted and rested on her walking stick. She stared across the river, trying to separate what she was now aware of from what she had been aware of then. 'I knew nothing at all about politics, you see.'

'Surely you knew the name Kevin Barry?' I was incredulous that the first great legendary hero of Ireland's troubles could have been so thoughtlessly dismissed – even at the time.

'No. Nobody knew.'

'But there is a famous song about him!'

'Not until he was dead,' Annie stated drily. 'I know it now, of course.' And she sang softly, '"Another martyr for old Ireland, Another murder for the crown . . ."'

I shook my head. 'It seems incredible to me that you didn't know. Or care.'

She turned to face me with controlled impatience. 'Bill, the British press kept the injustice in Ireland a secret for forty years – then blamed the Irish for letting it happen.' She strode on leaving me standing.

And that was true. It wasn't until 1969 that the mainland really found out what was going on. And by then it had been going on for over forty years. I caught up with Annie.

She added, 'You have to sympathise with the poor Protestants, as well. Suddenly the British government tells them to stop doing what a score of British governments have actively encouraged them to do – for generations!'

'They must have known it was wrong.'

Annie clambered onto a large flat-topped rock. She gave me a bitter little smile. 'Governments don't care about what's right or wrong. They only know what's likely to keep them in power.'

Celia Grenville lived in one of the old mansions on Bayswater Road. They were already much reduced in status from their fashionable heyday. The two uppermost floors were in use and the servants' quarters were now in the basement, built into what had once been the vast kitchen and storage area. Annie

37

mounted the stairs under the high ornate porch with as much self-assurance as she could muster. She was shown up to the drawing room where Mrs Grenville and Miss Sartain waited for her. Immediately she realised how over-dressed she was for the occasion.

Mrs Grenville rose to meet her with a smiling welcome. 'Good morning, Miss Jeynor. You're very prompt. I'm glad you had no trouble finding us.' She half-turned to include her friend with a gesture. 'I asked Miss Sartain to join in. You don't mind, I hope.'

'Not at all,' Annie said, wondering if the second pupil was going to pay cash.

Miss Sartain smiled and gave what she intended to be a cheery wave. 'Actually,' she said, 'my foxtrot needs more doing to it than Celia's.'

'Darling, that's because you've spent so much time trotting after real foxes.' Both ladies laughed and Annie joined in politely. Celia went on, 'Well! Shall we begin?'

'All right. But first we'll have to roll this back.' Annie moved briskly to the corner of the room and bent to grasp the edge of the carpet.

Celia stopped her. 'Miss Jeynor! You'll find it rather . . . heavy.' She leaned towards a bell-pull. 'We need help, I think.'

To Annie it seemed obvious that they did *not* need help. Three healthy women could easily roll back a carpet – but not, apparently, if two of them were ladies. They waited for the manservant to come up from the basement, staring idly out of the windows through the foliage of the kerbside trees towards the wide plain of Hyde Park.

During the rest of November the dancing lessons at Mrs Grenville's house continued, but often Mrs Grenville herself wasn't there. Miss Sartain was, though, and Jamie often appeared and insisted on helping with the tuition in the drawing room as well as wholly taking over as driving instructor.

Once or twice they stopped the car in the park while Jamie recounted the events at lively parties he'd attended. He laughed a great deal over drinking sprees and social indiscretions. The girl laughed too, but really did not find the stories very funny. She thought that Jamie and his friends spent a great deal of time and money enjoying themselves, but that the enjoyment seemed to depend on what *other* people did.

Nevertheless, their life had more variety than her own and she began to imagine what it might be like if she were married to Jamie. If lords were willing to marry chorus girls, why shouldn't a mere gentleman marry a dance hostess? Of course, no progress to that end could be managed if they were alone together only on increasingly wintry mornings. And he never came alone to the Garden.

It was another month before she saw Bert again and he came directly to her digs in Houndsditch with his kit-bag. He seemed to take it for granted that he would live and sleep with her when he was in London. This Annie found both unsettling and reassuring. It was unsettling because, though she didn't think her bed overcrowded with him in it, her room certainly was. The reassuring aspect was the fact that he didn't have a wife or other woman he wanted to spend his time with. So she responded to the invasion as though she too had expected this new arrangement.

She stowed his kit-bag under the sink. On it were stencilled official-looking numbers, and she asked, 'Have you joined the Army again?'

'No. I'm still an auxiliary.'

Obviously he thought he'd told her how he was employed. She hazarded, 'Is that like a territorial?'

'No.' He grinned and hugged her again. 'Just a helper. In Ireland.'

And he'd brought another present. This time it was a silver and amethyst necklace. Again the jewellery was wrapped in a piece of Irish lace and had to be very carefully disentangled. Annie wondered why the Irish shops didn't use boxes to pack their goods. She immediately tried on the necklace. It set off her hostess's black dress perfectly.

Bert admired her admiring herself. He asked, 'Do you have to go to work today?'

'Yes, of course! There are plenty of girls after my job.'

He started unbuttoning her dress.

39

Annie protested, 'And I have to go to work now!'

'This won't take long.'

'Bert! When I come back.'

He chuckled close to her ear. 'When you come back . . . as well!'

Annie sighed and let the dress slip to the floor.

As well as being a wholly satisfying lover, Bert was a lively man. And he had a keen sense of humour which chimed well with her own. She usually managed to arrange to have the Saturday off when he was home, so that they could enjoy the whole weekend together. They often went to the music hall where both joined in the singing, rocking from side to side, arm in arm. She found it rather endearing that he was so readily moved by the sentimental songs. And he did not hide it. Often he borrowed her handkerchief to wipe away the tears.

But mainly his was a laughing, live-for-today attitude. That was something he had in common with most of the young men who'd come through the war. He never talked about that or about the future. Instead, very flatteringly, he gave the impression that his life had really started when he met her. When they were together she was the only girl in the world. He never asked about her life before they met and she did not care what his had been as long as their present was such a delight.

By the spring of the following year Annie was convinced that she and Bert could make a real go of it together. And he seemed to think so too. On his first leave when the weather was warm enough, he took her down to Southend for a break. They went bathing and, resting on the sand afterwards, Bert started making plans for their future once he was back in London permanently. 'I've been savin' up quite a bit, y'know. I'll have time to look around to get a job that suits me.'

Annie turned on her side so that she could stroke his sand-encrusted arm. 'What sort of job would you want?'

'Oooh, somethin' with prospects, that's what I'd want.'

'What though?'

'The police, maybe. Don't pay much at first, but I'd see to it that I got promoted pretty quick.'

'I'm sure you would.'

'An' I've made a lot of contacts that'll stand me well, once I'm back in Blighty.' He rolled over on his stomach and raised his head to take in the sprawling families and screaming children on the beach. 'Wouldn't want any kids, though.'

To Annie this seemed a sudden jump that left out a crucial stage. 'You would want to get married, though?'

'Of course.' He glanced sharply at her as though the matter had already been settled between them. 'Don't you?'

'Oh, yes! Once I've got the job *I* want.'

'Annie, love, you can't go on dancin' all your life.'

'Well, not at the Garden, anyway. They'll soon be turning that back into a theatre.' She stretched out on her back again and covered her eyes with a forearm to block out the sun. 'No. Dancing is just a start for me. I want promotion too.'

This seemed to puzzle the man. 'I thought you said you wanted to get married?'

'Bert, actresses aren't nuns, you know.'

He grinned. 'So I've been told.'

'I mean, they get married the same as anybody else.'

'They don't get married to *me*,' Bert said.

Annie did not pursue the subject. She was well content with the intention which had been declared. The actual decisions could be put off until Bert's job in Ireland was over.

As the spring of 1921 brought a heady scent to the night walks through the market, Annie devoted a lot of her free time to preparing the ground for her advancement. As part of this determined programme she regularly bought magazines which celebrated the life she intended to lead. Each new issue of *Queen, The Illustrated London News* or *Vanity Fair* was carefully examined for information on how those who had money threw it away. She noted, too, how these alien women were dressed; how they held their wine glasses; how they stood and sat and how their make-up was applied. Of equal interest was the interior decoration of their homes – though in Annie's personal opinion they were all hopelessly cluttered. Why, she wondered, did people like Loelia Ponsonby, Lady Morrell and Maud Cunard put up with such a mass of unnecessary furniture and pointless bric-à-brac when they could afford to have *space*? But the puzzle did not for a moment deflect her from the intention to compete with the same extravagant bad taste when she had money.

A recurring feature in the illustrated society magazines was the latest fancy-dress party. That looked like good fun. Somehow, even débutantes looked human when dressed in ridiculous costumes; especially if they were drunk.

The opportunity to assess such an occasion at first hand came when Mrs Grenville – probably at Jamie's instigation – asked her to stay for a weekend. There was to be a fancy-dress evening at the Grenvilles' country house. It had been arranged to coincide with the regatta at nearby Marlow.

Annie accepted the invitation but begged to be allowed to attend only the fancy-dress. She explained that her work did not allow her to take the whole weekend off. But that was a lie. Really, she did not have, nor could afford to buy, the seven or eight changes of clothes which a full weekend would demand. She could, though, manage a suitable fancy dress – even if she had to make it herself. But that did not prove necessary.

One of the first shows she'd seen when she came to London was a Variety bill which featured the Houston sisters. Much of their act depended on dressing as, and behaving as, children; Renée as a little girl and Billie as a boy. Annie intended to imitate Billie Houston. At the time she made that decision there were only short-term advantages. First, the costume was cheaply and easily acquired. There were plenty of street vendors – youths dressed in well-worn breeches which would fit her. That would be the basic garment which she could augment with finer hose, colourful braces, a high kerchief stock and a stylish flat bonnet. She could also imitate one of the traditional cries. The whole ensemble would, she was sure, charm Mrs Grenville's guests at Marlow.

The party was held in the long, sloping garden which had once been an orchard. Coloured lights were strung between the blossoming fruit trees and a bright assortment of young people paraded with shrieks of laughter in the expensive costumes they had hired, or even had specially made.

Annie stood on the terrace, looking down towards the river.

42

Now that she was there, it seemed as though she was going to spend a very lonely evening. Jamie had said hello before he went off with Miss Sartain and her particular party to the gazebo. They were all in groups, Annie noticed, clustered or moving between the trees and she did not know any of them well enough to attach herself to any group. She smiled as she watched their high-spirited antics which so effectively excluded her. They were all pleasant enough people and if they were more than usually foolish it was because they could afford to be. Annie longed not for their money but for their luxury of being foolish. Meanwhile, in self-defence as much as to occupy her time in this charade, she put herself to work.

'Mrs Grenville!'

'Yes?' Celia turned. 'Miss Jeynor! How amusing you look. What is it you're supposed to be selling?'

'That's the trouble. I have nothing to sell. But if you lend me a basket I could help by carrying food around the garden. It'll save your guests walking back and forward to the house all the time.'

'What a good idea!' It did not trouble Celia that Annie, too, was one of her guests. She was grateful enough at being offered practical help to keep the sprawling party in full swing.

So the very attractive street urchin was soon a necessary focus of attention. Everyone thought she was 'really sweet' and a couple of the young men insisted on taking turns at carrying her basket. They asked where she'd got such a stunning idea for a costume. She told them it had been suggested by her friend, Billie Houston. The lie was accepted with gurgles of delight. They, too, had seen the Houston sisters and hoped Annie would be a chum and introduce them to her friends. She said she would. But secretly she was amazed at how easy it was to be accepted if you told the right lie to the right people. The trick was getting into a position where the right lie was feasible. It was a lesson she never forgot.

In fact, the young men told her, they were themselves loosely connected with the theatre and insisted that she must meet 'old Cocky' – a friend of *theirs* – who was right there that night. 'Old Cocky' turned out to be C. B. Cochran, the theatrical impresario.

He was a small and plump middle-aged man, dressed incongruously as a pixie. They found him in the drawing room, drink and cigar in hand. It must have been the latest of several drinks because 'old Cocky' was clearly several sheets to the wind. The young men introduced him to Annie. They said she was an actress friend of theirs, and of the Houston sisters. That was another lesson: people will make your lie their lie if it reflects even a little favourably upon them.

Mr Cochran seemed quite interested in a fuddled way. The urchin smiled her most delightful smile and denied only that she was an actress. 'No. I'm a dancer,' she said.

'Any speciality?'

'No. Anything at all, if it's to music,' she assured him.

Cochran gave her an encouraging nod before his attention was claimed by a horsey young woman who announced that she herself had had absolutely *no* theatrical experience, *but*... Her accomplice took that as a cue and started pounding the piano with the hit song from the latest Cochran revue. The impresario, drunk or not, did not let his smile even flicker as he faced yet another incidental hazard of his trade.

The horsey young woman went on to prove conclusively why she would forever lack professional experience. Annie moved away, wondering why anyone who had neither talent, nor need to be a performer, should want to be one. This was a London phenomenon, of course. It was considered daringly fashionable and great 'fun' to be on the stage in London. Elsewhere in Britain it was no fun at all.

In her efforts to find an escape from the noise, Annie came upon Jamie. He was in a distressed condition, slumped in one of the library chairs and quite plainly weeping. She stood where he could see her, ready to leave him alone if he showed any sign of annoyance. But he did not. In fact, he half-raised his arm as though to beckon her in. The girl sat in the chair opposite him, silent and perfectly still. She watched him recover some of his composure but determined that he should be the first to speak.

'Not . . . ,' he said at last, glancing down at his costume, 'not a very good advertisement for the Hussars.'

Annie smiled.

44

He pulled out a handkerchief and started to dry his face. 'The thing is, I'm in a bit of a jam.'

Annie waited.

'Emily thinks it's time we got married.' He sighed very deeply. 'And it is! It is!'

'Well,' Annie said, 'I suppose she's been waiting for you a long time. During the war, I mean.'

Jamie shook his head. 'No. We met after the war.'

'Even so, it's four years.'

Again he disagreed. 'Hardly. She hardly decided she wanted to marry me the first time we met.'

'She could have,' the girl suggested, and thought it more likely a certainty.

'Well, I didn't think about it . . .' He sniffed and applied his handkerchief again. 'Haven't thought about it until quite recently.' Another sigh. 'Until Emily started mentioning it, in fact.'

'When do you plan to get married, then?'

'I don't.' He shook his head vehemently. 'That's just it! I don't intend to get married at all.'

'To Miss Sartain?'

'To anybody. That's what she can't understand.' He leaned forward and stared into Annie's eyes. 'Can *you* understand that?'

The girl considered the question. There was obviously no point in asking him *why* he didn't want to get married. If he could explain that then clearly he would have explained it to Miss Sartain, and she would have understood. Nor did he really want to know if he was understood by Annie. He merely wanted to be comforted. So Annie said, 'Yes, of course.'

Jamie smiled. 'I thought you might.' He sat straighter. 'Yes. I thought you would agree with me. Because you don't want to get married either, do you?'

Annie shook her head.

He went on, 'You're about the only girl I know who isn't looking for a husband.' He was unaware that this went a long way to explaining his attachment to the little dance hostess. A girl who was not looking for a husband was still rare – even four years after the war when boys who'd been too young to fight were now entering the grievously depleted market.

'That's right,' Annie said. 'I'm not looking for a husband, but I *am* looking for a dancing partner.'

Jamie suddenly leaned forward, framed her face in his hands and kissed her lightly on the nose. 'Then we must see what can be done for you,' he said.

They rejoined the party and Mrs Grenville told her brother that Emily had left suddenly. Jamie nodded, his composure and good spirits quite regained. He led Annie to the group gathered round the piano.

Cochran was still there, and still in the deadly thrall of the horsey young woman. He seized upon the newcomers as a chance of relief; though he had to be reminded that Annie was the friend of the Houstons. He asked her to demonstrate one of her dances. She settled with the pianist upon a tune which would also allow her to sing. Then she and Jamie took the floor.

That was how she auditioned for her first stage show. And – with Jamie's willing help – that was how she got the job. Before the evening was over she became a temporary-replacement Cochran young lady. And she had every intention of making it permanent.

Albert did not approve at all of his girlfriend becoming an 'actress'.

'That's a bit above you, ain't it?' he said, and slunged a sponge-full of water down his back. The tin bath was set in the middle of the room and Annie watched as the soapy bubbles were swept from his gleaming skin.

She reminded him, 'Well, you said I couldn't dance all my life.'

'But what do you know about the-aters?'

'Not much. But I'll learn.'

He shook his head and applied himself to the undersides of his raised thighs. 'Never! You got to have trainin' for that, gel.'

'They'll train me.'

'You're not doin' it.' He raised a leg clear out of the water to get at his toes, which were long and curiously bent.

Annie watched this operation for a moment before she declared flatly, 'Yes, I am!'

He stamped the raised foot back in the water with a splash

which threw drops of water as far as the open fire. Puffs of hissing steam rose from the glowing coals. Bert turned right round and glared at her. 'I say *no*, Annie! I don't want you playin' around with that lot.'

'Why not?'

'Never mind why not. They're not for the likes of you.'

'What makes you so sure?'

'I know their sort. Take my word for it. I know all about *act*resses.'

'How do you know? Where did *you* ever meet any actresses?'

'Annie! I'm tellin' you . . .'

'And I'm not listening.'

'Damn it, I'll make you listen.' In a great whoosh of water he got to his feet.

The girl stood her ground. 'I'm going to do it, Albert.'

'If you do, we're finished.'

'Oh?'

He grinned. 'That makes a difference, eh?'

'No, it doesn't!'

He stepped out of the bath, soaking the rug, and moved towards her. He grinned. 'We'll see about that.' He flung his arms around her and pulled her against his wet body in a painful bear-hug. Annie tried not to utter a sound. She'd noticed before that he seemed to get a lot of pleasure from her pain in their often rough love-making. The water from his hair dripped over her face as he increased the pressure. 'Give in!' he growled in her ear.

Annie shook her head vehemently, not trusting her voice. She could feel the water on his body seeping through her clothes. The pressure on her trapped arms and her back was intense.

Suddenly he threw her away from him and she stumbled back against the armchair. He shouted, 'I'm warnin' you, gel. Stay where you belong!'

The argument ended, as most of their arguments ended, with sex. But on this occasion it did not change Annie's mind. She realised that what he objected to was the jump in her social status. As a dance-hall hostess she was obviously the paid servant of any man with sixpence to spare. On the musical comedy stage she was much less vulnerable because she was

47

out of reach of the people who were paying for her services. And, it seemed to Albert, she'd got above him too.

In the cast of the Cochran revue there were two 'improvers', both of them well-educated, upper-class girls. One of them might even have been paying for the privilege of appearing in a fashionable theatre. But the other, Rosemary Gill, undoubtedly had talent. She'd recently moved to London and was looking for someone to share an already acquired flat. On the acquaintance of one morning's rehearsal, she asked Annie if she'd be interested.

'No, thank you. I have a place out in the East End which is comfortable enough. And cheap.'

'But that's so far away!' Rosemary exclaimed. 'And the area can't be very nice.'

'I'm used to areas that aren't very nice,' Annie said. 'I feel more at home there.'

'Annie dear, one doesn't come to London just to be at home. That ruins the whole point of it!'

'If the show runs, maybe I'll be able to afford something better.'

'Why don't you come and see my flat at least? We could have such fun together. Do say you'll give it a try.'

'Not at the moment,' Annie said. It was true that she did feel comfortable in the run-down, poor quarter of the city. It had more life, more warmth. And it did seem important that she should be able to do as she pleased. There was her young man to consider as well. He must be free to come and go and it would be foolish to place anyone so attractive as Rosemary in his way.

The change from dance hostess to chorus girl was certainly a big move in the right direction. Annie loved her new life and, of course, she earned a lot more for less work. Eight performances a week seemed leisurely compared with the daily eight hours on her feet at Covent Garden. But there were disadvantages, too. In particular, she missed seeing her 'regular', Jamie. When she had told him she was no longer going to be a hostess he expressed regret, but had not suggested that they should continue to meet.

The following month Albert seemed to have forgotten their argument over her new job. But on that particular weekend he did seem uneasy. As they strolled towards the East End markets he more than once glanced quickly behind to check if they were being followed. It was August Bank Holiday weekend, when everybody had the Saturday morning off as well as the Monday. The streets were very crowded. Annie wore the beautiful lace shawl Albert had given her, tied loosely around her waist to set off her new nigger-brown dress with its dipping hemline and floating panels.

They were both startled – and Albert threw up his fists in defence – as a passing figure suddenly confronted them, blocking their way. Then Annie laughed. It was the boy from whom she'd bought the essential item of her fancy dress. His grin faded as he drew back from Albert's threatening gesture. But almost immediately he recovered and slapped his thigh to indicate his pride in the new serge trousers he wore.

'Oooh! What a gentleman!' Annie exclaimed.

'Who is it?' Albert asked, then to the boy, 'Who are you?'

'Only the bloke as warms your lady's britches,' the youth announced loudly.

The man cuffed him lightly on the head and he sped away, laughing, into the noisy crowd milling around the barrows.

That evening Albert was in the audience at the theatre. It was the first time he'd seen Annie on the stage. But when they met at the stage door afterwards he said hardly anything about the show. He was plainly in a fever of anticipation. Waiting for the Aldgate tram, he drew her away from the street light and pulled her abruptly towards him. His hands gripped and rubbed at her body. Annie offered no resistance, though uncomfortably aware of the looks and nudges being exchanged by the other women at the halt.

When they got to the digs, Mrs Willet stopped them halfway up the stair. 'Been a fella lookin' for you,' she said.

Albert whipped round to face her. 'Me?'

'Not you, luvvy. I don't rightly know who you *are*. No. Annie.'

The girl felt Albert's strong hand clench on her upper arm and his voice hissed, 'Who? Who would that be?'

Mrs Willet expanded on her message. 'Di'n ask for you by name. Jest if you was in.'

'What did you tell him?'

'That I minds me own business, ducky . . . within the lawr, that is.'

'Good for you, missus,' Albert said and hustled Annie quickly up to their room.

Knowing how jealous he would be, the girl expected an outburst as soon as the door was closed. To her surprise, he said nothing more about it but just started to strip off his clothes. In her relief at being spared another bawling match, she vied with him in the urgency of undressing.

Next morning when they woke he announced that he intended to leave immediately after breakfast. Since he normally stayed for at least three days and more often a week, Annie was astonished. 'Why? What's wrong?'

'Who said there's anything wrong?' Albert challenged. 'I got business to do out of town.' He knew she wouldn't pursue him on that. He considered it part of her charm that she asked so few questions about anything and none about his 'business'.

And he was right. Annie just shrugged, uncoiled his arms so that she could get out of bed, and set about preparing food. But even if she did not express curiosity, she did wonder what had caused this sudden change of plan. She connected it with his unease all the previous day and what had looked very much like fear over the unknown caller the previous evening. In the looking-glass to the left of the stove she glanced at Albert's reflection as he sat naked on the edge of the bed, scratching his head.

When he'd eaten and shaved and dressed he left abruptly. She stood on the landing and called down to him. 'When will you be back?' It was information he usually offered.

He did not pause as he clattered down the long flight of steps but called over his shoulder, 'I'll let you know.'

Scarcely an hour later, the girl heard heavy footsteps ascending the stair and smiled. It didn't surprise her that he'd suddenly changed his mind. She ran across the room and threw open the door. But it was not Albert. The stranger was a short, red-faced, youngish man. He was burly rather than plump and he walked right in.

50

He said, 'So you're the piece, are ya?'

'What? What do you want?'

'Practically everthin' ye have, girlie,' the Irishman said. Annie tried to get past him and through the still opened door but he blocked her way and slammed it shut. 'Who are you?'

'Who I am will be no bother. It's *what* I am will cause ya to worry.'

Annie backed away to a safer position and the man sat down at the bare table. He seemed perfectly sober and though there was nothing really threatening about his expression there was in it both contempt and authority. After a long pause she asked, 'Have you come to see Albert?'

The man grunted and hunched over the table, his hands clasped before him. 'Oh, I saw Albert, though he didn't see me.' His small dark eyes looked her up and down. 'So you're what he fucks when he's at home, eh?' Annie said nothing and he went on, his voice gradually taking on a ragged edge as he tried to suppress his anger. 'He's good at that, as ye'll know. He's a great fuckin' man altogether, is Officer Lane. Oh, yes! And likes a bit o' protestin'; bit of a struggle, eh? For it's *rapin'* he likes best of all.'

Dazedly, Annie repeated the unfamiliar title, '"Officer Lane"?'

'He's the one. And one of His Majesty's best – a man with all his heart and tool in the job, as every good Tan should.'

'I don't really know what Albert does,' the girl stammered.

'Is that a fact? Well, I'm the very wan that can tell ya. He's a bastard 'n Black and Tan! That's what he is. He's a murderer, a rapist and a looter. Nothin' less.'

The girl protested. 'No. You've got the wrong person. Albert is something to do with the Army.'

'That's right! There's an army *of* them.' The enormity of the fact seemed to constrict the man's throat for a moment. 'He's one of the army of occupation in Ireland.' He made an obvious effort to relax his throat and his tense shoulders. He sat back in the chair and sighed. His quarrel was not with the girl.

'He brings ya presents, does he not, from Ireland?'

'Yes.'

'Certainly! They all do. Would you show me what he has

51

brought?' As Annie turned towards the chest of drawers he stopped her. 'No. First, let me describe what I am lookin' for.' It had occurred to him that this girl could well be ignorant of how her man spent his time. If he could identify objects from memory, that should prove he spoke the truth. 'There are two things. One is a little oval brooch set in silver. There's a young girl's head carved into the stone. The other is a necklace with little bars o' gold makin' the chain and a pear-shaped locket at the end o' it.'

Annie nodded as the horror began to grow upon her. 'I'll show you everything he's brought me.'

One by one she placed all the gifts on the table. And now she understood why they had not been properly wrapped; and why there were dull patches on the gold or silver. The inscriptions they once bore had been erased.

The man's rather podgy fingers picked delicately through the accumulated hoard. He separated the cameo brooch and the pendant from the other items of jewellery. He held up the brooch he had accurately described before it was placed before him. 'This belonged to me mother. The necklace was a present I gave *my* girlfriend.'

Annie dared not ask what had happened to these women. 'Take them,' she said.

'Yes. I will take them,' he said softly. 'And now I'm sure which Tan it was, I'll take your man's life before we're much older.' He looked down sadly at all the other gifts on the table. 'Whose these are, I do not know.'

'You can find out!' Annie exclaimed, sweeping everything across the table towards him. 'Take them all!'

The man shook his head. 'Oh, no. That's too great a burthen of sadness for me.'

'But how can I keep them, now?'

He ignored her question and stood up, pushing the two chosen items into his pocket. 'I have what I came for and I bid you good day.'

When he had gone Annie stared at the objects on the table and saw in them a world of brutality and greed she had not known existed. She felt a terrible regret for the women from whom these things had been stolen. But, more strongly than that, she felt anger against exterior forces which had implicated her in actions which were not her responsibility. It was cruelly unfair. Albert had been cruel *and* unfair. And the accusing problem remained of what she was to do with the precious cargo now spread on the bare table. For what was merely decoration to her was precious to the unknown women who'd lost them, and the unknown men who'd first chosen them as gifts.

If, as now occurred to her, the British government condoned rape and pillage in Ireland there was no point in applying to officials in London. They would not return the plunder to its rightful owners. And she herself had no way of tracing those owners, nor time and the means to do it. Unless . . . Suddenly and aloud she said, 'Eileen!'

Eileen Docherty might know what to do. She was from Dublin and she'd no great faith in men, though she'd come to London in search of a fiancé who'd deserted her. In that pursuit, perhaps, she'd had dealings with those who knew the inside of the close-knit Irish community in the city.

Annie's first obligation was to wrap the items with more care than Bert had shown. From the newsagent's across the street she bought several large sheets of white tissue paper. She cut it into neat squares and folded them around each of the dozen or so 'gifts'. The remaining pendant, the brooches, lockets and earrings occupied little space, but the shawl, the ruffed-lace halter and the silk cape – when interleaved with tissue – had greater bulk. Annie looked around for suitable means of carrying everything safely. She did not have a large enough handbag and her suitcase was too big. Besides, the suitcase had her name indelibly printed inside the lid.

Annie had to make another excursion, this time to the street market. There she bought a mock-leather valise which had a lock clasp and a tiny key dangling from the handle. She went back to her digs and met Mrs Willet on the stair. The landlady admired her purchase. 'Just the thing, luvvy, for a nice weekend. You goin' away somewhere?'

It was only then that Annie realised that she must, as a priority, find somewhere else to live. 'Oh, yes, Mrs Willet, I was just going to tell you. I'll be moving out at the end of the week.'

'Well! That's what I call sudden, Annie. Nothin' wrong, I hope?'

'No.' Annie tried to squeeze past her on the stair. 'No. Just a change. I'm moving to a place nearer the theatre.' And before she had reached the door of her room, that spur of the moment excuse became for her a fact. She remembered the invitation from Rosemary Gill – the colleague in the chorus – to share a flat with her. Annie had declined the offer, largely because she wanted to be free to do as she pleased on her own. But sharing a flat now seemed an ideal safeguard against her own foolishness with men. She needed protection from herself.

With the valise packed and locked, she set out for Covent Garden and got there far too early. Eileen wasn't on duty until four o'clock. With at least an hour to wait, Annie went up into the balcony and sat at a bare table where she could maintain a clear view of the dance floor and the hostess enclosure. The valise she placed on the floor, out of sight and clasped between her ankles.

And now the fear started to grow. What if the Irishman had alerted others? They could have waited and followed her. She glanced up as every shadowy figure passed along the narrow corridor which once had led behind the theatre boxes. Then her attention quickly switched back to the dance floor so that she'd catch the first glimpse of Eileen when she arrived. The time seemed to drag. Even the band seemed to be playing very slow tunes to the sparsely attended afternoon session.

A shadow fell across the table. Annie looked up. A tall young man with a ragged moustache smiled down at her. She gripped the valise even tighter with her ankles. 'May I sit here?' the man asked and, before she could reply, sat down. The girl was reassured by his English accent. Probably he was just a young masher. He signalled a waitress and, very sure of himself, ordered tea for both of them. Annie caught a glimpse of the familiar tall girl at the hostess enclosure and leapt to her feet. Grabbing the valise, she rushed away before the young man could cancel his now redundant order.

When she reached the dance floor, several of her former colleagues called friendly greetings, but Annie could only wave to them and hurry on. The long wait had greatly increased her fear. At any moment someone could block her path and defeat her purpose. And that purpose now had taken on the force of a sacred mission. The big Irish girl was astonished by the urgency of her arrival. 'Annie! Are ya out o' work already?'

'No. It's not that. I must talk to you.' She raised the valise, clenched in a tight fist. 'Can I leave this in your locker? Just for a few minutes.'

'Sure, ya can.'

When the goods were safely hidden Annie felt some relief. She immediately proffered sixpence to her former colleague. 'Now. I'll buy one of your tickets.'

Eileen laughed. 'Don't be silly!'

'Yes. We can't talk in here.' It seemed important that none of the other girls should overhear, and that neither customer nor manager should interrupt. In the afternoons – when men were scarcer than ever – women often danced with each other. Eileen took the money and issued a ticket. 'Right ye are, then. Wan thing, though – *I'm* to lead!'

The smaller girl managed to smile and nodded agreement.

When they were dancing, Annie found it easier than she'd anticipated to get to the point of this strange assignation. Eileen knew Albert and, though she was horrified to learn that he was a 'Tan', quickly appreciated the fix in which her friend had been placed. 'So, what are ye goin' to do wit' the stun?'

Annie swallowed hard. 'I thought you might know somebody I could pass it on to.'

'A Fenian, ya mean?'

'Yes. Somebody in authority. Somebody here in London.'

'There's no Fenian leaders in London that I know of,' Eileen said. 'But there's an IRA transit . . .' She was about to give the address when it occurred to her that a girl who'd slept with a Tan for so long *could* have known that he was . . . and could have agreed to this trick which would discover an IRA transit house.

Annie felt her friend's fingers tense on her back as they

danced expertly around the floor. 'Where?' she asked. All this Irish business was new to her. She'd no idea what the difference was between the Fenians and the IRA. Nor did she care which of them lifted the appalling burden from her shoulders. It would never have struck her that she could be considered a spy, least of all by a friend.

The music stopped and they walked slowly to the side of the floor. Eileen said, 'Maybe better if ya let me take the stuff.'

And now, in her turn, Annie's background prompted in her an unwarranted suspicion. She really did not know Eileen all that well; not personally. But she did know the Irish girl was always short of cash. Was there not a possibility that she would just sell the valuables? Even in a pawn shop they would raise a lot more than could be earned by twice daily dance sessions for quite a while. 'No,' she said. 'I must deliver them myself. It's the least I can do for having them at all.'

The music started up again. A quickstep. The girls watched the dancers for a few moments without saying anything. Then Eileen decided to take a chance; though secretly she intended to put the word out about the Irishman Annie had mentioned. If that was true they were on safe ground and in any case precautions could be taken. She said, 'There is somebody you could go to . . . though it would be a brave lass, or man even, who'd go there not invited.'

'Where is it?'

'Ask for Ma Duggan at 28 Conlan Street, Kensal Town. She's a flower-seller during the day, so she won't be home for a couple of hours yet.'

Annie nodded. 'I'd better take that stuff out of your locker.'

Eileen dissuaded her with a hint of alarm in her voice. 'No, no. Best leave it there till you're goin'.'

'But I can't wait here for two hours.'

'Sure ya can! Have a walk around an' chat to the girls.'

Annie realised there was some duplicity in the Irish girl's hearty manner but could not do other than she was instructed.

When she emerged onto the street again clutching the valise it was already dusk. She went down into the Covent Garden Underground station and consulted the wall chart. She could go from there to Piccadilly and catch the Bakerloo to Kensal Green. That should be near enough. And if the business was done quickly she'd be back in the West End in plenty of time for the evening performance.

It did not prove quite so easy in practice. By the time she reached Kensal Green it was quite dark and up there only the main roads were gaslit. She stopped several people, including a lamplighter, to ask directions and thus, very slowly, progressed to the warren of streets on the other side of Harrow Road.

Conlan Street was at the very centre of an overcrowded slum. There was a great deal of shouting behind closed doors and, in uncurtained lamplit rooms, she saw large boisterous families gathered at their evening meal. Children plunged along the uneven pavement at startling speed. Everywhere there seemed to be a threat of violent unexplained eruption. Even her proudly confessed preference for such communities was not proof against this vibrant, dangerous expression of it.

The windows of number 28 were not lit, either upstairs or down. She knocked on the door, then drew back in alarm at the immediacy with which it was pulled open by a heavy, bearded man.

Annie struggled with a feeling of panic. Her voice was out of control. 'I'd like to see Ma Duggan,' she said.

The door was pulled wider and she went in to a narrow hallway which smelled of boiled cabbage. A door opened at the end of the passage and the greenish gaslight fell at an acute angle on the opposite wall. There seemed little doubt that she was expected. Annie recalled how Eileen had delayed her at Covent Garden. No doubt she had sent someone to make enquiries and warn the transit house to expect a visitor.

There were three people already in the room. Another heavy-set man, a thin, spinsterish-looking woman and an old woman who was seated at the table. The man who had answered the door pushed Annie forward to be inspected by the old woman. This was Ma Duggan. Her face was old but her hair was dyed jet black and heavily dressed with oil to make it glossy. This unreal-looking hair was drawn severely away from a centre parting in a style the old Queen had favoured. And that accentuated the broad, Slavish cheeks and short, thick nose of Irish tinker-people. But the most striking feature of her appearance was a deeply scored hare-lip. As was usually the case, this abnormality was linked with a cleft palate which gave a snorting, nasal quality to her voice. She said, 'You have somethin' for me, dearie?'

Annie placed the valise on the table and, with strenuously maintained control, unlocked the clasp.

The old woman picked it up and emptied the contents onto the table. She spluttered with satisfaction and made a guttural remark to the thin woman who moved closer to the table and helped unwrap the gifts. Ma Duggan snorted another question, then looked sharply up at Annie's face.

Annie couldn't make out the words and turned to the bearded man for help.

He rephrased the question. 'Is it a hooer ye are?'

'No!'

The old woman pushed herself to her feet and moved slowly round the table. Very gently she took Annie by the shoulders. The girl shuddered with fear. The scrawny hands tensed on her shoulders, moving her closer to the gas-mantle. Ma Duggan stared into her face. 'Ach, no,' she said at last. 'This is one of ours. Eh, dearie? But a lass wit' a great likin' for men.'

Annie said nothing but stared at Ma Duggan's upper lip which moved curiously when she spoke.

The thin woman was less easily satisfied. 'She must be blind that could not see what was clearly stolen.'

'Any woman,' said the old matriarch, 'is blind between her legs.' Her fingers tightened on Annie's arm. 'And that was the only gift ya really wanted, eh?'

'I was very stupid,' the girl confessed.

'But ye'll be wiser now?'

Annie nodded, longing to rush from the stifling, smelly room and away from the nasal, spluttering voice of the old woman whose display of gentleness carried such threat.

'Out ye go then, dearie. And say nothin' of this to a soul else.'

Before Annie could reply or give any assurance she was yanked backwards by the man and bundled out of the house.

Then she ran. She ran all the way back to the station, stumbling and tripping on the uneven pavements, panting for breath and glad to escape unpunished – or so she thought – from so great a folly.

Rosemary Gill's flat was in Catherine Street, up from the Aldwych. There were two large bedrooms and a sitting room as well as a fully equipped kitchen and a bathroom. Annie was delighted with it, though her first task was to move a lot of the furniture out of the room which was to be hers into the 'common room' as Rosemary called it. And within a few days she knew she was going to be happy there. The two girls got on very well together. At first it was just because they were so different in nature and upbringing. Each was fascinated by the other's way of looking at things and doing things. It seemed impossible that they'd ever run out of surprises. Nor was there any question that one of them had a better attitude or ability. They were different, that was all. If mature opinion would have it that one of them had moved up the scale and the other had moved down, such a notion did not occur to the girls. They had their work in common.

Fortunately, Annie was kept steadily at work. When one show finished she moved directly into rehearsals for another; still in the chorus but with occasional solo spots doing her urchin routine. And that was how Eileen Docherty found her again. One night after the show at the Pavilion she walked into the din and flurry of the chorus dressing room. Annie, bending to take off her stockings, caught sight of her in the mirror and felt a sudden stab of fear. But she turned brightly enough and shouted, 'Eileen! Come in.'

Her former colleague and friend looked a lot more than three years older. Her face was thin and drawn and she moved into the glare of the dressing-table lights with heavy-footed weariness. 'You're lookin' well, Annie.'

'So are you,' Annie lied. 'Did you enjoy the show?'

'To tell ya the truth, I've not seen it.'

'Oh!' Annie busied herself replacing the costumes on her rack in proper running order for the next performance. While doing so she reasoned that if Eileen hadn't seen the show then she must have sneaked in through the stage door – which indicated there was some urgency about this meeting. Whatever it was, she didn't want to discuss it with all the other girls milling about. She called over her shoulder to the doleful young woman:

'We can't talk in this noise. Hang on a minute and we'll go round the corner for something to eat.'

Eileen nodded and, with little interest, observed the bustle which surged around her.

Annie led the way across a rain-slicked Piccadilly Circus which reflected long zig-zag streamers of coloured light. She had in mind a supper club in Denman Street which catered for the theatre trade and which was too expensive to attract her fellow chorus girls. When they'd settled in a booth it was clear that Eileen was impressed by Annie's affluence. She said, 'Oh, this is a nobby place, sure enough. The money must be good, eh?'

'Not that good. Four pounds a week. But I get ten and six extra for the solo spot. And we're trying to get half a crown on top for the midnight matinée.' It had occurred to Annie that Eileen might be about to ask her for money. She certainly looked as though she needed money.

'Four quid! That's a sure grade better than fourpence a dance.' She loosened her coat in the warmth of the restaurant and Annie noted the lapels were threadbare under the fox fur.

'What have *you* been doing since the Garden closed?'

Eileen shrugged. 'Och, a turn at the Lyceum for thru'penny bits, four times a week. I'm at the Paradise now, though, supervisin'.'

'Supervising!' Annie managed to sound impressed but, from what she knew of Paradise Danceland, it seemed likely the supervisor would be chiefly employed as catfight separator and referee. Eileen had the height and raw-boned bulk for that.

She went on, 'And I'll tell ya who comes in regular there.'

'Who?'

'Your man Bert.'

'Bert Lane? Are you sure?' Annie felt the room suddenly go out of focus.

'Of course I'm sure. Doesn't he ask for you!' Eileen smiled.

'Asks me all the time if I've seen ya and where y'are now.'

The supper dish and a bottle of wine were brought to the table and there was silence between the girls as they started to eat.

Annie tried to cope with a turmoil of emotion. First, she was greatly relieved to know that Bert was even alive. She'd felt sure the Fenians would have killed him before he left Ireland. Added to that sense of relief was an undeniable excitement. So much had been packed into their short passionate affair, and her body responded to the memory of it, regardless of the consequences. There was some satisfaction, too, in knowing that he hadn't forgotten her. Fortunately, however – and above all – there was a strong sensation of fear.

Eileen said, 'He wants to know if you'd like to see him again.'

'Did he say that?'

'Sure, am I not tellin' ya? He asked me to ask you that.' Fear won. 'No,' Annie said firmly. 'I don't want to see him again.'

Her former confidante did not seem surprised. She nodded. 'I'll tell him. He's a policeman now, y'know.'

'Oh?' Annie bent her head and continued eating. 'Yes. He mentioned he might have a go at that when he came back.'

Eileen ate heartily and, between mouthfuls, revealed why she of all people had undertaken this errand. 'There's trouble enough at the Paradise wit'out fallin' foul o' the police.'

'I suppose so.'

'It's on his beat, y'see, so he gets his dancin' free. And whatever else is goin'.'

They finished their supper more lightheartedly, with talk about their respective occupations. Once or twice Eileen did make comments which normally would have led Annie to mention her flatmate, Rosemary; and, indeed, to say where they were living. But without wishing to give offence, she guarded her tongue. She felt strongly protective of her new friend and was determined that nothing should disturb the happy life she had attained after such a disastrous start.

For several weeks after Eileen's visit to the theatre Annie went home by roundabout means, but as the end of the revue's run, and spring, approached, the threat again faded. Both she and Rosemary would be away from London for most of the summer.

Rosemary took a long summer holiday. On a couple of occasions she went to Berlin which was rapidly becoming the place for bright young things with a yen for adventure. But Annie scorned so unnecessary a thing as holidays. If she was free she joined established companies at seaside resorts where the drill was twice nightly and the halls were humid with sweat.

If was after just such a season that she came back to London in 1924 and accepted an invitation which changed her life. She was friendly with Lionel Sillers, a writer for the Charlot revues, and he suggested she might like to see some 'real' theatre. Annie was sceptical. The sort of theatre she was in seemed real enough to her. She had no highbrow pretensions. However, Lionel was a pleasant man with a lot of good contacts and there was no harm in humouring him. That is how she came to be at the New Theatre to see Sybil Thorndike as St Joan. And she saw it every night for all of the following week. Nothing so immediate or overwhelming had ever struck her before.

She watched that rough, gawky, young woman and listened to that throbbing, imperative voice. She saw the actress transform herself in the course of the evening into sheer spirit; from boorish peasant to incandescent saint. And Annie was aware, all around her in the audience, that this was real indeed. This was more real than the most fabulous reality the exterior world could offer. At the end of each performance she sat shaken and exalted. 'How long, oh Lord, how long?' would it take her, she wondered, to do what Sybil Thorndike could do with a play and an audience – *every night*.

The acting lessons started immediately. And stopped just as suddenly. Annie tried several teachers in quick succession and on each occasion paid advance fees for lessons she refused to take. The teachers were well-recommended. But they were all retired or out-of-work actresses. And all of them wanted to make Annie what they had been at her age. Not what they'd hoped to be but what they actually were; even in fond retrospect. None of them could see the virtue in trying to develop the qualities which were already there. What they did develop was her breath control and voice projection. That accomplished, Annie saw no virtue in any further training to be an out-of-work actress.

She said as much to Madam Daltry. The gaunt old lady reared to her full height. 'You are presumptuous, Miss Jeynor. At the moment your abilities ensure that you will be a never-*in*-work actress.'

'I'm in work at the moment.'

Madam Daltry sniffed. 'Ah, yes. The music hall, I believe.'

'In the theatre. Entertaining a paying audience.'

'The audience will take what it gets and pay if it's fashionable, Miss Jeynor. I am talking about dramatic *art*. The tradition of excellence enjoyed by the serious English stage.'

'And I,' said Annie, 'am talking about *me*.'

'You must surrender yourself to the disciplines of the art.'

Annie did not want to offend the old lady by pointing out that surrendering to art should offer greater reward than a high crumbling flat in Bayswater Road, teaching whoever had enough money to pay for it how to breathe. 'Yes, Madam. I'm grateful for your advice, but I won't waste any more of your time.'

Madam Daltry was quick to point out, 'The fee is not returnable.'

'That's what they all say.' Annie smiled, and bade the lady goodbye.

Once outside the tall, flaking house she took a deep breath to the full extent of her expensively achieved capacity and set off across the park. It was a dull autumn day and the fallen leaves were held down by moisture after heavy rain. As she moved briskly along the path towards the lower basin of the Serpentine she, at first, paid little attention to the figure of a man huddled on one of the benches. But, as she passed, it did strike her as odd that the tramp was so well dressed.

Hearing the girl's footsteps he turned uneasily, but did not open his eyes. Annie stopped short, then slowly retraced several steps to look closer. There was no doubt. The dirty, unshaven young man in the mud-spattered clothes was Jamie Northcott.

He was dimly aware that he was being inspected. He cursed

drunkenly under his breath and with a wide uncoordinated gesture of his arm waved her away.

'Jamie!' she said, and laid a hand on his shoulder. The coat was damp. His eyes were open now, but still he did not recognise her. Annie shook his arm as though he'd been merely asleep and not sunk in an alcoholic stupor. 'Wake up!' she said. 'It's Annie.'

He made an evident effort to raise his head and focus his running eyes. Probably he did recognise her, dimly, but linking the recognition with any sort of positive response was quite beyond him. He let his head fall back against the boards of the bench and again closed his eyes.

One or two other strollers were now giving some attention to this encounter. Annie decided that nothing could be gained from trying to rouse him. She turned abruptly and walked away; but not in the direction she had been taking. Instead, she veered off the path and branched back across the parkland towards Bayswater Road. Though this was none of her business, she had always had an affectionate regard for Jamie. And he had been kind to her. Now, obviously, he needed help. His sister could and should provide it.

The urgency of her march across the park was impeded by the fact that her narrow heels sank at each step into the soft earth, and fallen leaves accumulated in a wedge under her instep. Before she rang the bell of Mrs Grenville's house, she spent some time trying to clean her shoes.

Celia met her on the landing and showed her into the drawing room. Though she spoke the usual pleasantries and Annie replied in standard fashion, it was as though Jamie's sister was expecting bad news. She looked drawn and the usual conscious grace of her movement and gestures had given way to a jerky nervousness.

Annie did not waste her time. 'Mrs Grenville, I've just seen Jamie in the park. I think he needs help.'

'In the park!'

'Yes. On a bench by the Serpentine.'

'Is he hurt?'

'I don't think so.' Annie hesitated to report that he was hopelessly drunk. 'But he does not look well.'

'Maybe he was on his way to see me.' There was clear relief in Celia's voice.

Annie nodded. It was possible that the young man had intended to sober up a bit before calling on his sister.

Mrs Grenville crossed to the fireplace and rang for the man-servant. Having given him instructions to find and bring 'Mr Jamie' to the house, she turned again to Annie. 'Please sit down, Miss Jeynor. I'm glad you came.' She sat on the couch beside Annie. 'The fact is I haven't seen Jamie for some months.' She controlled her voice. 'And on that occasion he was threatening to take his own life.'

Annie remained silent.

Celia Grenville approved of the girl's composure. She went on, 'There is nothing for him to do, you see, which would make up for the war. Or, that would equal the excitement of *being* at war.'

The girl understood that without difficulty. It was the same urgent need for a purpose allied with excitement which had drawn Albert Lane into the auxiliary policing force in Ireland. When a country primes its young men to kill, it may not, thereafter, offer them anything less. Annie said, 'I don't suppose there's much excitement in the shipping business.'

'No. He'd never consider going back to a dull routine office job.'

'He could be a professional dancer.'

The older woman looked at her as though this was hardly an occasion to joke. But, perhaps, it was not a joke. She responded obliquely. 'Oh, I wish he were so keen on dancing now as he used to be. Apparently, he's never had a partner as good as you.'

'I'm sure there's plenty good enough. If he got used to their style.'

But Mrs Grenville had no intention of discussing the style of various dance hostesses. Her brother had talked about this girl on many occasions. It was puzzling. She said, 'Jamie seemed to value your friendship as well as your dancing ability.'

'Oh?'

65

'Oh yes, indeed. He has a very high opinion of your intelligence.'

Annie smiled, 'I think that's only because I don't want to marry him.'

Celia's eyes widened. The girl was a constant surprise to her. Laying aside even the wildly unsuitable idea of such a marriage, she contented herself by observing, 'That is wise of you. But I wish someone would marry him.'

Annie got to her feet. 'I think it would be better if I left before he gets here.'

Celia who'd been about to offer tea, decided against it. There was little doubt it would be embarrassing for all of them if Annie remained. 'Perhaps you're right. Thank you again, Miss Jeynor, for your concern.'

Annie took her hand briefly then turned for the door. Celia accompanied her down the stairs. 'Have you kept up with your driving?'

'No. I haven't had any practice recently. And I live quite near the theatres now.'

'We must come to see you.'

They lingered uneasily in the echoing hall. 'Oh, I'm not in anything at the moment,' Annie told her. 'But I'm trying to do something as a serious actress.'

'Really?' Mrs Grenville said with bright interest, though for her the terms 'serious' and 'actress' were incompatible. 'I do hope you succeed. Goodbye, Miss Jeynor.'

Over lunch one day Rosemary remarked, 'I've been asked to read for a straight tryout.'

The word 'straight' indicated a non-musical play and 'tryout' a speculative venture which might or might not be produced; and even if it were, they'd probably hire a completely different cast.

'Not worth it,' Annie said.

'It's not worth it for *me*,' Rosemary mused, keeping her eyes on her plate. 'I can't act for toffee – though I *look* marvellous.'

Annie smiled. Her flighty friend was always on the alert for offers of work which she'd no intention of taking herself but which she casually pushed Annie's way. It was Rosemary who got all the offers partly because she did look marvellous, but also because she was part of the social circle to which many theatre producers aspired. Annie asked her, 'You think it might be worth it for me?'

'It's at the Court.'

'Sloane Square, I suppose, not Windsor.'

'Lucky for you! At Windsor you'd have to shout your lines above the bagpipes.'

'Who's the author?'

'I believe it's that little Scotchman with the American backer.' She meant Sir James Matthew Barrie.

'What does he need with a tryout?'

'Darling, I've no idea! I wasn't consulted about that at all. I was just asked to read for a part and . . .' She shrugged and smiled.

'And . . . ?'

'I said I couldn't but I knew a fine young actress who'd be absolutely right for it.'

'Uh huh. Who did you say this *to?*'

'The producer. He's a fearful snob, so . . .' she cleared her throat and stated firmly, '. . . so I also said you were a niece of Lord Exeter.' Seeing Annie's rising indignation, she added loudly and quickly, 'Exeter won't mind. He has loads of nieces. Some of them are even related to him.'

Annie laughed.

'You will try for it, won't you?'

'Oh, yes. But I'll have to borrow your pearls again.'

'Of course, darling!' Rosemary erupted from the table. 'I'll get the script.'

While she was gone Annie considered the advantages. The Royal Court, even for a Sunday tryout, would be a big step in the right direction – if she got the part. The theatre was being run by Barry Jackson whose reputation stood very high indeed. The resident play was the long-running comedy, *The Farmer's Wife*, but there had been several successful one-performance tryouts at Sloane Square. The author of this one was, of course, the author of *Peter Pan* – a rich and successful playwright, even before the war. It seemed strange that a commercial management would not go for full production right away on anything he wrote.

The reason for their caution was clear in the script. It was a curious family drama called *Soldiers Were They*, which at a particular point suddenly veered into Celtic mysticism. But there was also the question of bad taste, for it was set in Ireland. The play celebrated the end of the 'troubles'. And indeed, the troubles had ended. After more than two years as its own master, the Irish Free State was calm. Only the renegade De Valera stirred dissent against the new order.

The audition went well and Annie returned to the flat late in the afternoon with high hopes of having secured the part. As she ascended the broad stone stairway to the first floor her mind was on the script. It startled her to see the highly polished boots of a man on the top step. She glanced up sharply and stared straight into Albert Lane's smiling face.

'Hello, Annie,' he said and extended his hand to aid her on the last few steps.

'Bert! How did you find me?'

'I asked at your stage door.'

Annie fumbled for her key. 'They're not supposed to tell people where we live.'

'I was in uniform. They'll tell a policeman anything.'

He was not in uniform now and the girl, in an entirely detached way, was very conscious of how handsome he looked. She indicated that he should follow her into the flat. But, once there, they just stood uneasily in the middle of the sitting room.

At last Annie remembered to lay down her bag and the bulky script. She said, 'Didn't Eileen give you the message?'

Bert was his old assured self again. He nodded whimsically. 'She did that. But I was sure you couldn't mean it.'

'I did mean it. There's no point in us getting together again.'

'How do you know that, till we try?'

'I don't want to.' She retreated several paces and repeated with the utmost conviction, 'I really don't want to.'

'Right now you don't.' He moved slowly towards her. 'But

I'm sure I could change your mind – even if there is another fella.'

Annie seized on that. 'Yes. There is.'

He didn't believe her. 'What's his name?'

She said the first name that came to her mind. 'Jamie Northcott.' And now she stood her ground, hoping he wouldn't touch her.

They were interrupted by Rosemary. She hadn't heard them come in and now, entirely naked and wet, she came bustling out of the bathroom to search for her cigarettes. She stopped, swept the hair out of her eyes and stared brazenly at the man.

'How very embarrassing for you,' she said.

Albert muttered, 'I'll see you later, Annie,' and hurriedly left. The girls confronted each other.

'Rosemary. Thank God you were in.'

'Was he bothering you?'

Annie tried to sound casual. 'No, no. He's just a friend.'

'Oh, good. I don't mind a friend getting a free show.'

'He's a policeman.'

'Really! Then perhaps I should have done a little dance as well.'

'Get back in your bath.'

'As soon as I find my cigarettes.'

When Annie was alone in the room she sat down abruptly. The shock and uncertainty was even greater than she'd feared. She had thought about Albert and what it would be like to see him again. Gradually she built up a defensive anger with herself for being so callous – and so vulnerable. She reminded herself of what he had done. That could not be forgiven. She recalled how quickly he'd run out on her when he thought himself in danger. Now he was safe, that arrogant assurance she had once admired seemed less a natural quality than a pose.

From the bathroom came Rosemary's muffled voice. 'Did you get the part, darling?'

'I think so.'

The part Annie got was that of the wilful daughter of one of the De Valera rebels and, a couple of weeks later, she started rehearsing it. She had no trouble with the Irish accent, and her own natural energy as well as her vulnerable appearance commended her to the author. Sir James asked, 'Are you Irish, Miss Jeynor?'

'No, sir.'

'Well, you are very convincing. And you have a fine strong voice.'

'Thank you.'

He studied the highly polished toecaps of his boots with great attention. 'Of course, we wanted someone with fair hair.'

'Why?'

He looked up sharply. 'What?' He was quite unused to anyone questioning his opinion.

'Surely there are more dark-haired than fair-haired girls in Ireland.'

The playwright made an impatient fanning gesture with his hand. 'Oh, that may be. Less sympathetic, though.' He peered closer at her to make sure she understood this. 'Fair hair is more sympathetic than dark hair.'

Annie did not feel like offering to dye her hair blonde for one performance. She awaited further intelligence.

Barrie said, 'Of course, fair-haired girls usually have tiny voices.' He gave a wan smile. 'On balance . . .' Again he leaned forward. 'I say, on balance I'd rather be sure the audience can hear my lines than sympathise with whoever is speaking them.'

Annie chuckled obligingly. The playwright nodded several times in approval then walked carefully away to resume his hunched position on a bare rehearsal chair. This was the first of many pointed, humorous, and mutually enjoyed exchanges she had with the author.

And yet, to the girl, J. M. Barrie was a sad little man. He had a pale triangular face, with a deeply lined broad forehead and a pointed chin. And everything pointed down. His eyes drooped at the outer corners, his cheeks seemed to sag, his straggly moustache tailed off. Annie thought it rather ungrateful of him to be both sad and successful. But perhaps he felt that his greatest successes were already over; for he could not hold out much hope with regard to *Soldiers Were They*.

However, the event was well-advertised and there was a

70

small but rowdy demonstration in Sloane Square before the curtain went up. The Sinn Feiners were annoyed at what they took to be London support for the men who'd killed Michael Collins. Their protest was usurped by a column of striking miners. They had been holding a rally in Hyde Park and, when all the speeches had been delivered, came marching down Sloane Street waving red banners. Finding their way blocked by the Sinn Feiners, they vented their more general frustration on the Collins adherents. This soon developed into several running fights across the square.

Inside the theatre there was another sort of protest as the play unfolded. The audience grew silent and then restive at being given serious political comment by a writer they had always relied upon for amusing whimsy. Possibly they would have been more tolerant if they had not been forced to gain access to the theatre through ranks of rival political demonstrators. It really was a bit much expecting them to enjoy on the stage what they'd done their best to avoid outside.

In the dressing room afterwards, there was gloom. Most of the cast were experienced, sought-after actors. For them a Barrie play should mean success and esteem and a long run – none of which could now accrue from the occasion.

But their professional disappointment did not affect Annie. For her it was more than enough that she had played her first straight role and that a good number of management representatives and producers had seen her do it.

And there was at least one distinguished member of the audience who was impressed and wanted to say so. The playwright W. S. Maugham was brought backstage by the author, because apparently he had insisted on meeting Annie. This astonished several members of the cast. It was well known that Mr Maugham admired few actresses and liked even fewer. Certainly he was intimidating – a short, hawk-nosed man, with black hair brushed scalp-tight and a permanent expression of disdain. He also had a bad stammer. To Annie he said, 'What a surpr*i*sing perf-f-formance, Miss Jeynor.'

The young actress, ready to express gratitude, was stymied behind the ambiguity of the remark. 'In what way surprising?'

'In its v-v-vitality!' He made a rising gesture with both hands and half turned towards Barrie. 'Sir James does not deserve *all* of that.'

The little Scotchman consulted his boots and shook his head dolefully. 'Not *any* of it – as things have turned out.'

Maugham patted his shoulder and smiled. Then he turned directly to Annie. 'I hope, sometime in f-f-future, you will do as much for me, Miss Jeynor.'

'I'd be very grateful for the opportunity, Mr Maugham,' Annie said.

The short exchange came to an end. As soon as the play-wrights had gone, there was the present uncertainty to face again. But Annie was much cheered by Rosemary rushing backstage to congratulate her.

'Annie, dear! You were quite superb. But it couldn't have been much fun, surely?' She leaned over Annie's shoulder to freshen her make-up in the brightly lit glass. To Rosemary, a night at the theatre had to be, above all, a social occasion. She judged such events more by the celebrity of the audience than the quality of the performance. 'But of course one can't expect Sunday night in Sloane Square to be madly fashionable,' she said through pursed lips.

'Did you hear every word?' Annie asked.

'Oh yes, darling. Every single one. You were *extremely* loud and lovely. But in all those words there weren't many laughs, were there?'

'I don't think it was meant to be funny.'

'Then how well it succeeded,' Rosemary said, and smiled broadly at Annie's reflection.

Annie daubed the nose of her friend's reflected face with a smear of cleansing cream.

When they got out of the theatre the audience had gone, but there were still a few vendors hanging around. One of them was a flower-seller, there to persuade those ladies who were going on to a supper party that they needed a corsage. But this old woman was not waiting at the front entrance. She stood at the top of the alley from the stage door. The girls had passed her when she called out.

'Fresh flowers, dearie!'

Annie jolted to a stop but dared not turn round. That nasal, snorting sound of the old woman's voice could not be mistaken.

'Sweet posy, just for you?' Ma Duggan hobbled up to them and thrust something into Annie's hands. It was a small box decorated with a bunch of violets. 'Take it as a gift, dearie!'

Annie stared at the wrinkled face of the old woman, half shadowed by the marquee lights. Ma Duggan was smiling and the deep split in her upper lip gaped. 'Thank you.'

'Just a little gift. Maybe what you always wanted.'

Annie started away from her, clutching the box. Rosemary was bewildered by the incident but turned her sweetest smile on the old woman. 'You are very kind,' she said, then ran to catch up with her friend.

Ma Duggan nodded her head, still smiling, and snorted with pleasure.

When the girls were seated in the Tube for the short journey back to the flat, Rosemary lifted the gift from Annie's lap and sniffed the violets. Then she undid the careful wrapping around the box, but under the wrapping the lid was tightly sealed. And the corners of the wooden box had been waxed. Thwarted, she handed it back to Annie who assumed that one of the women who'd had her property returned wished to show her gratitude and had chosen Ma Duggan as the intermediary. But she was unwilling to discuss the matter in case her friend should ask questions she did not want to answer.

She had never discussed Albert with Rosemary and had not even alluded to his brief appearance in the flat. She certainly did not want to explain why she should be singled out for a gift from the old Irish flower-seller. When they got to the flat, Annie hurried into the kitchen where she managed to prise the box open.

Her scream brought Rosemary running from the sitting room. Annie waved her back. 'No! No! Stay there!'

'What is it?'

'Please. Don't look.'

Rosemary ignored the warning and came to see the contents of the box which lay open on the kitchen table. 'Ugh!' she wrinkled her nose. 'It's meat.'

Annie, white-faced, tried not to look down again at the crammed, bloody lumps of flesh in the box. The 'gift' from Ma Duggan was the severed testicles and penis of a man.

After a moment, and without looking, she pressed the lid back in place. Then in a frenzy of activity she covered it, rolled it and tied it in the table cover. Rosemary stood back, amazed and frightened at Annie's wild burst of activity. She said nothing. Nor did she follow when her flatmate rushed out carrying the strange bundle.

Annie forced herself not to run as she moved downhill towards the river. In her mind she kept hearing the old woman's loathsome voice. 'Just a little gift . . . what you always wanted . . . what you always wanted . . .' It was now quite late on Sunday night and Aldwych was very quiet as she crossed to Lancaster Place then out on to Waterloo Bridge. There were several people on the bridge and she paced herself so that a large enough gap should grow between her and them. She was very near the centre of the span when she hurled the bundle over the rail and continued walking.

It was another hour before she could bring herself to return to the flat. During that time the horror subsided and she was able to consider whether or not she deserved such retribution. What Albert had done was terrible. And now both of them had suffered the consequences. But surely her part in the wrongdoing should not be paid like this. She had done everything she could, as soon as she could, to make amends. If it was not enough there was nothing more she could do and it would be foolish to try. 'God damn them all,' she muttered to herself as she recrossed the bridge. Then again, with angry vehemence, 'God damn them *all*!'

I was unwilling to question Annie any further on Albert Lane. She tended to flare up if I tried to back-track on what she'd already dealt with; as if it was my fault the edges of the past were not properly aligned.

Indeed, our method of work was proving more exhausting than I'd bargained for. I began to sympathise with the actors and directors who'd worked with her, and been drained in the process. She *was* exacting. I had to ask all the right questions the first time. During that recollection she was patient; as though I were her defence counsel leading her through some tricky evidence. If I came back on it, though, my role had changed. Now I was the prosecuting counsel. She was willing to be examined but hated like hell to be cross-examined. So, with regard to Albert, I referred to the Sleavin biography.

Dr Sleavin had interviewed Lady Straven – formerly, Rosemary Gill – at some length. It was not surprising that such a gruesome episode had stayed in her memory. Armed with Rosemary's information, Dr Sleavin had combed the newspaper archives. The murder of Constable Albert Lane had been widely reported; as was his admirable record as a soldier in France, an auxiliary in Ireland and a policeman in London. He had been found stabbed to death and – the paper said – mutilated.

His wife was mentioned but, apparently, he left no dependants. That was something I felt bound to ask Annie about.

She said, 'Yes. It wasn't until I read the papers that *I* knew he'd been married. Before the war. It seems, when he was just a boy, he married an older woman. When he came out of the Army, they didn't get on and separated.'

'So really he had no intention of marrying you.'

Her voice strengthened. 'Oh, I think he had.' She nodded her head decisively as though this, at least, was something she could salvage. 'I think he did want to marry me.'

'Surely not? That would be bigamy.'

'Yes. It would.'

'Could you have faced that?'

The old lady raised her eyes to give me a fierce unblinking stare. 'After rape and looting and murder,' she snapped, 'bigamy is no great matter.'

JAMIE NORTHCOTT

Five months later, on a sharp spring evening in 1926, the houselights dimmed in the Old Vic for the opening performance of *Twelfth Night*. On the stage, the setpiece was revealed for the short opening scene in which the lovesick Duke Orsino waits to hear news from the haughty lady with whom he is infatuated. 'If music be the food of love, play on . . .' That established, the action moved on, to a sea shore where survivors of a shipwreck – one of them a young girl – wander onto the alien land of Illyria. The girl, a waif-like creature, asks, 'What country, friends, is this?'

When Annie Jeynor turned to face the audience and spoke the line, a stage legend began. Years afterwards, people who were in the theatre that night would swear the first scene never happened. They were convinced that in this production the play opened on Viola's entrance. What is more, they could vividly recall scene after scene in which she appeared. She transformed the part to something it had never been before. Almost, it seemed, by an act of will she made the role a testament of vulnerability, shining spirit and love. Here was a perfect Viola who poses as a boy so that she can be a servant to the man she loves. But the task he gives her is that of messenger; conveying his adoration to another woman.

Annie had heard of Shakespeare before she could read. But she had never seen any of the plays until she was cast in one. For all her dreams of a career on the stage, it had never occurred to her that she might act a classical role. The part of Viola had been offered to her, she thought, because of her performance at a 'tryout' at the Royal Court. But though the producer had seen her in the Barrie play, he wasn't much impressed. What

77

changed his mind was her comedy routine as a street-vendor at a party. Aware that she could act with great strength and concentration he then saw how mischievous and graceful she could be. And what a sense of fun she conveyed. That was what he wanted; to offset the pathos in the role of Viola. There was also the considerable bonus in how well she looked in those breeches. The girl had style.

Now, after weeks of painstaking rehearsal, Annie had to prove he'd been right to take a chance with her. She was very nervous to start with, and fearful. Even before that first scene was over, though, she knew she was going to be all right. In fact, she felt a sudden joy at the prospect of the long evening ahead. Scene by scene she could feel the excitement building. Upon every entrance she moved closer to the audience until it felt as though they had thrown their arms protectively around her from the dark. It was as though they and she were necessary to each other if the events of the plot were to have a happy conclusion. That was the secret. They were not mere listeners to the tale of unrequited love. They were active allies on her side, anxious and determined to clear away all the misunderstandings which stood in the way of her happiness.

But this was not at all the way the production had been planned. The producer had paid a lot more than Lilian Baylis would have paid to get the actors for the three main comedy roles of Sir Toby Belch, Sir Andrew Aguecheek and Malvolio. It was meant to be a vehicle for the talents of a very funny Malvolio. However, Annie had won all of the audience's attention before any of them appeared and, try as they might, they could not win it back.

The actor playing Toby Belch alluded to this at the interval. He stopped Annie in the dimly lit crossover behind the set. 'Of course, pet,' he said, 'I suppose you know you've ruined it.'

The smile froze on the girl's face. 'What?'

The actor explained, 'They don't want to laugh at us when we're *on* in case they hurt your feelings – though you're *off*!'

And that really was the case. The audience could not forget Viola's predicament, even when the stage was occupied by the most expert clowning. At the curtain-call it was clear the audience wanted to single her out, but she kept her place. So wave after wave of applause for her was received by the comedy actors. That was how the curtain-call had been rehearsed. And no one could have guessed beforehand that the 'breeches' part would steal the show.

The fact was roundly confirmed next morning. All the critics singled out Annie Jeynor for their highest praise. It was unanimous. At the theatre, the producer could sniff a West End transfer and went through his list to determine the order in which he would approach the commercial managements. He also sized up which theatres would be available, and how soon. And for each of the houses he worked out what percentage of the box-office gross he could reasonably claim above his fee for restaging this winner.

At the flat, Rosemary was ecstatic. First thing when she woke, she rushed out and bought all the papers. Then, very quietly, she let herself in and opened each paper at the review page. She folded them neatly over the back of the sofa before she woke Annie to inspect the triumphant array.

The new darling of the critics moved from one paper to the next with a grave expression on her face. It was all so difficult to take in. She had not changed. But the world had changed for her. Somehow she had not realised that the warmth she had felt between herself and the audience must have touched the critics as well. They were part of the magical conspiracy which had enveloped everyone the night before. And they had not forgotten it. When she had read all the notices she turned to Rosemary and stated with quiet wonder, 'And after all this, I'm going to do it *again*. Tonight!'

Rosemary hugged her. 'Yes. And the next night, and the next, and on and on. Oh, my dear Annie, I'm so pleased.'

'So am I. And I've you to thank for getting me that tryout.'

'Oh rubbish. That had nothing to do with it.'

'That's where they saw me.'

'They also saw you doing your much-loved – and overrated – impersonation of Billie Houston. That's what did it, darling. The loveable urchin.'

Annie threw herself full-length on the sofa and pulled the

papers down on top of her so that she was literally covered in praise. She smiled up at Rosemary. 'Thank God there are so many boyish girls in Shakespeare.'

'And so many girlish boys in the theatre!' her friend drily observed. 'They're going to love you.'

But Rosemary was mistaken about that; at least as far as Annie was concerned. About two weeks into the packed four-week run at the Old Vic a deal was concluded with a West End manager. As soon as it became known, the three male principals announced that they would not sign new contracts for the transfer unless the role of Viola was re-cast. They were really doing Miss Jeynor a favour, they told the producer. She was a sweet girl, but really she did not have the training or experience to cope with a long commercial run. In their view she was being sustained on this 'high' by no more than nervous energy, and that could not last. They had their own reputations to think about and her rapid collapse would be damaging.

The producer listened to all this with an increasingly grave face. When they had gone he called Annie in. She was hurt, amazed and depressed. This was the first occasion – though by no means the last – when she came up against the ruthlessness of the 'established' theatre stars. This first time, she had no way of dealing with it. Stunned by so sudden and unfair a change in her fortunes, she just hung her head and wept.

She knew – and the producer knew – it had nothing whatever to do with her lack of training or experience. They wanted her out of the way because they could not bear playing second fiddle to a brilliant newcomer. During the performance that night they were as charming as ever to her face. And something of Annie's spirit returned in her effort to show she could transcend their envy. She blazed even brighter on the stage. Then she went back to the flat and waited up for Rosemary to return from a party so that she could share the bad news and thus try to lessen its impact.

However, the snobbish 'old guard' of the classical theatre had reckoned without the crass financial judgment of the West End manager. As far as he was concerned, at that moment this unknown Annie Jeynor was as big a draw as Alice Delysia. When the producer reported his principals' ultimatum the manager did not hesitate for a moment. He said, 'Fire *them* instead.'

The producer gulped. 'What?' He had his own career to think about and other productions for which he would need the good will of the leading actors. He shook his head. 'I don't think that would be possible.'

'Really? Well, I'm sorry to hear that.' The manager sighed, knowing well what the outcome would be, but willing to indulge the producer's hypocrisy. 'You must do what you think best, of course. They are very fine actors . . .' he paused '. . . I believe. But if Miss Jeynor does not continue playing Viola, then I couldn't take the show.'

And that was that. The producer went back to the other side of the river. On the way, he decided what his plan would be. First, he reported that there would be some delay in obtaining a suitable theatre (which was true) and that the transfer arrangements would have to be put off until that was done (which was not true) – 'including any possible recasting'. That gave hope to everyone.

Meanwhile, he went ahead planning the changes in his production; shifting the emphasis away from the clowns, providing Viola with a more romantic Duke and ensuring the whole thing would now revolve around Annie. Not until the last night at the Vic did he tell his new leading lady that she would keep the part. He swore her to secrecy and advised her to get an agent.

There were plenty of agents eager to have Annie Jeynor on their books. But Annie could see no virtue in giving up a tenth of her salary for what seemed an unnecessary service. Since by her own efforts she'd got herself into a position where they wanted to represent her, it seemed obvious that she was perfectly capable of representing herself.

Thus, unknowingly, she erected another barrier between herself and the mainstream of the profession. Her independence was resented, for managements are happier dealing with agents, and agents deal with each other all the time. They were all to find it easy enough to label Annie Jeynor 'a difficult bitch' when the only difficulty was their lack of success in getting her to part with ten per cent.

During the lay-off before the West End opening Annie took the opportunity to relax. She'd been rehearsing or working for almost eighteen months without a break and now felt the need to restore her energy. As always, this meant finding the warmth and reassurance of a man.

There had been quite a number of light-hearted flirtations during the summer seasons at various resorts. But those – it was clearly understood by Annie and the respective partners – were strictly for the duration of the season. On each occasion they bade each other goodbye with much affection but no regrets.

One of the things men liked about Annie was her unfailing sense of realism. She was not a girl greatly attracted by romantic illusions, and so they did not need to devote any effort to out-of-character pretence. Nor was there much out-of-pocket expense. So the summer season affairs were all happy.

In London the situation was different. Apart from the fact that she had been so busy advancing her career, there lingered the awful warning shadow of Albert Lane. He'd been the first man with whom she'd really felt herself to be in love, and yet, when the crisis came, there had been only panic and emptiness. His initial escape, leaving her to face the consequences, proved that he had not been in love with her either.

Increasingly her thoughts turned to the other regular dance partner, who was as unlike Albert as any man could be. She wondered if she might be able to help the broken and depressed Jamie Northcott. His sister had come to see a performance at the Old Vic, but in the crowded dressing room afterwards there had been no opportunity to ask about Jamie. Celia had, though, invited Annie to spend a weekend at Marlow when the house in the country was opened for the summer. That would be around the first week in May.

The date was almost upon her, but Annie had not heard anything further about the house party. Of course, she did not want to spend the time with Mrs Grenville and her friends if Jamie was not going to be there. And considering his condition when she'd seen him six months earlier, and his sister's fears for him, it seemed unlikely he would be.

But Annie continued to think about him and gradually she began to wonder why she'd not made a greater effort in his direction. He'd been a very amiable, light-hearted man who obviously liked her a great deal. She chided herself for what seemed now a foolish disregard. But at the time she had been so engrossed with Albert there had seemed little point in pursuing her friendship with Jamie.

Things were very different now. And Jamie needed her help. Her realistic approach to life might be just what was needed to pull him out of the despairing, aimless depression which had engulfed him. Surely it was not too late for them to come together in a closer, more sustaining, relationship? Maybe, this time, love was possible. Indeed, her preoccupation over many days led her to suppose that, for her at least, love had already staked a claim.

More information was needed. She sent a note to the Bayswater house, suggesting that she'd like to call to discuss arrangements for the weekend at Marlow. By return of post Celia invited her to tea. She reported that Jamie, too, was very much looking forward to the visit.

As befitted a girl who'd become an overnight sensation and whose picture had appeared in several newspapers as well as the glossy magazines, Annie now took a cab all the way. But though it was late April, she made a point of wearing exactly the same clothes she'd been wearing the day of the previous October when, in very different circumstances, she'd called on Mrs Grenville at home. It was perhaps a pointless gesture, but in making it Annie felt she was keeping faith with herself.

She grinned in the looking-glass as she pulled on the same hat and recalled that she had worn it when she'd been sent packing by the formidable Madam Daltry as a person who had no place in the serious theatre. The mischievous thought occurred to her that, since she was going that way, it might be satisfying to call on Madam Daltry again – just to prove her wrong. But really there would be no justice in that. Madam Daltry had been right, as far as her own experience went. She was not trained to cope with an exception, or imaginative enough to recognise one.

Celia and Jamie were waiting in the drawing room and, as the actress was shown in, they were sharing a joke. Annie was amazed at the change in the man. Of course she had not expected that he would remain unshaven and dishevelled, but she was amazed to find him so obviously glowing with health and high spirits. He came forward at once, embraced her warmly and kissed her on the cheek. 'Dear Annie, what a pleasure it is to see you again!'

His sister smiled. 'And an honour, to entertain such a celebrity.'

It was the sort of remark Annie still had no idea how to deal with. She had no doubt that Mrs Grenville intended only to be welcoming and flattering but success was new enough to her to feel such remarks undeserved or undeserving.

However, talk about the play did manage to bridge the first awkward moments of the meeting and Annie was able to report with some relish how she had almost been robbed of a wider public.

Jamie was indignant. 'Serves them damn well right to get the sack! I'd no idea that actors were so spiteful to each other.'

'Nor did I,' Annie said, 'but I'm learning.'

Then Jamie told his news. He had been recruited by the shipping inspectorate of the Allied Control Commission. This was a watchdog organisation set up under the Treaty of Versailles which limited the permissible size of the German Army and also kept close watch on restricted exports and imports.

Seeing that her brother's voluble enthusiasm was leaving out some relevant information, Celia explained, 'You see, the family firm did a lot of business with Germany before the war. Jamie was involved with that until he went into the Royal Navy.'

'So I know something about it,' Jamie said. 'And the job gives me a lot of opportunity to travel – which suits me fine. I'm sailing for Hamburg next week.'

'Hamburg?' Annie was puzzled again, and also disappointed. It was not merely that Jamie had no need of the help she had come prepared to offer. If he was leaving the country there was now no possibility that their friendship could progress.

She did not pay much attention as he continued to talk about the League of Nations, of which Germany had recently become a member and to which he would be attached. Nor did she pay much heed to his idealistic chatter about the marvellous chance it offered to prevent any further conflict in Europe. That, he was insisting, was what made him so keen on the job. It wasn't just the travel, it was the chance to do something really useful.

Annie continued to nod and smile but she was thinking she'd come too late. She'd been too late in realising that Jamie Northcott was the man she needed in her life. And now he would always be out of reach.

'So he'll miss our party at Marlow,' Celia said.

There was a pause. Jamie gave his sister a sharp questioning look but she, bending over the tea trolley, seemed unaware of it.

And suddenly Annie knew that it was at this point Mrs Grenville should have repeated the invitation to her. But she did not. And so it was clear, also, that it was Jamie who'd wanted to see her. Perhaps to underline the end of their relationship.

Celia gave a faint gasp of annoyance and got to her feet holding a plate of pastries. 'This really will not do,' she said. 'Excuse me.'

As soon as his sister had gone from the room, Jamie moved closer to Annie and took her hand. Evidently he felt she had been snubbed and wanted to reassure her. 'I daresay you're very busy these days.'

'Yes, I am,' Annie said, thinking of the weeks of idleness which lay ahead until the play reopened. 'Very busy.'

The young man relaxed his grasp of her hand and lay back against the cushions of the sofa. 'What I'd really like to do tonight is dance. But Covent Garden's an opera house again.' He grinned. 'Such a waste!'

'There are other dance halls.'

'Full of girls who can't dance!' He turned suddenly to her as though he had not planned to say what he was going to say. 'Annie you're the best partner I ever found.'

'Thank you.'

'And I'd like you to have dinner with me tonight – at the Embassy Club. Then we'll dance the night away. Would you?'

'I'd love to,' she said, though she could not avoid betraying a note of surprise that this simple request had needed so much rehearsal.

She was greatly impressed by the opulence of the Embassy Club. The long room with its sage-green panelled walls with gold moulding, the crystalware and silver gleaming on the tables set on either side of the dance floor and, at the far end, the bow-shaped balcony – again picked out in filigree gold decoration. In the balcony, overlooking the length of the dance floor, sat the orchestra in evening dress. Below them the beautiful gowned ladies, jewelled and elegant, moved with their escorts in a murmur of laughter and perfume.

Annie wore the better of the two new long dresses she'd bought with the West End contract payment. It was turquoise silk with a high, halter neck and severe lines to make her seem taller. The colour flattered her complexion and her freshly cut and shaped auburn hair. She was conscious of looking 'right'. Jamie, of course, could not avoid looking right in that company. But she quickly saw why he had preferred to dance at Covent Garden. Both women and men here were simply awkward dancers. It seemed they had no innate sense of rhythm and moved to the music as though trying to accomplish some difficult exercise in calisthenics.

In such company Annie and Jamie could not help but shine as they swept effortlessly through their well-honed routines. Annie, for the first time since she'd come to London, felt that she belonged there. This was part of the new life towards which she'd striven for so long – and it was accepting her. Jamie, who had always accepted her, proved that his rehabilitation was complete. As they sat at their table sipping wine, he was full of enthusiasm for his new job.

Yet Jamie seemed to be holding something back – an excitement which could not be accounted for if all he was going to do was keep watch on German shipping. When he saw her home, he promised that he would keep in touch and for her part, she was grateful for their perfect evening. But she did not expect to see him again.

*　　*　　*

As events turned out, it would not have been possible to join the house party at Marlow in any case. The following week, after a day or two of reported crisis, the General Strike was declared.

Rosemary's father, Colonel Gill, knew what to do. He'd been an organiser of the Citizens Guard during the 1919 insurrection. In fact, he still had a large stock of the brassards, which he was eager to distribute.

Rosemary declared, 'He's asked me to round up all my friends who can help.'

'To do what?' Annie wanted to know.

'Darling, whatever needs doing. Will you help?'

'Not Mr Baldwin, or the mine-owners – but I'll help *you*.'

'Oh good! I've put you down for the field-kitchens in Hyde Park.'

'Why?' Annie asked.

'Because you can cook the sort of stuff the rabble likes to eat,' her friend replied.

'So I'm not to be a field scullery maid!'

'No, I've already recruited the scullery maids.' She chuckled. 'From Debrett. They can't cook *any*thing!'

At that point Rosemary's boyfriend, Freddie Bolen, arrived. He'd been to the flat several times before, but now he was reporting for duty and seemed more serious than usual. He was a thin German youth with dark curly hair, a pale face and sensitive manner. And he was totally under Rosemary's spell. His attitude to Annie was friendly enough, though formal and polite.

'I have several fellows waiting,' Freddie informed them.

Rosemary nodded briskly. 'Good. We'll need several men to load the stuff at the depot.'

'What do we load the stuff *on?*' the student asked.

'A lorry, of course.'

'But we have no lorry.'

Rosemary swept her blonde hair back with a careless gesture. 'Then you'll have to steal one, darling.'

'Oh, yes,' Freddie said, then looked for support to Annie. 'From where do we steal a lorry?'

Annie shrugged. 'Maybe from a goods yard at a station.'

'Do that now,' the commander instructed. 'Then come back when you've got it.'

'Very well.' Freddie bowed and went out.

Up in Hyde Park, Annie soon tired of preparing mounds of sausage and mash, mutton stew and gallons of strong tea. She happened to mention to a hungry ambulance driver that she could drive. He suggested that she should ask the coordinating committee to get in touch with St Thomas's so that she could be transferred to more valuable work. Annie said she would, but instead she just took a stroll around the store tents, removed her apron and returned to tell the man that she'd been re-assigned.

She climbed into his driving cab and, to prove her worth, took the wheel. The young man directed her down Grosvenor Place to the casualty pick-up at Victoria Station. He told her that help was needed both for Outpatients and Emergency. Drivers were sent out on their own and had to depend on local help getting the patient into the ambulance when they arrived at their destination. Everyone, he told her, was very willing to help.

There were not many casualties laid out on the concourse at Victoria, and most of them were victims of traffic accidents. All sorts of motor transport were being driven by unskilled volunteers and their errors of judgment took a steady toll on pedestrians. There were a lot of broken legs, broken arms and concussion. So far, nobody had been killed.

Annie helped pack the ambulance with the walking wounded and sat with them in the back to be driven across Lambeth Bridge. But there was a tremendous snarl-up of traffic on the other side. The ambulance was stalled for half an hour. During that time, two of the patients decided they'd had enough mercy and got out to hobble home as best they could. Annie got out, too, and walked the rest of the way to the hospital.

She reported for duty at the Emergency desk and lied about the amount of experience she'd had as a driver. Without much trouble she was given a Red Cross brassard to replace the old Citizens Guard one and told to wait in the yard for a vehicle.

She waited a long time and grew hungrier by the minute. It would have been wise, she now realised, to stoke up on the sausage and mash before she left Hyde Park. The afternoon shift of drivers was fully engaged. There would be no changeover until the night shift.

Eventually, she found her way through the vast rambling building to one of the courtyards. And there she emerged out of the gloom onto a scene which looked very much like the meadow at Henley during regatta week, except for the lack of the river.

Set out in the quadrangle were long trestle tables covered by damask table cloths and decorated with elaborate arrangements of flowers. Wine bottles and glassware gleamed in the bright sunlight. A host of young people in colourful summer clothes formed animated groups on the travelling rugs spread on the grass. The volunteers had transformed the space between the high grey walls into an alfresco canteen. And a high quality canteen, at that. Plates and dishes were piled with the very best cold buffet which Fortnum & Mason could provide. New hampers were arriving all the time, carried over the grass by liveried chauffeurs. And the volunteers themselves, who were paying for this marathon picnic, ate and drank, chatted and laughed together before dashing off again for another exhilarating spell of strike breaking.

In many ways it was unfortunate that Annie had applied at the Emergency desk. Apart from the night duty there was the realisation that her area would be the Lambeth slums, for soon there was proof of a fact which the nurses took as a matter of course. It is that rich people get ill mainly during the day while for poor people the crisis normally comes at night. So there were not to be many calls to Westminster where she could readily find her way, but a great many to Lambeth which she knew hardly at all.

She needed a guide. And after her first sortie that night she hired one. He was a boy of fourteen called Eric, ragged and thin, who claimed he could run through the area blindfold. Indeed he had run to the hospital on behalf of a neighbour suffering severe chest pains. He was elated at the prospect of riding in an ambulance and probably would have taken on the job for that pleasure alone. But Annie insisted she would pay him half a crown per shift. That seemed generous to Eric, but he was less keen on the lady's insistence that his mother should be consulted.

'Wot you want to tell my ole woman for?'

'So that she'll know where you are.'

'She won't care where I am at two an' a tanner a night.'

Nevertheless, Annie drove the ambulance to the entrance of an old tenement court and urged Eric to lead the way. Only when they were on the dim, narrow stairway did it occur to the girl that Eric didn't want his mother to know what he was earning because she would claim it for his keep. Annie plucked at his jersey.

Eric stopped. 'Wot now?'

'I'll tell her I'm paying you two shillings a shift.'

A smile began to erase the truculent expression on the boy's face. ''Ow abaat one an' a tanner?' he bargained.

Annie shrugged and nodded. 'All right. One and six.'

The woman kept them standing at the door. And though she readily agreed to her son's employment she seemed more than a little irritated that she'd been disturbed on such a slight matter by a total stranger. The irritation was part fear. She was wary of this nicely dressed, proper-spoken, slim young lady with her official armband who'd knocked at the door and had not come in. That meant trouble. And her Eric was looking worried. All the woman asked, God knew, was to be left alone so that she could cope. She slammed the door in her relief at having got through another trial.

Eric was elated at being on the move again. And now the headlights were required, he leaned forward eagerly with his hand on the horn, ready to honk it at any suggestion of hazard on the road ahead.

The first night was uneventful, and there were lengthy spells between calls. Only a doctor could summon an ambulance, and to do that he had to be fetched by a neighbour or member of the family. If he decided the call was necessary he then had to get to the patient, assess the need, send a runner with a note or get home again and call the hospital. Only then was the ambulance sent out.

Thus, by the time the ambulance arrived the crisis was often past, or the patient was dead. In the latter case, the corpse was taken to hospital so that it could be declared Dead on Arrival. The polite fiction of DOA gave the comforting impression that the doctor had made adequate response, only to lose his patient in transit.

There were no such occasions for Annie on the first few nights, which gave her a chance to get used to the heavy vehicle she was driving. She also got used to Eric's shouted commands, for he soon insisted on travelling on the running-board of the ambulance with his elbow hooked over the open window, mixing his direction calls with loud abuse at other road users who showed any inclination to get in his way.

Annie usually got back to the flat before Rosemary went out to her temporary job as switchboard operator at her father's city office. Switchboard manning was a favourite among girl volunteers from the theatre. Never in the history of the Post Office before or since were calls received and connected, enquiries answered or messages relayed with such spirited charm and vivacity. Besides, the girls themselves could take advantage of unlimited free calls to gossip and rearrange their social calendar. All Rosemary's friends agreed: the strike was really such *fun*.

On the fifth night Annie had a real emergency to deal with. A young man came to the desk on behalf of his pregnant wife. She was long past her time and the midwife wanted the duty doctor to take over. The husband sat with Annie while the porter went to wake the obstetrics clerk. 'She's in terrible pain,' he said. 'Nigh on eight hours now everythin's been awaitin' but it won't happen.'

'Is this her first?' Annie asked.

The man nodded. He was still panting slightly from the exertion of his long race through the dark streets. His young, fearful, face shone with sweat in the gaslight of the waiting room. He gulped. 'Midwife, she says Beryl ain't got the space for it.'

Annie said nothing but was puzzled. She recalled that as a girl

91

she'd seen many births accomplished in open fields without the aid of midwives or doctors. To her, childbirth was a natural, even humdrum, event which did not require the intervention of strangers.

When the doctor was ready they went out to the ambulance. Since the husband was in attendance, Eric's services as guide were not required and he gladly went off to scrounge tea and a sandwich at the porter's lodge.

The address was in Laud Street and when they got there several women – waiting with every sign of impatience – were caught in the headlights. They signalled greater speed. The young doctor-in-training snatched up his bag and threw open the door. He called to Annie, 'We'll be taking her back. You'd better come up and help.'

Annie unhooked the stretcher from inside the ambulance and followed him up the narrow, peeling stairway. The only light was from the doorways of neighbours on the landings. All of them seemed very annoyed at the time it had taken for help to arrive.

The young woman lay drenched in sweat and still in great pain. The doctor immediately snapped open his bag for needle and capsule. The light from a single lamp threw his shadow on the wall as he bent over the pregnant woman to inject her. While waiting for the drug to have effect, the midwife reported the long period of labour, the time several hours ago when the contractions indicated that birth was imminent. That done she gave her own strident opinion that her patient's condition had been forgotten by the doctor who'd last attended her. ''E knew it would 'ave to be cut out,' she asserted. 'Why 'aven't you takin' 'er in?'

'We're taking her in now,' the doctor said.

'Too bloody late!'

The patient was calmer now the pain had eased and Annie moved closer while preparations were made for transfer onto the stretcher. She was young; younger than Annie, but about the same build. Annie took her hand.

'You'll be all right. We'll get you to the hospital right away.'

The girl squeezed her hand tight and looked up at her and, in

92

something of a daze, murmured, 'Didn't know it would be as bad as this. Oh God, it's cruel bad!'

'It'll soon be over.' Annie lifted her shoulders onto the stretcher.

The girl kept a tight grip of her. 'I'm not made for it,' she said. 'Nor you, Miss. Don't . . . don't ever have a baby.'

The doctor and the husband carried the stretcher downstairs with awkward bumping and manoeuvring round the narrow stairwell. Annie had left the headlights on and now ran to open the back of the ambulance. When they were safely in she roared away in the wrong gear, imbued with a dreadful feeling that her urgency would be wasted.

It was not until the patient had been admitted for an immediate caesarean operation that she relaxed enough to consider the wholly new situation with which she'd been confronted. The pregnant girl and Annie *were* so similar. Both had very narrow hips. It was likely that she, too, had a pelvic structure which made the birth canal narrower than would allow passage for normal birth. As she waited for news of the operation she felt an irrational sense of anger that nature could be designed to frustrate its own purpose. It was desperately unfair that the girl could conceive and bear a child to which she could not naturally give birth.

She saw a nurse from the ward whisper to the duty Sister who then called her over. 'Miss Jeynor, I'm told the operation was successful.'

Annie sighed. 'Oh I'm so glad.'

The Sister eyed her coolly. 'But the mother died.'

Annie, who had been turning away in relief, now spun round with an expression of shock and indignation. 'What kind of *success* is that?'

After nine days the General Strike was called off by those unions who could not control their members – which was all of them except the miners who, without gaining anything, stayed out for another six months. For Annie, however, the gain had been considerable: her self-assurance was greatly enhanced. And Rosemary made a substantial gain as well. At one of the volunteers' parties she had met and fallen in love with the younger son of a marquess.

The flatmates held a breakfast meeting to plan their future, which indicated that Annie should take immediate sole possession of the flat. She protested.

'But surely you can stay here until you get married?'

'Oh, no!' Rosemary said. 'Wish I could. But I'll have to get into training at home.'

'Training for what?'

'To join the aristocracy, darling. That takes a *lot* of rehearsal. And of course I'll have to leave the stage immediately.'

'I don't see why.'

'Why, to give everyone time to pretend to forget I was ever on it.'

'That's a pity.'

'Nonsense. It was fun while it lasted but it's no great loss to me – or the stage.'

Annie smiled across the table at her friend. 'It's a loss to me,' she said. 'I'll miss you.'

Rosemary leaned over and gripped Annie's hand. 'And I'll miss you. But that'll only be for a short time.'

'What do you mean?'

'Well, darling, I'm not going to be locked in a castle. Being married is not like being in prison, you know. They let me out after the wedding.'

'It won't be the same.'

Rosemary tossed her head. 'I should hope not! Or marriage has been greatly overrated.'

'And you'll have a title,' Annie warned her. 'Lady Rosemary . . .'

'No. *Douglas*. I'll be Lady Douglas Straven.'

Her friend laughed. 'I think it's ridiculous.'

'That', Rosemary informed her with mock hauteur, 'is just because you are a peasant, darling. And mad with jealousy, into the bargain.'

'Of course.' Annie smiled. She really was delighted to see her friend happy.

And she had some cause for satisfaction herself. While the

strike was on she'd had a long letter from Jamie Northcott in Hamburg. Apparently he was enjoying his work for he wrote at great length about that. But the passage which captured all of Annie's attention was his offhand suggestion that she might care to spend a holiday in Germany – 'sailing up the Rhine'. She wrote back reporting on her most recent activity and noting that she'd very much like to take up his offer, as soon as she was free to do so.

The West End theatre which had been secured for the reopening of *Twelfth Night* was the Criterion in Piccadilly Circus. The year-long run of *Hay Fever*, which had started at the Ambassadors, was ending there. Its star – the already legendary Marie Tempest – had decided she needed an extended holiday before her next vehicle was ready to roll. And so Shakespeare was being allowed a six-month limited run at one of the most beautiful theatres in London. Of course, the advertising of this commerical venture did not stress that the play *was* by Shakespeare – or anyone else, for that matter. What the theatregoers were being offered was 'a poignant love story' centred upon the glittering success of Annie Jeynor.

As was the custom, the leading lady of the coming attraction called upon the leading lady of the closing attraction. The Old Vic producer took Annie to see *Hay Fever* and introduce her to Marie Tempest. Annie enjoyed the play and was quite captivated by Miss Tempest as Judith Bliss. In particular, she noted the veteran actress's flawless comedy technique; the effortless precision of her delivery which shaded the most delicate nuances with utmost clarity; the perfect timing of pauses, positions, gestures which brought forth roars of laughter even when nothing had been said. None of this prepared her for meeting the lady offstage.

As soon as she walked into the dressing room the first striking fact – which occurred to both women – was how alike they were. Marie Tempest, without the elaborate hair piece and make-up she wore on the stage, could have been taken for Annie Jeynor's mother. They were exactly the same height. And whereas Miss Tempest had a fuller figure – as became a woman in her early sixties – their proportions and stance and features were the same. The same round face with upturned nose, the same pouting upper lip and strong chin, the same challenging eyes.

The older actress commented on the resemblance (with forgivable leniency on herself), 'well, my dear, now you know what you will look like at fifty.'

The producer, who knew exactly when Marie Tempest was born, allowed his eyebrow to quiver but gave the expected response. 'I'm sure Miss Jeynor will be immensely comforted to think so.'

Annie quickly agreed. 'Oh, yes. But I think that would be expecting too much.'

The older woman, who had not missed the eyebrow quiver, turned sweetly to the producer. 'I wonder, Mr . . . er, if you could leave Miss Jeynor with me for a few minutes.'

'Of course.' The producer withdrew.

In the lively conversation which followed, other similarities were discovered. Miss Tempest had started her career as a singer and then moved on to musical comedy before making the decisive change to the 'straight' theatre.

Annie was delighted. 'Really? Why did you change over?'

'To increase the opportunities. And give myself more time.'

'More time?'

'Of course. Singing and dancing is for girls. If you must depend on being a girl you will have a very short career.'

'Yes. But it's hard getting the opportunity to change.'

'You have to make the opportunity. At least, I had to,' said Marie Tempest.

The personal emphasis was not lost on the younger woman. She could see very clearly that this veteran actress must always have known – as she was learning – that the important thing was not the role but herself shining through the role. It was contrary to what all the drama teachers had taught. It seemed to be against the whole idea of acting and yet there was something in her which suggested that the way to get to the heart of a character was through her own heart. She asked Miss Tempest if that could be true.

The lady shrugged but there was no false modesty in her reply. 'It's true for me. It was true for the few great performers I have ever seen.' She sighed. 'I don't know if it will be true for you or not. But if it is, *insist* upon it.'

'Insist?'

'Yes. Don't listen to those who haven't got it. Listen to the audience which recognises that quality. Insist on showing it.'

The Criterion run was a great success for Annie. All the ballyhoo which had attended the opening at the Old Vic was repeated. Indeed, the press reception was even more intense because now the popular newspapers and magazines took it up. And there was one front-of-house photograph which captured the imagination of all the picture papers. It was of Viola's entrance and showed Annie in the tattered, flimsy dress of the shipwreck scene.

The press devised endless variations to link Viola's arrival in Illyria with Annie's arrival in the forefront of theatrical celebrities. She was greeted with applause when she entered restaurants. If there was a musical ensemble, they immediately struck up the Mozart rondo which was used in the incidental music of the play. Pretty soon, people started addressing her as Viola because it suited the glamorous image much better than the unromantic 'Annie'.

The production played to near capacity for all of its six months. And before the run was over, the British Council made urgent bids to secure a European tour. At first the management turned the idea down. They were more interested in taking the play to Broadway. Unfortunately, this was forestalled by a recently mounted American production of the same play which suddenly flowered. There was no doubt that the astonishing commercial success of *Twelfth Night* in London had prompted the native enterprise in Manhattan.

So the British Council's offer was taken up in a modified form. The company would tour selected German cities when a suitable itinerary could be arranged. Meanwhile the cast were given time off, and Annie decided that now was the perfect opportunity to sail up the Rhine with Jamie Northcott. It would give her a chance to visit some of the theatres she was likely to play in, and she hoped to learn some German.

Jamie came aboard the Northcott freighter as soon as it berthed in Rotterdam.

He had changed a good deal since the last time Annie had seen him. Apart from the fact that he'd gained weight, he had grown a beard. Now there was nothing in his manner to suggest the erratic youthful dreaminess with which he'd protected himself against postwar reality. He gave the impression that his age had caught up with him, and he was more than willing to accept the fact. But his greeting was as warm and expansive as ever.

'My dear Annie, how well you look! And how glad I am to see you again.'

'Hello, Jamie. I'm very glad to see you too.'

'How was the trip over? Did they look after you all right?'

'Like a princess,' Annie said. And in fact she had been surprised and then delighted by the care and attention she'd received from the moment she embarked at Southampton. She was a guest of the owners and nothing had been too much trouble.

Jamie had known how rough the passage might be on the normal ferry service. Sailing on a Northcott ship in excellent private accommodation would, he felt, make a relaxing start to her holiday.

'Right! Let's go ashore and have lunch.'

'But what about my luggage?'

'Everything will be taken care of – packed, transported and unpacked in your cabin on the steamer.'

'Really?'

'Oh, yes!' Jamie smiled at her incredulity. 'All part of the service.'

The cruise was to be a leisurely progress up the Rhine. There had always been pleasure craft on the middle sections within Germany, but this new venture was being run by the Netherlands Steam Ship Company, on a three-hundred-mile stretch from the mouth of the river to Mainz.

They had lunch in an old restaurant full of decorative copperware and floored with plum-coloured tiles. It was here that Jamie explained another purpose behind the cruise.

'I hope you won't be annoyed, Annie, but I think I should tell you in case you think I'm being rather odd.'

'Tell me what?'

'Behaving oddly, I mean, on the steamer.'

'I don't care how oddly you behave on the steamer.'

'The fact is – it's not all pleasure for me.' He gazed earnestly across the table, then quickly added, 'Though I'm sure it will be.'

'Jamie, please tell me what you want to tell me.'

'I'm an observer,' he said. 'We suspect that this new steamer service is being used to break the embargo on materials getting into the Rhineland.'

'Smuggling?' Annie suggested.

'Sort of. You know about the demilitarised zone?'

'No.'

'Ah!' Jamie tried to conceal his astonishment at her ignorance. 'Well, after the war, it was decided that the land to the west of the Rhine . . . that is between the Rhine and the French border . . . would be kept as a sort of safety zone. There were to be no German troops there, or guns or any armaments.'

'A sort of no-man's land,' Annie hazarded.

'Well, no-armed-German's land, certainly. Since the idea was mainly to protect France against a surprise attack, the French are virtually in control of the Rhineland.'

'So, you are working for them?'

'No. I'm working for the Control Commission.'

'Why?'

Jamie smiled ruefully. 'Because we suspect France would rather make a profit than be safe. And there are a lot of Germans, too, anxious to supply all sorts of equipment to the Rhineland.'

'And you've to try and catch them at it?'

'Yes. We suspect that the starting point is here in Rotterdam and one of the ways they're getting the stuff in is by pleasure steamers. They call at ports on both sides of the river.'

'Which is the wrong side?'

Jamie chuckled. 'The *wrong* side is the right side. Going upstream.'

Annie shook her head in bewilderment. 'I'll keep my eyes open. And let you know if they start unloading any tanks.'

'Keep your eyes open for drums of petrol,' Jamie said. 'We think they're stockpiling petrol.'

'Petrol!'

'Yes. If there's another war, it will be a fully mechanised war. Petrol will be more precious than blood.'

They were both silent for a few moments. Then Annie remarked, 'I'm glad you've told me this.'

'I hope it won't spoil your holiday.'

'I'm sure it won't,' Annie said, but was not really convinced. She began to wonder which idea had come first – the surveillance mission or Jamie's invitation to join him on a carefree cruise. Obviously, her role was as a kind of decoy. A young English couple on holiday would arouse less concern than a British official travelling alone. But she was impressed that Jamie had taken her into his confidence *before* they went aboard the steamer. She decided that he had not lost his respect for her intelligence. Now he was watching her with some concern. She suddenly smiled at him. Decoy or not, she was determined to enjoy herself.

When they boarded the paddle steamer *Sieglinde* late in the afternoon, a cocktail party was already in progress in the forward saloon. Annie was shown to her cabin and was immediately enchanted with it. First of all, the scale was right for her. Everything was slightly smaller than normal, but so beautifully designed and fitted there was an impression of spaciousness. The woodwork and louvred doors were in rosewood and all the fittings were polished brass. The drapery and carpet were not patterned but of deep enough colour to make the glossy rosewood seem light. There was a sitting room, a bedroom and bathroom. And there were large oval windows, not portholes, through which the river could be seen brimming only a foot or so below the sill. Everything was so neat and uncluttered. Annie decided that, if ever she needed an interior decorator, she would employ a naval architect.

And as Jamie had assured her, the luggage was unpacked and everything put away in perfect order. She went through to the bathroom and filled the gleaming brass basin with warm water to wash her hands and face before joining her fellow passengers in the saloon. There were surprisingly few, considering the size of the steamer, and all were travelling first class. Apparently, this new river service was aimed at the top end of the market and nothing was spared in comfort and good taste to make the cruise worth the exorbitant cost. Presumably, Annie thought, the British taxpayer would be picking up the bill for herself and Jamie.

In the forward saloon, the other passengers were talking and drinking. Mainly, they were middle-aged and German – the women beautifully dressed and rather noisy, the men stodgy-looking and quiet. But there were two young Scandinavian couples who – Jamie had already discovered – could speak English. He introduced Annie to them. While they chatted, it became clear that Jamie had also let it be known to all the passengers that his lady friend was a famous actress. She became aware of how she was being carefully scrutinised by the other groups of people around the saloon. Probably she and Jamie were the only unmarried couple on board. A young English gentleman on the loose with a flighty, and probably immoral, actress suited the purpose of the surveillance mission.

The *Sieglinde* did not cast off until after nightfall. This was a prudent move by the operators. Sailing through the grimy, industrial heart of Rotterdam in daylight would have made a depressing start to the cruise. By next morning they should at least have got clear of the offensive wharves.

It was impossible to tell whether they had or not. During the night a thick drizzling rain had set in and it was impossible to see the river banks. Indeed, the combination of fog and rain made it difficult to see even the river. There is no more complete isolation than a long rainy spell in the Netherlands.

Obliged to remain below, Annie decided to make profitable use of her time. She started to learn German. At first, it was only with Jamie in a corner of the day-lounge. But the German passengers soon became aware of the enterprise and gathered round. It was a very enjoyable diversion for them and they were quite captivated by Annie's good humour and eagerness to learn. The role of principal tutor was quickly usurped by Frau Mosen.

She was an energetic little woman with very prominent front teeth. These gave the impression she was smiling all the time, even in repose. Her hair was thick, inflexibly permed – and violently hennaed. She could speak a little English and saw this as an excellent chance to learn more. Annie became her pupil, to their mutual advantage.

Herr Mosen, a fat, easy-going banker, was heartily grateful that something could keep his wife fully occupied. Now he was able to drink as much as he chose, and snooze as long as he liked, quite free of her nagging attention.

It took three fog-bound days to reach the German border and the first stop at Emmerich. Annie was in Jamie's cabin as he dressed to go on deck.

She asked, 'Is this where they could unload petrol?'

'No, no. We've still to go through the Belgian sector. This is just a fuelling stop.'

'Then why are you going up to watch?'

He smiled. 'So that they get *used* to my watching. I want the crew to get the impression that I'm a harmless crank who enjoys watching other people work.'

'*I* like watching other people work,' Annie said.

'All right. Put on a mackintosh and we'll both go up.'

The *Sieglinde*'s engines had been stopped. She was being winched into fuelling position under a huge dockside gantry. Jamie and Annie stood as far aft as they were allowed and watched as the bunker hatches were opened. Then a sealed leather chute was lowered from the gantry into the openings on the deck. When that had been secured, there was a dull roaring sound as coal was poured down the chute into the bunkers. While this was being done, other stores were loaded aboard. Jamie made a point of getting on friendly terms with the crewmen engaged on these heavy duties.

Annie was less entranced. Three days chugging into a downpour – lightened by the event of watching coal being loaded – was not her idea of a holiday.

At this point in the progress of the *Sieglinde* I asked Annie, 'Why on earth did you go ahead with it?'

'I'm very glad I did,' she said.

It was a bright, sunny winter day and Annie had decided this was the perfect opportunity for me to see Loch Lomond and the new crown of snow on Ben Lomond. These sights were only four miles from Dumbarton and I'd driven her car to a vantage point on the shores of the loch. 'Surely,' I said, 'you could have found a better way to spend your holiday than acting as a wet decoy.'

'I wanted to be with Jamie.' She lit a cigarette. 'And it wasn't wet all the way. Once we got into Germany the weather improved.' She leaned back against the headrest and smiled. 'It turned into a perfect holiday. One I was often glad to remember.'

'Because of Jamie?'

'Yes. He was a delightful man.'

'I'm glad to hear that.'

'Why?'

'Don't you remember?' I turned slightly in the driving seat to face her. 'The first time you saw me you said I reminded you of Jamie Northcott.'

'That's right.' She nodded firmly, expelling cigarette smoke. 'You are like him in some ways. You're taller, of course. And not so – fascinated.'

'Fascinating?'

'No. Fascinated,' she insisted.

I waited for her to explain. But she didn't. I tried another tack. 'Have I become more, or less, like him?'

'Less,' she said.

'Why is that?'

Annie wound down the window a little to let the smoke out. When she turned to face me again she shrugged and smiled. 'You're married and very dependent on Barbara. And though you're about the same age as Jamie was the last time I saw him, you seem a *lot* older.' She settled herself once more against the cushions. 'He was always quite independent, free – and young.'

Rather crassly, I asked, 'Is he still alive?'

'I don't know. The last time I saw him was in London in the 'fifties.'

We both gazed out at the still beauty of the loch under a

perfect blue sky. Slowly, I became aware that I was irritated at what she'd said about my dependence on Barbara. It was true, of course. What was worse, Barbara knew it was true. The very fact of my being there with her in Scotland was just the latest proof that she took the decisions for both of us.

Right at the moment, though, I was resentful that in some way I hadn't measured up to Jamie Northcott. I suddenly asked Annie, 'What do you mean, he was "fascinated"?'

She'd been thinking of something else and narrowed her eyes in an effort to locate the allusion. 'Ah! He saw things very – *freshly*. Every new day seemed to be a total surprise.' She chuckled. 'He was fascinated by the most ordinary things – and the most boring people. He didn't discriminate between people . . . who was acceptable and who was not. Or which one was clever and which one stupid. He didn't think it was any of his business to have opinions on such things. I suppose that's why everybody liked him.'

'And you loved him?'

'Yes. Though I only realised it afterwards. I realised I *had been* in love with him.' She snorted with disgust at her own fallibility. 'Normally, I jumped at the slightest excuse for being in love.'

'Maybe you idealise him just because you *didn't* become lovers.'

Annie leaned sharply forward. 'Who said we didn't?'

'Well, you haven't said that you did.'

She relaxed a little. 'I don't tell you everything, you know.'

I smiled. 'All right, then. Tell me. Tell me how things improved on the *Sieglinde* . . . who was Sieglinde, anyway?'

'What does it matter?'

'The reader will want to know.'

'Then the reader can look it up!' She snorted. 'I've reached over eighty without knowing.'

Once over the German border, the weather improved almost immediately and it was possible to spend a lot of time on deck. This introduced a whole new vocabulary to Annie's German lessons. There were team games and idle lounging in the sun.

There were also excursions ashore at Wesel, Ürdingen and Düsseldorf. But after dinner each evening Jamie and Annie made a point of setting themselves apart from the other passengers. Even the ubiquitous Frau Mosen was excluded from the little corner they established on the upper deck. From there, lulled by the beat of the great paddle wheels in the water, they watched the lights sliding by on the riverbank.

Once, when the boat was having difficulty moving forward against the current at a headland, they heard singing. It sounded as though a celestial choir was afloat somewhere ahead of them. They strained their eyes in the dusk, but only when the boat had cleared the headland and found slacker water did the Wagnerian chorus take shape.

There was a bonfire on the flat riverbank and, around it, a throng of young people in shorts. Some were standing silhouetted against the flames, some stood armed with flaming torches. They continued singing and, softly at first, the passengers lining the lower deck joined in. Annie, smiling with delight at this serenade, asked Jamie, 'What is that song?'

'"Die Wacht Am Rhein",' he said, and waved at the eager young faces around the bonfire. 'They are the *Wandervögel*.'

'"Wandering birds"?'

'Birds of passage,' he corrected. 'There are thousands of young people like them all over Germany, travelling about in groups.' The 'Watch on the Rhine' was growing fainter now as the steamer left them astern. 'Nomads, orphans, idealists and rebels. They've renounced all material values in favour of love and nature.'

'*I'm* in favour of that,' Annie said. She stretched out over the handrail to catch a last glimpse of the enchanted circle and the line of fire which still glowed along the wake of the *Sieglinde*.

Jamie put his arm around her shoulder and squeezed gently. 'So am I. But we can't all run away with the raggle-taggle gypsies.'

Annie stiffened under his caress.

'What's wrong?'

'Some day,' she said, 'I will tell you about the raggle-taggle gypsies.'

105

Jamie did not pursue the remark. Instead, he told her about his own youth. 'Of all things, I wanted to be an explorer. I read every book of exploration and archaeology I could lay my hands on. They really gripped me, but I was a little angry at them as well.'

Annie was puzzled. 'Angry?'

'Yes. It was annoying to think they'd already done all that – and maybe left nothing for me to do.'

She chuckled. 'I see.'

'My father had a huge world map in his study. I used that to score out what had already been discovered.'

'But surely everything on the map had already been discovered, or it wouldn't have been on the map.'

'Mmm. That's what my father said. It was very disappointing.'

'I'm sorry.'

'It's all right. I got over it.' He flicked the butt of his cigar in a glowing arc over the stern. 'But I never found anything else I wanted to do nearly as much as explore.'

On another occasion, as the steamer was swept by the current under a sheer promontory, they both gazed up at a castle which soared against the night sky. Moonlight glistened on its steep roofs and spires. Annie gripped Jamie's hand and gasped at the theatrical grandeur of it. He drew her closer and softly recited:

> '"*On such a night*
> *Stood Dido with a willow in her hand*
> *Upon the wild sea-banks, and waft her love*
> *To come again to Carthage.*"'

Annie said, 'How beautiful it is.' Then, after a long silence, 'Have you ever been in love, Jamie?'

'Selfishly, you mean?'

'What?'

He explained. 'In love, like having somebody all to yourself. Your own personal property.' His voice was curiously bleak. He seemed defensive.

'Well . . . yes! I suppose so.'

'Yes. But it's wrong to consider another human being as

106

property.' He made some effort to reclaim lightness. 'Since then, I have been in love in *general*. Frequently, I still am.'

'I'm not sure I understand that.'

'In love with life. In love with the world. In love with humanity. That is the most beautiful feeling of all.'

'I daresay,' said Annie sceptically.

It was not until they reached Cologne that Jamie's surveillance was rewarded.

Everyone was on deck as the boat rounded a wide bend in the river. At the same moment they all caught sight of the fretted twin spires of the cathedral dominating a great mound. Then, high over the river, the bows and lacy ironwork of the Festerbrücke. Bit by bit, the bridges and towers and monuments came into perspective and stretched away from them in the bright sunlight.

The itinerary showed they were to spend two days in Cologne. As Jamie pointed out, that meant they would be moored overnight near a large depot which was in the demilitarised zone. Indeed, it was the only city on the 'wrong' side of the Rhine. No doubt it was that fact, and the excellent network of railways and roads, which made it the foremost crossing point for Hitler's army many years later. He reclaimed the Rhineland across the Festerbrücke.

Among the first people aboard was a representative of the city's tourist organisation. Coloured pamphlets and brochures were laid out in the day-lounge. In one of these, Frau Mosen discovered that her local theatre company from Hamburg was on tour. They would be performing in the Altes Stadttheater all of that week. She insisted that Annie and Jamie must join Herr Mosen and herself to see them. Jamie declined.

'But Herr Northcott, why?'

'I'm not feeling well,' Jamie said.

Frau Mosen was not convinced. In fact, she was deeply puzzled over Herr Northcott. She wondered why a man would take a girl on a romantic cruise and behave like an elder brother. To the best of Frau Mosen's knowledge – and it was comprehensive – Fräulein Jeynor and Herr Northcott never spent the night together on the *Sieglinde*. They never even seemed to kiss, for all the time they spent in that secluded corner of the top deck. And the young man *never* went ashore with the young lady. That was reasonable enough at Wesel or Ürdingen (particularly Ürdingen) but Köln was a different matter.

In the afternoon Annie went ashore with the Mosens and their first stop was to book seats at the Stadttheater. Frau Mosen loudly supervised her husband during this simple operation – making pointed asides to Annie (who stood well back) to the effect that it was a great pity the company was not doing Shakespeare; how surprised the company would be when they found out there was a famous Shakespearian actress in the audience; how novel it must be for Frl Jeynor to be in the audience instead of on the stage.

All of this had the desired effect upon the front-of-house manager who happened to be in the box office. He came out and introduced himself to Frau Mosen who lost no time introducing the famous Annie Jeynor. The manager said how honoured he was and kissed her hand. He further insisted that Frau Mosen and her party should be guests of the management that evening. Annie was wracked with embarrassment. However, she managed to maintain the smiling gracious composure that was now expected of her.

The play being given by the Hamburg company was *Hedda Gabler*. It was a vehicle for the veteran actress Gerda Ritter. For the mousey second lead she was being supported by Emmy Sonnemann, an actress from the Weimar company whom Frl Ritter found compatible, and no threat. Apparently she did alternate seasons at Weimar and Hamburg. Their scenes together were the high spots of the evening. Annie made no secret of her delight when she went backstage to meet the cast. She could tell her praise meant a great deal to them, particularly the plump and jolly Frl Sonnemann. Gerda Ritter was equally pleased but, as a star in her own right, less able to show it.

Over breakfast, Jamie's eyes gleamed with excitement. He was now feeling very much better, since he had watched the cargo-handling all night and was able to report that more than a hundred barrels of petrol had been unloaded onto unmarked trucks. There was no doubt that this luxury steamer was engaged in violation of the Versailles treaty.

'What do you do now?' Annie wanted to know.

'I must report to the Commission's office here in Cologne.'

'But what if they're in on it?'

'What!' He spluttered over his coffee. 'The Control Commission?'

'Well, this can't be the first time it's happened, so somebody here must know what's going on.'

He looked at her in amazement. 'That would be an impossible situation.'

Annie was unmoved. 'It's not impossible if they're getting away with it. Who runs the Commission office here?'

'The French, of course.'

'Of course.' Annie raised her eyebrows and shrugged. 'As far as I understand it, the reason the British sent you was because they didn't trust the French.'

'The French traders, yes.'

She stuck to her point. 'I shouldn't think there's much to chose between French traders and French officials. In my opinion you'd do better to telegraph your office in London.' She paused. 'If you're sure you can trust *them*.'

Jamie threw back his head and laughed. 'Dear Annie, I'd no idea you were so cynical.'

'I'm not cynical in the least. It's perfectly obvious that you don't tell the fox there's a gap in the chicken wire.'

Jamie telegraphed London. Then they had the rest of the day to themselves. They clambered over the old walls of the city, hand in hand. Drawn by music, they watched a band parade in the Neumarkt.

They strolled further and found the quiet and beautiful Volksgarten under the wall of the outermost ring. The scent of flowers was strong in the hot afternoon sun. Annie took off her shoes and stockings to walk along the sandy paths. They ate ice cream, fed pigeons and talked about the future. Annie wanted to get Jamie to commit himself to a definite plan but he lightly dismissed the idea. He jumped up from the park bench and exclaimed, 'We are here now and we're happy, aren't we?'

'Yes! Of course. But looking forward won't make us *un*happy, will it?'

'It very well might.'

'How, Jamie?'

'It's a danger to make promises we might not keep. Bad enough if you do that in secret. Much worse if you tell someone else.'

'Even if you tell me?'

'Especially if I tell you! With *you* knowing I'd mind much more if I fail.'

'If that's so – then you'd try much harder to succeed.'

'Annie, I have succeeded already. I am me! I intend to go on being me.' He slapped his hand on his heart. 'There is no point in making promises to the future that I intend to be somebody else.'

She saw the point of that; but saw, too, the necessity that *she* should be somebody else. Jamie had been born lucky with no need to change. In her own life change was essential because it was the only means of escape. And that escape was now well in hand.

In the evening, as the *Sieglinde* drew away upstream from Cologne, there was dancing. The upper deck curved far out over the paddle-wheel casing on each side, making an almost circular dance floor. And now, with a small accordion band on board, dancing became the main after-dinner recreation. By day, too, the cruise was enlivened by more striking scenery where the Rhine flowed through its most picturesque region between Bonn and Coblenz.

Freed from his secret duty, Jamie reverted to the laughing, careless young man that Annie had first known. But now they were much closer than before. They felt entirely safe in each other's company and completely at ease, and with that degree of affection between them, it began to seem impossible that they could become lovers. Annie did think about it – and recoiled from the thought as though from incest.

A few months later, the *Twelfth Night* company started its tour of the northern cities. There was a gala opening performance in

Hamburg and Annie renewed her acquaintance with Frl Ritter and Emmy Sonnemann. There too she met again a young man she had completely forgotten.

He tapped on the open door. 'Miss Jeynor, I wish to say that you have given a very fine performance.'

Annie turned, smiling, to look at the man. 'Thank you.' He was tall and aristocratic-looking, in his late twenties. His black hair was carefully groomed and his pale face had a rather prim expression. With a gesture she invited him to sit down. And it was the way he sat attentively on the edge of the chair and the earnestness in his voice which Annie identified. She was instantly reminded of the shy youth waiting for Rosemary to get ready.

'Freddie? Freddie . . .' She couldn't remember his second name. Then it came. 'Freddie Bolen!'

'Yes. You remember me?'

'Of course! How lovely to see you again.' She got up from her own chair and hugged him. 'What are you doing here?'

At last he smiled. 'I am here to see how wonderful and famous you have become.'

'Do you work in Hamburg?'

'No. In Essen.'

'What are you doing now?'

'I am a manager of the smelting operation, at the moment.'

Annie put on the delighted and impressed look she was learning to adopt when anyone told her something incomprehensible. 'Really? And do you enjoy the work?'

'Oh, yes.'

'How did you hear about this production?'

'I read the papers. As you know, I am very interested about the theatre. Also, the company has a policy to support the arts.'

'I'm glad to hear it.'

He got to his feet. 'But now I should leave you to complete your changing.' From the door he added, 'Perhaps, when the play comes to Essen you will have dinner with me.'

'You're very kind. Yes. I'd love to have dinner.'

'I will call you. Good bye, Miss Jeynor.'

*   *   *

The dinner after the show in Essen was not a success. Freddie brought two friends with him, an elderly couple whose names she did not catch. They spent the evening comparing Annie with German actresses they had seen in Shakespeare. In particular, the marvellous Gerda Ritter. And, like many Germans who spoke English, they thought the playwright's native language did not serve him as well as the translation to *their* native language. Annie was amused and irritated by the idea.

But really, she later confessed to herself, the irritation arose from the fact that they'd come to see her and talked only of other people.

Freddie said very little but whenever he did say anything the elderly couple immediately deferred to his opinion. Annie thought they did so merely because they were his guests. It turned out to be a good deal more than that.

Back in London, towards the end of 1928, Annie soon came to realise that one Viola does not make a career. After a short break in which she was happy enough to lounge around the flat all day, the need to work again claimed her attention.

Her friends assured her that, now she was ready for it, there would be no trouble in finding the new modern play in which she could demonstrate the range of her talent. But there *was* trouble.

At first the main difficulty seemed to be the lapse of time. It was now two years since her sensational debut in *Twelfth Night* and meanwhile quite a few bright and fascinating girls had surfaced in the hectic, ever changing bustle of the West End. And none of them had taken much time off or gone away on a long tour outside the country.

London's theatre-land was a very clannish community and dedicated to the principle that no better theatre could be found anywhere in the world. Anyone who sought to disprove that was considered something of a traitor – unless they went to New York. New York was acceptable. Germany was deeply suspect.

Behind this was an even more reprehensible attitude. It went back to the leading actors who had been snubbed when *Twelfth*

112

Night had transferred to the West End. Those well-established stars had not forgotten how an upstart had dimmed their light. And even though it plainly had not been Annie's fault that they were replaced, she became the target for their enmity and the distrust they bred in their friends. So when discussions were held about the casting of new plays there was always someone with good drawing power who insisted in the nicest possible way that it would be a mistake to engage Annie Jeynor.

Months passed, then, in despair and some anger, Annie appealed to Marie Tempest. Miss Tempest, it might be thought, was a pillar of the stage establishment and able to influence received opinion. Annie was invited to tea at the house on the edge of Regent's Park.

The veteran actress, dressed exquisitely in dove grey and pearls, was welcoming and friendly, but when she discovered the nature of the young woman's problem she could offer no comfort.

'All I can say, Miss Jeynor, is that what is happening to you happened to me a long time ago.'

'To you?'

'Oh yes!' the doyenne of the English stage assured her. 'The grand people then did not want to share the stage with an impudent chit from Daly's.'

'And what did you do?'

'I went to New York and earned pots of money.'

'Did that change their minds in London?'

The older woman gave a mischievous, throaty chuckle. 'Indeed it did! Once you can prove you don't need them, they start panting to have you back.'

'Perhaps *I'll* have to go to New York, then.'

'If you can get work there, that is what I would advise. Of course, you would probably have to go into musical comedy again; to start with, at least.' An idea occurred to her. 'You've worked for Cochran, haven't you?'

'Several times.'

'Well, he's casting a New York production of *Bitter Sweet* for later this year. Noël's having dinner here some time next week. I could mention you to him if you like.'

'Mr Coward already knows about me,' Annie said. 'I don't think he'd be interested.'

'He's a brilliant director. Pity he's such a snob.'

Annie smiled and shook her head. 'I'm afraid to go into musical comedy again in case I never get out of it.'

Miss Tempest nodded sympathetically. 'That is a danger.' She took the girl's cup and poured more tea before making a tentative offer. 'The only other thing I can suggest is that you wait in London till the autumn when I shall be doing a new play. I could offer you a part in that.'

Annie brightened. 'Oh? What is it?'

The woman gave her a puzzled look. It was difficult for her to keep in mind how her position now ensured that she was given 'first refusal' of about a dozen new plays each year. 'I don't know yet what it will be,' she said. 'All I can be sure of is that the leading role will suit me perfectly. I cannot guarantee a role which will perfectly suit you.'

'You are very kind.'

'But there's a danger there, as well.'

'What's that?'

'Everyone will know that you got the part because I wanted you to get it.'

'How will they know?'

Again the woman had to explain something which should have been self-evident. 'Because, my dear, my contract always allows me full approval of casting.' She smiled. 'And I always use it.'

Annie nodded. Of course. That was the point. That was exactly the system she was fighting against – the veto of the crowd-pulling 'name'. There seemed little to choose between being on the inside or the outside of the hive. The only security was to become a queen bee.

She thanked the rather dumpy little lady who was just as capable as the rest of using inflexible prejudice to get her own way. The only real difference was that Marie Tempest had earned that power the hard way. She had fought the system and won. Annie promised to consider her offer. But even as the taxi was drawing away from the steep front steps where the sunlight

114

flashed on the burnished handrail, she had determined that another solution must be found.

Back in the flat she at once phoned Rosemary, as she'd promised, and reported the interview. Having specified the options she concluded, 'So it seems the only chance is trying to get Broadway to buy my comic urchin. My rapidly ageing comic urchin!'

'Darling, I am sorry. And I must say that doesn't sound a good idea.'

'What else can I do?'

There was a slight pause then Rosemary stated the obvious course of action which had eluded her other friends, Marie Tempest and Annie herself. 'You could go back to Germany.' The line crackled. 'I mean, if part of the trouble is your success in Germany . . . why not make *use* of that success?'

There was a pause while Annie digested the sheer simplicity of this.

Rosemary's voice came louder in her ear. 'Hello? Annie?'

'Yes. Yes, I heard.'

'Well doesn't that seem sensible? You're fresh in their minds over there and you've learned the language. Make use of that as well. And you've made some good friends in Hamburg, you said.'

'Yes.' Annie felt her spirits rise. 'In fact I was invited to do something there.'

'Accept the invitation, darling. I prophesy, you will become terribly grand and international.'

And though Rosemary's 'prophecy' was light-hearted, Annie would remember the dark moment in which it was made long after it came true. For the present, she merely laughed and promised to make enquiries.

In preparing the way, Annie wrote to her friends in the State Theatre in Hamburg, the Mosens, and to Freddie Bolen. Fortunately, in her letter to Frau Mosen, she mentioned the other people she was contacting. By return of post she got a very excited letter in which Frau Mosen stated her belief that this 'Freddie Bolen' who worked in the steel industry at Essen was really Frederik von Bohlen, a prince of German industry and nephew of Gustav Krupp von Bohlen und Halbach – who was undisputed king.

The information filled Annie with dismay. She immediately phoned Rosemary who confirmed it.

Annie spluttered, 'But why didn't you tell me before?'

'Before *when*, darling? At the time I first knew him he was just a student at the Poly and after that his name didn't spring regularly into our conversation, as I recall.'

'No. But he must think I'm very stupid.'

There was a well-calculated silence at the other end of the line.

'Rosemary!' said Annie warningly.

'My dear, I'm sure he'll think your total ignorance is quite beguiling.' She paused. 'Just as I did.'

After a few minutes chat on other matters Annie hung up. But now she was alarmed at the prospect of meeting Freddie again. Having spent some time in Germany she knew with what awe the Krupp empire was regarded. She was aware, too, of the exalted social position enjoyed by all members of the family. They were absurdly rich. Freddie himself would have automatically become a millionaire as soon as he was twenty-one. And they were powerful. It was easy to understand the excitement in Frau Mosen's letter. It was also easy to understand her incredulity that Annie did not know who her friends were.

In Dumbarton, fifty years later, my own credulity was stretched more than somewhat. Annie and I had been walking down the long avenue in Levengrove Park against a strong wind blowing up from the river. I stopped and turned my back against the blast while I came to terms with the astonishing piece of information she'd tossed lightly into the air. Several paces away, Annie turned to give me a puzzled look. Then she walked back so that she could stand in my lee, as it were, while awaiting further questions. She looked up at me, alertly. The strength of the wind had made her eyes run and her cheeks glowed almost girlishly pink. 'Krupp,' I repeated at last. 'He was a nephew of Krupp, the war criminal?'

116

'But not then,' she said. 'This was about ten years before the second war.'

I pulled my collar higher around my ears. 'But he was a criminal even in the *first* world war.'

'No, no. They didn't have war crimes in the first war,' she pointed out. Then added, 'Luckily for Haig.'

'But Krupp made Big Bertha.'

Annie gave a hoot of laughter. 'Nightly!'

It really was difficult getting things in perspective with the old lady. I'd been referring to the great gun manufactured by Krupp, but Annie immediately thought of Krupp's wife after whom people had named it. We resumed our walk and Annie explained how fortunate it was that she'd written to Frederik.

'You see, the Krupp company was a great patron of the arts and the Prussian state theatre got a lot of money from them. When Frederik told them about a good English actress, whom they already knew, there was . . .'

A gust took her breath away for a moment: '. . . there was absolutely no difficulty about inviting me to join them.'

'I suppose not.'

But I was still thinking of the Krupps who eventually gave up sponsorship of the arts in favour of the Nazi party. Not that they financed Hitler's rise to power – that would have been too speculative a venture. They waited until he actually *achieved* power. But then their support was generous.

Yet money was not the crime. At Nuremberg after the war, Gustav Krupp was indicted by the War Crimes Commission on charges of using thousands of prisoners as slave labour. He was too old and ill to stand trial, so the Americans obliged his son, Alfried, to take responsibility instead. Alfried got twelve years, but was released after three and allowed to reclaim his fortune. That was Frederik's cousin.

We had reached the esplanade and Annie grasped the hand-rail, head raised, staring out across the white-capped waves. I asked her, 'Was Frederik one of the directors charged at Nuremberg?'

She turned her head sharply and the wind tugged at the loose tail of her headscarf. She seemed irritated that I was still on the same subject; and far ahead of the period we should have been considering. 'No. He was dead by then.'

'Oh! How did that happen?'

She resumed her survey of the stormy river. 'Frederik died of hunger and cold during the siege of Stalingrad.'

Arriving by boat in Hamburg was not calculated to give the best impression. It was like Newcastle, only more so. About ten times more so, along the vast, clanging waterfront. But away from the docks it reminded Annie of Glasgow. There was the same grimy, solid, built-for-business look about the streets and, as far as she could judge, the same energetic warmth in the people.

She had dinner with Jamie near his flat on Niedernstrasse. They'd not really been in touch since the previous summer and Annie had intended to ask him the results of his surveillance. But she forgot. Instead, they talked about their happy times together in London. He also reported that, at last, his sister was going to remarry. 'I've met the fellow a couple of times. He's much older than Celia.' He chuckled. 'But of course *she's* not a bright young thing any more.'

Annie, who did not think Mrs Grenville had ever been a bright young thing, said, 'I'm glad to hear it. Your sister was always very kind to me.'

'He's investing in the business. In fact I'm selling out to him.'

'But I thought the business was doing well.'

'Yes. It is.' Jamie smiled. 'Which is why he wants to buy into it, I should think.'

And why he's marrying Celia, thought Annie. But she did not pursue the matter. Nor did she realise how fortunate the deal was for Jamie. He was now quite free of all business obligations and, having realised his assets all at once, independently rich.

After dinner he started to drive her out to the Mosens' villa in the fashionable Eimbüttel area, north-west of the city. But just as they were about to cross the Lombardsbrücke, he stopped the car. Annie turned to him with surprise. 'Is there something wrong?'

'Yes. Yes, there is.'

At first she thought it must be some trouble with the car or the traffic. She looked around. The broad tree-shaded embankment was clear ahead. On their right side the broadening flood of the outer Alster sparkled with reflected light from pleasure craft, to the left the complete half-circle of the inner basin framed Jamie's bearded, shadowy profile.

He went on, 'I'm afraid I haven't been quite square with you, Annie.'

'About what?'

'About anything, really.' He switched off the ignition. 'Remember last summer when you asked me if I'd ever been in love with anybody?'

'Yes. I remember that very well.'

'And I gave you some sort of high-flown talk about nature and so on?'

'Yes,' Annie said.

'Well, that wasn't true.' He removed his gloved hands from the steering wheel and clasped them on his lap. 'During the war, I was in love with a girl in France.' He started kneading his hands together and the leather gloves squeaked in the silence of the car.

'Was she in love with you?'

'Oh, *yes*. Yes.' His voice grew louder. 'And we did plan to get married as soon as it was possible. She was on her way to . . .' He faltered.

'What happened?' asked Annie softly.

'She was on her way to meet me at a rest and recreation station . . .' He repeated the word bitterly. 'Recreation! That was the worst part of it. She was pregnant. My child. And she was killed . . . *they* were killed. There was shelling, you see. Some fell short and some fell wide. These were well off their target. A whole busload of people were killed.'

Annie turned her head to look out of the car towards the water, criss-crossed with dancing trails of light. There could be only one reason why Jamie was telling her this now. Before he said anything further she prepared herself for a decision.

After a long silence the man continued. 'I swore I'd never suffer like that again. Never *lose* again. Never care too much

119

again. But that was twelve years ago – and now I do.' He grasped her hand and she realised he was trembling. 'I'm in love with you, Annie. And I want you to live with me. Let's go back. Now.'

'Jamie, there's no sense in making sudden decisions like that.'

'It's not sudden. I've thought about it a lot, since last summer.'

'But I haven't,' Annie said. 'It's not something which has to be decided right this minute. And the Mosens are expecting me.'

He relaxed his grip on her hand. 'Yes, of course. But will you consider it?'

Annie realised he was determined to have an answer. She already knew what her answer would be, but had hoped to ease the situation over a longer period. However, there was something to be said for getting it done with immediately. 'I have considered it,' she said. 'In fact, I considered it before you did.' She sighed. 'Jamie, I can't . . .'

She was startled as he suddenly reached between the seats for the starting handle and got out of the car. In the headlights his face was grim. He cranked furiously to restart the engine. And she felt relieved that he was angry. The anger wouldn't last. They crossed over the bridge and drove on in silence.

The Mosens' house was impressively large and fully lit in welcome. The front door was thrown open before the car stopped and three figures emerged. There were her host and hostess, of course, but behind them – standing at the top of the steps – Annie was astonished to see Freddie. Closely flanked by the Mosens and followed by Jamie, she ascended to meet him.

He bowed, took her hand, and smiled. 'My dear Annie, welcome back to Germany.'

'Thank you.' Annie was glad he'd reverted to using her first name, for it meant that, although she could no longer call him Freddie, she did not have to worry about the proper formal address for him. 'And thank you for coming to meet me, Frederik.'

Frau Mosen beamed. She did not think it odd to have one of her guests welcome another to her own house. He was a Krupp

120

and she was perfectly happy that he should call her house his own. Her attitude to Jamie was less well-defined. There was that curious behaviour on the Rhine to think of. However, once Annie's luggage had been unloaded, the hostess did make great play of pressing the Englishman to spend the night there. Jamie declined, bade them all goodbye, and drove back into the city.

The arrangement was that Annie would be Frau Mosen's guest until the actress found a suitable flat nearer the theatre – probably in the spring. Meanwhile, the hostess would continue the task she had begun on the Rhine steamer as language teacher, guide and confidante. It was a role in which she took great pleasure. She also insisted on sharing all aspects of Annie's life, particularly in the theatre. The world of backstage drama was now open to her and she found the activity stimulating.

To begin with, she persuaded the theatre director that Annie's work in rehearsal would be greatly eased if she, Frau Mosen, was on hand to comfort and counsel. Then she wangled a reserved free seat at all opening performances so that she could offer 'the patron's view' to her friend. Pretty soon she was recognised as a sort of agent and unpaid social secretary for the English actress. Annie accepted all of this with some amusement and genuine gratitude. She did, though, decline to have Frau Mosen as her dresser.

FREDERIK VON BOHLEN

It was during that first season with the Prussian State Theatre in Hamburg that Annie started to change into the person the press and public decided she must be. Once it was established she would never escape from it – nor really wish to. But the change was not sudden. Only gradually was she estranged from the trusting, unassuming girl who merely wanted to lead a happy life working at what she did best.

Now she began to grow into the exacting, fanatical worker and – above all else – the star performer. It came to her later than it had to others. She was almost thirty before she saw that the only real happiness lay in *being* the best. Occasionally she felt sad about it and more than once, offstage, she tried to ignore it. Always she was forced to realise that having accepted and used the great gift of her talent there was no way in which she could wrap it up again and return it to the sender. It had to be used.

To Frederik von Bohlen, Annie Jeynor was desirable because so many men in the audience desired her. She was fascinating to watch on the stage and by the time he got to know her well the stage persona had taken over off-stage as well. So he need not have blamed himself for being so blind to her attraction when they'd met several years earlier. The woman he fell in love with in Germany was not the woman he'd met in London.

Much of the transformation was accomplished by Gerda Ritter's example. That first season was Frl Ritter's last in Hamburg. Her magnetic ability had been recognised and she had been invited to Berlin. Before she left, however, she gave a crash course in sheer bravura performance to a young woman who happened to have the ability to make potent use of it.

To begin with, Annie shared the supporting roles with her friend and colleague Emmy Sonnemann. Their job, mainly, was to *react* to Frl Ritter. Emmy had been doing this quite happily for several years at Weimar and now in Hamburg. She would have gone on doing it for more leading ladies if her private life hadn't intervened. Annie, however, could not prevent herself shining more brightly than she intended. The fact was not lost on Frl Ritter and, instinctively perhaps, she realised she was sharing the stage with one of her own rare kind. After that, their performances became exciting duels which were relished by both; and which held the audience entranced.

Frl Ritter – a dark-haired, lean-faced beauty then in her fifties but playing thirty – showed a generosity which talent affords only to others who have it. She decided to groom this newcomer to take her place after only one season. And right at the start she identified, without difficulty, the essential qualities which commentators and critics spend unsuccessful years trying to define in unique performers. 'My dear, there are two things. One for them and one for you.' By 'them' she meant the audience. 'For them – Apprehension. For you – Insularity.'

'I don't understand that,' Annie said. She was seated on a hard chair while Frl Ritter sprawled on the couch, spreading cleansing cream over the fine bones of her face.

'You do not have to understand it at this moment. Just remember I have told you. Also, without any doubt it is true.'

Annie persisted. 'I think I could use it sooner if I understood it now.'

Gerda Ritter smiled. 'I do not *want* you to use it until I am safely in Berlin. Just remember the words: Apprehension and Insularity.'

The following evening Annie paid particular attention to the audience while Gerda was on the stage. And for the first time she noticed something which must have been obvious all the time. Although the play was well-known and most of them must have seen other productions of it, they were constantly surprised by Frl Ritter. She made them forget that if a play has begun it must have an ending. She instilled in them a feeling of uncertainty by convincing them that she did not know how it ended. In fact,

124

from moment to moment, it seemed as though she didn't know what was going to happen next. Consequently, they had the unsettling sensation of *fearing* what she was going to do next. In a word, they were apprehensive. And yet their apprehension was a kind of tingling, excited thing – a conviction that something wonderful was going to happen. And, of course, many wonderful, spontaneous things did happen. Frl Ritter had painstakingly rehearsed every one of them, and the role, to within an inch of its life.

The other quality – insularity – was one which could not be seen or appreciated from the stage. It was something the audience saw. And it was, moreover, something which could be deployed only in the leading role. By the time Annie graduated to leading roles in Hamburg she had the quality of insularity as well.

Frederik was a regular witness of the transformation. He made a point of travelling from Essen to attend every first night. That was a rail journey of 220 miles and required that he stay overnight in Hamburg. He chose the Palasthotel on Jungfernstieg and waited for Annie to join him there for supper after the performance. He never took part in the dressing-room crush of well-wishers. Indeed, for some time it seemed he wanted to give the impression that his interest was merely that of an arts patron. He was the representative of the Krupp empire on a courtesy mission from the Villa Heugel to demonstrate publicly that the iron giant had a heart.

Annie, revelling in her new identity, was eager to try out her powers of flattery and charm. This took longer than her former direct approach, but she found the game had surprising fascinations. Formerly she would have thought those long conversations which got nowhere a waste of time. Now she took some delight in the duplicity other women had always enjoyed.

She was aware that Frederik was falling in love with her. Her own feelings, she thought, were completely under her control. To her, he was an attractive young man anxious to prove that he had matured. He was using his friendship with her as a sort of testing ground for worldliness. That was an aim she was willing to encourage.

Thus, she listened with great care to his vision of the new Germany and the celebration of its old glories. She asked relevant questions and with every sign of astonishment and admiration followed each step of whatever explanation he offered. Occasionally, though, she found herself actually impressed as well as seeming to be impressed. He really was a very intelligent young man. And he was handsome.

Before long she was looking forward to his visits to Hamburg and missing him when he was away. In a letter to Rosemary she wrote, 'I can't imagine why you thought he was such a ninny. Maybe he was when you knew him but he has changed a lot. Anyway, I've been invited to spend a weekend at the Villa Heugel, if I can persuade them to let Emmy take my part for a few performances.'

With great good humour, Emmy agreed to learn an extra role in her already onerous repertoire. And once Annie had explained why she wanted the time off, the director was anxious to facilitate her visit to the awe-inspiring holy of holies at Essen. It was the family home of the Krupps. An invitation to the Villa Heugel was a summons which chancellors, presidents, foreign statesmen, royalty . . . all had obeyed.

And all had been met at the station by a horse-drawn carriage. The growing popularity of the motor car had not altered that ritual. The host thought a motor car all very well for business journeys or carrying luggage but undignified for any other purpose.

Frederik seemed nervous and she was too overwhelmed to say much. She had not realised what was oppressively obvious as soon as she emerged from the station. The whole centre of Essen was the Krupp steelworks. The great sheds, railway sidings and gantries were the core. Smoke from the huge chimneys dominated the horizon to the west and around that central complex of industry, grouped like vassal colonies, were the workers' housing estates, all named after members of the family. The sheer size and vigour of the enterprise was intimidating. And that, probably, was why visitors were obliged to arrive by train. No one could fail to be impressed by the might and power of the reigning Krupp von Bohlen und Halbach. The sound of the horse's hooves on the cobbled street was drowned out by the steady deep roar of furnaces and the tympany of steam hammers forging new wealth.

Annie said, 'How can the people sleep through all this?'

Frederik smiled. 'It is the same people who are making the noise,' he said. 'They work in shifts, day and night.'

'But what about the people who don't work for Krupp?'

'There are very few people in Essen who do not work for Krupp, one way or another,' Frederik said. 'And even they *wish* they did.'

Then came the drive between the long rows of groomed poplars, identical as guardsmen, before the country estate opened upon a great expanse of parkland rising gently towards the house. And the house itself seemed small and merely decorative, compared with the grand preparation. However, it was only the white painted façade which was modest. Careful landscaping concealed the real extent of the buildings.

Once the guests had been settled in, it soon became apparent that life at the Villa Heugel was sternly High German, or Victorian – which is the same thing. What irritated Annie immediately was the segregation of the sexes. The ladies behaved as a sort of decorative audience to the men during the weekend. They were to appear punctually, en masse, full of enthusiasm and as given to mindless repetition as any chorus in Gilbert and Sullivan. As a longtime chorus girl to a whole series of male clowns, this was a part Annie could play with distinction. And she brought to it a quality the other ladies lacked – a well-rehearsed vivacity.

Gustav Krupp was a good fifteen years older than his wife: a stocky man with white hair and a curiously pointed face. Both his nose and his chin were pointed. His skin was very fine and glowed healthily pink. He smiled, and indeed laughed, without opening his narrow lips. Annie thought anyone as shrewd as he was must realise that everyone deferred to him in a quite ridiculous fashion. But no doubt he'd got used to it, and now was not surprised that every guest's personal opinion on any subject entirely coincided with his own.

After dinner the scenario was slightly different – then the

127

ladies were expected to talk to each other instead of only reacting to their lords. To do this they retired to the drawing room under the direct command of their hostess.

Frau Bertha Krupp led Annie aside and settled for an earnest conversation. That was the first indication the young actress had of the real purpose of this visit to Essen. It was an assessment course. She was being sized up in the matrimonial stakes. Annie was amused. The journey, the drive and the carefully arranged party seemed to her a wildly extravagant way of holding an audition.

Her hostess was a distinguished lady, then in her early forties. She could not speak English but she had the courtesy to face Annie across the table in case lip-reading might be helpful, and to speak in slow, careful German. She began, 'Miss Jeynor, it is a great pleasure that you have come to visit us.'

'It is a great honour for me, Frau Krupp.'

The hostess nodded, knowing it was. 'We have not had the pleasure of seeing you on the stage.' She raised a heavily jewelled hand regretfully. 'But we look forward to it when, perhaps, you are in Berlin. That is, if you intend to pursue your career in Germany.'

Annie now cast herself in an ingénue-with-dowager scene. She widened her eyes and stated with great earnestness, 'Oh, I *do*. Working in the German theatre has been a great joy to me – though I do not think I'll ever be offered a role in Berlin.'

'If you're good enough, you will be. What does your family think of you spending so much time away from home?'

'Frau Krupp, I have no family. I am an orphan.' She just managed to resist the gesture of lowering her eyes and turning slightly aside. And to suppress a giggle. The whole thing was getting dangerously near 'little Nell'.

Frau Krupp patted her hand. 'My dear Miss Jeynor, I am sorry to hear it. For we are such a large family and depend so much on each other. It is difficult to think of someone being entirely alone.'

There was a sudden hubbub across the room as each of three ladies disagreed in unison. The one with the loudest voice was Frederik's sister, Marta, who now got up and stalked around

128

the table, demonstrating whatever it was they'd been arguing about. The other two laughed and Frau Krupp smiled benignly before turning her attention again to Annie. 'Marta is a charming girl. And Frederik is a delightful young man.'

'Yes, indeed,' Annie said. 'They are both quite delightful.' Clearly it was for Frederik she was being considered. Yet *his* parents were not there. Only the head of the clan, it seemed, could decide who should be admitted to the clan.

Her hostess went on, 'Both of them spent some time in London. I believe you met them then.'

Annie had not met Marta but suspected Frederik might have reported differently. 'Yes. We had a mutual friend. Lady Douglas Straven.'

Frau Krupp seemed particularly interested in the name and Annie spent some time explaining, as far as she knew, the styles and titles of the Marquess of Duncryne and those held by his sons, the second of whom Rosemary had married. The older woman tried to convert these titles into German equivalents. At last she said, 'So – it is important to have influential friends.'

'Oh, I agree,' Annie said. 'Without influential friends I would not be here.'

'Is that so, Miss Jeynor?'

'Surely you know, Frau Krupp, that your family's patronage of the arts is very highly valued.'

Frau Krupp's elegant composure weakened or, perhaps, softened. She was about to say something, thought better of it, then made a deprecatory gesture and smiled broadly. Her estimation of the English actress increased with this forthright confession that Annie knew exactly who she had to thank for her career in Germany. But the fact had been decorously stated – and that was a virtue too. Most young people, she found, took so little trouble with the way in which they told the truth. She said, 'We have always had the greatest admiration for genuine talent. And Frederik has such good taste in these matters. We place great trust in his judgment.'

And that, Annie knew, meant she had passed the test. Frederik would be encouraged to pursue his courtship. Before that, though, he was pursuing another important purpose of this visit to the villa. While Frau Krupp had been interviewing Annie, Frederik was arguing with Gustav Krupp about funds for a worthy cause. He was urging that now would be a good time to make a contribution to the electoral expense of a new right-wing political party – the NSDAP. The Krupps' friend and rival, Fritz von Thyssen, had already done so, as had Emile Kirdorf, the coal tycoon. Like them, Frederik had the view that the NSDAP was the party of the future, and a sure bulwark against both the communist menace and union power.

But the old man would not be swayed. To him the NSDAP were a crowd of ridiculous Bavarian romantics who'd get nowhere in the hard north. It was impossible they'd ever live down the Beerhall putsch. 'Suppose they tried that in Dortmund with our money?' he scoffed. 'We'd be the laughing stock of the Ruhr.'

Frederik protested. 'Nobody need know if they get money from us.'

'*I* would know,' his uncle insisted.

Reporting this to Annie as they drove back to Essen, Frederik added, 'I'm sure he'd change his mind if only he would meet Hitler.'

'Hitler?' This was the first time Annie had heard the name. 'Yes. Adolf Hitler. He is the leader of the NSDAP.'

'I thought you said it was the Richthofen pilot?'

'That's Göring.'

'Yes. I've met him.'

Frederik seemed impressed. 'Where? Where did you meet him?'

'Oh, at some theatre function in Weimar,' Annie said vaguely. 'He was there with his wife.' Really she had little interest in this talk about obscure politicians and wondered when the conversation would turn to more important personal matters.

'Ah, yes! Göring is very interested in the theatre.' Frederik nodded approval. 'I haven't met his wife yet. She's Swedish – a countess, I believe.'

'She's very beautiful,' Annie said, and wondered why the whole Krupp family seemed obsessed by titles.

Frederik did not propose that day, or that week. Annie had

to face the conclusion that she'd made much less of an impression on Frau Krupp than had seemed apparent at the time. Only later did it become clear that she had indeed been approved of, but Frederik had been advised not to marry until he returned from his American trip. It was assumed that his intended bride would naturally hold herself available for eighteen months or so while he went off for further training in American business methods.

But when Frederik applied to take up his long-arranged posting with the American steel corporation they withdrew the invitation from the entire Krupp party of managers who were to accompany Frederik. The situation had changed. Floundering in the grip of the depression, the Americans were laying off scores of their own managers. It was no time to entertain a bunch of foreign freeloaders. And besides, all that could be learned in Cleveland now was basic survival. Nobody knew more about that than the Krupps of Essen.

So Frederik was free to marry immediately. Once free of more important commitments he lost no time in proposing. Annie knew there could be no other purpose when she was taken for a second visit to the Villa Heugel. This time it was an entirely family party and she met Frederik's widowed mother who gave her blessing. Or that, anyway, was the assumption, though the brief confused conversation left a lot unsaid. For it was now clear why Frederik's mother had been kept in the background. Frau Caroline von Bohlen was quite obviously insane. She had to be attended and carefully watched by a rota of nurses, day and night.

The rest of the family, and Frederik himself, overcame her disability by simply ignoring it. Annie felt desperately sorry for the wrecked old woman. She spent as much time as she could sitting beside her, stroking her bony, spasmodically twitching hand. Frau Bertha Krupp commented upon this solicitude.

'You are very kind, Annie, but I do not think it necessary.'

Annie intuitively realised that her concern was being interpreted as an effort to curry favour. The colour rose in her cheeks.

'Frau Bertha, I do not do it because it is necessary. I do it because I'd like her to know somebody cares.'

Bertha smiled sadly and shook her head. 'Poor dear, she has no conception of that.'

'But *I* have, Frau Krupp.'

The great lady seemed puzzled and raised an eyebrow. 'Her understanding is very limited.'

'That may be. But it is not her understanding I care about. It's what she *feels*.'

Frau Krupp was offended by the fierceness in Annie's voice but she did not intend to debate the matter further and turned away.

Frederik proposed and Annie accepted in the afternoon. The engagement was announced to the whole family by Krupp after dinner and toasts were drunk for their future happiness. Nor was it intended that that should be delayed. The marriage was set for a Wednesday, six weeks later. It was a date which the principal members of the family would do their best to keep free.

Only when the date was set did they consider the difficult problem of who could be found to give Annie away. The bride-to-be was able to suggest only two names: Jamie Northcott or Rosemary's husband. Frau Bertha thought the latter more suitable so it was Lord Douglas Straven who led her down the aisle. Rosemary herself was unable to attend because she was in the final stage of pregnancy. Jamie was there, though, together with the Mosens, Emmy Sonnemann and most of the Hamburg company.

'Why did you marry him?' I asked Annie.

'Mainly because he wanted to marry me.' She shrugged. 'I was almost thirty, remember, in a foreign country with no security, and my season at Hamburg was coming to an end. It would have been very hard to crawl back to London and beg for work.'

'Surely, with your ability, you could always get work.'

She wedged herself tighter into the corner of the window seat. 'Yes. Doing what though? You must understand, Bill, that acting's a *climbing* profession.' She snorted. 'No! Worse than climbing. It's like a moving escalator. You can appear to stand still as long as you're on the way up. If you're going down, though, you have to scramble just to stay where you are – and *every*body knows you're going in the wrong direction.'

'So you married him just for security.'

'No. As I said, mainly because he wanted to marry me. And, more important than that, even – he was in love with me.'

'But you weren't in love with him.'

The old lady sighed. It all seemed too remote now to be so particular. 'I was very fond of him, and I was flattered.'

'But not in love,' I persisted.

'No. I knew I wasn't in love because I'd been in love before – with Bert Lane . . . and with Jamie.' She turned to stare through the window down the long slope of the garden. 'Being in love with a man is no great guarantee of anything.' Her attention was caught by a sudden squabble of blackbirds high in the trees to her left. 'I married Frederik because it seemed the best thing to do at the time. And for a while I was sure I had made the right choice. When my contract in Hamburg ended, he took up a position in the firm's Berlin office and we moved there.' She raised her head in enthusiastic recollection of that move. 'It was marvellous to live in Berlin. Rosemary was right. Even when *I* got there it was still the most exciting city in Europe.'

'It must have been rather *more* than exciting for the Jews,' I said.

She turned to face me again with an expression of great impatience. 'Oh, Bill! Always the sniper in the hindsight, aren't you? I'm talking about 1930. The persecution hadn't begun. The Nazis had no power at all. Nobody had any idea of what was ahead.'

'Frederik was a sympathiser, though. He must have known what the Nazis had in mind.'

'Yes!' she said sharply. 'Yes. He thought he knew. And Baron Fritz von Thyssen thought *he* knew. Maybe even some Nazis thought they knew. But they were all wrong.' She got up and strode angrily away down the centre of the huge empty room. Her voice rose sharply in denunciation of the fallible past. 'Oh, you are safe enough – looking back! What people knew or must have known is perfectly obvious to *you*. From *here*!' She turned with a swinging, wide contemptuous gesture. 'Hope!' she exclaimed. 'That's what you safe snipers always forget. Hope. We *hoped* things would be different. Better. Happier. And because we hoped strongly enough, we convinced ourselves we knew.' She held the defiant position for a moment. Then the spirit seemed to desert her and she slumped in one of the chairs by the fire.

It had never occurred to me before that I was a sniper. 'A sniper in the hindsight', as she very neatly described it. There are a lot of us. And we, I now realised, are somewhat vengeful persecutors of the past. We are judges and blamers of hopes that failed. We exact retribution from influential people who are old – for no better reason, it seems, than that they survived into our world. Powerless to alter the present (for which we are responsible), we try to alter the past – which is none of our business. I certainly am one of those who bear no responsibility for the rise *or* the fall of the Third Reich, since I was born the year war was declared.

Glancing down the long shadowy room to the old lady slumped in the armchair, it seemed reasonable to assume that, even though she was there at the time, Annie Jeynor didn't start the war either.

The newly married von Bohlens settled into a large flat on Ziegelstrasse. It was north of the river and only a short walk to Frederik's office in Oranienburger. It was convenient, too, for the Deutsche Staat Theater. There, the highly regarded Max Reinhardt was again director and continuing his long success in productions of Shakespeare. It was natural that he should want to engage a celebrated actress from the home of Shakespeare so Annie got a job there entirely on her own merit. What was less stimulating was the fact that he wanted her to play Viola again. Everyone wanted her to play Viola again. Of course it was prudent to make her Berlin debut in a role she knew so well, but Annie wondered if she would *ever* get out of the damn breeches.

Before that, she spent a lot of time furnishing her first real home. It was a high, airy flat and from its tall windows gave

134

wide views over the city. Following the long curve of the river to the east she could see the domes and towers of the cathedral rising above the trees of the Lustgarten. To the west was the broad, quartered dome of the Reichstag, framed in the open stretches of the Tiergarten whose lakes glittered in the sun. Between these imperial markers, wide avenues converged south through great quadrangles of government buildings, gilded monuments and old palaces.

Gazing out over all this, Annie was struck by the sharp brightness of the air. It seemed possible to pick out fine detail over long distances. And, walking in the streets, she found that same air intoxicating. There was so much bustle and cheerfulness. In the long pavement cafés under the trees, in the beergardens, in the open squares where children played or street performers entertained, there was the constant impression of some festival in progress. But there was no special event being celebrated. This was part of the normal vitality of Berlin before the wave spreading out from the Wall Street crash in New York had time to cross the Atlantic and swamp Germany. Meanwhile, the reckless investment of American money in previous years afforded buoyant employment and scope for enterprises of spectacular risk.

But the wave was coming; and with it the conditions for violent political change. When Brüning was appointed chancellor that spring, Frederik predicted there would have to be an election before the year was out. He tried to explain to Annie why this was so. But all she gained from the instruction was the galling fact that if she'd waited until the end of the year to furnish the flat, it could have been done for a quarter of the price.

She asked him, 'Will you be selling steel at a quarter the price?'

'If Brüning stays, we'll have to . . . *and* cut production.'

'And cut the workforce?'

'Certainly. We're already doing that. So, you see, the people we were paying won't be able to buy furniture; so the people who *make* furniture will lose their jobs; so the people who sell furniture will have to compete with each other for fewer customers – so the price goes down.' He shook his head dolefully. 'And if Brüning gets elected again he'll let everything drift lower and lower. The only way out of this is for Germany to invest in itself. Brüning hasn't got the imagination to do that. But the Nazis have.'

'Then why don't the Nazis tell Brüning how to do it? For the good of the country.'

Frederik laughed and crossed the room to give Annie a quick hug. 'Dear Annie, governments don't exist for the good of the country. They exist for their own good. That's about the only thing you can gamble on.'

'Even so, surely they must do something good to get elected.'

Frederik shook his head. 'No. It's what you can force them to do so they'll be *re*-elected that does the good.'

Annie did not entirely appreciate the cynicism of this observation, but she did realise for the first time how little her husband trusted the people he'd urged his uncle to support. As the crisis deepened through the early summer of that year, he made fresh efforts in the same direction. There were several secret meetings. The secrecy was necessary because he was going against the company's policy dictated from Essen. It was against the interests of the government as well.

Usually these covert negotiations were arranged at the weekends and Annie was invited along to give credence to what seemed to be harmless outings in the Grünewald or Tegel forests outside the city. In warm summer weather the sheer beauty of those great open areas of parkland, lakes and trees was incentive enough without considering the real purpose of being there. Indeed, with bright sunlight sparkling on the Wannsee, where squadrons of sailing boats leaned to and fro, it seemed impossible that anything sinister could be accomplished. And Frederik was always in such high spirits.

On Sunday mornings they drove off immediately after breakfast with a large hamper of food stowed on the back seat. On the first occasion Annie also took along her bathing suit but that proved unnecessary. To Berliners, nude bathing was practically obligatory. As the car swept out through the fashionable villas of Charlottenburg, then turned south, the young married couple joked and laughed. Their respective events of the week were

136

recounted and embroidered; the forthcoming social occasions had to be discussed and planned. But often Frederik also explained the object of the particular mission they were engaged upon that day.

'This time I'm going to meet their Berlin gauleiter. You might like to meet him too.'

'Oh, no,' Annie protested. 'These men you talk to are all so dull.'

'But this one's a playwright.'

'Really?' She held her hair against the wind as she turned her head.

'Yes. He had a play on last year, I believe.'

'Then why does he want to bother with politics?' She faced into the wind again. 'What's his name?'

'Josef Goebbels. His job is to organise the party workers in the city but it seems he's pretty close to the main bunch in Bavaria.'

'What's the point of talking to any of them if you can't offer them money?'

'That may change. And when it does, I want to have a few good concessions agreed in advance.' Frederik swung the big open car down a dirt track road away from the day-trippers. 'You see, they don't know Krupp is against making any contribution. They think the only reason we haven't put up any money so far is because we haven't had a good enough offer from them.'

'What can they offer?'

'That depends on who I talk to. And Goebbels has more authority than anyone so far.'

He pulled into a copse and stopped the car. About a hundred yards ahead was a small clearing in which stood an abandoned forester's cabin. The scent of pines was very strong in the warm air and the drowsy sound of bees was amplified under the canopy of branches. 'Are you sure you don't want to meet him?'

'I'm sure,' Annie said. 'I'll wait here.'

Frederik got out of the car and walked towards the clearing which shimmered slightly in the rising heat. It was carpeted by a mass of bright yellow flowers. Annie kept her eyes on the door of the old cabin but there was no movement there.

137

Suddenly, away to the left there was a flash of light which, at first, seemed to be a signal. But really it was only the sunlight reflecting on the glass of another car door opening. The car itself was completely hidden in the undergrowth.

Her husband must have heard footsteps, for he suddenly turned to face in that direction. Two men emerged out of the tangled green wall and moved slowly towards Frederik. The first, a tall muscular man, was obviously a guard – probably one of the SA commandos in civilian clothes. Following him came a short, slight man. He had a pale face and jet black hair. This, Annie thought, must be the playwright, Goebbels.

In his careful negotiation of the rough ground he moved with difficulty. Then it became obvious he had a club foot and walked with a decided limp. The guard stood aside as Goebbels and Frederik greeted each other. She saw Frederik make a gesture in her direction. The guard asked Goebbels something but he shook his head. Then all three went into the cabin.

After a few minutes Annie opened the walnut-veneered compartment on the dashboard and took out her handbag. She lit a cigarette and the acrid fumes of the match seemed much more intense in the pure forest air. It had been her intention to take a stroll back down the track but then she remembered smoking was forbidden in the forest. She did not want to cause trouble with the Grünewald rangers who patrolled on horseback. They were properly obsessed by the danger of fire, and diligent in their pursuit of wrongdoers. So, she remained in the car with the brass ashtray pulled open.

About an hour later, the three men emerged from the cabin. Annie sighed with relief. She longed to plunge into the cool waters of the Wannsee and noted with impatience the time-wasting formalities being performed in the clearing. Finally, Goebbels gave the straight-arm salute and Frederik, rather self-consciously, returned it. The little, intense man hurried as best he could back to his hidden car. Frederik watched them and waited until the roar of the engine receded in the other direction before running back along the track to his wife. He seemed elated and lightheartedly jumped high over fallen logs as he came towards her.

138

She asked, rather unnecessarily, 'Did it go well?'

'Very well indeed,' he said and sank into the driving seat. But he did not relate the substance of the conversation, as on other occasions he'd done. Annie did not notice the omission. Nor, at that moment, did she care. It was enough for her that now they were driving on the main road again towards the cool water.

As the summer progressed, Frederik was often away on business trips and Annie took advantage of his absence by entering into the hectic life of the city. There really wasn't any work for her to do until rehearsals started in mid-August.

But she had already met one or two members of the Reinhardt company. She was most favourably impressed by the actor, Helmar Schüstiger. He was a man in his early fifties, courtly and self-assured. As a native Berliner he was an ideal guide, though he'd been brought up in the rough working-class Neukölln district on the southside. There, he told her, children like himself had thought of Unter den Linden and Wilhelmstrasse as parts of a fabled country they might never see. Now he was a careless habitué of the Adlon Hotel which stood at the crossing of these great thoroughfares. And he had an apartment nearby to prove that, having climbed out of the gutter, he intended to stay out.

Like Annie, his elevation was due to the most private of enterprises – hard work on the exploitation of personal talent. He was a Reinhardt discovery when the director first came from Austria to Berlin in 1905. With only amateur experience, Schüstiger was given leading romantic roles as a new pro-fessional. 'Max took a chance with me. And that was all I needed – one good chance.'

He and Annie were strolling round the victory monument in the Königsplatz after lunch. 'He's still taking chances,' Annie said, thinking of herself.

Helmar scoffed at the idea. 'No! With you it is not chance. You are the marvellous Frl Jeynor. For you he took a special trip to London.'

Annie was astonished. 'What? He saw me in London?'

'Oh, yes.' Helmar stopped and turned the girl to face him. 'And he came back with that smile which says everything.'

'But he has never mentioned that.'

'Naturally. If he'd said how anxious he was to have you here, the fee might have been too much. And you couldn't speak German *then*. He asked about that.'

Annie laughed. 'Did he really?' She threw back her head to gaze at the soaring stone pillar on which a huge winged figure was perched. 'What victory is this for?'

'The defeat of the French,' Helmar said.

'We have a column for that, too.'

'Any country which defeats the French deserves nothing less,' Helmar noted. 'But this one is much higher than the one in London. Also, as you see, God sent Germany a golden angel for the job. To England He sent only Nelson.'

'*And* four lions,' Annie protested.

The actor seemed to consider how much of a difference that could make, then remarked, 'I have never understood what the lions *did* at the battle of Trafalgar.'

Smiling, they walked through the shadow of the brazen victory to find a bench in the Tiergarten.

All Helmar's information on Berlin was tinged with sardonic humour. Indeed, that characterised his attitude to any displays of national fervour, whether they arose from Prussian imperialism or the Weimar Republic. His philosophy in personal matters was equally relaxed and spiced with amusement. Annie, who'd been getting used to the fact that she was married to a rather intense man, much younger than herself, found the easygoing maturity of Schüstiger quite captivating. She did not have to worry about hurting his feelings inadvertently. That was always a danger with her husband.

And Helmar was romantic. The flowers, little gifts, effortless compliments and flattery were all delightful and harmless. In fact, Annie felt rather guilty about enjoying the surface of things so much. To be cherished by an attractive man merely as a decorative and amusing companion was a sort of luxury for her. If indulged too often, she thought, it would blunt her sharp view of reality.

Yet, increasingly, she looked forward to those afternoons. There was never any suggestion that the relationship should become more serious. Helmar had an estranged wife in

Dortmund and, in Berlin, a mistress who was a buyer in a fashion house. So each evening he went back to his mistress, and Annie went home to await Frederik's return from the office.

Very often, of course, Frederik was away for several days at a time. When he came back he always behaved as though he'd been away for months. Then something of the enthusiastic boy she'd first known burst through his reserve. He bustled around the flat, admiring any changes she had made in his absence, insisted on hearing what she'd been doing, where Schüstiger had taken her and what she'd thought of it. He was grateful to Herr Schüstiger and admired him a great deal as an actor. So Annie's early fears that her husband might be jealous were quickly dispelled. To Frederik, his wife's guide was simply a charming old man, and an amusing one.

Annie continued to be happy as rehearsals started. But then, too, the full weight of the economic depression had added thousands of Berliners to the lines of unemployed, just as preparations for the national election reached a peak of activity. Most visible of all the parties were the Nazis. Probably they'd been much in evidence for some time. On the north side of the river, beside the theatres and the university, Annie had not particularly noticed them. Now, though, she had to attend rehearsals at the far end of Friedrichstrasse – going at mid-morning and returning late in the afternoon. There was a SA Standarte quite near the rehearsal hall and the broad pavement outside the local headquarters was always thronged with brown-shirted, peak-capped troopers.

From there they were sent out with collecting cans. Indeed, once or twice a week, uniformed collectors tramped loudly upstairs and halted the rehearsal with their 'polite' but insistent presence. On the first occasion the stage manager had been unwise enough to turn them out. The following morning the cast found the floor ankle-deep in rubbish and debris. Thereafter the collections were tolerated.

The same thing was going on all over Berlin, either for the communists or the Nazis. Often there were running fights between them which always caused damage. More than once, Annie's taxi braked sharply to avoid running into these straggling noisy pursuits. She noticed that, mainly, the Nazis were strong, burly young men, whereas the communists tended to be thin and weedy.

Once, when her taxi was halted in a traffic jam, a young communist jumped on the running board. Annie recoiled from the cut and bloody face pressed against the window. Glancing beyond that, she saw the brownshirts in pursuit. The young man tried to open the door of the taxi and Annie moved clear so that he could get in. But the vehicle started off again and he lost his grip. He fell sprawling on the cobbles and was soon surrounded by a mass of SA troopers. As the taxi pulled quickly away she looked back to see the pursuers still kicking and stamping on the body in the middle of the busy road.

The communists seemed to be badly organised. The Nazis favoured combined operations. That is, compact units comprising bill-posters, collectors and guards. So, a group of about a dozen would arrive at a location which was to be posted. While that was being done by two men, three or four collectors would fan out, rattling their cans among the pedestrians. The remainder of the detachment would form a wide protective ring around this activity. The communists, on the other hand, sent their men out singly or in twos. It was not surprising that they made less of an impact. They were ambushed, their posters ripped off half-pasted and their cans stolen by superior forces.

When Annie reported this to Frederik he said, 'The trouble with communists is, they are all generals or want to be.' He smiled. 'Great plotters and talkers but not enough *do*-ers.'

'Who do you think will win the election?'

'We will.' The words were blurted out and he gave a rather worried and shame-faced glance at his wife.

She returned a quizzical look across the breakfast table. 'We? Who do you mean by "We"?'

It was then he told her he had joined the Nazi party. On one of his trips after the last meeting in the forest he'd been in Munich and had gone to hear Hitler speak. Apparently the leader of the NSDAP had made a big impression and Frederik had taken up the offer of 'concealed' membership which Josef Goebbels had suggested.

142

'But why didn't you tell me?' Annie asked.

Frederik shrugged uneasily. 'Well . . . just because it is a *concealed* membership.'

'Concealed from *me*?'

'Annie! I know you are not in the least interested in all this political manoeuvring.'

'I'm interested in what you do.'

He smiled. 'I'm not required to do anything. But Hitler does see a way out of the mess we're in. They're going to re-arm. That means work and investment and profit.'

Annie nodded and seemed to continue placidly with her breakfast. Thanks to Jamie and his work for the Control Commission, she knew re-arming would mean a great deal more than that. It would mean tearing up the Treaty of Versailles and breaking all the agreements which guaranteed the stability of Europe. Of course, she did not believe the Nazis would be elected. And even if they were, she knew they'd never get away with re-arming. Britain and France would not allow it. But she did not point these things out to her young husband. It would have been a pity to dampen his new found, if naive, enthusiasm. She was glad, though, that she had not told Frederik about Jamie Northcott's activities.

Election fever had a bad effect on the box office and for about a week after the opening of *Twelfth Night* a lot of the Deutsche Theater subscribers stayed away. Then the results were announced and everyone wondered what all the fuss had been about. In practical terms there was no change. Brüning's government remained in power and Hindenburg was still the president. Of course the Nazis had increased their share of the vote, but so had the communists. What seemed a great deal more important was that the Deutsche Theater increased its share of the audience.

Frederik seemed to lose interest, if not faith, in the profitable cause. And he agreed with Annie when she said, 'Just as well Krupp didn't give them any money.' She put up her umbrella as another heavy shower started teeming down. 'It would have been such a waste.'

'Yes.' He stared for a moment at the significant figures boldly printed on a newsvendor's bill, on which the ink had already started to run, then he took her arm to cross the Potsdamer Platz. 'Of course, it could be that the extra money would have made a difference.'

Annie did not reply but concentrated instead on negotiating the traffic moving in all directions, and making sure her heels did not get wedged in the slippery tram rails. During the lead-up to the election the weather had been unfailingly dry and bright, but now it rained constantly, peeling away the posters which marked every available surface near the government buildings. They hurried along Voss to Wilhelmstrasse where a taxi would more readily be found. Lights blazed through the gloom from every window of the Chancellery. Frederik, bending slightly under the umbrella, nodded in that direction. 'Let's hope old Brüning makes a better job of it this time.'

'Maybe he would if you'd give *him* some money.'

'No. It would only go to pay reparation.' He darted forward to secure a taxi before it was snapped up by one of the horde of officials flitting endlessly between crisis meetings. The Weimar Republic, having enjoyed 'Hitler weather', was enduring another Pyrrhic victory in the rain.

After the success of *Twelfth Night* plans were immediately in progress for *A Midsummer Night's Dream* in which it was intended that Annie would play the magical, mischievous boy Puck. In the event, Reinhardt's *Dream* became the theatrical marvel of the decade, but Annie wasn't in it. She had declined the chance of being one of that legendary cast because she just did not want to play another boy – even a boy who was not a girl in disguise. Instead she took the chance to work with Erwin Piscator at the Theater am Nollendorfplatz on the southside. It was in a revival of Hauptmann's *Rose Bernd*. And the part suited her perfectly. It was that of a wanton, working-class girl struggling against circumstances over which she had no control. Unfortunately, the play also suited the communist agitators who adopted the production as their own. And thus, in turn, it attracted the wrath of the Nazi Sturmabteilung.

Now it was not a mere inconvenience of Party collectors

at rehearsals. During performances, in a side street off the Kurfürstendamm, the studio theatre was frequently under siege. The communists mounted a protective cordon but that never held for more than half an hour. During that time it was difficult for the audience to hear much of what was being said on the stage because of the uproar of shouting and fighting in the alley below. Then the stormtroopers broke through and marched up the stairs, singing loudly, and hammered on the securely bolted door. Only then was it permissible for the stage manager to call the overstretched police. They always arrived before the stout and fortified door gave way; but often it it was touch and go.

Frederik was appalled by the danger in which Annie was placing herself and brought Helmar Schüstiger to see a performance and try to dissuade her. But Annie was determined to go on. 'I am not going to give up the first great part that I fully believe in.'

Helmar said, 'What a pity the communists believe in it just as strongly, but never see it.' He squeezed Annie's hand. 'And the audience which wants to see it spends the time watching the door instead, and listening to the Horst Wessel song.'

'The whole thing is quite impossible,' Frederik said. 'Those thugs are going to get in one of these nights and tear the place apart.'

Annie compressed her lips and resisted the impulse to point out that those 'thugs' represented a Party which he wanted to put in power.

Helmar sighed. 'It isn't really the best play to put on at the time of an election.'

The beleaguered actress slammed her hairbrush down on the table. 'When, in God's name, is there *not* an election going on in Germany?'

Frederik smiled weakly. 'We are great believers in democracy.'

And that seemed to be the case. For two whole years there had been nothing but elections; either in progress or in preparation. There had been state elections, national elections for the Reichstag and national elections for President. In the long

145

and bitter contests of Hitler v. Brüning, Hitler v. Hindenburg, Hitler v. Von Papen and even Hitler v. Schleicher there had been virtually no rest period. Nor was there until January 1933 when President Hindenburg finally bowed to the overwhelming, democratic will of the people and appointed Hitler as Chancellor.

'I remember it was a Monday afternoon,' Annie said. 'We were in the flat just lounging about after lunch and we heard the announcement on the wireless. I could see the excitement growing on Frederik's face. His eyes were gleaming but he didn't say anything. Then, within fifteen minutes of the announcement the telephone rang. It was Gustav Krupp calling from Essen. He wanted Frederik to go and see him as soon as possible to discuss exactly how a substantial contribution could be made to the new government's Party funds. Frederik was delighted. He packed an overnight bag and left immediately.'

I grunted. 'Krupp didn't waste much time.'

'He didn't waste *any* time. And he didn't waste any money. He did nothing to help the Nazis into power. But once they *had* power there was no limit on what might be available to keep them there.' She smiled grimly. 'That's good business judgment. I mean, those foundries in Essen weren't making pianos.'

The point of this allusion was lost on me. 'Pianos?'

'Yes. Like Bechstein. He was one who gave Hitler financial backing from the very start – and for what? The Nazis never promised there would be a Bechstein grand in every home. But they *had* promised to re-arm Germany. Naturally the contracts would go to friends of the Party.'

But the pianos were still bothering me. 'My mother has a Bechstein.'

Annie looked at me in some perplexity. 'Yes?'

'But my mother's Jewish.'

'So was Bechstein.'

It was clear that she did not consider this tenuous coincidence worthy of note and I was left wondering why I'd insisted on pursuing the matter. Only later did I place it as yet another example of the heightened susceptibility with which those who did not live through the Nazi era look back on it. There was, too, the error of generalisation. Annie did not generalise, unless with humorous intent. Her world was populated exclusively by individuals, not by classes of people or by masses of nationality.

She now continued with a more striking incident which arose from the appointment of Chancellor Hitler. 'While Frederik was on his way to the station, there was another phone call. This time for me. It was Emmy Sonnemann, and she was very excited. She was in Berlin, at the Kaiserhof Hotel, and begged me to come and have tea with her because she had some really important news.

'I hadn't seen Emmy since my wedding, though we always sent each other telegrams on opening nights. In the taxi going to the Kaiserhof, I more or less made up my mind that the great news must be that Emmy had finally been offered work in Berlin. I felt happy for her and glad that I'd have an old friend in close touch again. But that wasn't the news. She wasn't in Berlin to rehearse a play. She was there at the express invitation of Hermann Göring to watch the Nazi victory parade.

'At first I thought it could not possibly be *the* Hermann Göring. But it was. Emmy's new lover was the President of the Reichstag who'd just been appointed Prussian Minister of the Interior.'

'President? But I thought . . .'

Annie silenced me with a gesture. 'President of the *Reichstag*. That's like the Speaker in the House of Commons – but without the wig.' My interruption had thrown her recall of that eventful Monday in 1933. She rose, clutching her drink, and started pacing the reception room.

'You were at the Kaiserhof having tea with your friend,' I reminded her.

'Yes. And I remarked that Göring's wife must be a very understanding woman. Emmy laughed. It was difficult to get her to *stop* laughing that day. She told me Karin Göring had been dead for a couple of years. And Hermann hadn't wasted much time after her death in paying court at Weimar. Apparently he'd met Emmy when he was there drumming up support for the Party in the Thuringia provincial elections – shortly after I moved to Berlin. The affair blossomed after that. And now that the Party was finally in national control, the person Göring wanted with him to share the glory was Emmy Sonnemann. He'd called her on the Sunday evening and sent a car to collect her.' Annie finished her drink in one gulp, banged the glass down on the coffee table and threw her arms wide as expression of the sheer incredulity she'd felt that day.

I remarked, 'From what you've told me about her, I got the idea that Emmy wasn't a very good actress.'

Annie shrugged. 'She wasn't brilliant.' Then added warmly, 'But she was a very nice woman. Amusing and sweet-natured and kind. *And* she was over forty. That's why . . . once I got over the shock . . . I was delighted with the news. She was just so happy, and willing me to be just as happy with her. Of course, I didn't expect the affair to last. But it did. They were unofficial lovers for a couple more years, then they were married in the cathedral with Hitler as best man. It was a marvellous wedding.'

'Did you meet Hitler, that day at the Kaiserhof?'

'No. Though he was staying there. And Emmy invited me to come and watch the parade with her, so I could have. But I had a performance in the evening and I'd have had to go down through the centre of the city to Nollendorfplatz. I'd need plenty of time. In fact it was practically impossible to get to the theatre at all! The centre of Berlin that night was one huge mass of people; all waiting for the parade. The main streets were closed to traffic and my taxi got stranded about halfway down Friedrichstrasse, so I got out to see what they were all watching. I climbed onto the top deck of an open tram which was crammed to capacity and going nowhere.

'The legions of the SA were assembled in the Tiergarten. It was a cold dry night and in the darkness behind the Brandenburg Gate you could see the flames of thousands of torches being lit. Before long the bands started up and everyone craned forward, or climbed lamp posts or pulled themselves up on ledges to get a better view. Then this huge *army* with their banners and bugles and drums came marching out of the shadow of the Brandenburg into the street lights and floodlights which had been set up on the Linden. This was Hitler's private army. Before, I'd only seen them as roving squads of bully-boys, but now they came on like guardsmen.

'The reflected light flared on the silver mountings of their standards and flashed on the band instruments. And I'll never forget the sudden, frightening noise of the crowd. It was like one single huge animal roaring and I felt as though I was crouching in its stomach. After that everyone was screaming and clapping and men were pounding at each other's shoulders while their eyes ran with tears. The tram shook and rocked as all the feet stamped in time to the music.

'But the parade didn't reach us. It wheeled to the right down Wilhelmstrasse. Apparently, Hitler was waiting to take the salute at the Chancellery window. Suddenly there was a stampede as the people on the tram decided to get off and follow. I hung onto the overhead handrail at the top of the stair but my hat was dragged off in the rush. And still more columns of Brownshirts kept marching out of the Brandenburg Gate. And more bands. And beyond them, dimly in the Tiergarten, you could see what was like a comet's tail of torches snaking between the trees. The crowd massed deeper and deeper at the Wilhelmstrasse corner – right under the windows of the British Embassy. They were getting more and more hysterical.' Annie was standing, stretched upright in the middle of the room as though still desperately clinging to that handrail while Berlin went wild all around her. Then she relaxed and smiled. 'It was pure theatre, Bill.'

'Did you get to *your* theatre?'

'No. And it didn't really matter. There was no audience that night and the performance was cancelled. We were to find that that always happened when the Nazis staged a parade. I remember Max Reinhardt saying, "The contribution of Goebbels to street theatre will never be matched – please God!"'

By the time Annie became pregnant both she and Frederik knew their marriage was already beyond saving. Yet, it was the realisation that something was needed to bring them together which persuaded Annie she must suppress her fear of childbirth. Frederik had wanted to start a family as soon as they were married, but she kept putting it off. The reasons she gave him were the needs of their separate careers. Really, though, she was haunted by the girl in the Lambeth slums during the General Strike.

As soon as the pregnancy was confirmed she insisted on tests to establish that a normal delivery would not be possible. She also had it clearly recorded on her medical record that a caesarean operation would be required if the pregnancy reached full term. Delay and a doctor's blunder had killed the girl. They'd forgotten she was to be operated upon in hospital. Annie was determined that she was not going to die of a clerk's oversight.

The change in Frederik had probably started when he secretly joined the Nazi Party, but his behaviour altered markedly when Hitler came to power. For then the head of the family, too, became a Nazi supporter and Frederik no longer felt obliged to hide his feelings or prove what a dutiful, caring husband he could be. In fact, he had been dutiful and caring. And the happiness they'd shared had been genuine. But, as Annie had realised from the start, *he* was the one who'd been in love. Now he was no longer. Another ideal had taken Annie's place. Now the Romantic excitement of a great Germany reborn claimed all his energy. His work and the secret dream became one.

He spent more and more time away from home, much of it on Party business. And even when he was at home it made no great difference. They did not have rows. There just didn't seem to be anything worth saying any more. Annie tried to keep up the same sort of conversation they'd enjoyed before. Now he found it trivial and irritating. That led to long silences, then rather formal good manners. It was the politeness which Annie could not stand. To her, politeness meant not caring.

Before long, she did not care what became of Frederik either. And she quietly resented the fact that she was carrying his child, which would oblige her to face what seemed a dangerous operation to give it birth.

Another grievance was that she'd had to give up her work in the theatre. But the Berlin theatre seemed to be paralysed in any case. The influential people she'd worked with had gone. Reinhardt and Piscator had both fled to America at the start of the Nazi regime. So had Bertolt Brecht. There was a steady exodus of artists out of Germany, and writers, and people of excellence in all professions. Annie could not understand that. If they'd been Germans before, why were they not Germans still?

'Because,' said Helmar Schüstiger, 'it is not enough to be a German any more. These days, the only safe thing to be is a Nazi.'

'Or the wife of a Nazi?' Annie suggested contemptuously. Helmar nodded. He was paying the first of his many calls to the flat now that Annie found it awkward to get about. Standing at the window he looked southward over the city. His eye was caught by the huge blue repair tarpaulin which was still stretched over the dome of the Reichstag. 'You must have had a good view of the fire from here,' he said.

'No. It happened in the middle of the night. We were asleep.' She lowered herself onto the couch. 'We saw the book-burning, though, in the Opernplatz.'

Helmar turned away from the window. 'Yes. They held that at a decently convenient hour.'

Annie was still thinking about the famous deserters. 'But what about the people who have to put up with it? What about the people who can't afford to go to America?'

He shrugged, lighting a cigarette. 'It seems to me, if they can't afford it, America probably wouldn't have them anyway.'

Annie spread her legs and writhed against the cushions, trying to get into a position where her back didn't ache. 'I think it's very selfish for theatre people to rush off as soon as the wind changes.'

'My dear Annie, it's easy for you . . .'

'*Nothing* is easy for me at the moment.' She patted the great mass of her belly. 'Look at that! Can it possibly get worse?'

'I mean, it's easy for you to feel safe. Because you *are* safe.' He turned his head to blow a puff of smoke away from her. 'As you say, you are the wife of a Nazi. You are also Frau von Bohlen, of Krupp von Bohlen. *And* you are a friend of a dear friend of Hermann Göring.' He turned to smile solicitously. 'Does she visit you?.'

'Emmy? Yes, occasionally. She's living in Berlin now – with him.'

151

'When does she come to see you?' There was more than idle interest in the question.

Annie immediately noted the change of tone. 'Why do you ask?'

Helmar waved the cigarette dismissively. 'I just wondered if she keeps up with her theatrical friends – now that she's moving in such exalted circles.'

'Of course. Emmy doesn't give a damn about all this "master race" nonsense.'

Schüstiger tilted his head and winked. 'And why should she, now that she has won the "mistress" race?'

Annie laughed but had the feeling that he'd angled the conversation in order to establish her continuing friendship with Emmy Sonnemann. He wanted to join that circle. For no one realised more clearly than Helmar Schüstiger that he was going to need influential friends, now that practically all the theatres in Berlin were under Dr Goebbels' direct control. So the next time Emmy proposed to visit her, Annie specified a time when Helmar would be available and saw to it that he just happened to be on hand.

There was another, more unexpected, visitor to the flat on Ziegelstrasse during that seemingly interminable year of 1933. Jamie Northcott phoned from Hamburg suggesting he might come and see her since he had business in Berlin. It was not until some time later Annie realised that *she* was the business. At the time, she was puzzled by the fact that his conversation was devoted to asking about Frederik's work; what companies he was seeing and what government contracts Krupp might be engaged upon at Essen and elsewhere. Just before he left he said, 'Annie. Does Frederik know that I was coming to see you?'

'No. He's been away all week.'

'Oh, yes. You told me that. In Kiel.' He ran his hand nervously over the bald patch on his head. 'The thing is, I'd rather you didn't tell him I was here.'

'All right. But he'll find out anyway.'

Jamie gave her a quick worried look. 'How?'

She shrugged. 'The neighbours. Particularly Herr Lusik on the ground floor. He's bound to mention it. He mentions everything he thinks might do him some good.'

'Is he a Nazi?'

Annie smiled at the naïveté. 'Oh yes!' And she remembered Helmar's observation. 'A Nazi is the only thing to be nowadays.'

Jamie pulled on his overcoat. 'Maybe *you'll* be joining the Party next.'

'No. They have too many bloody elections – and I've never voted in my life.'

'But you intend to go on living in Berlin?'

'Of course.'

'Good.' He moved towards the door. 'Do keep me up to date on all developments.'

Annie took this as a reference to her pregnancy and probably that was the main intention. But there was, too (and underlying everything he'd said) a clear suggestion of future complicity.

Meanwhile, the dread of the actual birth had to be faced. There seemed to be no aspect of it from which she could draw comfort. The bright hope in conception had been so illusory, the experience of pregnancy so unpleasant and the eventual outcome so frightening that it seemed more like the sentence for a terrible crime than the joyful event so many women pray for.

What remained was anger. As the time for the operation drew closer she became increasingly frightened and her natural response to that was anger. In the final weeks, day by day, she stoked up a smouldering anger against the unborn baby, and against Frederik who was wholly responsible.

He visited the hospital sometimes twice a day and it seemed to Annie – somewhat befuddled with drugs – that he came to gloat at her weak, ugly condition. Sometimes she became hysterical and railed against the threatening bulk which would ruin her life. When he didn't respond to that, she threatened she'd have nothing to do with the child once it was born.

But Frederik remained calm, so thereafter she pretended to be asleep. That was her only defence against visitors. And lying there with her eyes closed she plotted a kind of revenge against the injustice which had led her to such a wretched, vulnerable state.

Gerda, a healthy baby girl, was born on 16 February 1934 and at once Annie's resentment against the child vanished. She was quite enchanted with the infant and wept with joy when she first held the tiny little girl. But now *all* her unpurged resentment was directed against Frederik. And he had placed in her arms the perfect weapon of revenge. She would use his love for the child against him. Nothing could be more effective than that.

But it did not work. Back at the flat, a resident nurse had already been engaged. Annie ordered her out and screamed at Frederik. Neither of them took any notice. And there was worse to come. As soon as the infant had been weaned under the nurse's supervision, Frederik informed his wife of the plans which had been made while she'd still been awaiting the birth.

'Gerda is to live at the Villa Heugel,' he said.

'What?' Annie felt a sudden weakness in her limbs. 'What did you say?'

He sounded as calm and reasonable as he'd always been. 'It's been agreed that since you did not really want the baby it would be unfair to force the responsibility upon you.'

'Who said I don't want the baby?'

'You said so.' There was a melancholy bitterness in his voice now. 'You told me so, many times. You blamed me and now I will take the responsibility.'

'But that was *before*,' Annie protested wildly. 'That was before, when I was sick and frightened.'

'Nevertheless, that was when *I* had to consider what should be done.' He moved away from the stricken expression in her eyes. 'And it would be best in any case. You will wish to go back on the stage and we . . .'

'*We?*' Annie shouted.

'My family is anxious that Gerda should be brought up as a German.'

Annie fought the overwhelming urge to break down in an abandonment of tears. But as she stared across the room she was astonished to see that Frederik was weeping. It was then she decided that she could, and must, prove herself stronger than he and all the Krupps. Tantrums and wailing would not do it. No. Nor could she battle with the nurse, snatch the child and run. But she would find a method to make them pay. All that remained of her marriage was the opportunity and prospect of revenge. She would make sure, too, that her daughter formed no part of the dynasty at Essen.

Annie was furious when she read that passage.

Barbara, Elspeth and I were seated in the dining room having lunch when suddenly the door was thrown open and she stood there brandishing a section of the typescript in one hand. It was quite a theatrical entrance. In keeping with that, I was astonished at the impression of size and authority the actress now imposed on us. Not that she was particularly well made-up, or dressed, to do so. In fact, she had on an old housecoat, her hair was in some disarray and she wore no make-up at all. Nevertheless, the air fairly crackled with electricity. Of course, anyone who can hold an audience of two thousand attentive on a whisper has no difficulty in stunning three people in an ordinary room.

Apparently she'd been resting in bed and catching up with the material most recently typed by Elspeth. Then she was seized with great indignation. This had to be voiced immediately.

She now moved to the table while the three of us watched her as though hypnotised. She slapped the manuscript down with intentional force and declared, 'You are as bad as that bitch Sleavin!' Her voice rose a couple of notches. 'What you don't know you guess. What you can't guess you invent.' She gripped the back of a chair. 'Either way, it's a bloody lie . . . and I won't have it.'

I could feel the colour drain out of my face and saw Barbara take in the fact. It was she who spoke first. 'Annie? What's wrong?'

The betrayed actress made half a circuit of the table before she answered – as though fighting for control enough to answer. 'Revenge!' she declared. 'I'm accused of *revenge.*'

Of the four of us, Barbara was the only person in the room who didn't know what this meant. Elspeth, who had typed it, gulped as though fearing that that, in itself, was sufficient offence. I, who had written it, sent my brain spinning in search of justification. But again it was Barbara who spoke. 'Have your lunch, Annie,' she said.

In answer, Annie swept her place setting off the table,

155

scattering glasses and cutlery across the floor. Then she confronted me. I kept my eyes on her eyes but was aware of scurrying activity to my left as Elspeth made her escape. Barbara was made of sterner stuff; in fact, the same stuff with which I now had to cope. At last I demanded, 'How would you describe what you did if it wasn't revenge?'

'What I did?' She shouted at me across the table. 'It's not your job to find excuses for what I did!'

'Reason, then. There must be a reason.'

'Yes. *My* reason. Not yours.'

'And what is your reason?'

'Love! Always, love!'

The argument would probably have raged for a good while right there but my wife put things in perspective. Now that she knew it was no more than a matter of words, she calmly resumed eating her lunch. The old woman knew a theatrical ace when she saw one and, with a look of infinite contempt at me, swept from the room.

When she'd gone, I turned to Barbara. But she stopped me. 'Don't!' she said. 'Don't tell me about it. Just think of a good reason . . . for *her*.'

I nodded and tried to eat. This was not the first altercation between Annie and myself over the way in which I was telling her story. But, to date, it was the most serious. The other occasions had been to do, mainly, with a fictional verbiage turned to a herbiage which she called 'Rambling Iris'. Her point was that she had never in her life indulged in much thinking. She was a *do*-er. In particular she had never analysed her own actions or feelings in literary terms. For me, the solution to these objections was simple. I took out all the long internal bits I'd written as her thoughts. It was a great improvement. She cured me of 'Rambling Iris'.

But her present anger was about something more important and I was determined not to give in. After lunch I got dressed as usual for our walk and went down to the reception room to wait for Annie. She was already there and also prepared to go out.

But, first, the reason for her change of heart with regard to the Nazis had to be dealt with. She had reclaimed the sheets of typescript and now read the offending sections aloud to me. '"Annie fought the overwhelming urge to break down in an abandonment of tears. But as she stared across the room she was astonished to see that Frederik was weeping."' She read it well. There was no unfair sneering in the tone of her voice.

'Well?' I asked.

'Why do you think Frederik was weeping? You report *that* as I told you but you don't say *why*.'

'Because I don't know why.'

'Oh, really!' I could hear the gurgle of anger in her throat again, and not far from the surface. 'When you don't know why Frederik does something you keep quiet. But when you do know why I did something, you change it.'

'Can we sit down?' I suggested. The conversation was being conducted over the threshold of the open door.

'*You* sit down,' she said.

I did so. 'Then perhaps you'll tell me why Frederik was weeping when he took away your child.'

'Of course! It was either because he was still in love with me or because he was remembering the way he had once loved me. Whichever it was, nothing more could come of it.'

'I don't see that it makes much difference.'

'It makes a difference to this.' She raised the script and continued her recital. '"It was then she decided that she could, and must, prove herself stronger than he and all the Krupps. Tantrums and wailing would not do it. No. Nor could she battle with the nurse, snatch the child and run. But she would find a method to make them pay. All that remained of her marriage was the opportunity and prospect of revenge. She would make sure, too, that her daughter formed no part of the dynasty at Essen."' She stared balefully at me over her spectacles. 'First, it was not because Frederik was weeping that I decided to be strong and fight them. Second, I was in no fit state to decide what I was going to do. Third, what I eventually did had nothing to do with any of this and most certainly was not for revenge.'

'Please, Annie, sit down for a moment and listen.' After a pause, she did and I continued. 'The point of that paragraph is to prepare the reader. They've got to have some reasonable explanation of why you suddenly took to *spying*. And it has got to be a good enough motive for you to go on pretending to be a devoted Nazi wife, hob-nobbing with the top people while – at the same time – you were feeding all the information you could get to British Intelligence.'

'Huh!' She threw both her arms in the air and slumped back against the cushions. 'And you think *revenge* is a good enough reason to do all that?'

'Yes.'

She shook her head decisively. 'No. My only reason for getting into that business was because I'd found another lover.' She leaned forward and shrugged. 'It just happened that he was a British Intelligence agent.'

'"Just happened"! Annie don't be ridiculous. He was instructed to get in touch with you.'

She nodded. 'At the suggestion of Jamie Northcott. He was in British Intelligence, too, though he never told me.'

'Then how can you say it just happened? It was planned.'

'Oh, Bill!' Impatiently she got to her feet again. 'I would have fallen in love with Rolf anyway. It "just happened" that he was a British Intelligence agent. If he'd been a French agent, or a communist agent – I would *still* have fallen in love with him. And spied against anybody he asked me to spy against.'

'I don't believe that.'

From the other end of the room her voice rang clear, suddenly charged with that piercing intensity which made me uneasy. 'This book is not about what *you* believe. And it's no⁺, God knows, about what you'd *prefer*!' She advanced upon me, down the very centre of the room, building the speech as she moved.

'You seem to think I should always have other people's reasons for what I did. But there is no State which owns nor ever owned me. I'm not a chattel of greedy politicians – so! – to hell with allegiance and patriotism. Those were the virtues that killed millions in the Great War.' She was so close now that her eyes seemed to be giving off sparks. 'No country ever gave me anything from the goodness of its heart, so I'm a bit short on sentiment where countries are concerned. I'm pretty short on nationality as well. It leads to slavery. Slavery of *other* people – who are not the right colour, or don't live in the right place.' And now she stood directly in front of me. 'You've been brainwashed, Bill, and you're a credit to society. Whereas I have always had to make do with just being a credit to me.'

I took a deep breath. 'Yes. I think I understand that.'

'Fine.' There was a long pause, then she patted my shoulder and her manner changed dramatically. 'As long as you understand, it doesn't matter if you believe me or not.' She smiled. 'But love is the best reason to do anything.'

'Love might be.' I returned her gaze defiantly. 'But I don't think sex is a good enough reason.'

'Who can tell which is which, at the time?'

'You could tell,' I reminded her. 'You've told me it was entirely sex.'

She was immediately defensive. 'That doesn't make it any less real. Or exciting. And some good came of it.' Having laid the manuscript on the table she moved towards the door.

I rose to follow her. 'Do you want me to take out the bit you read about revenge?'

'I don't know. It depends on what sort of person is likely to read the book. If they're like me, take it out. If most of them are like you then perhaps you'd better leave it in.' As she walked out into the hallway she repeated incredulously, 'Revenge!' She selected her walking stick from a stand by the front door. 'Why in God's name would anyone waste an ounce of their energy on revenge when there's so much *else* to do?'

We took a sedate walk along the Havoc shore and it was as though there hadn't ever been the slightest disagreement between us. Annie Jeynor, who didn't believe in revenge, didn't believe in sulking either.

ROLF TEMPLAR

When Gerda and her nurse had been safely installed with the Krupps at Essen, the von Bohlens were obliged to come to terms with the new situation. Having no excuse to do otherwise, they began accepting invitations to go out together. Indeed, they were soon considered an asset at artistic and political gatherings. And quite separately – for quite different reasons – each enjoyed the atmosphere of barely restrained excitement which seemed to whirl around the city like a turbulent rising tide. For Frederik (who'd been proved right about the Nazis) it was a surge of patriotism mixed still with idealism. For Annie it was like a burst of adrenalin which jerked her from a state of lethargy and regret to one of constant activity.

There was also the plain fact that she wanted to get back to work again. She knew from her experience in London that nothing could be gained by trying to beat 'the establishment'. The Nazis were quite definitely established now. Both theatre and films were under their control. The one man who held the future careers of actors – and, particularly, actresses – in his grasp was Dr Josef Goebbels. And since Goebbels was the first Nazi leader whom Frederik had dealt with, it seemed natural that Annie's desire to start work again should be made known to him.

They were asked to a large theatrical party at Goebbels' ministry in Wilhelmplatz. One of the guests was the English actress Lillian Harvey who had been working in Germany for some time. She reported that conditions out in Babelsberg were excellent. And the money much better now that the film studios were a state enterprise. Another guest who seemed genuinely pleased to meet Annie was the tall and strikingly beautiful Leni

Riefenstahl, full of plans for filming the next Nuremberg Rally. Indeed, there was a great deal of talking shop, and part of it was Annie's contribution. Everyone seemed well aware of her fine performances at Weimar, Hamburg and in Berlin.

Frau Magda Goebbels was a svelte, ash-blonde, impeccably groomed woman whose eyes glittered with intelligence. She moved, smiling, around the large room. Already it was well known that the Minister was tirelessly engaged in a whole series of affairs with aspiring actresses. Evenings such as this enabled her to prove that she didn't care – or, at least, have it believed that she didn't care. But it was in her mind at every introduction that here might be someone her husband was sleeping with, especially if the girl was tall, long-legged and a blonde.

'Frl Jeynor! I have heard so much about you,' said Frau Goebbels in the hubbub of clinking glasses, chatter and occasional laughter. She spoke in English with a strong American accent. Her smile was convincing as always, but the sad eyes noted with some relief that this petite actress had auburn hair, and was no longer a girl. Probably, therefore, she would have to get work on her feet. 'Have you met the Minister?'

'No. Not yet.' Annie nodded across the room to a noisy group of guests who surrounded and quite concealed Goebbels. 'He seems to be very busy.'

Frau Goebbels cast a disdainful glance in the direction of the sycophantic throng. 'Not too busy to meet you, Fräulein.' She was about to take Annie's hand for an immediate foray across the room.

But Annie stopped her. 'Frau Goebbels, may I introduce my husband, Frederik von Bohlen.'

Frederik came to attention, then bowed low over Frau Goebbels' hand.

The lady was even more impressed. This small foreign woman with the auburn hair also had a husband who came with his wife to parties! 'What a delightful couple you make. But tell me Frl . . . Frau von Bohlen, why have we not seen you on the stage for so long?'

'I've been having a baby.'

'Ah! Better still. But now you feel ready to work again?'

Frederik said, 'Annie feels very depressed unless she has something to do.'

Frau Goebbels, a fiercely devoted mother of several children, let that pass. She said, 'Of course. And it is such a waste of talent if she does not.' She glanced over her shoulder. 'My husband has escaped, I see. Let me introduce you.' She hesitated several paces away. '*Both* of you.'

The Minister was all smiling charm and extremely well-informed. He knew what plays Annie had appeared in, who had written them and who'd directed them. Probably he was the only person in that crowded room who dared mention the disgraced names, Reinhardt and Piscator. But, since he did, Annie decided to test him. She said, 'Herr Reinhardt is an excellent director. What a pity he is no longer working in Berlin.'

The heavy lids of Goebbels' lizard eyes flicked. 'He was at the Deutsche a long time. No doubt he needed a change.' He turned his large head to one side and his smile invited friendly argument. 'The theatre is always looking for new blood. That is what stirs the imagination.'

Frau Goebbels laid a hand on Annie's arm. 'The one *I* can't understand is Brecht. For years, a devoted communist – and where does he run to? Not to the Russians, no! He runs to America, the capital nation of capitalism.' Her husband nodded encouragingly and she went on, 'Now that is what I call a triumph of imagination over principles.'

They all laughed. And Annie did so genuinely. She had not cared at all for Brecht. In fact she had a deep suspicion of all middle-class intellectuals with proletarian convictions.

Another well-reported social occasion they attended that summer was at the invitation of Emmy Sonneman. At last, she had reported to Annie, Hermann's grand new hunting lodge was complete. Money, time and the best of German craftmanship had been lavished on the baronial country residence, situated in the forest of Schorfheide to the north-east of Berlin. Emmy did not seem at all put out that the mansion was called Karinhalle, in honour of the former Frau Göring. Frederik and Annie were asked to stay the weekend for the housewarming.

Among the guests were a number of foreign diplomats, including English and American representatives. There, too, was Rolf Templar: a tall athletic man, who was introduced as a cultural attaché at the British embassy. He seemed out of place and distinctly uneasy in the house but, apparently, made a great impression on the men who accompanied Göring on the carefully staged hunting trip into the forest. Frederik said the Englishman was a remarkable shot and a born woodsman.

Annie nodded and smiled, already aware that it was not his prowess in the forest which caused the familiar tingling sensation in her throat. After dinner that evening she decided to find out more about him. And he seemed more than willing to be detained away from the card tables in a dimly lit corner of the huge room. 'Can I get you anything, Frau von Bohlen?'

Annie smiled up into his dark, amused eyes. 'Not at the moment, thank you. Mr . . . Templar, isn't it?'

'That's right. British Embassy.'

'Why do *they* need such a good shot?'

He was startled. 'I beg your pardon?'

She saw she would have to take things a bit slower. 'My husband says you're a fine marksman, and I wondered how that sorted with your training in the diplomatic service.' In fact, what she was truly wondering about was how long it would take him to sit on the deep couch beside her.

'As a matter of fact . . .' He sat down and Annie half turned to face him. '. . . I'm not a career diplomat. They needed a cultural attaché.'

Annie tried to keep her face straight. 'So, naturally, they recruited an expert woodsman.'

He laughed at the incongruity and leaned back as though abandoning any further pretence. For indeed his posting in Berlin was a pretence. But he tried one last excuse, out of loyalty to his superiors. 'No. What they really needed was someone with the right background who could speak the language well enough.' He shrugged. 'My mother is German and I spent a large part of my youth here.' His admonitory finger forestalled any further quibbling. 'Where I also learned to shoot.'

'How long have you been at the embassy?'

'Almost a year now.'

'Ah! I was wondering why I hadn't met you before. But I've been out of cultural circulation for a while.'

He raised his eyebrows. 'Is the circulation restored now?'

'Quite, thank you.'

'So we're likely to meet in future?'

'I'm quite certain we shall.'

Next day, Rolf did not go out with the huntsmen. He kept Annie company. And before the weekend was over there were clear indications that the attraction between them was mutual. Almost casually, they made an arrangement to meet in Berlin, after a decent interval. Rolf promised he would call her to confirm their date.

That arrangement was shattered at the end of June, when the whole social and diplomatic life of the city seized up in a panic of fear and uncertainty. The source of this eruption was the Hanslbauer Hotel outside Munich. There the first murders were carried out in 'the night of the long knives'. The following day, as the purge of Röhm's SA continued, communications were cut in all parts of the country. It was virtually impossible to make a phone call in or out of Berlin. It was difficult if not dangerous to be on the streets and all foreign embassies had restriction of movement imposed on their staff.

Annie paced about the flat, hoping that somehow Rolf Templar would manage to deliver a message confirming the time and place of their meeting. Finally she decided she would go to the hotel on Kreuzberg just on the chance that he might be waiting for her. But Frederik thought her agitation was due to fear of the political upheaval. Considerately, he insisted on staying at home with her until the crisis was over.

The ban on freedom of movement and communication was lifted a few days later. But that was too late. The courier the British Embassy immediately sent to London was their intelligence agent Rolf Templar. And he was kept there, pending the reorganisation of his department. He and Annie did not meet again for almost a year. And it was as a result of two very different but equally well-publicised events.

*　　*　　*

Hermann Göring and Emmy Sonnemann were married at the Protestant cathedral in Berlin on 10 April 1935. Just over six weeks later, on 28 May, Marie Tempest celebrated her jubilee, fifty years on the stage, at Drury Lane.

Annie was guest at both occasions, as many newspaper photographs bore witness. Parochial as ever, the London press seemed to concentrate on the 'West End star' with the unknown German bride of Göring (the fat one among the German leaders). Unkindly, they pointed out that the bride was not nearly so fat as the groom, and certainly taller. Miss Jeynor, on the other hand, was identified as 'petite and glamorous' and a godsend to the German theatre – as what West End star would not be?

In Germany the wedding was treated as a state occasion. The celebration started days before the event and continued long after the happy pair had departed to their honeymoon at Wiesbaden, then the Adriatic. Immediately before the wedding day there had been a gala evening in the Opera house, and the wedding service itself brought the whole of central Berlin to a stand-still. The procession of cars, led by Hitler, moved from Brandenburg Gate, along the full mile of Unter den Linden, under the bright green spring foliage of the decorated trees and triumphal arches. The air was very fresh after overnight rain and the sun glinted on the immaculate phalanx of motorcycles which formed a moving arrow down the broad avenue.

The glittering cavalcade proceeded through densely packed cheering crowds to the cathedral. There, royalty, diplomats and an Almanach de Gotha of distinguished guests waited, the gentlemen in full orders and the ladies wearing long court dresses and jewels. Frederik and Annie were placed well back, but close to the centre aisle.

Hitler took his place, sitting in a huge carved chair at the foot of the altar steps. During the Protestant service, and in the sermon by Reichsbishof Müller, he was frequently deferred to – as though this drab-uniformed, piercing-eyed man with the small moustache was really an incarnation of the divinely-guided monarchs of a restored Holy Roman Empire.

The reception was held at the sumptuous but gloomy Kaiserhof Hotel. Once there, Emmy did her best to dispel the tense atmosphere of high Nazi ritual. She circulated freely, laughing, joking and making sure all her theatre friends were enjoying themselves. She insisted on introducing Annie to the Führer who kissed her hand. Emmy reported to him that Frl Jeynor was working on an historical drama for UFA and Hitler asked a few idle questions about that before moving on with a renewed smile to another guest. His smiles seemed to be requisitioned from some interior store. They wore out very quickly and there was always a slight delay before a replacement dropped into position.

Emmy immediately asked, 'What did you think of the Führer?'

'Impressive,' she said. 'But I think he takes himself too seriously.'

'He has a great deal to be serious about,' Emmy said.

Annie suggested, 'Maybe that's his own fault.'

Her friend smiled. She thought Annie had said seriousness was the Führer's *only* fault.

It was the publication of Annie's name in friendly association with the Nazi hierarchy which singled her out in the estimation of British Intelligence as a likely source of information. Enquiries were made and Jamie Northcott was asked for his opinion. He reported how helpful Miss Jeynor had been in his mission through the Rhineland seven years earlier. He also reported her potentially useful marriage to Frederik von Bohlen. The department instructed him to get in touch with her. Before he could do that, she wrote to him saying she'd be in London for the Tempest jubilee.

So it was at Drury Lane, in the presence of King George V and Queen Mary, that Annie was recruited. Jamie introduced her to Rolf Templar. He and Annie pretended they had not met before. And that in itself was an admission of the charged feeling which formed an almost tangible link between them. If Jamie was aware of the link he counted it an advantage and left them together in the bar during the interval.

Rolf immediately asked, 'Is your husband with you, Frau von Bohlen?'

'No. He is very busy at the moment.'

He smiled. 'Of course. There is a great upsurge of industry now . . . with the new regime.'

'Yes. But he's also started on a new project for General Göring.'

'How interesting! What sort of project?'

'Something to do with industrial research.' She changed the subject. 'Have you known Jamie a long time?'

'Not long. No.' Rolf smiled and shrugged at the apparent oddness of it. 'In fact, I met him for the first time last week.' He leaned across the marble-topped table. 'Where are you staying in London?'

'At the Dorchester.' By gesture, she invited him to light a cigarette for her. 'Where did you meet?'

Rolf seemed a little startled. 'At Karinhalle, don't you remember. You were there with your husband.'

'Yes. That's where *we* met. But I was asking where you met Jamie.' While he made an obvious effort to cope with that she added, 'And *why* did you meet him?'

He laughed unconvincingly. 'I can't remember. Does it matter?'

Annie decided it would be pointless to force a satisfactory answer. But as she puffed decorously at her cigarette she made several obvious deductions, based on past experience and the present coincidence. It seemed likely that both men were engaged in the same sort of work and that Jamie had been called in as intermediary. And whereas Rolf Templar was a cultural attaché in Berlin, his duty would scarcely include a jubilee binge in London, unless . . . 'How often have you seen Marie Tempest?' she asked.

'I'd never seen her until today. Heard of her, of course.'

'Of course.'

Rolf was aware that some explanation was needed but the only reasonable explanation he could think of was the real one. Yet he couldn't be too specific right away. 'To be honest, I came here just to meet you. I've wanted to meet you again for a long time. Ever since . . .'

'The *first* time we met?' Annie suggested helpfully.

'Yes. Then, ever since the Röhm purge. I really did try to

reach you.' An earnest, soulful expression clouded his eyes. He bent his head as though about to make an unworthy confession.

To his astonishment, Annie laughed. 'You don't have to do all that!'

'What?' His composure was shaken. 'Do what?'

'The strange fascination from afar act.' Too late she saw he couldn't cope with such directness – at least, not yet – and hastily tried to restore his confidence. 'I mean, it must have been obvious, at Karinhalle, that I wanted to meet *you* again. Don't let's spoil things by asking pointless questions.'

That suited Rolf very well indeed. He didn't want to ask any questions until he was sure of what the answer would be. The interval bell rang and he took her arm to lead her back to the auditorium.

There the houselights dimmed, and the enchanting Marie Tempest re-enacted many more of her famous scenes. She also, most affectingly, *sang*. The huge audience was enraptured by nostalgia as well as affection when they listened to that throaty, rather cracked little voice which still managed to fill the house, singing 'The Goldfish Song'. She indicated they should join in. There was hesitation because this was such a grand occasion. The rather plump little figure, all alone on the stage, appealed to the royal box. The stern, bearded man in the royal box responded immediately.

> *'A goldfish swam in a big glass bowl,*
> *As dear little goldfish do.'*

For the first couple of lines it was a duet for the actress and the King of England. Then, for the chorus, the sheer volume of massed voices from stalls, grand circle and way up into the gallery practically shook the old theatre to its foundations.

> *'And she said it's fit, fit, fitter,*
> *He should love my glit, glit, glitter,*
> *Than his heart give away*
> *To the butterflies gay,*
> *And the birds that twit, twit, twitter.'*

It was all such nonsense and so trivial but there was, too, in that very special community singing, a feeling of great love for the ageing woman in the spotlight. For so many years she had promised nothing more than to entertain, and, with superb artistry, had never failed to keep her promise.

The following evening Rolf took Annie out to dinner and after dinner to his flat in Cadogan Square. She spent the night there. And it was a quite surprising night for both of them. Rolf was surprised to find that his well-honed seduction routine was quite unnecessary. In fact it made Annie laugh because, she said, it reminded her so much of the peacock-parading in French stage romances. And whereas the eyerolling and *double-entendre* behaviour was all very well in public, or even in the living room, it was ridiculous when practised by a comparative stranger in bed.

But Rolf surprised Annie, too. All the pretences of his background, training and technique seemed to be stripped away with his clothes. He became exuberant and boyishly playful. That made her laugh as well, but now she was laughing with him in shared enjoyment of their physical delight in each other. She was astonished to feel so young and carefree again. And she was grateful that she'd found exactly the man she needed at such a testing and dangerous time in her life. Of course, she did not know quite how dangerous it was going to be until the following morning. Rolf, fully clothed again, told her the truth about his work in Berlin; and of the service it was hoped *she* would undertake when they returned.

She asked, 'You are going back to Berlin, then?'

'Oh yes! We would be partners there.'

Reassured by that, at least, she mentioned what seemed to her an obvious difficulty. 'I'd be willing to help, but nobody's going to tell me anything which would be the slightest use to British Intelligence.'

'Darling, they will if you ask.'

'I wouldn't even know what to ask.'

Rolf laid down the hairbrush and crossed the room to sit on the edge of the bed. He squeezed her thigh under the bedclothes. 'You must start taking an interest in your husband's work. I'm perfectly sure that whatever he's doing for the Party is not ordinary research. Let Frau Göring tell you about *her* husband's worries. Get invited to the right parties at the Villa Heugel or Karinhalle or the Berghof. Become friendly with *Frau* Goebbels. Hitler trusts her.'

Annie sighed. 'Frau Goebbels is far too intelligent, and discreet, to let anything slip. And she's a dedicated Nazi.'

'Of course. They all are.'

'Emmy isn't. They wanted her to join the Party and she wouldn't.'

Rolf lay back against her raised knees. 'You see, we don't expect you to steal plans, or sleep with the High Command. We want to know where who is, when, and why. A sort of strategy by social calendar.'

Annie had the impression he was quoting this job description, but asked, 'What good would that be?'

He leaned forward and kissed her brow. 'Leave that to our boys. They'll know how to interpret whatever you can find out.'

'I think it would be a waste of time,' said Annie flatly. 'Much better if I could get them to hire me to spy on *you*.'

Rolf drew back as though stung. 'What? But you wouldn't . . . I mean this is your country . . .'

'But not *really*,' Annie assured him quickly. It bothered her that he could be so dense. 'I mean, I would pretend to be working for them – passing false information to you. And from you to them. You see, that would mean we could meet without trouble.'

But this idea was far outside Rolf's brief. He needed instructions on how to proceed. When those instructions came he drove her to a country house at Rickmansworth. There she met his superiors and was briefed on the task they wished her to perform. A few days later, she returned to Berlin.

Unlike Rolf, his superiors saw at once the advantage of having her seem willing to work for the Nazis. It was a strategy which, when war came, they were to use with astonishing success. By then there were several German spies in Britain, but all of them had been coerced by British Intelligence. They continued sending back false information without ever being suspected by their original employers.

Like them – though still in peacetime – Annie was given some bait to carry back to the Nazis. One of her co-stars on the film she was then making was, she knew, the current mistress of Goebbels. The girl asked about Annie's holiday in England. That allowed Annie to boast about the parties she'd attended and about the influential government personalities she'd met. She reported herself astonished at what these men told her when they were drunk, or in bed.

Naturally, this item of gossip reached the ears of the Minister. Doctor Goebbels invited her to discuss a future film project in his office at the Ministry. And the interview did take place in his office. That was a comfort. For she'd heard from more than one young actress that beyond the office was a self-contained luxury flat, with bedroom kept in constant readiness.

Goebbels, seated behind a huge desk, seemed very business-like. He made a pre-emptive strike almost at once.

'Frl Jeynor, I must tell you that we are disappointed in your recent work at Babelsberg.'

'I am sorry to hear that, Minister.'

He shook his head regretfully and consulted some papers on his desk. 'These reviews of your last films are not as good as we'd hoped.'

Annie forbore to point out that since he controlled the *Völkischer Beobachter* that could easily be set right. She lowered her head. 'Perhaps the subject wasn't really suitable for me.'

'What subject do you think *would* be suitable?'

Annie mentioned several properties which she knew were being considered by UFA. But the Minister plainly was not enthusiastic about her participation in any of them. Soon they reached the unavoidable conclusion that Annie could well lose her place in the German film industry. But the actress did not for a moment believe it. This, she knew, was just the softening-up process. Goebbels had used the same technique many times before with other actresses – though the object of the softening-up was different on those occasions.

As though to give them both a break from a depressing

172

discussion, the Minister asked about her recent visit to London. And here Annie had to use all her skill in order to let slip the essential information without betraying that she was aware of it. Nor did Goebbels betray that he'd picked it up; though of course, he had. His was the nimblest, most subtle and best educated mind of all the Nazi leaders. He let her ramble on and she knew he'd check several sources to establish the likelihood of her story before anything else was done.

Finally, when they were back on the subject of her work again, he suggested it would be no bad thing if she agreed to make an outright propaganda film for the Ministry. Annie reacted as though she'd been thrown a lifeline and agreed on the spot. Goebbels smiled. His strategy always worked.

While she was waiting for the Ministry to check the story she'd told, Annie had to weigh up the possibilities of obtaining information she could take back to London. They did *not* want mere 'social calendar' gossip. Whitehall was much more interested in Hitler's erratic strategy with regard to Germany's neighbours. When Annie and Rolf conferred on their future method of operation she suggested that he might be best in that area. He attended diplomatic functions and was well able to charm the wives of ambassadors. Her own activity seemed to lie in making use of the friends and acquaintances in the Nazi hierarchy. Unfortunately, the most highly placed of these persons were not friendly with each other. Magda Goebbels and Emmy Göring sustained a mutual dislike. And that antipathy carried over to their respective circle of friends. A choice would have to be made.

Of the two women, Magda was by far the more intelligent. High-born and used to wealth and influence, she was a long-time insider and dedicated to the Party. In fact, she believed more sincerely in the Nazi ideals than her husband. But her husband didn't tell her anything. Moreover, she was likely to have a basic reserve with actresses – considering the reckless lack of reserve the Minister displayed towards so many of them.

Of course, it shouldn't be too difficult to become Goebbels' mistress, and Annie considered the option. She asked Rolf, 'What do you think?'

His handsome face showed instinctive disgust. 'You couldn't!'

'I could if you think it would be worth it.'

'He's a puny . . . *cripple*.'

'Not where it counts, I understand,' Annie observed drily.

Rolf tried hard to overcome his personal repugnance to the idea. He pointedly asked, 'Have any of the women he's slept with ever told you anything of any importance?'

'About *government* strategy, you mean?'

'Yes. Is he likely to give away any secrets?'

'No.'

'And his mistresses don't last long either.'

Annie was quick to agree. 'That's true.'

So the Goebbels' connection was abandoned.

'What about Eva Braun? You've met her haven't you?'

'Yes. At the Berghof. Poor girl, she never seems to get *away* from Berchtesgaden.'

'She must know something.'

'Only about snow.'

'Be serious, Annie.'

'Yes. That's not being fair. She also knows about clothes, and men. But in the talks I've had with her, that really is all she has in her mind . . . and it's more than enough to fill it.'

Emmy Göring still seemed the best bet. But here Annie had her own scruples. She hated the prospect of trading on real friendship. Big, easy-going Emmy was such an amiable, kind woman. It seemed a shame to gain her confidence only to betray it for national gain. But she was a valuable informant because her husband *did* tell her things, and listened to her, and did his utmost to satisfy her wishes – even when they clashed with Party policy. She was an outsider who had never been a Nazi. And she was an actress. That provided a good deal of cover for the operation. Of equal importance was the fact that Göring had his own personal intelligence organisation; and the less negotiable fact that Frederik was a member of the Marschall's staff.

'Maybe you could stage a reconciliation with your husband,' Rolf suggested.

'No. I wouldn't do that.'

'He could be very useful. At least, get him to take you to the right gatherings. The Party likes its husbands and wives to stick together – in public.'

'We do still get invited out.'

'So? Accept!'

'The trouble is that if I started going out with Frederik again, he'd want to come home with me again. And he wants another child.'

Rolf saw the difficulty there. 'That could keep you out of circulation when you were urgently needed.'

'Also,' Annie retorted, 'I'm damned if I'll carry another cannon ball for the Krupps.'

While I was working on the passage above it struck me that Annie might be able to answer a rather trivial question which had often occurred to me. With regard to the Nazi leaders, I asked her, 'Is the song really accurate? I mean, the words of the song.'

'What song?'

'The wartime song that goes to the tune of "Colonel Bogie".'

'I don't know it.'

That surprised me. But of course Annie had not spent any time in Britain during the war. So I recited it to her.

> *'Hitler has only got one ball,*
> *Göring has two, but very small,*
> *Himmler has something sim'lar,*
> *And poor old Goebbels*
> *Has no balls at all.'*

Annie laughed. 'I have no reliable information on Himmler. But Eva, Emmy and a score of actresses would assure you the song isn't accurate. Particularly about Goebbels. His balls and everything else in that area were large and hyperactive.'

My efforts to check other details for the story at this point in Annie's career were not nearly so successful. I was forced to an astonishing conclusion. It is that the control of information in

Nazi Germany during the late 1930s was less severe than the control of information still operated by Her Majesty's government in the late 1980s. It is also true that the suppression of facts and subjugation of the Press is more effective in Britain now than it was under Goebbels during the Third Reich. It was he, of course, who invented the 'news management directive' which we adopted and now call 'the lobby system'. This enabled him (and still enables our governments) to put out undiluted propaganda as though bestowing a privilege.

But we have gone further than Dr Goebbels in some respects. Among other things, he could dictate what reaction his film critics would have to any film. He could also have the papers print exactly what he or any of the other leaders had said, verbatim. He could not, though, prevent any editor printing a discovered truth. His only recourse then was to close down the offending newspaper. This he often did. But the fact that the paper no longer appeared was in itself an indictment of the system. In Britain, on the other hand, the truth can be suppressed and the editor forbidden to say it has been suppressed. Yet the paper continues to be published as reassurance to the gullible lieges that a free press is being maintained.

I came to these conclusions with a sense of amazement when I tried to check the facts which Annie had supplied for this section of the book. Naturally I applied to the keepers of various Foreign Office archives. Before they would even confirm or deny what she had reported to me, they wanted to know why *I* wanted to know. And then they wanted to see the manuscript of this episode. After a month or two it was decided that the middle section (which should be here, where this explanation is) was in contravention of the Official Secrets Act.

And that, as Annie said, is a hard act to follow. It is certainly a hard act to circumvent. The normal 'thirty year rule' does not apply. It goes on forever. So there is a large gap here to prevent your learning of the stupidities and petty rivalries among bureaucrats, long dead, who ignored or misinterpreted the information which – notionally, at least – could have ensured a greater state of readiness in Britain for war than eventually was the case. When I made that point to one of the civil servants who agreed to talk to me, he conceded the possibility with a smiling shrug. 'Who can say?'

'*I* can say, if you'll allow me to say it,' I said. 'At least, Annie Jeynor can certainly say.'

He stared at me evenly across the leather-topped desk. 'We discussed these matters at length with Dr Sleavin some time ago.'

'So it was you who told her Miss Jeynor was talking nonsense?'

'We pointed out how unlikely these spy stories were.'

There was no doubt that Angela Sleavin toed the official line. Naturally. She had had the training for it. Academics always know on which side their next research grant is buttered. But I, deprived of such incentive, believed Annie Jeynor.

However, the discussions did add to my understanding of the issue. I always thought the Official Secrets Act was operated solely to protect the guilty, but now a more positive aspect was brought to my attention. Of equal importance is its use to inspire confidence in the gullible electorate. Strong objection is raised against anything which illustrates the incompetence of a government department. They honestly think it better that the public should believe an illusion.

The illusion is that the country's security is, and always has been, in the hands of intelligent and trustworthy people. There is no objection, though, to the publication of any secrets which happens to be complimentary to the State. This admirable attitude was one which Goebbels tried to impose but, unlike successive British governments, he had no law to help him and so was less successful.

I returned to Dumbarton determined to find some way round the problem. Annie was not optimistic. She did suggest the American reports published not long after the end of the war. Apparently the Americans had captured documents in which the Nazis identified Frau von Bohlen as a spy who had successfully duped them. There were even details of her escape, just as the SS was about to arrest her. Since the Americans don't have an Official Secrets Act – and don't give a damn about ours – these discoveries were published in America in 1950.

177

'That's great,' I said. 'So those stories must have been copied in the English papers.'

Annie shook her head. 'No. They were told not to reprint the story.'

'But how could anybody stop them? If those were Nazi documents published by American journals it had nothing whatever to do with Britain.'

'But it had. I was spying for Britain.'

My throat tightened on a lump of incredulity. 'And the English papers *swallowed* that?'

Annie gave me a wintry little smile. 'The English papers will swallow whatever they are told to swallow.' She seemed to accept it is a natural fact of life and was not put out by it.

'That's difficult to believe,' I said.

'Not at all. It was a small matter. They've kept quiet about bigger stories in the past.' She shrugged. 'God knows what they're keeping quiet about right now.'

For several years Annie was employed as a go-between, making frequent visits to London where she relayed the information she had collected. Then she reported back to Berlin whatever story she had been told to tell. It seemed odd to her that the stories the Nazis wanted Britain to believe were all to the effect that Germany and Britain should be allies, whereas the lies from London to Berlin were always to stress Britain's readiness for conflict.

In 1939, when it seemed obvious that war was imminent, her controller in Berlin decided there would be no more London visits. She would now remain in Germany and spread the good word among influential foreign visitors. This order was delivered as she sat with the official in the waiting room of the Underground station in Wilhelmplatz. It was one of three meeting places they used, and Annie always found it depressing. The other spots where it was thought the public might not be surprised to recognise her were the Adlon Grill and the Deutsche Theater bar. At both those locations Rolf, too, was an acceptable face in the background – ready to engineer a 'chance meeting' soon after the controller had gone away. Here, in the Underground, the timing was trickier. He varied his method. Sometimes he arrived to take a southbound train and sometimes got off one which was northbound.

When she was given the stunning news that she would be permanently detained in Berlin, Annie's first instinct was one of fear that she'd been found out. She reacted with simulated anger. It was a drastic imposition on her freedom. And the Propaganda Ministry was just across the square. This would have to be settled at the highest level, without delay. She got to her feet and started moving towards the exit stairway. The controller was taken by surprise. He had to run several paces to catch up with her. He knew how highly she was regarded by his superiors. The fear that she might be able to overrule his judgment added to the strength with which he stopped her. His hand clenched hard on her arm and he spun her round. 'It's no good,' he said. 'This is a decision of the Minister.'

'I don't believe you. Let him tell me.'

'He's not there. And from now on you are forbidden to enter the Promi.'

'Let me go!'

'Frl Jeynor, this is for your own safety. It would be dangerous for you in England now.'

That was reassuring, but still Annie strained to get away from him and reach the stair. Then, at the top of the stairwell, she caught sight of Rolf. His grim expression reminded her in an instant that she could never afford to be herself and react as her nature dictated. Her relationship with the controller was another role that had to be played. She suddenly went limp against him. 'I'm sorry,' she said. 'You are right, of course. I can be much more use in Berlin.'

Rolf passed them without a hint of recognition.

But it was this change in the situation, together with the increasingly uncertain negotiations between Britain and Germany, which brought another problem. Annie began to worry obsessively about her young daughter, Gerda. By then it was two years since she had been allowed to visit the child. Indeed, she had to make an appointment even to meet Frederik so she could plead with him. He now lived in the top flat of a friend's large house in the Charlottenburg district.

Her visits never did any good. His argument was always the same. It would be wrong to upset and confuse the child by re-introducing a mother she hardly knew. Better to let her maintain the ordered, familiar life in which she was happy.

Annie protested, 'But it's not my fault she hardly knows me. It was you that fixed the time I was allowed to spend with her.'

Frederik was calm and inflexibly reasonable. 'Annie, I don't say it's your fault. But the fact is, she hardly knows you.'

'You saw to that.'

'It seemed wise – since you had your career and . . . other interests.'

'So had you.'

'Yes. And that is why she has been given a proper family life at the Villa. We agreed on that, Annie.' He attempted a reassuring smile. 'And she is perfectly happy there.'

'But *I* am not happy, Frederik.'

He seemed to be concerned. 'I am sorry to hear it. But I don't think we should jeopardise *her* happiness so that *you* will feel better. We must do what is best for Gerda.'

It always ended like that. Frederik knew, because he was in the position to know, what was best for the child. And he was always so calm and reasonable that Annie felt she had to re-examine her own motives. She knew that if she were suddenly granted full custody again she'd find it impossible to cope. The situation was so different now. She was engaged on a dangerous activity which required her complete freedom of movement. And yet there was the increasing danger that her real purpose with Rolf might be discovered and she'd find herself in jail, or worse. As things stood she could not be a mother to Gerda. But that realisation did not ease the growing panic she felt.

Day by day her tension grew. It was fuelled by exterior evidence that a crucial event was about to break. Whether at the studios, in the streets or in night clubs, where she now habitually spent her evenings, there was a growing, unsettling atmosphere. It was the same excitement she'd sensed in the people the day

180

the Nazis came to power. It was a kind of guilty, but gleeful, anticipation shared at every level. Whatever had been held in check would not be held for much longer.

She discussed her fears with Rolf when, as usual, they met secretly in the office of an abandoned warehouse by the canal. There seemed to her no question of what must be done, but she proceeded cautiously; even with her lover. 'I've got to be sure that Gerda is safe.'

'She's with the Krupps. You can be sure they'll keep her safe.'

'But if I'm not allowed to see her I feel so vulnerable. Like a part of me was being held hostage.'

Rolf said, 'I don't think you want the little girl mixed up in this.'

'How could she be?'

The man showed little care in expressing his thoughts. 'Well, if you start seeing her again, and then they catch you . . . Well, that would be pretty final. You'd be shot. How would the kid take that?'

Annie moaned. 'Oh God!'

'Maybe things are better the way they are. Easier for her to forget.'

'I don't want to be easy to forget.'

Rolf drew her closer on the rug they'd placed in the corner of the derelict office. He spoke softly against her ear. 'I won't forget. As long as I'm in any condition to remember.'

They held a tight embrace. Then Annie drew back, and stated the plan she had come prepared to insist upon. 'I want Gerda safe in England.'

Rolf drew away from her. In the spill from the street lights she saw consternation on his face. 'But you can't leave now, Annie! You can't give up at the most important time.'

'No.' She stroked his face. 'No. I'll stay in Berlin. But I want you to take Gerda to London.'

'They won't let her go. The Krupps, your husband . . . they'd never even consider letting her go.'

Annie nodded. 'That's why you must take her.'

He gave an exasperated gasp at this wild suggestion. 'It can't be done. Apart from the fact it would be impossible to snatch

181

the girl, I've got to stay here too. We're a team. We've got to keep the information flowing. It's more important than ever, now.'

'Yes. I suppose so. Though they don't seem to make much use of it.' She dismissed the thought. 'All right. You remember Jamie Northcott.'

'Yes. He's still a commissioner in Hamburg, isn't he?'

Annie nodded. 'If you can get her to Hamburg, I'm sure he'll get her to London. So you wouldn't have to leave the country. It's just that you are the only one I can really trust to get her away from that house.'

Whatever his doubts, Rolf listened to the rest of the plan which Annie outlined. He had been to the Villa Heugel in his diplomatic capacity. Together they knew the house quite well. Annie could not take part in the kidnap since she would be the immediate suspect. But she could find out when Frederik would be visiting his daughter and could arrange an alibi for herself. And his visit would be a good opportunity because he always took Gerda out for the afternoon to some amusements in Essen. That overcame the main obstacle of actually getting into the house.

Rolf asked, 'But what will happen to Gerda in England?'

'That,' said Annie, 'is something else that has to be arranged in your message to London. I want to get in touch with Lady Douglas Straven in total confidence.'

Rolf shook his head despondently. 'The department won't do it. They won't deal with any personal messages.'

'They will this time,' said Annie firmly, 'or I'll just pack up and go home. Tell them that.'

'But this is criminal, Annie. Kidnapping is criminal.'

'Then don't call it kidnap. Call it furthering the escape of a very important refugee.'

While these arrangements ground through the system, Annie was forced to consider another refugee.

About two o'clock one morning she was awakened in the Ziegelstrasse flat by a soft yet insistent tapping at the front door. Only gradually did she become aware of the sound, because her conscious senses kept interpreting it in her dream. But at last she did wake and identify the source. When she opened the door, the draught from the back service stairway set the hall light swaying.

For a moment she did not recognise the man. He pulled off his hat to reveal silvery hair streaked with blood. It was Helmar Schüstiger. She helped him in and closed the door. His overcoat was sodden with rain and his shoes were thick with mud.

His voice was very soft. 'Annie, my dear, I need your help.' He tried to smile his familiar world-weary smile. It did not succeed because there was a terrible, real weariness now, and three of his teeth had been knocked out.

'I'll do what I can,' she said.

Having been severely beaten up, and having dragged himself perhaps for miles along the margin of the river to reach the flat, the actor was exhausted. He slumped unconscious. Annie struggled to take off his soaked overcoat and shoes. Then, having determined that he was really asleep, she covered him with a blanket before bathing his more obvious injuries. He slept on. She turned up the heating, set a chair close by him and chainsmoked through a long vigil.

She was not surprised that the Gestapo had finally come for Helmar. Things had been going badly for him for some time. Indeed, once his patron, Max Reinhardt, had fled to America it could have been predicted there would be lean times ahead. At first it was not the fact that he was Jewish which caused a slackening in the work he was offered. It was professional resentment. Senior actors whom Reinhardt and Piscator had ignored in favour of Schüstiger seized their chance to push him out of the limelight.

It was likely he could have found rewarding enough work in the provincial theatres. But he adamantly refused to leave Berlin. He was born and bred there in the slums of Neukölln. For good or ill, it was his city. But, increasingly, he was made to feel an alien at home. He fought against the injustice in his own way, writing and performing cabaret monologues in various fit-ups and clubs where the spirit of the satirical tradition clung on. That was what had brought him to the attention of the SS. He had gone too far.

All night Annie tried to find a way through the difficulties which confronted her. Schüstiger would have to stay in the flat until some method was found to enable his escape. She was sure Emmy would help, as she had helped many others. Both Himmler and (on his report) Hitler were losing patience at Göring's appeals on behalf of this actor or that writer. But the Marschall could never deny his wife's pleading when she put her mind to it, and Himmler had always decided he could not afford to offend such a powerful colleague. Or not yet, anyway.

When the old actor dazedly opened his eyes, his hostess was able to offer a little hope. It had occurred to her that she could combine two possible escapes in one. If she could arrange to visit Emmy at the time Frederik was next due to visit Gerda, then an alibi was secure. Particularly if she was in the company of Göring's wife at Karinhalle – a long and time-consuming distance from Berlin. That would be part of the plan. The other part was that she intended to take old Schüstiger with her to the grand hunting-lodge at Schorfheide. Emmy knew Schüstiger and would be quite incapable of refusing him in person.

When they'd had breakfast Annie set about getting in touch with Emmy. Of the five luxurious homes she could be living in, her Press secretary finally tracked her down to the Reichstag palace and connected Annie's call. Both of them knew (as did Emmy herself) that the telephone conversation was being taped. As always, Emmy was immediately prepared for a long chat and gave the impression there was absolutely nothing else she would rather be doing. Whoever got the job of tapping her phone had to be ready for a lot of overtime.

But Annie came as quickly as possible to the point. 'Emmy my dear, the reason I'm calling is that I really have to get away for a few days.'

Her friend's tone changed immediately to concern. 'Why, Annie? Aren't you well?'

'No, no. I'm fine.' She had already calculated the next part of the conversation. 'The thing is, I'm rather deeply involved with a gentleman at the moment.'

'Ah!'

'And it seems there's nowhere safe we can meet.'

'Sweetheart, I understand,' Emmy said, and was perfectly sure that she did.

'I was wondering if you could give us shelter for a day or two.'

'Of course! Which shelter would you like to use?'

'Well . . . he has never been to Karinhalle and . . .'

Emmy interrupted. 'When would you like to come?'

'At the end of the week. Friday evening, say. Would you be there then?'

'I *shall* be there. I often spend the weekend at Schorfheide. Hermann's in the south until Sunday.' By this she meant at Berchtesgaden. 'But I'd be delighted to see you both. What's his name?'

Annie, guilty at the duplicity, gave an embarrassed giggle. 'If you don't mind, I'd rather keep that as a surprise.'

Emmy's hearty laugh crackled from the receiver. 'Just as you wish.' She deduced – as was intended she should – that Annie was playing fast and loose with somebody else's husband.

'But we'll need an invitation. You know how difficult it is getting through all those guards round the estate.'

'Indeed I do! A lot of nonsense. Sometimes I'm not sure if they're going to let *me* through! But I'll have Helene send you an invitation for two. "Frau von Bohlen and Friend". How would that do?'

'Lovely,' Annie said. 'And I am looking forward to seeing you.'

'Until Friday, then. Goodbye, my sweet.'

It was Tuesday morning when this was arranged. Annie's next job was to warn Rolf that his kidnapping must be scheduled for the following Saturday. With so many agencies engaged on surveillance it would have been foolish to phone him. But their next scheduled meeting at the condemned property by the canal was not until Thursday evening. That would be far too short notice. Nor could she afford to be seen with Rolf so near the event. Somebody would be sure to notice and mention it to Frederik. The whole city was rife with suspicion. Neighbours, colleagues and even complete strangers were encouraged to spy on each other.

That is what gave Annie the idea. Although she was a spy, she would go disguised as a spy to see Rolf – and have him report it. 'So, back to the breeches,' she thought. For her stature and slim figure still enabled her to dress as a convincing boy. She knew there were some Hitler Youth uniforms in the Nollendorfplatz Theater wardrobe. It would not be difficult to go in as herself to see the play, then slip backstage and change at the first interval. With any luck she'd have time to visit Rolf and return to her seat at the end of the performance.

To Helmar Schüstiger she merely reported that they were invited to Karinhalle for the weekend. He was very grateful, but immediately started to worry about his appearance and his clothes. Annie assured him that his suit could be cleaned and pressed in good time. As to the bruising – assiduous bathing with hot and cold compresses, then the subtle application of make-up would ensure he'd be his handsome self to meet Frau Göring.

'But, what about my teeth?' he wailed.

'For God's sake, Helmar! This is an effort to save your *life*, it's not a bloody audition.'

He was immediately contrite. 'Yes, of course. Bless you, Annie.'

'You just have to stay here in the flat, completely out of sight for a few days.'

'But what if some of your other friends should come in, or your husband?'

'Then,' she told him, 'you can play French farce for all it's worth because you'll have no trousers.'

In fact she took his suit with her when she went out to the theatre. In her glamorous evening dress and cape, she hailed a taxi and asked to be taken to a Chinese cleaner's. The taxi driver was sure he couldn't have heard right, but the imperious lady repeated her instruction with no hint of amusement. Having deposited the bundle, she then walked the short distance to the theatre and joined the fashionable crowd going in to see a Schiller adaptation specially tailored for Party consumption. It was a reworking of *Kabale und Liebe* – an appropriate title, Annie thought, in the circumstances. The naïve idealism of the young

186

poet was here interpreted as a denunciation of the Weimar Republic.

The front-of-house manager insisted that such a distinguished patron should have a box to herself, so there was no difficulty about getting backstage unobserved. And she used the chorus staircase to get up to the wardrobe department – which, during a performance, was deserted.

A short time elapsed before a handsome member of the Hitler Youth emerged from the stage door and started running west along Tauenzienstrasse. As he dodged in and out between the pedestrians they did not pay him much heed. Perhaps he was late for a band practice at the massive Kaiser Wilhelm church which stood at the end of the street. But before he got at far as that, he stopped in the forecourt of a fashionable block of flats. At the clerk's desk he asked to be announced to Herr Templar. The clerk raised his eyebrows. It had not occurred to him before that Herr Templar was an Englishman of *that* persuasion. But of course, he reasoned to himself, it was said that *all* Englishmen were.

When Rolf opened the door he immediately recognised Annie but, to her great relief, reacted as her apparel suggested he should. Once inside the flat, little time was lost in establishing the order of priorities. And now, for some reason that had become instinctive, Annie did not tell her lover that the alibi she'd devised would include Helmar Schüstiger. It was not that she feared misplaced jealousy. It was just that she'd learned to keep different aspects of her life in separate compartments. She trusted Rolf to rescue her child. There was no reason to test how trustworthy he was in conspiring at the escape of a Jew.

He told her that the arrangement with Lady Straven had not yet been confirmed with London. That couldn't be helped. Annie knew Jamie Northcott would keep Gerda safe until her destination was secure. What had been approved and would be made available was their privileged diplomatic transport from Essen to Hamburg. The consulate in Essen would provide a car for Rolf. What had to be confirmed was that Frederik would be visiting the Villa Heugel as anticipated on Saturday.

'I'll call him,' Annie said.

187

'What?' Rolf stared as though she'd lost her mind.

She shook her head. 'No. Not to ask if he is going. I'll ask if I can go with him.'

'That's taking a risk, isn't it? What if he says yes?'

'He won't. I'll manage to sound hysterical on the phone.' She smiled wryly. 'As I often am. That way, even if he'd been thinking of skipping the visit he'll make a point of going just to reassure me. But having me there in a tantrum will be the last thing he wants.'

Rolf smiled admiringly at the shrewdness of this. He said, 'Annie, you're a great girl.'

'No. At the moment I'm a great boy. And it's time I got back to the theatre.'

The man was disappointed. 'Oh. I thought we'd have time for . . .'

'No. And, as soon as I leave, you must report something suspicious to the clerk.'

Rolf did not grasp that immediately either. 'What do you mean?'

'Well, unless you normally entertain fetching members of the Hitler Youth, he will want to know why I was here. Make up a scandalous rumour about one of the neighbours. Say I told you.'

As she was about to leave he asked, 'Is our Thursday meeting still on?'

'Of course.'

'I look forward to it, hard floor and all.'

'So do I, darling.'

They kissed, and the uniformed youth sped off again in service of the Party, to the greater glory of the Reich.

Frau von Bohlen was back in her box by the time the third act ended and applauded very loudly – more to mark her presence than her approval. She found Schiller hard enough to take in his original form. When the visionary dream turned out to be a swastika in the follow-spot she was even more sceptical. The trouble with idealists, she found, was that although their heart was always in the right place, it was never there *long* enough.

*   *   *

The expedition to Schorfheide was not without its alarms. Annie had made a point of asking for a signed invitation, but not because she wanted to avoid delay getting through the many guard-posts around the Karinhalle estate. There would be delay there in any case, but no danger. Her primary concern was getting out of Berlin with Helmar Shüstiger. And that was why she had not wanted to have him named. Until he had gained the patronage of Göring, he could be arrested on sight.

In a large hired car they drove out of Ziegelstrasse into the upper reaches of Friedrichstrasse, and thence onto the old Oranienburg Allee. This was not the most direct route, but it avoided the busier junctions which would have to be crossed in heading for the normal exit from the city at Prenzlauerstrasse. Police and SS agents tended to loiter at junctions. Thus, the car was heading more directly north than north-east. Annie drove at a sedate pace and Helmar sat upright and apparently relaxed beside her. Most of the bruises on his face had faded to no more than shadows. And the dressing over the large cut on his temple was masked by a wide-brimmed hat.

The most striking difference in him was his silence. He said as little as possible because the front teeth that had been knocked out impaired his hitherto faultless diction. He complained. 'Now I sound like an illiterate labourer from Neukölln.' Annie smiled. That, she knew, was exactly what he'd been before Reinhardt pulled him out of the gutter. She drove on and, clear of the city traffic, increased her speed. Suddenly, a large black car overtook, then slewed in front of her. A spotlight positioned above its back bumper flashed a warning that she was to stop. She drew to the side of the road. The car in front braked more sharply and there was almost a collision as she came to a halt.

It was a Gestapo agent who got out of the passenger seat. Even in his well-cut civilian clothes she could tell immediately. She wound down the window. The agent leaned slightly in and rested his elbows on the frame.

He said, 'I think I know you, Madam.'

'I should hope you do!' Annie retorted with all the hauteur she could muster.

'Frl Jeynor, is it not?'

189

'In the cinema and the theatre, yes. But I am Frau von Bohlen.'

'Ah!' The agent straightened a little. 'And Herr von Bohlen?'

Annie gave him an affronted stare. 'Certainly not! This is a workman I am transporting to do a job for a friend.' She could feel Helmar subtly altering his pose and expression to fit this identity.

'I see.' The agent leaned sharply forward again and demanded of Helmar, 'Your name is?'

'Sigurt Alversonne,' Helmar spluttered then, in his very broadest Neukölln accent went on, 'I repair drains. Better, I *find* leaks in drains that cannot be found.'

The agent eyed him warily for a moment then turned his attention again to Annie. 'Is this your car, Frau von Bohlen?'

'No. My husband is using our car. I have hired this one.' The agent's expression lightened considerably. 'That would explain the matter,' he said; but did not explain what the matter was. 'Good afternoon, Frau von Bohlen.' He doffed his hat and returned to his own vehicle.

But they did not move off. Annie waited for a few moments, then spent a few moments more fumbling to find the reverse gear, before she was able to edge away from the still flashing light and veer onto the road again. She left the SS car far behind, still parked by the roadside.

There was another stop in Oranienburg but only because the small town was so crowded. This was pay-day for the servicemen at the nearby General Headquarters of the Luftwaffe. But, a few kilometers further on, both Annie and Schüstiger felt an instantaneous surge of dread. Driving through a picturesque little village they were suddenly confronted by what looked like a roadblock. Three staff cars were drawn across the carriageway. There were two troop transporters parked under the flowering trees at the roadside. Schüstiger swallowed hard and murmured, 'Totenkopf.'

For all of these vehicles were manned or packed with black-uniformed, jack-booted SS. One officer confronted them with hand outstretched, signalling them to stop. Annie braked immediately and, with her free hand, started searching in her bag for the signed invitation. Men of the Death's Head units were a law unto themselves and could not be held accountable for their actions. Annie glanced covertly at Helmar and saw a sudden sweat running down his cheek. She gripped the large steering wheel very tightly to prevent her hands trembling.

But having stopped them, the officer did not approach the car. Instead he turned back towards the other vehicles and signalled beyond some trees. At once a convoy of half a dozen transporters rumbled out from a concealed farm road.

The roadblock had only been set up to allow this traffic onto the main road. The heavy trucks, all packed with black uniforms, threw up clouds of dust as they roared back towards Berlin.

When they had gone, the officers got into their staff cars and followed the convoy. Annie heard Schüstiger's long sigh of relief as she started up and moved on through the village. At the far end, he glanced out to read the name-sign which was done in rustic, poker-work. '"Sachsenhausen." What on earth can be so attractive to the SS in Sachsenhausen?'

Annie shrugged. 'Who knows?'

There was the inevitable delay getting through the four security cordons on the Karinhalle estate, but Emmy was out in front of the enormous house to greet them when they finally got through.

She embraced Annie, then her eyes widened with surprise when the second visitor emerged on the other side of the car. 'Herr Schüstiger! I thought you'd left the country.'

'Frau Göring, I wish that were so.'

Annie moved close and grasped her friend's arm. 'Emmy, there's something I must explain.'

'But not here, sweetheart,' said their hostess quickly. She gave a slight but definitely warning glance at the guards and servants grouped around. 'And first you must relax after that long drive.'

'Longer than usual this time,' Annie said.

They moved over the gravel towards the long monolithic porch. The front door of Karinhalle resembled the entrance to an Etruscan tomb. The servants followed in dutiful file, but the guards remained where they were.

Emmy Göring, for all her scatty behaviour, was no fool. She

191

knew at once that Annie was not having an affair with Helmar Schüstiger – not even a single weekend fling. And that meant there must be a more serious purpose in the suddenly arranged visit. She was glad, therefore, that Hermann was safely away from home. Things could be arranged much better when she was able to present a request in her own time – and in her own way.

Waiting for her guests in the long sitting room (which looked like a stage set only slightly modified from Bayreuth) it occurred to her that both Annie and Schüstiger must want to get out of the country for different reasons. She saw no great difficulty in making suitable arrangements for the actor, but Frederik von Bohlen was on Hermann's staff. Her husband would never connive at a Party wife's desertion.

Over cocktails, this misunderstanding was quickly corrected. Helmar explained why he'd sought shelter in Ziegelstrasse and Annie confirmed that it was really for the actor's sake that they'd come to Karinhalle.

Most pertinently Emmy asked, 'But why did you not contact me yourself, Herr Schüstiger?'

Annie answered for him. 'He didn't think he knew you well enough.' It was important to conceal the fact that her own reason for being there was to establish an alibi. 'And besides, he probably would have been arrested if he'd been on his own. The Gestapo is out in force between here and Berlin.'

Emmy nodded. 'Everything is unsettled at the moment.'

'That is why I must get away soon,' Helmar said.

'And where would you go? Out of the country?'

'Oh no, Frau Göring. I would like to settle in Dortmund.' Emmy raised her eyebrows with theatrical exaggeration and smiled across at Annie. '*Dort*mund?'

'Yes. I have a wife there.'

Emmy laughed and Helmar joined in, covering his mouth with his hand.

Annie added, 'It is the only place where Helmar has a wife. As far as I know.'

Their hostess shrugged. 'And what is to prevent you going to Dortmund?'

192

'Because my name is on the list of those to whom the Gestapo wishes to offer "protective custody". If I went there, they would follow – and perhaps offer to protect my wife as well.'

Emmy's expression became solemn. 'Ah, the list!'

'If my name could be removed from that, then I could be safely reunited with my wife.'

'Does Frau Schüstiger know that you plan this reunion?'

'No. I stopped writing to her some time before . . . before I lost my teeth.'

In matters like this Frau Göring saw no virtue in tact. 'Is your wife a Jew?' she asked.

Annie gave her an astonished look.

Helmar said, 'Yes. But *she* has not been performing satirical cabaret.'

Emmy did not respond to that. She took another sip of her drink. 'Herr Schüstiger, I will be honest with you. Certainly it would be possible to have your name taken off this list. But there would be another list. There *are* other lists.' She straightened against the uncomfortable, high-backed chair. 'One way or another, it seems to me, you will always be on a list. A single exemption is no guarantee of safety, for you, *or* your wife. Particularly if you are with her.'

Annie had never heard her friend make such a serious, cool speech. 'But Emmy, surely . . .'

Emmy stopped the interruption with a gesture and went on, gazing earnestly at Helmar. 'My advice to you would be to leave the country, as soon as possible.'

'But where would I go?'

'I cannot advise you on that. But I will do all I can to have your passport in order, and see that an exit visa is provided.'

Helmar Schüstiger thought only briefly of his long struggle to move from Neukölln to Unter den Linden. Probably no frontier would be more difficult than that crossing of the River Spree in his native Berlin. 'Frau Göring,' he said, 'I accept. And I am deeply grateful to you.'

Emmy smiled again. 'Good. Now let's all have another drink.'

In the conversation that followed it became clear that Göring, much to his annoyance, had been summoned away following a frantic telephone call from Hitler at the Berghof. Apparently most of the top commanders had received a similar call – or so their wives had told Emmy. Her impression was that it was something to do with the Italians. Count Ciano, she knew, had been with the Führer in Berchtesgaden for some days. Annie listened politely to this small talk, trying not to seem too interested. But she knew how important the information could be. Unfortunately, there seemed no way she could get it to London. It was Rolf who transmitted material for immediate assessment in Whitehall. And he was on his way to Essen.

Yet here was just the sort of chatter which could be of use to British Intelligence. On this occasion Emmy thought she was merely making social excuses for the absence of her husband. But Annie had taught herself to extrapolate from innocent phrases. First, the Berghof meeting had not been planned. That, taken together with the fact that it was a 'frantic' telephone call, suggested a sudden crisis. If the military commanders were called at short notice then it was not a matter of internal policy. If the Italian foreign minister was with Hitler several days before the crisis developed then there must be trouble between the Axis partners. And, following the same line of thought, if Ciano went to Berchtesgaden – which he found cold, damp and gloomy – then it must be something Italy wanted from Germany. Otherwise, Germany's foreign minister, Ribbentrop, would have been sent to Rome – which he loved.

But all this speculation was useless without the means to transmit the facts to those who could piece them together with information from other sources. So, Annie enjoyed her cocktails, and laughed, and soon found herself deep in nostalgic shop-talk with her fellow actors. They were joined at dinner by some local friends of the Görings and the whole evening passed very pleasantly indeed.

On the following morning Annie stayed late in bed, going over what would be happening far to the west, in Essen. Frederik would have arrived at the Villa Heugel and Rolf would be pacing his hotel room hoping the weather would stay fine so that Gerda's outing with her father would go ahead as usual. Annie had told him it would be after lunch, but she knew he'd be hovering around the gates to the estate long before then. A long day stretched ahead for both of them. And, at Karinhalle, there would be no way of knowing the outcome until long after the kidnap was well under way – or had completely failed. There were to be no telephone calls between the conspirators. Whatever the outcome, it was Frederik who would have to call Annie. And he'd have to trace her first. She had not left notice with anyone where she was going – because, normally, she never did. Annie calculated that it would be after six o'clock in the evening before she heard anything about the kidnap – or even the attempted kidnap.

Emmy had arranged an outing by the lake after lunch and Annie steeled herself to enjoy it. To her surprise, she found that Frl Ritter's advice for a star performer on 'Apprehension and Insularity' was remarkably apt in circumstances for which it was not designed. The apprehension about Rolf's success and her daughter's natural fear nagged constantly at her attention. But the well-drilled exercise of cutting her true self off from her exterior allowed her to seem a carefree companion to her friends. Emmy was as amusing and good-natured as ever and Helmar, relieved of his dread, had regained something of his old assurance and wit. They walked through the forest together, followed by servants carrying everything which could possibly be needed for a picnic in the sun.

In the house again, later, Emmy was showing Annie the latest photographs of little Edda – her daughter was just over a year old – when she was called to the telephone. But it was her own husband, reporting from the Berghof that it would be Monday or Tuesday before he'd be back.

Annie said, 'I suppose you won't be able to mention Helmar until then.'

Emmy pursed her lips dubiously. 'Well, it's not the sort of thing I'd care to discuss on the phone.'

'No. Of course not. So, Helmar will come back with me to Berlin and wait there.'

Emmy said, 'If they're already looking for him, that wouldn't be wise. Much better if he spent the time here – I mean in one

195

of the cottages on the estate.' She smiled. 'He won't be the first "refugee" I've put up until the circumstances were right.'

Annie hugged her friend. 'Bless you, Emmy. That really would be best.' She paused. 'I suppose he'll be safe enough here, even when you're in Berlin?'

Emmy made an expansive gesture and laughed. 'Absolutely. You see, our Jewish friend will be protected by four cordons of Gestapo!'

Frederik finally got through to Karinhalle after dinner. Annie took the call in a sound-proof vestibule completely lined with blue velvet. Her husband's voice seemed curiously high-pitched and staccato.

He reported that he'd taken Gerda to the fairground in Essen. One of the rides was a huge carousel. He'd stood well back and waved each time the little girl came round astride the elaborate wooden horse. Then it seemed the roundabout must be moving slowly for there was a longer interval. At first he thought he'd just missed her. He waited. But still she did not re-appear. 'Then I started to walk round in the opposite direction. Against the direction of the wheel. I stumbled a bit because I was concentrating so hard on the faces of the children.'

When he'd got back to his starting point he was sure Gerda was not on the carousel. He jumped on and had the operator stop it. Together they searched. It was possible Gerda had fallen from her mount and lay unconscious. But she was not anywhere on the machine. Perhaps she'd just got bored and jumped off to try something else.

The fairground manager was called and he put out a message on the public address system asking Gerda to come at once to the entrance pay booth. They waited at the pay booth. There was no response. Then another message was put out to the public thronging the acres of amusements. This was a description of the five-year-old girl and the clothes she was wearing. Anyone who saw the little girl was asked to bring her to the pay booth. Meanwhile, a team of fairground employees was sent all around the ground to search for her. More waiting. There was no response.

Finally, the police were called. Annie had said as little as possible while Frederik was speaking. Now she asked, 'When was that?' Her voice was very soft.

'What?'

'How long was it before the police were called?'

'Oh . . . it must have been . . .' Frederik's voice faltered as his responsibility for the loss was again forced to the surface. He cleared his throat. 'It must have been more than an hour later . . . after she disappeared.'

Annie made no comment, but thought that more than an hour later Rolf would be well clear of Essen and speeding north-east on the Ruhr autobahn towards Hamburg.

Frederik had then alerted other State agencies before he started trying to locate Annie. He tried the flat. He also tried the Press office at UFA, the Deutsche Theater, and several friends, and hotels. Finally he'd called his own office in the Reichstag in order to put them on the search. The phone monitoring unit at Alexanderplatz was asked to co-operate. More delay. Then, after another urgent appeal by the distraught father, the substance of a private telephone conversation between Frau von Bohlen and Frau Göring was released. By now it was after 9.00 p.m. and still no trace had been found of Gerda.

'That's six hours,' Annie said.

Frederik took this as an accusation about the delay in getting in touch with her. But really it was an involuntary remark. Annie was thinking that six hours after the kidnap, Gerda would be in the care of Jamie's housekeeper – and probably fast asleep.

On the phone, it was agreed that Annie would return immediately to Berlin. Frederik would join her that night at the flat in Ziegelstrasse. Then Annie hung up and went back to the dining room to tell her friends that Gerda had been kidnapped.

Emmy was deeply shocked. She seemed incapable of speech and the colour drained from her face. Still trying to croak words of comfort, she stumbled round the table and took Annie in her arms. It was almost as though she'd been told that her own infant daughter had been stolen.

In Dumbarton, on a gloomy winter afternoon, Barbara, Annie and I were gathered round the fire in what we had claimed as our sitting room. We'd all been drinking freely since lunchtime. Particularly Annie, who was now in a more sentimental mood than I'd seen before. She sat on the couch beside Barbara as we insulated ourselves from the unforgiving Scottish sabbath, windy and baleful outside under a dull sky.

Barbara said, 'I feel sorry for Frederik. He must have loved that little girl.'

Frederik, I reminded her sternly, was a Nazi who'd shown no qualms when he virtually kidnapped Gerda from her mother and held her in isolation at the Villa Heugel.

'Even so,' Barbara persisted. 'He probably did *that* because he loved her as well.'

I was about to protest at this loaded interpretation of events but Annie interrupted.

'Of course he loved her,' she said. 'He doted on her.' She finished her drink in a gulp. 'I felt sorry for him too. And for poor Emmy. I felt rotten putting her through that shock; knowing all the time that Gerda was perfectly all right.'

Barbara asked, 'What happened to Emmy Göring? Was she put on trial after the war?'

Annie shook her head. 'No, no. She was interned for a while, but they had to let her go.'

'Was there no evidence against her?'

'*No*! Not only was there no evidence against her . . . there was overwhelming evidence *for* her. People came from all parts of Europe and America. People she'd helped to freedom came back to free her.' Annie sighed. 'Dear Emmy. I'm glad she lived as long as she did – and died as contentedly as anyone can hope for. That was in . . .'

'In 1973,' I prompted.

'Yes. In Munich. I was invited to the party they held. It was to celebrate her eightieth birthday. We had a wonderful time, talking about the old days in Weimar and Hamburg. Göring's son was there – from his first marriage. Thomas. He and Emmy had always been such good friends.' There was a long pause. 'No. Emmy had nothing to reproach herself with. All her life she was kind. And she died immediately after that party.'

We all stared into the fire. Although it was only late afternoon the sky looked quite dark beyond the window. But none of us wanted to switch on the light. That would have spoiled the feeling I'm sure we shared that, for an hour or so at least, it might be possible to make sense of the past. And it was to the past that Annie referred when she spoke again. Possibly she had been reflecting silently on the difference between Emmy and herself at the age of eighty. Annie had a great deal to reproach herself with.

'Frederik,' she said. 'When I saw him that night in Berlin, all the stuffing was knocked out of him. That night . . .' She visualised it in the brightening flames of the log fire. 'That night, he was like the boy I'd first met . . . when he was just Freddie Bolen. He was totally exhausted. We went to bed without a word and he fell asleep in my arms. Helpless.'

Barbara said, 'If men were wiser they'd be helpless more often.'

Annie smiled wanly and nodded. Discovering her glass was empty again, she held it out in my direction for a refill. I poured myself another as well, remarking, 'The important thing was, the kidnap went without a hitch.'

'Oh, yes!' There was no mistaking the heavy irony in Annie's voice. 'That was the *important* thing. Gerda was saved from the Nazis. No more than three days later she was safely at home with Rosemary in Cumberland.' With a weaving hand, she accepted the refilled glass from me. 'Thank you, Bill. You always know what is the *important* thing. So – isn't it a pity things *change* their importance . . . through time. Without warning!'

Softly, Barbara sang, '"The youth of the heart, And the dew in the morning . . ."'

Annie at once joined in, '"Will vanish and leave you, Without any warning."'

It occurred to me that my wife, too, had probably drunk more than she should.

She asked, 'What happened to Gerda?'

Annie, with a gesture, invited me to go on with the story while she lay back in the deep armchair.

I recounted the facts. Rosemary put Gerda to school, claiming that this was her niece, Gerda Straven. That was a wise decision

199

because Britain was soon in the grip of a propaganda campaign which taught not only children but adults to hate all things German. And although Annie had insisted on Gerda being taught English in Essen, the little girl had a marked German accent.

Rosemary told her to explain that her family was in the diplomatic service and that she'd merely been sent to kindergarten in Germany. But 'kindergarten' itself was then a dangerous German innovation – easily confused with the infamous Hitlerjugend. Gerda was confused. At the Villa Heugel she had not realised she was a Nazi. Now all her new friends were Nazi-haters, so she started hating them as well. In particular, she hated her long-absent mother for marrying her father in the first place. All her baffled affection was now transferred to Rosemary – who did not make the mistake of rejecting it. But she did try to intercede on Annie's behalf. The little girl was unmoved.

In a very short while, the German accent had gone completely. And now the name 'Gerda' must go. When she was moved to a more senior school she insisted on being registered as Gertrude Straven. Later, when she was old enough to do so, that was the name she legally adopted.

During the war, of course, Annie had written to her from Hollywood. But it was Rosemary who had to reply. And after the war it was Rosemary who had to advise her friend that nothing would be gained by visiting her daughter. Annie accepted the situation. Gertrude's mind could not be changed because it had been made up at that early time in everyone's life when impressions leave indelible marks, and scars which will never heal are imposed on the heart.

When I'd finished this recital, Barbara and I both glanced at the old woman, stretched immobile in the armchair. Her eyes were wide and tears were pouring down her cheeks. But, now that I'd stopped talking, she thought she should make an effort to say something. It came very quietly but with a chilling resignation. Annie said, 'The worst thing was not that she hated me . . . I was never a very good mother. So – I was no great loss to her. The worst thing was that I deprived her of her *father*. I was so sure that I had to get her out of Germany, you see. But now I'm not sure which is worse – to be a loyal German, or an orphan.'

Barbara tried to lighten the atmosphere a little. 'Still, you were successful in getting Herr Schüstiger out of Germany.'

Annie, using the arms of the chair, dragged herself into an upright sitting position. 'Oh, yes. I did that, too.'

'What happened to him?'.

'He escaped. Emmy got him the clearance he needed and he crossed the border. Unfortunately . . .' And again that note of angry sadness was creeping into her voice. 'Unfortunately, the nearest border to Schorfheide was Poland. He settled in Warsaw, just before the outbreak of war.'

I drew a sharp breath. For a Jew to escape the Nazis by travelling to Warsaw seemed a great deal like fleeing from Baghdad, only to keep an appointment in Samarra.

'Did he survive the war?' Barbara asked.

Annie shrugged. 'I don't know.'

'Surely you could have found out,' my wife retorted sharply.

The old woman cried out. '*Why?* What could be gained by that?' She rocked from side to side in the chair, seeming to struggle in an effort to make the obvious plain. 'If I don't know . . . I can hope. I desperately hope he managed to survive. But if I tried to make sure . . . Suppose I had tried to make sure he was alive after the war. That was nearly forty years ago. But suppose I had tried to find him . . . and found instead . . .' Again the tears flowed, no matter how angrily she tried to stop them. 'It's very likely he died in terror. Thousands did, in the Ghetto. It's *more* than likely he died of starvation and disease even if he was not murdered . . . Would you have me live with that certainty for forty years?' She paused for breath and then went on with a kind of impossible pride swelling through her voice. 'But I remember Helmar Schüstiger as a witty, flirting, gentleman. I remember him elegant and graceful on the stage. I have . . . *carefully* . . . remembered all this for his sake. And I've had *hope* on my side. He cannot be alive now, because he was older than me. But still I hope that, when he died, he died with dignity, like a man and not a hunted animal.' She broke off to make a slight apologetic gesture towards Barbara. 'My dear, facts are

201

all right for people who don't care one way or the other. Helmar would never have forgiven me if I'd found out he finished up in the gutter – exactly where he started.'

Barbara said nothing.

I looked at Annie Jeynor with new eyes, and a new feeling of intense affection. Often, in the previous weeks, I'd thought of her as callous. Suddenly I knew that wasn't true. What I'd mistaken for callousness was a self-reliant bravery. My impulse was to gather her up out of the chair and embrace her. But I resisted the impulse.

Frederik continued to live with Annie. It seemed they were reconciled by his grief and feeling of guilt. For, of course, there was no news from Gerda's 'captors'. There was no ransom demand, no trace and no body. In time, the police reached the conclusion that the little girl had been taken by a child-molester, murdered, and the body disposed of. They did not confide this to the parents.

Annie, feeling equally guilty for her part in the plot, did all she could to sustain Frederik's spirits. He marvelled at her resilience and strength and was very grateful for it. She persuaded him that Gerda was still alive. This she was perfectly able to do because she was in a position to have no doubts on the matter.

Only a few weeks after the kidnapping, the situation between Britain and Germany deteriorated sharply. In the secrecy of their den at the Landwehrkanal, Rolf told Annie that the ambassador and all his staff would soon be recalled to London. The channel of information which they'd operated together would have no further purpose. Another system would be devised; a more complex, professional, wartime system, under different control.

'But I'm coming back,' he promised. 'As soon as I can be re-assigned I'll be back here in Berlin. And I'll need your help.'

'How long will it take?' Annie asked. It seemed inconceivable that she could remain long without him.

'A few weeks. A month, maybe. No more than that.' He drew her closer. 'When I get back to London I'll tell them how much you've done; and how much more we can do together.'

Annie snuggled against him on the pile of blankets in the corner of the ruined building. She wished she could stay there all night, since it was probably the last time she'd see him for some time. But Frederik would already be pacing the flat and driving himself into a panic at her absence.

That was on a Thursday evening. On Saturday, Rolf sailed from Hamburg. Among other British officials on the boat was Jamie Northcott. There was no need for the Control Commission, now that everything was out of control. Indeed, its work had been minimal for some years and by the end of August 1939 there was only a skeletal staff to be repatriated.

It seemed entirely reasonable that there would be a great deal of confusion in London as they tried to adjust the Intelligence service to its new role. Rolf's re-assignment was obviously delayed. But when all of September passed, then all of October without any message, Annie became seriously concerned. She dared not try to get in touch with him for fear of the greatly enhanced surveillance which had been introduced in Germany at the beginning of hostilities. But surely her former employers would not leave her stranded. Surely Rolf would be making every effort to get back to Berlin.

Towards the middle of November she was called to the Ministry. The propaganda 'short' which she'd been obliged to make had proved a remarkable success. She received official congratulations and was asked to make a personal appearance tour which would boost the film. Annie politely declined but, aware of her greatly enhanced status as far as Dr Goebbels was concerned, she suggested that now might be a good time to make the dramatic film she had been promised as reward for past co-operation. 'I'm sure you'll agree, Reichsminister,' she said, 'that unless propaganda is balanced against other work, it loses its effectiveness. The public has to be convinced that the person advancing the glory of the Party is worth listening to for other reasons.'

Goebbels lowered his heavy eyelids and smiled faintly. But he took the point. It was one he often advocated privately. Aloud, though, he seemed to parry the suggestion and asked, 'Have you done much wireless broadcasting, Frl Jeynor?'

'No, I haven't. Though I'm sure it is fascinating work.'
Goebbels lifted a telephone and said, 'Joyce.'

At the far end of the luxurious office a door was opened from an ante-room. The man who came in was William Joyce, later known throughout Britain as 'Lord Haw-Haw'. He was a stocky, fair-haired, fanatical Irishman who'd recently been recruited by Goebbels to broadcast to the rest of Europe in English. Having been introduced by the Minister, he led Annie to a small office near the top of the building.

Standing at the window, they looked out over Wilhelmplatz. The square, bordered with trees, was bustling with activity. At the centre was the Underground station. There the ordinary Berliners dodged and jostled with many uniformed figures around the newsvendor who yelled the latest report on the recent assassination plot against Hitler.

It had happened earlier that month in Munich. Hitler and all the Nazi leaders had left the Bürgerbräukeller before the bomb exploded, but many other people were killed. The *Völkischer Beobachter* posters declared that two English spies had been arrested for the crime.

Beyond that throng, on the far side of the square, a huge Nazi flag waved over the steep roofs and gables of the Kaiserhof Hotel which had been, for so long, the Party's Chancellery-in-waiting.

The open side of the square was bounded by Wilhelmstrasse – the Whitehall of Berlin. Its ministry-packed length stretched from Unter den Linden to Leipzigerstrasse. The broad pavements were crowded. Buses and trams vied with each other through the traffic, but stopped and immediately gave way for the frequent passage of huge black official Mercedes. They swept through, zig-zagging down the crown of the road, swastika pennants snapping on their bonnets while ahead of them a clear path was forced by motorcycle escorts whose lights incongruously blazed in bright daylight.

William Joyce slapped the window frame in satisfaction. 'We're at the centre of things here, eh?'

'It all looks very confident,' Annie said.

'And with good reason.'

He invited her to sit down and moved a chair from behind his desk so that he could sit near her in comradely fashion. 'It is because of our confidence that we can afford to joke about England . . . *to* England.' Seeing the actress hadn't understood that, he went on, 'In my broadcasts, I mean.' He brushed his hair off his brow. 'They will provide a lighthearted commentary comparing the growing certainty of Germany with the worsening state of England.'

'I don't see how I could help in that.'

He laughed and tried to cross his legs negligently. The gesture was not successful because his thighs were too short and heavy. At best, he could only rest one ankle on the other knee. 'Miss Jeynor,' he said in that condescending, Home Counties voice which cried out for mimicry, 'the mere fact that you are here – an Englishwoman who has made a dazzling success in Germany – is a great help. And there are many others like you who chose Germany. The British public must be told such things. It makes them wonder, "Why?"'

Annie shrugged and he went on to outline other methods by which he could assert Germany's superiority and breed alarm in the British. Part of the strategy would be to choose precise details of people and places and events in Britain; thus giving the impression to the impressionable islanders that their country was riddled with Nazi spies. He would also broadcast personal messages to individuals across the channel.

Annie's attention quickened at that. 'Personal messages?'

'Oh, yes! That will be part of the all-knowing accuracy which undermines resolve. And the persons to whom the message is addressed may well be influenced in our favour.'

'How very subtle,' Annie said admiringly. But really she was thinking this would be an excellent way to remind the spymasters in London of her existence. And it would assure Rolf that she was still free and waiting for him.

She devised a fairly cryptic message which seemed to use real names, but in fact used code identities. Joyce wanted her to broadcast the message herself. He was anxious to harness the celebrity value of Annie Jeynor. But the actress declined with the excuse that he would make a *much* better job of it. There was no difficulty in convincing him. He would refer to her by name, of course. But still there was something missing. Then he hit upon exactly the right device which could be used to open the programme.

Thus, several days later, listeners in Britain tuned to Lord Haw-Haw and heard him ask, 'What country, friends, is this?' There was a pause. He then answered his own question with his habitual opening words, 'Germany calling . . . Germany calling . . .' and went on to report a conversation with 'my dear friend, Annie Jeynor'. Lastly, he transmitted a rather bewildering 'personal message'.

At the time, Annie thought only of how effective it would be in making contact with British Intelligence officials who monitored every broadcast. Later, she was bluntly made aware that it had also been heard by a public of millions who did not know she had been working for their government. Quite naturally, they were convinced she *was* a dear friend of Lord Haw-Haw. And just as much a traitor.

Goebbels had finally agreed that a film should be made of Ibsen's play *Rosmersholm*. It was expected that Annie would repeat the great success she'd already enjoyed as Rebecca West in a Berlin stage production. But the film was to be much more ambitious than that – so the material had to be 'opened out'. To that end, there would be six weeks on location in the Harz mountains.

Ibsen's original play is set in Norway. Its climax is a suicide pact between the lovers, Rebecca and Rosmer. They throw themselves into a millrace and drown. On the stage, the event is merely reported by another character who is looking out of a window. In the film it can be seen happening.

There was a great deal of publicity about the film and the fact that the tiny village of Hildur, on the banks of the river Helme, would be reconstructed to look like nineteenth-century Norway. There was also some sniping at the actor chosen to play Rosmer. The role had not gone to the man who'd played opposite Annie on the stage, for the reason, apparently, that they wanted a younger man for a younger audience. But Annie was furious. Everybody in the business knew it was because he'd been a communist sympathiser in his youth. Casting under the Goebbels regime expected a full roster of those devoted to the Party. It was because of this slight on her former co-star that Annie insisted on having his wife as her stand-in.

She too was a fine stage actress. Her career in films had been limited only by the fact that she so closely resembled Annie Jeynor. This did not bother Nadia Kulp. She and Annie were old friends. And she was glad to accept the offer as stand-in, considering the exorbitant fee the star had negotiated for her.

While Annie was frantically engaged on preparation for the film she had little time to devote to Frederik. He did not resent it, but he did decide to shake himself out of the depression caused by Gerda's kidnap. He announced that he was going to give up his privileged position on Göring's staff and join the army. Annie did not try to dissuade him. In fact, she felt some relief that she would no longer have to cope with the nagging sense of guilt which his presence in the flat imposed upon her. Göring saw to it that he was given the rank of major, and when that was settled he was anxious to get away. He reported for duty with the Sixth Army at the beginning of February 1940.

Two months later, the film company and crew set out for the mountains. The weather was still very cold, and once they reached the snow line the convoy of huge trucks slithered and got stuck. The car in which Annie travelled with her stand-in had an easier journey, and they reached Hildur well ahead of the main party. Even so, it was late in the evening. After a light meal, Annie went to bed in the family-run hotel which had been hired in its entirety.

During the night she was wakened by the noise of the trucks arriving. Their headlights flashed across the ceiling of her room. There was much cursing and grinding of gears as the long, heavy vehicles were manouevred up the narrow lane to the field which had been reserved for them. Annie got up to watch, and wait until the disturbance abated.

The few street lights of the village reflected off the snow all around. Standing in the dark room, Annie was able to identify many of the muffled figures moving to and fro.

And she recognised Rolf.

It was his bearing and the way he walked which first struck her. He was dressed like all the other men in the trucking crew and seemed to be helping them. In fact he was just moving from one group to another, and Annie realised that he'd arrived by some other means.

He was waiting for her. She switched on the light and stood a little back from the window so that she would be plainly visible.

When he stopped and turned and looked up, he saw her at once. Quickly, he moved away again. Annie put out the light and waited. The waiting seemed to go on a long, long time. She wondered if she should get dressed and go out to find him. Maybe he was waiting somewhere, for her to come. She smoked several cigarettes, trying to make up her mind which course to take. Then without a sound her bedroom door opened . . . closed . . . and he was *there*.

She went to him before he had time to cross the room. They did not speak but stood, locked close together, embracing and kissing until the first emotional impact of the reunion had ebbed. Then Annie took off her dressing gown and got into bed to watch him undress.

He joined her and, once more in each other's arms, they conversed in whispers. The new Intelligence command had refused point-blank to consider Rolf's plea that he should be sent back to Berlin. It was pointed out that as he'd served as a diplomat at the British embassy in Berlin for a long time, he'd be far too easily recognised. Nor were they very keen to have him join the new operation somewhere else. But they had agreed to put him on a training course for MI9, and when that was successfully completed he was sent to Zürich.

MI9 planned and operated escapes routes from Germany and, later, Nazi-occupied Europe. Rolf had been given the job of trying to establish contacts along a route from Switzerland through Austria and Bavaria. He had been in Munich when he read the advance notice of the *Rosmersholm* film production. But it was not until he was in London again, some months later, that he saw the transcript of the message from Annie which Lord Haw-Haw had broadcast.

Only then did he learn that Annie had been totally neglected.

He stormed through several offices, in ascending order, denouncing the callous treatment of a former agent. They told him nothing could be done. Miss Jeynor was no longer useful to them in the changed circumstances. He could, if he must, make her a sort of guinea-pig in trying out the escape route into Switzerland. Rolf was amazed at their effrontery. But he desperately wanted to see Annie again and to make sure she was safe. So he agreed. Only then did they add a further rider. *If* his route was safe and worked, Miss Jeynor must stay in Switzerland when she got there. Having her in Britain would only be an embarrassment, considering the very public role she'd played in German society.

Rolf hotly pointed out that it was for *their* sake she'd taken on such a public role. Nevertheless, they told him, she would not be welcome in Britain for the duration of the war. Rolf wanted to punch their smug bureaucratic faces but he needed their resources and organisation to get into Germany again. Once more he moved up through Switzerland and Bavaria, timing his arrival in the Harz mountains for the period when he knew the film would be on location.

And here he was. He put the question to her. 'Will you come back with me?'

'You mean, *now*?'

'First thing tomorrow morning.'

'Down into Switzerland?'

'Yes. It's a safe route. You'll be all right with me.'

Annie kissed him. 'Oh, I know I'd be safe with you. But once you get me there, you'll be off again, won't you?'

He nodded. 'Yes. I'm afraid so. I wouldn't be much use if I spent the war in Switzerland.'

'Nor would I,' Annie said. 'There'd be absolutely nothing for me to *do*! I couldn't bear that.'

'Darling, at least the Nazis couldn't get you.'

'They won't get me in Berlin. They'd scarcely give me this expensive film if I weren't in favour with Dr Goebbels.'

'There's no telling what they might find out, though.'

'I'm not spying any more – what could they find out?'

'I don't know. But they're not fools. If they occupy any more countries, and overrun the embassies there, they could find quite a lot.'

'What do you mean?'

'I mean, from the time we were working together. I don't know how much of that information was passed on to friendly powers. Maybe even some note detailing where the information came from.'

Annie shivered slightly against his warm body. 'Surely they've been more careful than that.'

He sighed. 'I wish I could be sure. When you think of the stupidity of those clowns in London, I wouldn't want to take a chance on it.' They lay silent for a few minutes. 'Please come back with me, Annie.'

But she'd already made up her mind. 'I can't.'

Before dawn he drew away from her and got up to dress. As he was leaving he said, 'If ever I get the chance again, I will come back.'

She should have told him, no, it was too dangerous. Instead she replied, 'I hope so.'

Minutes later she stood at the window again and watched him disappear in a flurry of snow.

The filming of *Rosmersholm* continued without incident, and Rebecca West, with her lover, went spectacularly to death over the millrace.

But another plot was unfolding. Annie had been right in claiming that her stock was high with the Ministry of Propaganda. Other ministries, however, were more sceptical, and in particular, the SS was starting to pick at a mystery reported in Salzburg.

It was connected with some dissident Austrians who seemed to be involved in planning an escape route out of Germany and into Switzerland. According to the men they'd interrogated, the starting point was located high in the Harz mountains. The SS men were puzzled by such a ridiculous idea. But it had to be checked, even though it was so remote. Several agents were dispatched to investigate.

In retrospect it was ironic that the person who led the Gestapo to Annie was Rolf himself. And he'd put her in danger solely by trying to remove her from it. Basically, the mistake had been in thinking that German Intelligence must be as chaotic as the British system at the outbreak of war. But when war was declared, Germany had already been a police state for six years. There were agents and legions of informers placed in every locality. And, of course, the Swiss-Austrian border was bristling with them.

Towards the end of the film company's six weeks on location, two Gestapo agents in civilian clothes arrived at Hildur. And even in that picturesque little mountain village there were a few inhabitants who'd kept their eyes open and were willing to co-operate.

When she spotted them, Annie was horrified by the thought that the Gestapo had traced Rolf's route. But since they were still looking, they had not yet captured him. And, having satisfied themselves that all the film people in the village could be vouched for – and having found no other strangers – they went away, with no firm evidence that Hildur was an established starting point for an escape route. There was no sensible reason why it should be. They went back to check their sources, and to discover what the connection was between the reported Englishman and the village of Hildur.

The mere fact of Gestapo suspicion was reason enough for Annie to reconsider escape. Since she'd been more or less assured of official welcome in America, that would be her destination. There was no point in trying to get to Britain.

So, if it could be managed, she would make a bid for the United States. The problem was finding a way out of Germany. This task was made much more difficult by the fact that she was a Nazi celebrity and widely recognised public figure. Anyone helping her would certainly be held to account if she got away. There was no question of appealing to the anti-Nazi faction among her friends: it would be unforgivable to place them in danger of retribution. So characteristically, her instinct was to make an asset of a liability. How could she make the fact of her celebrity work to her advantage?

The first item to be considered was the matter of geography. It would be foolish to start an escape from Berlin. It was too far from any border. She wondered if there were likely to be any films on remote locations in which she could make a guest appearance – followed by a sudden disappearance.

That idea had to be abandoned. Such projects were beyond her control and subject as much to the weather as anything else.

It was while she was watching the pre-dubbed version of *Rosmersholm* that a much better idea occurred to her.

In a number of long shots, and even some rear-placed mid-shots, she realised the film editor had used the set-up footage. In these it was her stand-in, Nadia Kulp, who was on the screen and not Annie herself. The selected audience was convinced it was Annie they were seeing all the time. Made up and in costume, she and Nadia could be doubles.

Back in the flat, alone, the idea persisted. But no practical *use* of the idea presented itself until she thought of the occasion when she'd taken her place in the box at the Nollendorf theatre and then sneaked out as a Hitler Youth to visit Rolf. Other people watching that play had been sure she was there all the time because she was there at the beginning and the end. And in between, their attention had been directed elsewhere. Annie then thought: But suppose they are sure I am there all the time because they see me on the stage?

Suddenly the perfect stratagem fell clear and complete into her mind. She spent the rest of the night searching through her comprehensive library of plays. By breakfast time she'd selected half a dozen published scripts and piled them one on top of the other – all open at the cast list. After breakfast she read key scenes in all of these plays. Two of them she read the whole way through. By lunchtime she had selected an eighteenth-century comedy, *Die Gewährleistung*. This was the play she and her personally selected company would tour to entertain the troops.

The first person she got in touch with was Nadia Kulp. Her former stand-in agreed to call in later that day. But almost before Annie put the phone down she was beset with doubts. The plan required the total co-operation of the other actress. To gain that it would be necessary to give an explanation of the real purpose

212

to the tour. Nadia would have to be told of Annie's plan to leave Germany. Revealing that would be dangerous enough without revealing why. Again, the necessary evil of hood-winking a friend (though it was for her own good). It had to be done.

By the time Nadia arrived at Ziegelstrasse, Annie had a credible story prepared. It was a matter, she explained, of advancing her career. An offer had been made by Twentieth Century-Fox in Hollywood which she felt she could not refuse. But of course the Ministry would never let her go. They wanted her to go on churning out dreary propaganda epics in black and white. Nadia shook her head over the Ministry's stupidity. It wasn't the propaganda but the black and white which seemed so unfair, considering Annie's red hair and her beautiful skin.

Annie prompted her. 'So you do think I ought to take the chance.'

'Of course, darling! You'd be a fool not to.'

'And you will help me to get away?'

'Certainly. But I don't see how it can be done.'

Annie lifted the playscript. 'Do you know *Die Gewährleistung*?'

'Vaguely. We did it at the Academy when I was a student. As I remember, it's a standard comedy of the period.' Nadia thought for a moment. 'The English play, *She Stoops To Conquer*, has the same basic idea and does it better.'

'That may be. But in *She Stoops* – one character plays two roles. In *Die Gewährleistung* two roles can be played by one actress.'

To Nadia it seemed these were different ways of saying the same thing. Yet obviously it wasn't or Annie wouldn't be so excited at the discovery. 'I don't see,' she said.

Considering that her own life might depend on it, Annie was anxious that her friend should thoroughly understand the matter. 'Forget about *She Stoops*. Concentrate on *Die Gewährleistung*. Here we have a spoiled young lady who is tired of the rich and weedy young gentleman who wants to marry her. She'd much rather have a rough, strapping farmer's boy, but he's afraid of her grand airs. So – she gets a jolly little serving wench to teach her the delightfully crude manners of the peasant class.'

'Yes,' Nadia recalled. 'But the genteel airs of the lady rub

213

off on the jolly serving wench. That way, the more each of them learns of the other, the further they get from what they want.'

'Right!' Annie nodded decisively. 'Now – the spoiled lady and the jolly serving wench are two separate roles. They are played by two actresses.'

'Naturally, the situation . . .'

Annie stopped her with a gesture. 'But they *can* be played by *one* actress. For most of the time they're just reporting and demonstrating what the other has told them. There is only one very short scene where they are actually onstage at the same time – and even then, they're not meant to see each other. If it came to the point, *that* scene could be cut.'

'Ah!' Nadia said. And at last she saw quite clearly what Annie had in mind, though she could not yet appreciate what could be made of it. With much heightened interest she waited to hear the next step in this theatrical game.

'Suppose,' her friend put to her, 'I am cast as the spoiled lady – a role calculated to display my celebrated glamour, well-known tricks and deeply-loved mannerisms.'

Nadia chuckled and shrugged. 'But, of *course*!'

'Whereas, you are . . .'

'. . . typecast as the sluttish serving wench . . . however jolly.'

Annie nodded. 'Exactly. Now, we go on tour – doing a couple of nights at various towns in France – and both our names are on the cast list. And we play our respective roles – including that short scene where we are on the stage together. How*ever* . . . when we get to a certain town, my drinking will be getting out of hand. Naturally, that fact has to be kept from our brave lads who've only turned out in order to see me. Then, just before the curtain is due to go up, the callboy finds me hopelessly drunk. The stage manager is frantic. What's to be done?'

Nadia rose bravely to her feet. 'I will save the day,' she said. 'For it will then occur to me that, if we cut one little scene, *I* can play both parts.'

Annie applauded.

Nadia stilled this premature ovation. 'The stage-manager will be amazed.' She did the amazement. '"You mean," he will say, "you'll go on with the book?" "Certainly not," I will tell him. "If I did that, everyone would know that the lovely, glamorous and talented Frl Jeynor is canned senseless – as she *so often* is."'

Annie gave a hoot of laughter.

'"No",' her saintly colleague went on, '"I will play Frl Jeynor's role as though I were Frl Jeynor and thus save the tattered reputation of that fading star."' Now she signalled applause, and Annie supplied it.

And that was what they did.

At the house on the Clyde shore, Annie was propped up in bed. After much trudging about in January snow, she'd caught a severe cold. But she didn't want to hinder my work on the book, so we were having a bedroom conference. I was anxious to hear the details of her escape from Germany.

She blew her reddened nose again and regarded me wearily over the end of the bed. Clearly, she was not pleased at my badgering her on the subject. Rather crossly she said, 'This is the wrong sort of book for all that stuff.'

'All what stuff?'

She sniffed. 'There have been hundreds of books about derring-do during the war. Famous escapes with plucky heroines cowering in wayside barns. You know – books that tell you every time a stray dog pees.'

I smiled. 'Even so, it's important to get an accurate, personal recollection of the war.'

'Too many of those books as well. Like "I Was Churchill's Second Gardener From The Left".'

'That is not the sort of thing I want.'

She sighed wearily and levered herself up against the pillows again. 'I don't know which was worse, the tour or escaping from it.'

It was not until late September that *Die Gewährleistung* was staged at Cologne before setting out on its tour. And even then the convoy of trucks started off in quite the wrong direction for Annie's purpose. The itinerary specified the northern coastal towns of France, but all the escape routes lay through Vichy territory to the south.

After the surrender, France had been divided roughly in half. German forces occupied the northern section and all along the Channel coast. Work had immediately been put in hand erecting fortifications. To the south was the nominally 'free' zone under a puppet government at Vichy. This free zone extended east to the Italian border and south to the Mediterranean. To the west there was a narrow corridor of occupied territory along the Atlantic coast, down to the Spanish border.

Of course there were a lot of German personnel in the free zone too, but the fiction was maintained that they were there on various helpful or recreational pursuits. And Nazi law was enforced by French police.

A Gestapo agent and two armed guards went everywhere with the *Gewährleistung* company. This, it was alleged, was for the security of the actors themselves, as they were entertaining troops and sailors in very sensitive areas in occupied territory. And there was a genuine fear that Annie might be taken hostage. The kidnap of her child had never been cleared up and Himmler didn't want any more of the von Bohlen family placed at risk. So Gestapo agent Friml had strict instructions not to let the star out of his sight when they stopped at any town. He could relax only when the convoy was on the move, for then they had a military escort.

Everything went very smoothly in Boulogne, Abbeville and Rouen. But the servicemen's reception of the play was far from ecstatic. The audiences were made up mainly of Wehrmacht, with strong contingents of the Kriegsmarine now that the Navy had access to the French coast. All of them would have much preferred a strip-show from Berlin or a farce from Paris to this stilted period piece of German dramatic art. Annie was popular, though. If time allowed she sang to them when the drama was over.

And time was very much on her mind. However it could be managed, she had to be at MI9's departure station at Perpignan on the Mediterranean by 21 October. That was when a former Northcott freighter would leave Marseilles for Lisbon. Jamie had provided her with structural plans of the ship so that she knew where to stow away undetected once she got aboard. But she could go aboard only when the ship had been searched and cleared at Marseilles and was under way. That was going to be the most difficult part of the plan – assuming she could get that far.

The tour ran into a serious delay at Le Havre. They had done the three scheduled performances and were preparing to move on when the Kriegsmarine commander of the port had them detained without explanation. Annie protested to the agent, Friml, who reported to Berlin. The Ministry confirmed they were to wait at Le Havre. They told Friml why, but he would not divulge the reason.

In the boarding house which had been put at their disposal, Annie paced her bedroom and fretted. There were dates at Caen and St Malo to be filled before they could get to Paris where she was to join the 'Pat Line'. This was the efficiently run escape route to the south. The 'consignment' in which she had been given a place would not wait for her.

It was Nadia Kulp who discovered the reason for the delay. Friml had told her in confidence. Annie was in her room, staring at rainwater gushing from a broken gutter in the house opposite, when Nadia burst in and announced, 'We're waiting for a victorious "wolf pack". U-boats! Apparently, they've sunk dozens of enemy ships and expect a hero's welcome.'

'God!' Annie spread her arms and declared with bitter irony. 'And, of course, nothing would please a lusty bunch of submariners more than an overdressed, eighteenth-century comedy of manners!'

Nadia stilled this unpatriotic outburst. 'No, darling. It's not the play that's the entertainment – *we* are! And Hitler's coming to hand out medals in person.'

Annie was immediately alert. 'Friml told you that?'

'Yes. He's very excited.'

'And very friendly, it seems.'

Her friend tilted a defiant chin. 'It helps pass the time.'

'Nadia, be careful. We want Friml in the audience, not holding your hand in the wings.'

'What harm can it do?'

'None, when you are you and I am me. But when you are *both* of us, you won't have enough hands.'

Nadia gasped as she realised the danger she was inviting. 'Oh, yes! Yes! I *am* sorry.'

It was a further three days before the pack of seven U-boats got back to Le Havre. There was now no possibility of Annie playing the next two performances on the tour and getting to Paris in time to join the Marseilles 'consignment'. It was after Paris that Nadia was to take her place – when the company looped back through Amiens, Arras and Lille.

As she dressed for the reception she tried to assess her chances of making it on her own. Perhaps the moment had come to set up the excuse for her inability to play at Caen and St Malo instead. Certainly, if she was going to impress with her dependence on booze she could not choose a more memorable occasion than in the presence of the abstemious Führer.

A car had called to collect them and was waiting with its engine running when she called Nadia in to discuss this change of plan. Her friend's reaction was not encouraging.

'Annie, you can't do that.'

'Why not?'

'Because they'd cancel the rest of the tour instantly – and send you back to Berlin under escort and in disgrace. Your being drunk has got to be a secret within the company to make the plan work.'

Annie nodded. 'Of course you're right.' She sighed. 'But what do you suggest? I've got to get to Paris as soon as possible.'

'Why? What does a few extra days matter?'

Annie made a vague gesture. 'It's the Americans . . .' It was difficult to keep in mind what her friend did and did not know about the means and purpose of the exercise. The car driver blew the horn impatiently.

Nadia grabbed Annie's arm. 'We'll think of something. But we must go *now*.'

The reception was held in a drill hall within the secure zone

218

of the dockyard. There they were introduced to the U-boat captains who were to be their escorts for the evening.

The decorative services of the other ladies in the company had already been snapped up. Then everyone stood and waited for Hitler, his entourage and several admirals to arrive.

Annie was surprised at how well Hitler looked. He seemed to be in excellent spirits. His cheeks glowed and his eyes shone as he acknowledged the cheers of the packed hall. Close behind him limped Josef Goebbels, anxious to be seen at a genuine propaganda triumph. Behind him, in full dress uniform, marched Admiral Doenitz, thin-faced and disdainful; then in a close bunch about a dozen high-ranking officers. They grouped themselves around the Führer on the platform.

The ceremony was very much like a school prizegiving. But here the effort being rewarded was the destruction of thousands of tons of urgently needed food and the deaths of hundreds of seamen. The prize was a warm handshake from the plainly dressed little man and the halter of the Knight's Cross, cool against a well-scrubbed neck.

Hitler left immediately after the ceremony but Goebbels lingered on to enjoy the buffet, the wine and the chatter. He mingled with the victorious captains, all of whom towered over him. He also paid some attention to the ladies of his touring company. Annie took the opportunity to make a suggestion which had been prompted by a remark of her escort. Thinking it was something she must know, he'd alluded to the great U-boat pens at St Nazaire on the Atlantic coast. That was on the way south, down the Nazi occupied corridor.

Goebbels bowed over her hand. 'Frl Jeynor. It was good of you to wait for this celebration.' He knew perfectly well she had been ordered to wait and given no explanation.

'Reichsminister, I am very glad I did.'

'The tour is going well?'

'Yes. My only regret is that we can't bring live entertainment to more of our servicemen.'

He smiled slyly. 'We must conquer first, Fräulein, before we can play.'

'But in what has already been conquered!' she insisted. 'We

go only as far as St Malo. I'm sure there must be other places on the coast where we would be welcome.' She was careful not to name any specific place lest she get her informant into trouble.

'You are a tireless worker, Fräulein.' He signalled to an aide and sent him in search of the appropriate commander.

The tour was extended, to take in St Nazaire, La Rochelle and, at Annie's further suggestion, Bordeaux. If things had gone according to plan, that was as far south as she could have reached within the free zone in the time available. Her idea was that, having missed her 'consignment' place in Paris, she might be able to reclaim it at the MI9 clearing post in Toulouse – thus by-passing the assembly station in Marseilles. So, the only stretch she'd have to manage completely on her own was the short railway journey across the demarcation line.

At St Nazaire there were signs of increased vigilance on the part of Friml and the guards. Also, Nadia's flirtation with the Gestapo agent seemed to be continuing, despite her promise to keep him in his place.

In the dressing room after the performance Annie told her, 'You'll really have to be more careful.'

'I'm *being* careful. And surely it's a help if we know what he has in mind.' She paused and inhaled sharply to release the tight bodice of her costume. 'In fact, he seems much more interested in you than in me.'

'Oh?' Annie tried to sound casual. 'What gives you that idea?'

Nadia shrugged. 'Various things. He was asking about the *Rosmersholm* film.' She chuckled. 'He wanted to know if we shared a room on location.'

'What did you tell him?'

'The truth. He also wanted to know about your boy friends.' She stepped out of the collapsed skirt. 'Maybe he's jealous.'

'Maybe,' Annie said lightly. But she knew with chilling certainty that the Gestapo had managed to form the connection between herself and Rolf Templar. Her immediate reaction was to get away at once, yet perhaps that was why Friml had put these pointed questions to Nadia. Perhaps they needed some clear proof of her complicity or guilt. Making a run for it would

220

give them that. So it would be better to continue as before, though with much more care.

The following morning, when the trucks were being loaded for the journey to La Rochelle, there was a shock. Friml was out on the parade ground keeping an eye on the operation. Annie watched him from her room, then decided that now was the time to display results of heavy drinking. She hurried along the passage to tell Nadia and found she too was at the window, but waving and smiling to Friml in the square below.

When the two actresses emerged, Nadia was supporting Annie who looked a mess. Slowly they made their way to the car, which Nadia habitually drove. Friml watched from a distance as the star actress was gently lowered onto the back seat where she lay, flat out. Then Nadia gave the Gestapo man a wave, got into the front seat and drove off. Friml watched the car and turned to the stage manager who had been informed of the extra hazard of the tour. 'Is Frl Jeynor ill?'

The stage manager was embarrassed. 'No. Not really. Just a little too much to drink, last night.'

'But she will be able to perform?'

'Oh, yes! Yes, of course.' He glanced around. 'And I would be grateful, Herr Friml, if you did not mention this to anyone. We like to keep this sort of trouble . . . within the family, as it were.'

The Gestapo man smiled wearily. 'I quite understand.' It really was no part of his job to enforce sobriety among theatricals.

That evening the stage manager was informed that they'd have to delay the curtain because Frl Jeynor was indisposed. An announcement was made from the stage. Friml was out of his front-row seat immediately. He hurried backstage to make sure the reason was as he expected. In the dressing room he found Annie stretched out and Nadia applying cold compresses to her brow. Nadia gave him a long-suffering look and waved him away.

When the performance eventually started Frl Jeynor was entrancing as ever. Friml watched carefully throughout the evening and joined in the sustained applause. He did not know that it was the last time he would see Annie Jeynor in the role.

The following evening the play started exactly on time. The

vigilant Gestapo agent was reassured – although Frl Jeynor did not seem so good this evening. In fact, he was watching Nadia Kulp then; and on two further occasions after a long drive to Bordeaux. Annie herself was already in Toulouse.

The Hôtel de Paris was the collection point in Toulouse for escapers being conveyed along the 'Pat Line'. There, in the kiosk of the inner courtyard, sat Madame Mongelard. As scores of clients would remember, she was a squat woman dressed entirely in black except for a white scarf around her head. Annie entered the hotel and, as though already a guest, walked past reception right through to what had been a conservatory. The woman in black sat impassively at her desk, white scarf knotted securely under her chin. Annie strolled around idly inspecting the rockery then sat in one of the shabby lounge chairs which gave her a clear view of the kiosk.

If she had been able to join the line in Paris she would have been given cover and clearance as far as Marseilles. Then, before leaving that port, she would have been given new identity documents for the remainder of the journey. These identity documents were what she should present to Madame Mongelard. They would ensure that she was taken into hiding immediately. Without them, there was no safety, even in Vichy France.

As Annie sat there, idly turning the pages of a magazine, she considered the irony of her situation. A new identity had been created for her; meticulously forged documents already existed to prove it; a safe room had been prepared for her; brave and willing helpers were waiting to speed her to freedom. But all that could be achieved only if she could gain the recognition of this one Frenchwoman who sat only a few yards away.

Several men came and went. One or two had short, soft conversations with Madame, then an elderly porter was called and they moved away to ascend the stairway to their rooms. Annie noted that occasionally papers were produced for the woman's inspection. It was likely that Madame's only concern was with the *false* identities. She did not know who the escapers really were, so there would be no point in justly claiming to be

222

Annie Jeynor. *But*, the thought suddenly struck the actress, there was a more basic identity than that. Surely, since the consignments were made up of escaping British servicemen, there would on this occasion be only one false identity prepared for a *woman*.

Annie got to her feet and approached the kiosk. She smiled and in broken French made a statement which could be construed as faulty in grammar but perfectly innocent. 'Madame,' she said, 'I am the lost woman.'

Madame Mongelard stared amazed for a moment, then her large bosom heaved with suppressed amazement. 'Ah! Then perhaps I can help you.'

'I would be most grateful.'

A porter was summoned and he led Annie up the back stairway to the third floor. At the end of a narrow corridor at the back of the building he tapped on a door which was immediately opened by a tall, grey-haired man. And, after one comprehensive glance, the man made a decision. He opened the door wider and Annie went in.

There were three other men in the room, grouped around a table, playing cards in hand. All of them looked carefully at the new arrival, then one nodded firmly to the grey-haired man still guarding the door. He said, 'You have kept us waiting, Catherine.'

There were six men hiding in the Hôtel de Paris that week. All of them were to take the route to the Spanish border then over the Pyrenees and down to Gibraltar – the last remaining British outpost on the mainland of Europe. From there they would sail for England. But Annie was going to America. For her the escape route led only as far as Perpignan. Thereafter, she'd have only a little local help in getting aboard the ship from Marseilles that would take her to Lisbon.

She showed the men the hull drawings of the Northcott freighter, which would soon be given clearance at Marseilles. In particular, she drew their attention to the various compartments in which she could hide. Two of them were below the water line and one on deck.

'But how do you get on the ship?' the grey-haired man asked. 'It will not stop when it comes near Perpignan.'

'No. I must get on while it's moving; and in the dark. For that, I need a small fishing boat and a volunteer. Can you arrange that for me? I'm willing to pay for the man's trouble . . . and for the loss of the boat, if necessary.'

'The *loss* of the boat?'

'Yes. There's a risk it might be rammed by the freighter.'

'All of this is too dangerous.'

'Compared with what?' asked Annie bleakly.

They went more thoroughly into the plan, and special exercises were devised for Annie which made her limbs ache.

Five days later the little fishing boat set out down the river from Perpignan at dusk and headed out into the Mediterranean. There were two people in the boat; a man and a 'boy'. The man knew the waters well and had a good knowledge of regular traffic of ships which used the deep water just off the coast. By the time the dusk turned to darkness the fishing boat was tethered to a marker buoy. It put up no lights and became invisible.

In the cold, open boat Annie prepared herself for a considerable exertion. The rough woollen clothes she wore might restrict her movement, but were an essential disguise if she should be discovered. As the hours passed the leaking old boat had to be baled at frequent intervals. One or two large ships passed, but the fisherman said these were not the one. She had to trust him.

Then, at about four o'clock in the morning, long after the Northcott freighter was due, a ship started to materialise in the grey shifting light. The fisherman nodded vehemently. This was the one. He released his mooring on the buoy and let his boat drift into the current of the shipping lane.

Annie carefully re-coiled the grappling line which he would throw and she must climb. The distance between the boat and the retracted access ladder of the ship was not great. What mattered was the accuracy of the throw – so that the grappling hook caught on the ladder at the first attempt. If it didn't catch

224

first time the ship would be moving past too quickly for another try.

The mass of the freighter seemed to curl over them and the roaring hiss of its bow wave drowned out all the other sounds. Annie felt the fishing boat lift on the wave then slip sideways as it was sucked down the flank of the ship. The man stumbled past her in the wildly lurching small craft. He held the line ready. Then, as they bumped sickeningly against the steel hull he threw the grappling hook.

It seemed he must have missed. The small boat continued to slither aft of the freighter. But suddenly the line tightened. Their boat shuddered and changed direction. They were being pulled along by the cargo boat.

The fisherman heaved to pull in the excess line and Annie clambered to the bow to help. Now the boat was nuzzled against the sheer flank of the ship. And dimly above them was the grating of the access ladder. Annie strapped on the haversack with its change of clothes and basic foodstuffs. The man in the bow urged her to hurry. Neither he nor his boat could bear the strain much longer.

Annie gripped the rope. It was taut and rose at a steep angle to the grating about twelve feet above the water line. She stretched out, pulled and then hooked her legs around the rope and clamped it between her feet. This was a manoeuvre she had practised in the basement of the hotel. And she was heartily glad now that, at the grey-haired man's insistence, she had mastered the technique.

The water continued to roar as the space between herself and the boat increased. She was aware of nothing but the numbing effort of transferring her weight from her hands and arms to her feet. Stretch, then grip, then pull and clamp. Stretch, grip, pull, clamp. Very slowly she edged closer to the firm grating above her. It was when she could reach it there came the most difficult operation.

For a few seconds she had to support all of her weight on one hand. Then she hauled herself over the lip of the grating. Immediately, the grappling line went slack as the fisherman cut his boat free of the pounding turbulence at the freighter's side.

Annie sprawled face down on the grating and watched the dark shape of the fishing boat slip and spin away.

When she'd recovered her breath she edged up the ladder. Since it was retracted the steps were almost at right angles to her bruised knees. And between the steps she was now acutely aware of the foaming water rushing below her. She crawled upwards and reached the open and deserted deck. After a long careful look, she closed her eyes and visualised the drawings of the ship which Jamie had supplied.

There could be no delay. Already the sky was brightening. She pulled herself under the rail and moved cautiously away from the watch station towards the bow. There, she knew, was machinery housing large enough to conceal her. It was winching machinery which would not be needed or tended until the freighter reached port. And that port was Lisbon.

BEN TIERNEY

There were three or four studios in Hollywood which were anxious to get hold of Annie Jeynor. They knew she was on her way to America and started making plans which they'd put into operation as soon as she arrived in Los Angeles. Darryl Zanuck, the head of Twentieth Century-Fox, was more enterprising than that. He had already bought the rights to *Beloved Empress*, and the production was under way with Anne Baxter in the leading role. When he heard that Jeynor would be available for the part she'd played in the original German version, he took Baxter off the movie and cabled Annie when she was still crossing the Atlantic to offer her the part.

By the time the ship docked in New York the contract was waiting, together with a full-blown fanfare of welcome. Such publicity was too good to miss. And it was efficient. Fearing that any refugee from Nazi Germany must necessarily be under-nourished, badly clothed and in need of both hair styling and manicure, the studio had sent a posse of glamourisers to a hired rest-room at the ocean terminal who went to work on Annie before the press could get even a snap of her.

When the transformation was accomplished, she was hustled back aboard the ship and told to wait. The photographers had to be assembled. Then she walked down the gangway all over again, looking, as she said later, 'like I'd just escaped in a hermetically sealed bubble from Bel-Air.' The scrum of photographers expected nothing less. The journalists were not so pleased. If Elisabeth Bergner could give the impression of a war-tossed waif in the depths of peacetime, then Miss Jeynor had an obligation to look at least a little travel-stained.

'You been living well in Berlin, Miss Jeynor?'

227

Annie was alert to the implication. 'I haven't been starving, if that's what you mean.'

'Some people are,' another reporter challenged.

'I doubt it,' the actress said. 'There are so many delicious American imports.'

The feeling of accusation waned perceptibly. They had not been aware that American commerce was still doing a lot of business with Germany. Annie had taken the precaution of checking. If pushed, she was also in a position to name the volume of traffic and the products. Her antagonist tried another possible weak spot.

'Miss Jeynor, how did you manage to get clearance to work in Hollywood?'

Annie smiled as though grateful for the opportunity to answer. 'Through the generosity of your State Department. I met Under Secretary Sumner Wells in Berlin earlier this year and he promised to help me.'

That one slammed to the boundary as well. They had not known there were still apparently friendly diplomatic relations between the USA and the Third Reich. And they certainly had not been told of Sumner Wells' Berlin jaunt. Even so, there was one more threatening pitch.

'How come you went on working for the Nazis for nearly a year?'

'I work for myself and the audience, not the Nazis. After all, Hitler's been in power for eight years, and I have to earn a living.'

'But you're English. When the war started, why didn't you quit?'

'Why should I? Mistinguette is still working at the Folies Bergère. And she's *French*.'

The reporter growled, 'Mistinguette is an old whore.'

Annie leaned forward and fixed him with the battle glint in her eyes. 'Yes, she is. But she's an old whore with beautiful legs, even at sixty-eight . . . who can make an audience cheer if she moves her little finger . . . and send them home delighted that she's even *alive*.'

There was some laughter at this and a general sound of

approbation. They were not too clear what they were approving of, but suddenly it seemed a rather *brave* thing to go on working under the Nazis. The questioning moved to other subjects which had no accusation of treachery. Annie's heart slowed to its normal pace. It seemed her welcoming committee did not know she was still married to a Nazi.

Having passed unscathed through her first encounter with the press, Annie was hurried to Pennsylvania Station. There she began the long overland trip to Los Angeles via Chicago. It was meant to be a restful five days by rail, starting on the Twentieth Century, then on the Superchief. The journey was designed to tune her in to the new country. The studio boss could not possibly have foreseen how vulnerable he'd made the representatives who were accompanying Miss Jeynor. Zanuck's bid to steal a march on his rivals was about to backfire.

For, as the luxurious train rushed from one corner of the country to the other, it was turned into a cramped, contentious and swaying cockpit of negotiation. The film Annie was to star in was already in production. The various heads of department involved had all sent representatives to travel with the actress and get her to accept what they had already decided was best. This led to an unbroken and hectic series of meetings and shouting matches. For the lady, they discovered, had a mind of her own.

Having secured a copy of the script and having declined, so far, to sign a production contract, she was in a strong position. She had signed the studio contract on arrival. That meant they had exclusive rights to her services for five years. But she had not yet agreed to do this particular film. Nor – since they'd already replaced one star – did she think the studio was likely to start their association by suspending her. Given that, Annie was determined her first American vehicle should be as near what *she* wanted as her knowledge, value and inflexible will could devise.

She'd known too many actors who'd squandered their 'name' and earning power by believing that the studio knew best. So the arguments became heated and the American movie men, who'd promised their bosses that they'd have the new star 'all wrapped up' by the time the Superchief reached the Sierras, began to have crucial doubts. Some were in despair of even getting her as far as the Sierras. For the actress declared her intention of getting off the train in Denver unless negotiations showed some progress.

Thus by fits and starts – and *stops* – she ground them down. What they couldn't understand was why she wanted her leading man to be an established star. That, they felt, ran counter to what they saw as her unflagging egocentricity. Why in God's name would she want to share the billing, and get lost in the shadow of an actor who was already established in Hollywood movies? Surely she could see it would ruin her own initial impact on the audience? Among themselves they agreed that the studio couldn't afford another star fee on a fairly low budget costume-piece.

Annie held her ground. She said she wanted Tyrone Power or Basil Rathbone, who were already under contract to Fox. Or, better still, Joseph Cotten who could be had on loan from Universal. The front office representative blanched at the prospect of arranging – and paying for – such names. He and his colleagues stared out on the barren rocky plains of Colorado and wished they'd never left New York with this dainty little virago.

What she did not tell them was that her determination to have an established star as male lead was really no more than a bargaining counter. She knew perfectly well that such casting could ruin her own chances of success. It was her intention to give up this demand in exchange for a much more profitable one. Before the train got to New Mexico she was sure she could get a 'percentage of gross' deal. This arrangement, where an actor gets a share of the profit as well as a salary, was quite unheard of at that time in Hollywood.

At the stop in Ogden the front office man phoned Los Angeles with this novel suggestion. Annie had led him to believe it was his own idea. He also reported success in all the other matters outstanding since his last call. The money men needed time to consider and promised to telegraph a decision ahead to Oakland.

Meanwhile, sitting tight in her compartment, Annie now seemed willing to hear who *they* had in mind as her leading man. After a long build-up, about suitability, availability, sympathy and chemistry, the actor they named was Ben Tierney. Annie did not make the mistake of saying that she'd never heard of him. There was no reason why she should have. He was a competent, middle-rank, handsome supporting actor who'd been under contract to the studio for a long time. And he'd never caused any trouble. He, they told her, would be a perfect foil for her own sparkling talent.

Annie didn't say no. But she didn't say yes either, until she had the telegraph form which assured her of stipulated salary plus three per cent of gross on *Beloved Empress*. Then she signed the production contract.

Twenty minutes later, having won her first major battle, she walked out of Union Station into the warm hazy sunlight of the Los Angeles evening.

She had managed to achieve a financial arrangement which was to provide large benefits well into the future. Having established the principle with her first film, she insisted on a similar arrangement for every other film she made. But the strategy by which she had extorted these benefits had immediate repercussions which she had not foreseen. And for a time she was not aware of them. For the thwarted production team lost no time in putting it about that the star had definitely not wanted Ben Tierney in the movie. The way Ben heard it, she had fought tooth and nail to have him replaced. This hurt and dismayed the amiable actor. He'd never got in anybody's way and had been looking forward to working with the European actress he'd heard so much about. He just could not understand what she had against him. They'd never met and it was unlikely she'd seen any of his work.

Ben Tierney was the son of a farmer in Wisconsin. He was the youngest of a large, happy family. While still a young athlete in his teens he'd developed a passion for the silent films of the great Hollywood comedians – particularly the more athletic and acrobatic of them. He had no interest in acting. It was the sheer energy and physical activity which delighted him. For a long time he thought the movie actors did all their own stunts and so there seemed no possibility that he could join Hollywood's erratic open-air circus performing in constant sunshine.

Then he found out about stuntmen and realised that what he most admired about the movies was not done by actors at all. The performances which had sent *his* imagination soaring were those of anonymous young men. He could think of no better way to earn a living. He set out for California.

He got the stunt work he wanted without much difficulty and would have been happy to go on doing that. But he attracted other attention. Directors and feature-player actresses were quick to realise that the daredevil in long-shot had a lot going for him in close-up as well. This realisation came just at the time when the great change from silent to sound films was reaching its peak. And Ben Tierney had an excellent voice. It was deep and resonant and, even on the primitive recording equipment, conveyed great sincerity. He couldn't act. He certainly couldn't play comedy. But he knew how to play to camera, and everything he said or did had total conviction because he just was not trying to be anybody other than himself.

Of course many actors had become stars by doing no more than Ben Tierney did. What held him in a whole string of supporting roles was a total lack of ambition. He just did not want to be a star or to earn much more than his steadily increasing salary, guaranteed by a long term contract. His only regret was that by 1940 he was thirty-five and too old to do any challenging stunt work. His consolation was that he was by then happily married to a researcher who also worked for Twentieth Century-Fox. Her name was Geraldine, called Gerry. They had two young sons, one aged six and the other an eighteen-month-old baby.

Beloved Empress was a costume drama, and so Mrs Tierney had been involved with the script since the studio bought the rights in the earlier UFA film. And Gerry Tierney was there at the first production meeting after the actress arrived in Hollywood. She heard of the marathon travelling crisis on the Superchief and of the storm over the leading man. So it was Ben Tierney's wife who told him that the 'Empress' herself did

232

not want him. Nevertheless, he was *in* and must make the best of a bad job.

A party was arranged at the director's house in Malibu to introduce everyone before shooting began. It did not go well. Ben was subdued and excessively polite, Gerry was resentful, and Annie spent most of the time talking and laughing with Gig Young who had been assigned to escort her for the evening. When Ben Tierney was presented to her it was quite late and everyone had been drinking heavily. Annie turned to her handsome leading-man with genuine professional interest. 'I understand you used to do a lot of stunt work?'

'Yes, I did.'

'That's something I've always admired about American films. The action. In Germany everybody just stands about in deep shadow and talks a lot.'

Ben cleared his throat. 'I suppose it depends on what kind of movie it's supposed to be.'

Annie nodded brightly. 'Even so, I hope they get some action into this version.'

Geraldine, hovering protectively at his elbow, spoke up. 'They will if that's what you want, Miss Jeynor.'

Ben took a half-step back, fiddling with his tie. 'This is my wife, Gerry. She's been doing research on the *Empress*.'

'How do you do.' The actress smiled. 'I don't suppose you often have the chance to work together on a film?' She was making small talk while she tried to pin down the cause of the tension in the air. For she could certainly feel tension.

Ben said, 'I certainly am glad to be working on this one, after all.'

'After all?'

Gerry couldn't resist the opportunity. 'After all the actors who could have got the part.'

Despite the glow of alcohol, Annie could not help noting a rather spiteful edge in the researcher's voice. She also noticed an embarrassed flush on the actor's face. She knew something was wrong and guessed that the wife of this team was more likely to reveal what it might be. Handing her empty glass to Ben she said, 'Would you get me another, please?'

233

'Sure. Yes, of course,' he said and wandered away to the bar which was in another room.

The two women faced each other appraisingly. Annie asked, 'Was there any doubt about Ben getting the part?'

Gerry gave a short incredulous laugh. 'Surely you know that, Miss Jeynor.'

'That means there was, I suppose.'

'You *know* there was.'

Annie had never had any intention of changing the casting. So the fact that she'd used the threat to do so, as a bargaining counter, refused to connect in her mind with the polite man she'd just met. She asked, 'Who did they want instead?'

'*They* didn't want anybody else,' said Gerry bitterly.

Then the whole thing did connect and Annie was filled with embarrassment and shame. This was quickly supplanted by anger at the production team who'd abused her confidence. But she did not have time to add anything to the conversation before Ben returned with a fresh drink. Annie accepted it with a smile, though fuming inside. 'Thank you, Ben.' She raised the glass to him in a toasting gesture. 'Here's to our very happy association.'

Ben, after a quick glance at his wife, responded. 'To *Beloved Empress.*'

They were joined by gossip columnist Louella Parsons, who insisted on dragging Fox's latest acquisition off for a private chat. Annie knew who she was, of course. American film magazines had been scrupulously studied at UFA. What she had not realised was that Miss Parsons was a devoted instrument of the Hearst press. And William Randolph Hearst was an isolationist. His papers did all in their considerable power to keep America out of the conflict in Europe.

So, in talking to Louella Parsons, Annie had to take a very different line from that she'd adopted with the Luce journalists in New York. Now she was invited to recall the benefits which Hitler had brought to Germany; to sing the praises of a film industry under Goebbel's control; and to disparage the British film industry for not recognising her talent. All of this the actress tried to do. But she became aware that Miss Parsons wasn't really interested in all that 'political' stuff. She just wanted to show her employer that she was on the ball when the opportunity arose to exercise his hobby horse. When the chat was over the columnist clapped her heavily jewelled hands and a photographer appeared. This really was the purpose of the exercise. This would provide the evidence that it was Louella Parsons who'd gained the first interview with a new star.

Annie was reclaimed by Gig Young and looked around for the Tierneys, but they'd gone. It was annoying that she had not had the opportunity to clear up the misunderstanding.

When work on the film started, Annie went out of her way to be appreciative and charming to Ben Tierney. In the same compensating vein, she also saw to it that he got much more opportunity to shine than the script allowed. The director was amazed at her generosity, considering the stories he'd heard of her domineering behaviour at UFA. However, he went along with it since a strong man always makes the woman more credible. Lines and telling moments which had been cut from the script in anticipation of the usual star egomania were reinstated.

All this had a quite marked effect on Ben. He was quite used to playing second fiddle to the big names, both male and female. He found it astonishing that his opinion was being sought and his personal effect enhanced to the degree Miss Jeynor insisted upon. Apart from that, he was captivated by the woman who seemed to care so much about him, and charmed by her amusing, tomboyish manner off the set.

Annie was equally impressed with Ben. He was quite unlike any actor she had ever worked with, simply because he wasn't an actor at all. He was a stuntman who looked good and sounded right. The fact that he'd been engaged to play a courtier did not strike him as odd. When Annie pointed out that in the German version, his role – Master of the Horse – had been played by a real Hapsburg prince, Ben asked, 'How was he with horses?'

Annie laughed and had to admit, 'Not so good.'

Ben was quite serious. 'Well, I'm *very* good with horses. And if that Empress had any sense she would've hired a guy like me.'

He did have some worries, though. One day he came to

Annie's dressing room before a crucial scene to ask for her help. That in itself was typical of the difference in his attitude. An actor – or, at least, any actor Annie had known – would have considered asking his leading lady for help as demeaning and a confession of incompetence. Ben, easy-going and modest, was just anxious to do as good a job as possible.

It was a scene in which the Empress wrongly believes that the courtier she is in love with has secretly betrayed her. He will not provide the evidence that this is far from the truth. She dismisses him from her service and from the Court.

Ben said, 'What I don't get, Annie, is why he bothers to show up. I mean, I know that sister of the Empress has told her a whole bunch of lies about me. Just because I wouldn't hit the sack with *her*.'

Annie explained, 'If the Empress orders him to appear he must obey. That's his duty.'

'Suppose that sister, the Grand Duchess, ordered me to appear at Court. I'd have to go, right?'

'Yes, of course.'

'Then how come, when the Grand Duchess ordered me to strip off and get into bed with her, I *didn't* obey?'

'Because you're in love with *me*.'

There was a long and awkward silence. It was caused only partly by Annie's effort to find an explanation for the anomaly. It was caused much more by the look in Ben's eyes, and the flush on his cheeks, when Annie suddenly reported the Empress in her own person.

She had not done it intentionally. Ben knew that. But why did the bald statement seem to stand out from the rest of the conversation? In an instant the man was consciously aware, for the first time, that it was true. He said, 'Yes. So?'

Annie tried to bridge the awkward, pulsing silence that had developed. With some effort she gave a flippant response. 'There's a difference between getting you . . . him . . . to do his job . . . and . . . and . . .'

'And screwin' her.'

'The *sister*, yes.'

There was another pause while Ben moved around the trailer

recovering his composure. Then he said, 'What I want to know is, when the Empress tells me to get the hell out and never come back, how do I feel? What shows strongest on my face . . . the fact that I accept the order or . . . that I'm in love with you?'

And when he said it, there was no doubt that it was intentional.

'If I were you,' Annie advised him, 'I'd go for the blindly-obeying-an-order response. Leave the audience to know how he really feels.'

'Will the audience know how he really feels?'

'You can depend on it,' Annie said.

Ben smiled and nodded. 'Thanks Annie.' He turned to go but paused at the door to ask, 'How'd *you* make out with that real prince who played my part?'

'We didn't get on.'

The man grinned and slapped his script against his hand. 'No good with horses *or* women, huh?'

'No. But he was great at taking orders.'

Ben left the trailer whistling, and curiously light of heart.

For the two-month duration of the film, Annie had little chance to appreciate living in California. She was aware that the weather was better, but only very early in the morning and quite late in the evening. Those were the only times she was out of doors. The studio car nosed into the palm-fringed avenues of Beverly Hills at five a.m. to pick her up. Snuggled in the back seat, she observed the dawn brightening behind Mount Hollywood. The big, luxurious Buick zig-zagged between mansions in which everyone would be asleep for several hours. On the mornings when there was a late call she was able to watch sunrise from Sunset. Then on to Beverly-Wilshire and the Twentieth Century-Fox complex which was the most westerly of the major studios.

Lunch for all the cast was in the studio commissary. Annie usually ate in company with the other leading actors. Ben sat with his wife, Gerry, who was working on future productions. Occasionally they had the elder of their two sons with them. Ben led the little boy across the room to be introduced to Annie.

His name was Steven. He was a polite little boy, aged about six.

Annie's instinct was to kiss him, but she stopped herself. A six-year-old probably thought he was too big to be kissed by unauthorised strangers. When asked what his baby brother was doing, he gave the opinion that Martin was probably sleeping. Stepping close to Annie's ear he confided in a worried voice, 'He sleeps an *awful* lot.'

'Lucky Martin,' Annie said.

From across the room Gerry called rather sharply, 'That's enough Steven!' as though talking to Miss Jeynor might be hazardous to the child's health.

Late in the afternoon, there was usually a snack for which Ben joined Annie in her trailer, together with her dresser and, often, a wig man. Then more work until everyone was on the point of collapse and the director called it a day.

By the time the star had been unlaced from her costume and had scrubbed off the make-up, her Master of Horse had long since ridden home. And Annie was far too tired to notice as she plodded towards the waiting car to be ferried back to Beverly Hills. In the evenings her driver usually took the Speedway route north along the shore. Sometimes they were in time to catch the last few strands of cloud that had been reddened by the setting sun. Mostly, though, it was just a stretch of dark water. At the Spanish-style house, the drive and porch lights blazed a welcome. The housekeeper had drawn a hot bath and prepared dinner. By then it was about nine p.m. Dinner was followed by a couple of hours studying the scenes called for the next day. Then bed.

But sleep did not come immediately. Annie could not prevent her mind rerunning the main events of the day. And in most of these, necessarily, Ben figured prominently. He really was a thoroughly nice, amiable man. Also, he had great warmth. A comfortable man to be with, however ungainly or flustered he might occasionally be. She liked him very much.

But she was not in love with him. Nor did she take too seriously his evident belief that he was in love with her.

Annie had learned to distrust the effect she had on men. She

238

reasoned that, as she'd spent her life learning all the tricks of attraction and allure, it wasn't surprising if they worked. They worked without any conscious effort on her part.

'But,' she wryly observed, 'who can trust seduction on auto-pilot?' The situation wasn't as basic as that in Ben's case. But it did seem likely that he imagined he was in love with the person when he was merely infatuated with a well-rehearsed personality.

And yet, as the weeks went on, she had to admit this was no starry-eyed youth. He wasn't that much younger than Annie herself. And he had a thoroughly down-to-earth concern for the exacting job they were engaged upon. The fact that Annie made it *more* exacting than her fellow actors were used to, only seemed to increase Ben's quite evident admiration of her. Even when he was the object of her professional dissatisfaction, he bore up, made no complaint and sweated until he got it right. If that meant twenty takes just moving round a chair to kiss her hand, then that's what he was prepared to do.

Others in the cast took her perfectionist tendencies less well. In fact, it wasn't long before Annie was eating alone at lunch time. But when Gerry Tierney wasn't there, Ben joined her. And increasingly they were left alone during the afternoon break. When he started waiting for her after the day's work, however, the tongues really started to wag.

Her dresser said, 'Honey, watch out for Mrs Tierney.'

'What?' Annie was puzzled. 'When?'

'Any time now, I reckon. She been sniffin' aroun'.'

'Mrs Tierney is doing her job. She works here.'

'That ain't the job she been sniffin' *at*. An' she been askin' questions.'

'What questions?'

'Like what extra work her husban' he's doin' late at night.' The big coloured woman inclined her head portentously. 'An' plenty folks here willin' to think of reasons he never tol' her.'

Annie bent her head and gave great attention to the drape of lamé panels on her gown. Obviously Gerry Tierney had wondered at the change of routine which brought her husband home so late. And of course she was able to check the day schedule to see exactly when Ben should have been free to leave the studio. There was no doubt that jealousy was going to invade the scene.

The actress sighed and recalled other occasions when wives or mistresses of her leading men had declared wars of emotional attrition. Nobody won and the production suffered. But she'd learned how to deal with it. To her dresser she said, 'Then I'd better take the cow by the horns.'

At lunch she told Ben she'd be busy with contract business after shooting. Then she sent a message to the office asking Mrs Tierney to call on her that evening for a drink. They'd travel to Miss Jeynor's house in the studio car which would wait, then take Mrs Tierney home. It was not an unusual request. Gerry Tierney was already doing research for Annie's next picture.

When the star emerged from her trailer that evening everyone else had gone home, but the wife was waiting. Annie assumed the armour she'd developed for such occasions and greeted her warmly. 'Gerry, my dear, this is very good of you.'

'It's no trouble, Miss Jeynor.'

'Oh, I do hope not.'

They walked out to the car together. The drive to Beverly Hills was occupied with carefully monitored small talk about the current production. Annie made several astute observations on details which were the mark of really excellent research by Gerry. The researcher accepted the compliments gracefully enough and tried once or twice to open discussion on the next project. Each time, Annie complained that she'd really have to relax a bit before she could take it in.

At the house, the guest was invited to stay for dinner but she declined the offer. So, there was nothing for it but to pour the drinks and get down to the real purpose of the meeting. Mrs Tierney had no idea what that purpose was until Annie opened with a broadside. 'I understand you think I'm sleeping with your husband.'

Gerry froze with her glass within two inches of her lips. She looked away, placed the drink on the table and cleared her throat. 'I'm not here to discuss that, Miss Jeynor.'

Annie's expression was bland. 'Oh yes you are.'

'You asked me here to . . .'

'To discuss that,' Annie said firmly.

'This is very unfair.'

'I think it's much fairer to discuss it with me than with the tattle-tales on the set.' She indicated that Gerry should drink up and demonstrated the intention by taking a good slug from her own glass. 'I do want to be fair with you. And I can understand your concern. What I'd like you to be absolutely sure of is that the gossip isn't true.'

Gerry realised the subject couldn't be avoided. And now that she'd come to terms with the full-frontal approach, she intended to make use of it. She was a spirited and intelligent woman. 'You say you understand my concern?'

'Of course I do. Ben and I work together all day. He sees me more than he sees you. That leaves plenty of room for all sorts of stories.'

'And he's very fond of you.'

'I'm fond of him, too. I wouldn't want to deny that. Your husband is a very likeable, friendly man.'

'The way he talks about you is more than friendly.'

'To you?' Annie asked. 'He talks about me to you?'

'Yes. He talks about you a lot.'

'That doesn't sound very underhand to me.'

'Maybe that's the idea,' Gerry suggested.

Annie was astonished. 'You can't believe that. Ben has absolutely no guile. Don't give him any of yours.'

Instantly Gerry was on the attack. 'Maybe he needs some of mine. Against you. Maybe he should hear about some of the things I've heard from other places.'

Annie felt a small but acute sadness at this. It was all so unnecessary. 'Mrs Tierney, I'm sorry you feel threatened . . . or feel that your marriage may be threatened. All I can tell you is that it won't be by me. In fact I'll do all I can to reassure you.'

'You can stop seeing Ben.'

'Not until the picture is over.'

'I mean outside of working hours.'

'And what explanation should I give him for that?'

Gerry seized on this as though on a confession of guilt.

241

'You think he'll want an explanation?'

Annie sighed and got up to pour herself another drink. 'Of course he will.' She explained, 'Whether you believe it or not, most of the time we talk about the *Empress*. And how he can make a real breakthrough this time.'

'Really?' The wife was sceptical.

'And I think he *can*! But if I start treating him as a total stranger it will play hell with his confidence.'

'What about *my* confidence – in *him*?'

'It seems you've let that get a bit shaky,' Annie told her bluntly. 'Though it's none of my business, I'd suggest you are losing your grip, Mrs Tierney. And that's a pity because your husband could become a major star – if you'd give him this chance.'

Gerry did not follow the reasoning. 'What chance? The chance for you to break up our marriage?'

'No. The chance to keep his confidence in me – and himself – until the picture is finished. Please trust me that far, and I promise you I'll be of no further use to him.'

Gerry got to her feet and straightened the jacket of her square-shouldered grey suit. 'Why the Lady Bountiful, Miss Jeynor?'

'Because I can afford it, Mrs Tierney,' the star replied crassly. 'Financially, artistically and emotionally – I can afford it.'

Shortly thereafter, Gerry Tierney departed somewhat re-assured, but much incensed against a woman who seemed to be totally impregnable.

It was a quality which Annie had to flex, continually, both at work and socially. She made few friends during her early days in Hollywood. Among the leading ladies there was resentment. Anne Baxter got a lot of sympathy. They didn't like the idea of a foreign actress being imported when already there was fierce competition among the home-based roster.

Another obstacle was envy. Word got out that this upstart from UFA had put the squeeze on Zanuck for a percentage of gross. That was something even Myron Selznick hadn't been able to do for his clients. Using Annie as a precedent, they tried to alter their own contracts to include the long-term bonus.

But their employers would have none of it. Suspensions were threatened and the established actors came to heel. They had too much to lose.

The shining exception to all this concealed rancour was Marlene Dietrich. She called on Annie the very first night after the newcomer had settled in. Although it was ten years since Dietrich had been brought to Hollywood, she had not forgotten how strange and intimidating the place could be. Apart from assuring Annie of any help and support she might need, it was an opportunity to talk about the old country. In particular they recalled the beauty of the Rhineland in spring. There was also the pleasure of being able to refresh a long-neglected language. When they were alone together, she and Annie always spoke German.

Beloved Empress was completed without further hassle. And even before the editing had been completed it was general knowledge around the Fox lot that Ben Tierney was now a hot property. By then, Annie had gone off on a much-needed holiday to Palm Beach, with David Otrego to provide the relaxing therapy she needed.

Several months later, the première confirmed all the good reports of the film, and of Ben's performance. So convincing had he proved as Master of the Horse in the Austro-Hungarian empire that he was immediately rushed into a Western. The response to Miss Jeynor's performance was less enthusiastic. Sitting in that overdressed, super-critical audience in the baroque Pantages theatre, Annie could see why. Scene after scene proved a remarkable foolishness. She had committed a crime that no female star should ever be accused of. She had handed the picture to the man! And a *supporting* man, at that.

Annie grinned and bore the accusation with fortitude. At the party afterwards she greeted the Tierneys warmly. Ben's manner had changed since she'd last seen him. The fact that he looked the part of a new romantic leading man, Annie put down to his wife's efforts. But deeper in himself, too, was a relaxed assurance. There was no doubt that Annie's gamble for him had paid off – though she had not bargained that it would be to her own loss. They chatted idly about the Western Ben was doing and the drama which Annie was engaged on. Gerry couldn't resist the opportunity to crow a little. When there was a large enough circle of interested bystanders, she remarked brightly, 'We're so glad you took on this new movie, Miss Jeynor.'

'I don't know if I'm so glad. It's not an easy role.'

Gerry shrugged despairingly. 'What can you expect with second-hand property?'

Annie made sure her smile was fixed before she prompted, 'Second-hand?'

'Oh, yes! And cheap. We bought the story from Warner Brothers when Bette Davis turned it down flat.'

'Really?' Annie said, as though only marginally interested. But she was acutely aware of the avid, gleeful faces surrounding her.

Ben came to her rescue. 'Annie will make Davis wish she hadn't.' He put a protective arm around her shoulder. 'Won't you, Annie?'

'I'll do my best.'

Then he said something which quite astonished the silent snipers. 'If you do, it's bound to be great. Because this time you won't be hog-tied having to make *me* look good.'

That statement was so honest, generous, and true that it was immediately reported throughout the huge party. Apart from the novelty value of genuine modesty, it explained to everyone's satisfaction what they hadn't been able to pin down about *Beloved Empress*. For the remainder of the evening Annie noticed a remarkable thaw in the atmosphere. And several people quoted the gist of Ben's remark to her – under the impression he had made it to somebody else. However, when she went home that night, she solemnly promised herself that never again would she make the mistake of behaving like a human being when she was employed to be a star. Years earlier, the German actress Gerda Ritter had taught her that. The star performer must *insist* that when she is on, everybody looks at *her*. If she doesn't, nobody gets paid for long.

Shortly after that, she met Bette Davis at a dinner party and asked Warner's *prima donna assoluta* why she'd turned down the role Annie was currently working on.

'There was too much thinking in it. And not enough feeling.'

'How does that affect what you do in front of the camera?'

'Doesn't matter a brief goddam to the *camera*,' Davis said. 'It matters to the public, though. My public, anyway.' She drew on her cigarette as though she was obliged to consume it in one breath. 'They don't want to watch me thinking unless I'm thinking of *doing* something. And then I'd better do it, damn quick. But most of all they want to watch what I'm feeling.'

Annie thought she understood this, but wanted to make sure. 'With your face in close up . . .' The famous round eyes widened to their full extent. '. . . how do they know the difference?'

'They don't. *I* know the difference. That's what shows. They know I would not be wasting their time just thinking.'

'I see.'

Davis drove the point home. 'That story you're stuck with was written by some goon of a professor who thinks thinking for the sake of thinking is exciting, for chrissakes!' Impatiently, she waved a path through a cloud of smoke. 'Fine if you're Greer Garson discovering radium. Then, you've got something to show for it. Otherwise, the public doesn't want to look at women thinking.'

Annie was very grateful for this pertinent advice. It prompted her to demand changes in the script. Cuts were made in the long passages of internal maundering – which she was later to define as 'Rambling Iris'. Instead, the emotional content was topped-up, and always followed by decisive action.

When the film was shown everyone agreed that Annie was marvellous and Davis must have been crazy to turn it down. Only Annie and Bette Davis knew that it was, in a way, their joint performance. Ben was delighted when his prediction came true. He invited Annie out to celebrate her success. Unwisely, she accepted. A lot of time had passed, and a lot of changes had been accomplished since she'd taken steps to avoid his troublesome infatuation. There seemed no harm in establishing a new, entirely friendly relationship with a man whose company she enjoyed.

In fact, she was feeling quite bereft of men whose company she enjoyed. All the others she'd met so far were totally consumed by ambition. Often their sole interest in her was as a step up the ladder. There was also the fact that she was being snubbed by the English 'colony'. None of them came to the première. The group of distinguished British actors, who'd been working in Hollywood for many years, did not think it proper to extend a welcome to anyone they viewed as, at best, a reformed collaborator.

And that wasn't the only thing which bothered them. Doyen of the group, Ronald Colman, most perceptively noted that Annie Jeynor was 'common'. Madeleine Carroll and Merle Oberon declined to return courtesy calls. The De Havilland sisters, the Cedric Hardwicks, the Brian Ahernes, Leslie Howard, Basil Rathbone, Nigel Bruce and even old C. Aubrey Smith were markedly cool to Miss Jeynor. Between them, of course, they were a power-house of pro-British propaganda. Since Annie had never been autocratic enough to treat members of her audience as her subjects, this puzzled her. She wondered how they could feel justified in alienating such a large section of the ticket-buying public – those whose motto was 'America first'.

So the dinner with Ben came at an opportune time. Their table at the Trocadero was well back from the dance floor; and from the insistent rumba beat of Xavier Cugat's band. Ben had expected to find Annie glowing with triumph at having turned a stinker into a box-office hit. Instead, she seemed curiously deflated.

'What's bothering you?' he asked.

She shrugged. 'My past is catching up with me, I suppose.'

'Is that bad?'

'Not *all* bad. But not all beer and skittles either.'

He didn't know what that meant exactly, but took the implication. 'Do you miss England?'

'How can I, when England's right here? Alive and well and lording it in Hollywood.'

Ben reached across the table and took her hand. 'But it's not their country.'

'I can't be sure of that.' She smiled and softly paraphrased, 'Whose country, friend, *is* this?'

'Mine,' Ben said. 'And me and the American public are wild about you.' Before she could raise any objection he got to his feet, still holding her hand. 'Let's dance.'

Annie had not known he *could* dance. It was a fairly rare accomplishment in a city where everyone seemed to have learned all they knew from watching movies. Thus, whatever the music, they revolved slowly in a foot-square space, presenting alternate profiles to a notional camera. But Ben could dance and, in the dim light, Annie could close her eyes and imagine that she was back on the vastly greater space of Covent Garden twenty years earlier.

That illusion was oddly sustained by the manner in which Ben held and moved her. He felt like Albert Lane. She opened her eyes quickly, and an instinctive panic was immediately calmed by the gentle expression and the smiling brown eyes of her partner. Then she relaxed completely and enjoyed the sensation of their bodies gradually engaging in the fine focusing of move-ment which made them a single entity.

They'd been on the floor a long time before Annie noticed the waiter trying to attract their attention. He was ready to serve the meal.

As they ate it was clear that something had changed in their relationship. It showed in their conversation. They said less, but everything seemed to mean more. It showed in their faces as, over liqueurs, they listened to the band's rare tenor singing 'Besame Mucho' or 'Amapola'.

It wasn't clear if Ben felt the change as much as Annie. Probably the new situation was achieved by Annie's almost magical conversion to what Ben had always felt was true. And he did realise that he was managing to convey what he'd never really succeeded in conveying before.

Then they danced again to a new tempo. And there was no doubt where the rhythm would lead. Annie made no attempt to correct that impression. Nor was she in any position now to tell herself, or anyone else, that Ben was merely caught up in an infatuation. Or fascination. Miraculously on cue the tenor sang,

'The line between love and fascination, is hard to tell on an evening such as this . . .'

By the time they went back to Annie's house some hours later, that line was effectively crossed.

When Annie woke early the following morning in the high, airy bedroom, she immediately realised how much she had missed waking with a man beside her. Ben was still sleeping with the edge of the blue silk sheet tucked under his brown arm. She stroked his shoulder. He stirred but did not wake. She crouched down so that she could see how his face looked in repose. It looked absurdly boyish. Annie smiled with the sheer joy of being there with him. She wanted that suspended joyful time to go on and on – as though his waking might somehow alter a perfect relationship.

It was the noise of the housekeeper setting the breakfast, things on the patio which woke him. Having stirred, he opened his brown eyes very wide. Annie's kiss missed its mark and brushed his chin. He smiled lazily and arched his back. 'We'll have to do this more often,' he said.

'That's what I have in mind,' Annie told him.

Over breakfast, out by the side of the pool, it was as though this was their first meeting. The curiosity of people who suddenly find themselves in love kept them talking long into the morning. Annie was relieved to be able to share her secrets with him. And Ben recounted his youth and how he'd met and married Gerry.

As he told it, things had not been going well between Gerry and himself recently. His new status as sought-after leading man changed the image they had of each other. And of course there was a change in his work schedule which was damaging to the sort of life they'd had up until then. Before *Beloved Empress* his job as supporting actor required no more than three or four weeks on any film. And there were long stretches between films. But after his breakthrough – and a re-negotiation of his contract – the studio was determined to make full use of a suddenly discovered asset. He was rushed into the Western and, after that, into two more projects with scarcely breathing space between them. And now, of course, he was at work from the beginning to the end of shooting of every film.

So it was not that he'd started to neglect his wife, but the simple fact that he no longer had the time for such attention as he'd formerly lavished on his home. And she knew he hadn't. That did not lessen her resentment, fuelled by her dismay at her own loss of status in the marriage. Before, she was the driving force and the decider on what should be done both personally and professionally. Now Ben had other advisers and scores of people willing to do what he wanted. He'd gained confidence and earned the right to make his own decisions. Noting all this, Gerry herself had no doubt about who was to blame for the change. Then she found out they were seeing each other again. But this time she was chary of forcing a confrontation. Besides, she was convinced that Ben's love of the children would keep him tied down. As for Miss Jeynor, Gerry decided it was just a matter of biding her time until she was in a strong enough position.

In the spring of 1942 the affair was continuing. Gerry seemed to be reconciled to the situation and there was a degree of harmony between Ben and herself. This arose mainly because Ben and Annie were kept excessively busy on separate films.

Now that the United States was in the war, the studios were going flat out on patriotism and propaganda. For Annie it was a rather bizarre sensation. Having once trumpeted the glories of the Third Reich for Josef Goebbels, she was now cast as heroine for Darryl Zanuck and the good old USA. She had also been accepted by the English colony, for now that Britain and America were on the same side in the same war, she felt free to espouse the views that the Ronald Colman clique had been promoting all along.

Annie joined with great vigour in the ballyhoo of selling War Bonds. The fact that this patriotic duty could be linked to bumping up ticket sales for a movie was not lost on the studio. At the same time as it had dispatched Ben in one direction, it sent Annie off in the other, on a nationwide personal appearance tour with *The Brightening Land*. And she did great business; for the war effort, and Twentieth Century-Fox. Her impact was helped by the publicity department which, without her knowledge, published reports of her dramatic escape from persecution and starvation under the heel of the Nazi jackboot. Annie's astonishment was mixed with amusement when she thought of her luxurious flat on Ziegelstrasse – but she let it pass.

Then, in the knifing winds of Chicago, everything was torn to shreds. The evening started well enough. The packed audience loved the movie and cheered when it was over. Then the band struck up the 'Star Spangled Banner' and Annie walked onto the stage – bringing the cheers to a deafening pitch. She went right into her War Bonds harangue. In her case the speech which had been written for her was specifically aimed at helping the British war effort. Then the band struck up again and she sang 'There'll Always Be An England' which, as always, excused the rest of the United Kingdom from any war effort whatsoever. After that, the houselights came on. Spotlights picked out all available exits and at each one there was a table stacked with pledge forms to tempt the departing audience into doing its bit.

At the press call, reporters and photographers filed down to the front of the emptying theatre and Annie came down from the stage to stand before them.

One of the reporters was a lot more excited than this frequent chore required him to be. His name was Deely Connor, a burly, red-faced man with broken teeth. The reason for his excitement was that that afternoon he had received a quite astonishing call from a woman in Los Angeles.

When several of the usual questions and answers had been exchanged, Connor elbowed his way to the front and, innocently enough, asked, 'Can you tell us your real name, Miss Jeynor?'

She thought it was a standard movie magazine quiz request. 'Annie Jeynor is my real name.'

'I mean, your married name. You are married, aren't you?'

Annie took the opportunity to strike several poses for the sake of the impatient photographers. The prolonged battery of flashes suddenly seemed to her like an opening assault of heavy guns.

Connor repeated the question – and the mere fact that he could *remember* the question struck his colleagues as odd. 'You are married, aren't you?'

'Yes, I am. But my husband . . .' She tried roguishness. 'My husband prefers to be kept out of all this lovely publicity.'

Another reporter shouted, 'Any kids?'

Annie saw a chance to confuse the issue. 'Yes. We have a daughter. She's in England.'

'And where's *he*?' Connor, who knew, demanded that she say. 'Where is your husband?'

The confusion might still work. 'Somewhere is Germany.' It could sound as though he was engaged on a secret mission.

'What's his name?'

She smiled, and the effort made her cheeks ache. 'Frederik. That's all he'd want me to tell you.'

Connor stood very close now – a red-faced bar-room brawler who'd never quit, obliging the other reporters to crowd round. 'Hey, Miss Jeynor, I'm sure he wouldn't mind at all if you told us.' Hitching his trousers, he consulted a note. 'Isn't his name Frederik von Bohlen? One of the Krupps? Is that right, or not?'

It seemed to Annie she stared at him for a long time before she finally let go. 'Yes. That's right.'

There was a pause, then a wild babble of sound as all the other reporters clamoured for more information. But she felt incapable of saying any more and edged along the rail in front of the screen platform. At the pass-door to the backstage area she saw the white, stricken face of the Fox PR man. He opened the door for her as though he were an automaton and she found herself alone in the narrow, silent, stone-floored corridor.

Next day the papers were full of it. Connor's paper ran a large photograph and the headline, 'ANNIE JEYNOR IS FRAU VON BOHLEN'. In his story there was more than Annie had said. There was, for example, some damning background material on the Krupps. He knew, also, about the films she'd made for Goebbels, about her friendship with the Görings, her privileged position in the Berlin theatre and the fact that her husband was a member of the Nazi Party. Apparently, he knew exactly what Annie had told Ben. That was the most crushing realisation of all.

The sensational news was taken up by network radio. The PR man hammered on the door of her hotel room. He told her the studio had cancelled the rest of the tour. Annie asked him, 'What do they want me to do?'

The young man shrugged. 'Right now, Miss Jeynor, I don't think they give a damn what you do – as long as you do it well away from them.' He left abruptly. Almost mechanically, Annie continued to pack.

Then, separated by only a few minutes, there were two telephone calls. The first was from Marlene Dietrich. She already knew something of the circumstances in which the German propaganda film was made. She didn't approve of that but she understood it. There was only one thing she wanted to know now, before offering her unqualified support. Annie was glad to give her friend the assurance that she'd never been a member of the Nazi party.

Marlene believed her without question and advised that she return immediately to Hollywood for a further discussion of strategy. 'Come back to me, honey,' she said. 'You know the address. The name, you'll recall, is Maria von Losch.' She gave a throaty chuckle. 'Also Frau Sieber, naturally. Take your pick, you've got me.'

The second call was from Ben, in Florida. He sounded even more shattered than Annie felt and immediately confessed he must be to blame. But all he'd told his wife was that Annie was married to somebody called von Bohlen. The point of mentioning it to Gerry at all had been part of the reconciliation. It was to illustrate that Annie was not free to marry anyone else – himself for example – because she, too, was already married. Giving the name seemed natural and no danger. Now he reported, bitterly, that he would never forgive Gerry. He was cancelling his own personal appearance tour and flying back to Los Angeles. He'd be waiting for her.

Things began to seem less black. It was Ben's wife who was responsible. As a highly-skilled researcher she would have had little trouble tracing everything she'd told Connor from the simple facts she'd been given.

It was difficult to see what Gerry Tierney hoped to gain by this treachery. With Annie and Ben geographically so far apart, and both far away from Hollywood, it may have seemed an ideal time to strike. With any luck, Annie wouldn't come back at all, and Ben would come back appalled but grateful to have escaped from the pariah Miss Jeynor must surely become.

Her mistake lay in thinking that her husband's new confidence was illusory. Relying on the person she knew him to be, she was certain that when the scandal reached the papers Ben would take fright and run home. It was not that he was a timid man, but he had a deeply entrenched 'country boy' attitude to anything that might be considered unpatriotic. Together they had often prided themselves on working in Hollywood, yet staying aloof from the often lubricious lifestyle which surrounded them.

However, Ben did not run home. Certainly he felt what his wife had expected him to feel, but two powerful factors defeated her purpose. First, and shining above all, was his love for Annie. Second, there was his feeling of guilt. It had been through his carelessness that Gerry had heard the name 'von Bohlen'. Apart from the emotional imperative there was the need to do all in his power to make up for the damage he had caused.

His new-found confidence was not illusory. His worth and popularity existed by popular acclaim and could be measured at the box office. The studio believed in him and had big plans for his future. So – he flew back to Los Angeles. On arrival he went home only to pack a suitcase. Gerry was at work. Privately he asked the children's nurse to tell her mistress that he would not be back. Then he spent some time with the children and told the older boy that he'd been called away to do some work on location. Steven asked him when he'd be home again and Ben said he didn't know. The baby started to cry, upset by the intrusion. Ben ran from the house to the cab he'd kept waiting.

The problem for the studio would not go away just by ignoring Annie. Her cast-iron contract ensured that she must be paid for another three and a half years whether they offered her work or not. Only if she were convicted of an indictable offence could they abrogate the terms and get rid of her. So, after the first shock had passed, Zanuck saw clear need to weather the storm.

Reports from around the country suggested that a salvage operation might be tricky, but was possible. A few theatre fronts had been daubed with mud or tar and their marquee lights stoned. The distributors weren't happy with that but, so far, there was no great drop in the takings for Annie Jeynor films. The Defense Department banned her from any further War Bond tours. That was a pity but it did mean she could be put to work full-time in the studios – *if* a satisfactory story could be put out soon enough.

Annie was summoned to Zanuck's office, already crowded with publicity hacks, writers, lawyers, assistants and production staff. The loud chaotic meeting went on all day. What emerged was a masterpiece of defence dressed as attack. But, to begin with, they wanted to know how the defamation got out in the first place. Annie said Ben Tierney might know. He was called and told his side of it. When he left, his wife was called. And she was sacked on the spot. A virtue would be made of that. The astute Chicago reporter had been duped by a jealous woman. Deely Connor would thus have some excuse for a retraction piece, if everything else fitted together.

Another bonus was the fact that Gerda was in England. Annie was reluctant to say how that had come about, but when she did they whooped with joy. So the story was emerging of a grave misunderstanding. Some of it was true, a lot of it invented – but it held together. It was the tale of a very talented actress who happened to be working in Germany *before* Hitler came to power. She met and fell in love with a prominent industrialist who'd often been the guest of corporate heads in the USA. (If top Cleveland bosses did not spot him for a wrong-un, what chance had a mere slip of a girl?) They had a child whom the actress adored. Then the husband went bad and joined the Nazis. The trusting actress was appalled, but trapped in a dangerous situation. It was a matter of saving her child or saving herself. In order to ensure that the child could escape, she herself remained in Germany. Then, when the opportunity arose, she battled her way through several occupying armies to reach the promised land of America. Fearing the natural, understandable, shock that news of her marriage might provoke, she kept quiet about it. There were gallant friends still in Germany who had to be protected.

When the final draft of this statement was read over to the packed room there were audible sighs of relief and sympathy. There was also some applause. The general opinion was that it would make a great movie. Before that, however, it made great copy. A personal call from Zanuck was put through to Deely Connor in Chicago. It was important to cut any ramifications of the original exposé off at source. The shrewd reporter was quick to realise that he could get double mileage from the same gallon of gas. But he wanted a personal interview with Jeynor. Would the studio fly him down to California for a few days – as their guest? They would. He boarded a clipper the same day.

Ben insisted on being with Annie for the interview. She was very glad to have him there. For, whereas Deely Connor might have been on edge with a hoity-toity European actress trained on the classical stage, he got on like a blazing barn with ex-stuntman Tierney. The lovers sat shyly holding hands on the sofa and Connor was won over. Of course the love angle had to be discreetly handled and, at Ben's man-to-man request, it was.

When the story was published Annie came out a much-wronged heroine. And, of course, for Connor to get to that position he had to right his own wagon. He confessed that he had been duped. A jealous vindictive woman had set him off on a false trail. A woman consumed with envy of the glamorous European actress had tried to wreck a brilliant career. The reader could not possibly blame Connor for his error of judgment. They could, though, wonder a little *why* the woman had gone to such lengths. It was not at all clear that she was the wife of Annie Jeynor's lover. And the mother, what is more, of his two sons.

Gerry Tierney reacted strongly in the new situation. She had no job and little likelihood of employment with another studio – Darryl Zanuck would see to that. Within a few days she'd decided to quit Hollywood and go back east, where she came from. Until things quietened down, she and the boys would live with her parents in Massachusetts.

Meanwhile, Ben moved in with Annie.

*   *   *

255

I was obliged to do no more than skim through the von Bohlen revelations in Hollywood.

Annie was ill. Her cold had not cleared up and, to our alarm, her condition suddenly began to deteriorate. It was pitiable to see her so weak. Shocking, for the first time really, to see her *old*. When she was robbed of her vitality, her astonishing alertness of mind and the ability to move, I watched her and felt cheated. Here was no more than a sick old woman. Here, quite unfairly, was a stranger. Of course she deserved love and care and attention. That was given by the housekeeper, Mrs MacKenzie, by her secretary Elspeth and by her doctor. And Barbara was a devoted friend who happened to be there. But I had no authorised role to play. Naturally I was anxious for her, and willing to do all I could to help. But that was no more than could be expected of a passing stranger. It was unsettling to have the idea thrust upon me that I had no business with the real person. For I could clearly see – when I looked at that pale, wrinkled face lolling on the pillow – that this was *not* Annie Jeynor.

When she was taken to a private hospital in Glasgow, the nursing Sister asked, 'Are you her son?'

'No. No, I'm just a friend.'

'Is there no family?'

'Yes. She has a daughter.'

'Do you know the name?' the Sister asked coolly. 'And the address where I might contact her?'

Probably these were just routine questions. It would seem no more than prudent that such enquiries are made on behalf of a frail patient in her eighties. But to me, at the time, it sounded like the intimation of imminent death. I told the Sister I would try to get the information. At first, I intended to do only that. But by the time I told Barbara that evening, I'd more or less made up my mind that I must find Gerda.

Barbara said, 'Of course you must find her. If Annie is seriously ill her daughter should be here.'

'The trouble is, I don't know where to begin. Neither Mrs MacKenzie nor Elspeth have any idea about the daughter. In fact, Mrs MacKenzie didn't know she existed and Elspeth only knew what she'd typed for the book.'

'Is Annie herself no help?'

'No. She's semi-conscious. Incoherent.'

'Oh, God!' Barbara confronted me with staring gravity. She had not been with me at the hospital and had not realised how bad things were. 'Bill, you must leave tomorrow.'

'And go where?'

'Annie's friend will know. Rosemary, wasn't it?'

'Yes. Straven. Lady Douglas Straven. I suppose I could get in touch with her.'

'Of course. Phone her now.'

'Yes.' I wandered towards the telephone. 'But I don't know the number – or the address.'

Really, I did not want to do any of this. It all seemed to confirm that Annie must be dying. I stood, irresolute, in the middle of the room.

Barbara shouted at me. 'For Christ's sake, Bill, will you get a grip of yourself!'

'Maybe it's not really necessary.'

'How long will you wait to find out?'

She strode past me and I followed her to the study where all the books and papers were kept. I thought she intended to go through all the records and clippings for a clue. But she did something much simpler than that. She reached up to a shelf and pulled down a volume of Debrett. Then she left me to get on with it.

Annie's daughter was now fifty-three. She had not married and lived alone in a small but expensive house in Flask Walk, Hampstead. During my long telephone conversation with Lady Straven, I also learned that there would be no point in phoning there. Annie's old friend was sure Gertrude would refuse to go to Scotland. Indeed, she seemed anxious that I should not pursue the daughter at all. But she herself intended to drive up from Cumberland the next day. Probably she had arrived in Glasgow by the time my flight landed at Heathrow.

In the taxi moving towards the city I rehearsed the plea that I would make on Annie's behalf. For I intended to confront Gerda – or Miss Gertrude Straven as she'd resolutely chosen to be known – and insist that she visit her mother. Nor would I give her any warning of my arrival. Lady Straven's efforts to dissuade me made that seem the wisest course.

It had been strange, listening to that bright, optimistic voice on the telephone. I'd kept wanting to call her Rosemary. And probably she would not have minded. Then I checked myself and remembered that although this might sound like a young woman – and exist in my mind as a girl – she, too, must be at least eighty.

Such a confused perception of time was partly responsible for my uncertainty when I reached the house in Flask Walk. Although I knew for a fact that I was going to meet a middle-aged woman, I could not wholly free myself of the illusion that I'd come to convince an errant child: the little girl on the carousel at Essen who'd been whisked away.

I found Flask Walk to be a short and quite narrow cloister, reserved for pedestrians. The paving sloped from the house fronts towards the centre where there was a shallow gutter for drainage. Somewhat apprehensively, I rang the bell at the address I'd been given.

Gertrude Straven was a tall, thin woman. (Was Frederik *tall*? I wondered. Had Annie told me that?) She had clear blue eyes and her hair was beautifully set.

'Good morning.' I cleared my throat. 'Miss Straven?'

'Yes?'

'My name is Thompson. Lady Straven suggested that I should come to see you.'

'Ah!' She smiled. 'What is it you want to see me about, Mr Thompson?'

'About a personal matter.'

The smile waned a little. She was not hostile, she was just puzzled. 'Oh? Personal to you, or to me?'

'To you . . . and Lady Straven.' I was anxious to stress that I had sound credentials.

She opened the door wider. 'Do come in.'

That surprised me a little, but at once I realised she was not alone in the house. From a bedroom came the sound of a vacuum cleaner. Perhaps a daily-woman.

Miss Straven led me through to the back of the beautifully furnished house. She showed me into the sitting room. On the walls were several small oil paintings. All genuine, presumably. I had no great knowledge of paintings but clearly Miss Straven was a woman of taste.

She invited me to sit down, though she would remain standing until it seemed worth her while to do otherwise.

'Thank you.' I smiled for no good reason and wondered where it might be best to begin. 'The reason I've come is . . . I am a writer and recently I've been working on a book about Annie Jeynor.' From a quick glance upwards I noted that the smile had gone completely.

'Yes?' The voice gave nothing away.

'In fact I've been working with Miss Jeynor for a few months. My wife and I are living in the house.'

I wanted her to ask about her mother. To sit *down*. She did neither, and obliged me to continue. 'Unfortunately, Miss Jeynor recently caught a cold and now is seriously ill.'

'I'm sorry to hear that.' It was no more than a polite response. She would have said the same – and so would I – if told that a complete stranger was seriously ill.

I struggled on. 'The people at the hospital asked me if I would try to find the next of kin.'

'I see.' And now, to my great relief, she did sit down.

Her expression was calm and attentive. The striking blue eyes were alert and watchful. It occurred to me that Miss Straven was probably an excellent committee woman, if not a much admired chairperson. Now that I was facing her across the gleaming surface of the walnut coffee table I felt more competent myself. 'They are anxious that you should visit Miss Jeynor.'

'Surely not,' she said gently. 'It's unlikely the hospital staff has any opinion on which visitors their patient should see.'

'Of course, but . . .'

'And their interest in the next-of-kin would follow the death of the patient, surely?' She tilted her head a little to the side as though inviting me to correct a false impression. 'Perhaps you misunderstood them.'

259

Suddenly, and for no accountable reason, I began to feel frightened of this woman.

She went on. 'And in any case, I doubt if I am the next of kin.'

'You are her daughter.'

She nodded to accept that fact readily enough. 'I meant by legal definition. As you will know, I was adopted by Lady Straven.'

I shrugged, quite at a loss to know how I'd ever manage to state the real reason for my visit.

She prompted. 'You said Lady Straven suggested you come to see me.'

'Yes.' My voice faltered. 'I mean . . . I did say that. But she didn't, in fact.'

'Then would you tell me why you have come here, Mr Thompson?'

'To ask you if you would visit your mother.'

'Did she say she wants to see me?'

'No. She's not able to . . .'

'But you decided to do so?' At that point, whoever had been cleaning upstairs came downstairs and moved, unseen, into the kitchen. 'Excuse me,' said Miss Straven. She got up and left the room, presumably to give further instructions.

To be honest, I felt like bolting out of that house without another word. It was not that I could detect any bitterness in the woman's manner. Her tone of voice was cultured and even. Her questions, though pointed, were apt and polite. But altogether what was conveyed was a total estrangement. There was no chance whatever that I would persuade her to travel immediately to Scotland.

It was only when I'd reached that conclusion there occurred to me another use for my uneasy predicament. If I could shake off the burden of supplicant and become an inquirer, the interview could be put to useful account. That made me feel a lot happier. When Miss Straven returned it was to a different person. And her first question seemed to point in the right direction.

She observed, 'So, you are a writer, Mr Thompson.'

'Yes. And my wife is an actress. Her name is Barbara Cree.'

'Oh! I've seen Barbara Cree. A fine actress. I didn't know she worked in Scotland.'

'Normally, she doesn't.'

'Quite!' said Miss Straven.

'As I say, I've been writing the story of Miss Jeynor's life. A fascinating life. Of course, I'm doing it from only one point of view.'

'Is that wise?'

'Perhaps not. But I have no option.' She did not rise to the bait. 'The German period in particular is very interesting.' I could tell from her expression she knew exactly what I was trying to do. 'Of course the subject is not always as co-operative as one could wish. And now, of course, Miss Jeynor is very ill.'

She nodded sympathetically. 'Is the book nearly finished?'

'We've got as far as her time in Hollywood.'

'Ah! That's when my father heard the news.'

I'd got so used to her stonewalling that I almost missed the opportunity. 'What news?'

'The news that I was in England.' She leaned back in the chair. The point could be pursued. Perhaps she had an ulterior purpose of her own. 'The information about my abduction was published in the American papers, and all the enemy newspapers were monitored in Germany.'

'Yes. I suppose so.'

'So my family found out where I was.'

There were two expressions in close succession here which struck me as odd. She called them 'the enemy' newspapers and she referred to the Krupps (presumably) as 'my family'. Somehow that did not tie in with her hatred of the Nazis and her hatred of her mother for allying her with von Bohlen. I asked, 'Did your family do anything about that?'

'There was nothing they *could* do . . . during the war.'

An unlikely possibility presented itself. 'Did they try to contact you after the war?'

She gave me a rather surprised look. 'Oh, yes! After the war everything had changed. And of course the Krupps had their fortune restored to them. My uncle was in charge then. Alfried. He restarted the business.'

'And he contacted you.'

'Not me. I was still at school. They tried to reach an agreement with Lady Straven. She would have nothing to do with them.'

'That seems reasonable.'

'Most *un*reasonable,' said Miss Straven. 'Very foolish, in fact.' She sat a little straighter. 'So, when I was old enough to decide, I took up the offer.'

'What offer?'

'The offer of financial support. It seemed quite proper that if the family lost nothing by the war, I shouldn't either.'

'But I understood you hated the Germans.'

'I did when I was young. We all did. However, one can't live very comfortably on hatred.'

That was true. And indeed it did seem entirely proper that private morality should not lag behind state morality. After the war, the victorious powers had agreed that the Krupp empire should be broken up and the family's personal fortune confiscated. Such righteousness proved a luxury. For the company which had worked thousands in slave labour during the conflict was attractively able to employ other thousands on good wages when the conflict was done. The rehabilitation programme required an early change of mind. The Krupp family was handed back its millions.

And the daughter of Frederik von Bohlen got her share. I asked her, 'Did you go back to Germany?'

'Oh, yes. Exchange controls were very difficult after the war. The financial arrangements had to be made in Germany. And, of course, Lady Straven could not see that I was doing the right thing.'

'You mean, she threw you out?'

Miss Straven smiled at the crudeness of this description but, with a shrug, conceded it was true.

'When did you go back to Germany?'

'When they released Uncle Alfried from Landsberg prison. That was in 1951. In fact I lived in Munich throughout the fifties.'

'I wonder why you came back here.'

'Yes,' she said. 'Perhaps it was because I have a certain

262

position in England which I could not have in Germany.' She made an airy gesture. 'Due to my connections with the Duncryne family.'

Against my inclination I had to marvel at the woman. Here was a perfect example of having your cake and eating it. Well sustained by Krupp money she was better able to enjoy English society as the Honorable Gertrude Straven.

But if the Krupps could be forgiven, surely her natural mother was due some kind of amnesty. I asked, 'Why have you avoided seeing your mother?'

'There has been no reason why I should see her. In person, that is. I've enjoyed her films.'

'That's hardly the same thing.'

'Indeed. It is because it's an entirely *different* thing that I've been able to enjoy them.'

'Miss Straven, I . . .'

She raised an admonitory finger. 'Exactly. Not Frl von Bohlen. Nor is she now Frau von Bohlen. I was adopted and, as I understand it, there should be no contact with the natural mother.'

'But I would have thought you'd have some pride in being the daughter of Annie Jeynor.'

'Perhaps I would have – if I'd ever planned to go on the stage.' She smiled. 'You do see, don't you, that we have no common ground. I do not know Miss Jeynor. I can't remember her at all clearly.' She spread her hands resignedly. 'If we met again, what could be gained by either of us?'

I had to agree that she was probably right.

When I returned to Dumbarton there was heartening news. Annie seemed to be making some progress. In fact she had asked to see us. I telephoned the hospital to say we'd be there in the late afternoon. Barbara, on her way to the theatre, drove me up. And I was very glad to have her by my side, for Annie staged a little charade for our benefit which in itself convinced me she was on the mend.

When we were shown into the room the patient seemed to be unconscious or asleep. But she must have known we were

263

there for she performed an elaborate back-from-the-dead waking to reality. Her eyes opened, her head turned from side to side in bewilderment. She looked first at Barbara then at me. Apparently she was making great effort to say something. We concentrated avidly on her pale lips. Then the appropriate words formed. 'What country, friends, is this?'

I felt a surge of joy expand in my chest. The line seemed so apt, touching and characteristic.

Barbara smiled and gave the correct response. 'This is Illyria, lady.'

But although there were good indications of Annie's recovery it plainly would be some time before we'd be able to resume our routine for work on the book. Since both Barbara and I had to be back in London by the middle of April there was a danger that if I waited until Annie was well enough, there would not be enough time to finish the book. I thought it best, therefore, to go ahead with the section on Ben Tierney without her direct help. It was an episode which was particularly well documented by private papers and other publications, as well as press clippings. The story was quite clear.

With Deely Connor's help, the correction which the studio put out was widely accepted. Not only was Miss Jeynor cleared, she was triumphantly re-established as a favourite. However, the crucial relationships which had led to the crisis were not so easily dealt with. The movie fans were not bluffed in the way Zanuck hoped they would be. They saw Ben Tierney sitting there holding hands in Annie's house and knew perfectly well that his wife had behaved as she did because he'd deserted his home and family. It would not do.

Slowly at first, but steadily, attendances dropped for Ben Tierney movies. The distributors began complaining that they'd accepted bookings for a product they now could not sell. The fan magazines, led by a lethally destructive piece by Hedda Hopper, started baying for his blood. That drove Louella Parsons to join the assault, though she was careful to absolve Annie from any blame. The studio had to face the fact that Tierney had developed into a liability. The first thing they did was separate the bad apple from further contact with the good. They loaned Ben to the Canadian government for a 'good neighbours' propaganda piece being shot along the 49th parallel. Since it was taxpayers' money being used, the project was likely to last a long time.

Annie, meanwhile, made three feature films during 1942 – in one of them, the highly successful musical *Step Lightly*, she recreated her own past as a Cochran young lady. Her fans who'd thought of her as a woman of drama were thrilled by the 'new' singing and dancing Annie Jeynor. In a fan magazine interview she drily observed that she'd been nursing these 'new' talents for twenty years.

While Ben was in Canada, his wife filed for divorce. Naturally, she got custody of the children. When the judge came to decide what access should be afforded the father, all he had to go on was the pattern of the previous twelve months. That showed only one visit and did not show the physical impossibility of Ben getting to see his sons more often. The great distance and a demanding work schedule were not considered in mitigation. He wrote to Annie that he thought he would go crazy if he was allowed to see his boys only twice a year. He also mentioned the exorbitant sum of support and maintenance which Gerry had managed to have imposed on him.

Sheer distance seemed to play an important role in all the changes which took place. The three members of the triangle were literally at the furthest points which could be achieved in the geography of the United States. Gerry was now furthest east in New York. Ben was furthest west in Seattle. Annie was away to the south in Los Angeles. Of the three, it was undoubtedly Ben who was the real casualty. Annie's career was still on the crest of the wave while his was draining down the plug-hole. Heartsick and lonely, he'd taken to heavy drinking – though that was not at once apparent when, eventually, he got back to the studio.

But once again Annie came to his rescue. She was now in a position to choose her next vehicle and, to a large extent, her co-star. These factors, together with the knowledge that Somerset Maugham had recently surfaced in Hollywood to discuss screen adaptations of his stories, led her to devise a salvage package.

First she let Darryl Zanuck know of her previous association with Maugham. Perhaps he would write a screenplay for her. Zanuck said, 'If you can get him to do that we'll buy it.' By this time Maugham was already back on his American publisher's estate. She wrote to him and he replied saying how delighted he would be to see her. The story she had in mind was a short piece called *Louise*. The woman's role was one no other Hollywood leading lady would look at because it was so unsympathetic. But the leading-man part could be developed as a lifesaver for Ben. It was with this in mind that they set out together for a short break in South Carolina.

Maugham already had two celebrated houseguests staying at Yemassee, both highly-regarded as screenwriters. They were Dorothy Parker, whom Annie knew quite well, and Christopher Isherwood. Really the prospects couldn't have been brighter as Annie and Ben put up in an hotel in nearby Beaufort. They hired a car to take them back and forward to the house which had been specially built for Maugham by Doubleday.

According to reports by both Parker and Isherwood which were later published, 'the actress and her boyfriend' provided a welcome highlight on that week-end. Indeed, for Dorothy Parker is was the highlight of the whole three weeks she'd already spent in Yemassee. Here at last was a man who really liked women. What did it matter, in her opinion, if he was a lush? That was something she knew all about. She was less happy about homosexuals. But Isherwood, too, was impressed by Ben and found him 'a thoroughly agreeable big bear'. He certainly was the biggest member of the party. Maugham and Isherwood were both short, Annie and Parker were both petite. In the photograph taken in front of the loggia Ben looms over them, grinning like a benign giant.

Annie knew that Willie Maugham must already suspect that this visit had an ulterior purpose. It was something he suspected even when there wasn't one. So after dinner she came right to the point. The other guests were astonished that an actress should want to play the character Louise – a woman who wears out her husband by carefully staged little illnesses. She goes on to ruin her daughter's life with the same strategy. Nobody is allowed to walk out on Louise because she convinces them it would kill her. The husband, Tom, is an amiable sportsman whose strength and fitness are worn away by his love for Louise, and the constant attention she demands.

Maugham could see that it was a good part and, glancing across at Ben, he could also see why Annie wanted to play it. He prevailed on Miss Parker to consider the possibilities for comedy that were offered. She said she must read the story again. Annie immediately lent her the copy which she'd brought along. Next day the project got off to a good start. But not before Miss Parker got off to an even better start with Ben. It was agreed that *Louise* would be offered to Twentieth Century-Fox.

When that was settled, Isherwood and Annie took a walk together in the pine wood behind the house. Naturally, they talked about Berlin. But their memories of it were widely at variance. He had lived down in the slums of Wassertorstrasse, while she had been in the high town. This seemed to divide the weather just as effectively. For his memory insisted on almost constant rain sluicing down Kurfürstendamm while she recalled nude sunbathing on the shores of the Wannsee. They did agree, though, on the feeling of excitement and danger the Nazis brought to the city.

In a letter to a friend in London, Isherwood gave a very clear impression of what Annie Jeynor was like at the time he met her. He was struck by the beautiful control of her movement and impressed by her good humour. Lurking behind the charm, though, he detected great shrewdness and commented, 'That's what Willie Maugham likes about her. He thinks she is a calculating hussy. I think she's just been disappointed too often to take anyone at face value.'

Annie waited until Zanuck had bought the rights before she told him that for the part of the trusting, amiable husband she wanted Ben Tierney. This, she insisted, was not just her own judgment. Mr Maugham and Dorothy Parker had both voted him best choice for the part. She expected a battle but there was only token resistance. Zanuck was already angling to buy the screen rights to *The Razor's Edge* and had no wish to thwart the author.

It was when *Louise* went into production that the trouble started. Ben desperately wanted to see his children but it would be months before that was allowed. He was also aware that, as far as his career was concerned, this was definitely the last chance. His drinking was out of hand, and the whole situation was fraught with tension which made him difficult to work with. Annie persevered, but she had her own standards of excellence to maintain and could not always conceal from Ben that he was fouling things up.

Hedda Hopper had a scoop when she was able to report that trouble on the *Louise* set came to blows. Apparently, Miss Jeynor kept insisting on more takes of the scene she was playing with Ben Tierney. This was after the director had declared himself satisfied. The actor lost his temper and slapped the star on the face. She staggered but didn't fall. Then she slapped him right back. After a short cooling-off period, the actor apologised. Miss Jeynor accepted the apology – but still insisted on seven more takes.

Ben knew only too well that he was the cause of all the trouble on the film. He felt terribly guilty about placing Annie in such a mess. But his self-recrimination did nothing to ease the great despair which overwhelmed him. He drowned that in booze and it took an awful lot to dull his pain. That meant he had to get away from Annie's constant watching. He moved out of her house, promising to attend an alcoholics clinic. But really he moved into an hotel.

Soon he wasn't turning up for work at all. The schedule had to be re-drawn, and a lot of money was being lost. It couldn't be tolerated. When Zanuck threatened to cancel the whole production, Ben managed to stagger up to the office and plead that his part should be given to another actor. That meant re-shooting whatever work Ben had already done. And it meant Ben was finished.

With the idea of demanding to see his children, he got on a train heading for New York. But he never arrived. During the night he either jumped or fell from the observation platform onto the tracks. It was a day or two before his body was found. With his jacket caught in the hinge of the tailgate, he had been dragged a long way behind the train before the material finally tore free.

This was in October 1943. When they told Annie the news, she was already in a vulnerable state. In the cruel way that circumstance manages such things, she had just learned by letter from Rosemary that Frederik von Bohlen was listed among those lost at the siege of Stalingrad which had ended in February. Annie did not at first concern herself over when or how Rosemary came by the information. Probably she never learned that the Krupp family already knew where Gerda was. The message was passed by the Red Cross to Lady Straven.

Annie replied to Rosemary, 'It might have made a difference, if I had known Frederik was dead all that summer. There was nothing I could do for him. But his death meant I was free to marry Ben. Maybe if we'd been married I could have saved him. And if we were married perhaps his boys could have spent some time with us that summer. I think that really would have made a difference.'

SIR AUSTEN FRYSOR, BART

Like most people, Annie held politicians in amused contempt. She just could not see how it is possible to admire individuals whose only qualification for public office was that they'd signally failed at something else. Failed lawyers, mainly. But an alarming number of failed accountants as well. In fact, the dregs of all professions seemed to end up at Westminster. And whereas the best families had once sent the fool into the church, that was no longer an attractive solution. The church had lost even more credibility than public service. So it was up to the fool to get elected instead. There were always thousands of voters with severely damaged memory banks who would oblige.

It was in this frame of mind that Annie accepted the invitation to a dinner party at Betsy Carswell's London house in 1954, and it was there she met Austen Frysor, among several other political zombies, in company with a few puzzled artists. For Betsy saw herself as a latter-day Emerald Cunard, drawing together the talented and the powerful with those protégés who looked good bets in both these races. It had not occurred to her (though it certainly occurred to Annie) that these two groups were mutually exclusive. People with real talent have no urge to achieve power. However, they do need work. Politicians, on the other hand, need publicity more than anything else.

At the dinner party – not far from Lady Cunard's old house in Grosvenor Square – Austen Frysor did not make a sparkling impression on the actress. He was then fifty-eight and had been a widower for three years. His wife had died just a few months before the 1951 election in which he'd lost his seat. He'd been a junior minister in the Foreign Office, and now all his energy was devoted to getting back into parliament. He was a tall, elegant man, very much influenced by the notion that he resembled his ex-chief, Anthony Eden. And it was on Eden he pinned his hopes. Churchill was far too ill to continue as Prime Minister much longer. Informed opinion was that he'd step down in favour of his Foreign Secretary. It would be Eden, therefore, who would start the run-up to the next election. There was quite a lot of talk about that at Betsy's table.

The hostess asked Austen, 'Do you think Anthony is up to the job? He has such a foul temper.'

'I have always found him very wise and calm,' said Austen loyally. 'And I cannot think of anyone better suited to lead the country.'

'A foul temper is more interesting, though,' Annie said.

Austen smiled condescendingly. 'Why is that?'

'It gives the illusion of humanity. That and his hair.'

The ex-Minister involuntarily touched his own hair which was groomed in the same fashion of careful carelessness as his hero. There was laughter round the table and Austen felt a little uneasy. 'Miss Jeynor, I think you've been unduly influenced by the American cult of personality. That's not what matters in England.'

'Really? What *does* matter in England?'

'Why . . . serving the country with sound policies. Personalities are not important.'

'Ah! So, you wouldn't mind doing it anonymously.'

Austen felt there might be some danger here and parried. 'I'm not sure I follow that.'

'Well . . . if personality doesn't matter, you'd be quite happy to serve your country anonymously.'

'Yes, of course,' he lied.

'And if Anthony Eden already has sound policies – he doesn't need you to chip in, or to carry them out. Does he?' Annie smiled.

'No. He doesn't need me, in particular.'

'So there's no good reason why you, in particular, should get into parliament again, is there?'

Austen gave a hearty laugh. 'Oh, I think I could make a valuable contribution.'

'A *personal* contribution?'

There was more laughter as Austen fell into the trap. But the hostess thought he'd been baited enough, for the moment. She turned the conversation to what was uppermost in her own mind – the proposed desecration of Grosvenor Square. She reported that the whole west side was going to be rebuilt, to house the new American embassy.

'The Grosvenors must be mad,' one of the guests said.

Betsy agreed. 'Quite mad. I've seen some of the drawings.'

'Is it to be a sky-scraper?'

'No, darling. More a penitentiary. And that was the *artistic* impression! Can you imagine what the real thing will be like?'

They all sympathised with Betsy, and nobody pointed out that she'd been an American herself at birth, and for a good number of years thereafter.

With three of four theatrical guests, talk veered to stage topics. The best new play of the year, they agreed, was Ludovic Kennedy's *Murder Story* at the Cambridge. But best performance of the year was likely to be Peggy Ashcroft as *Hedda Gabler*. Annie had been out to the Lyric at Hammersmith for the opening and was entranced. There would never be a better Hedda than Peggy's, as far as she was concerned. Rachel Kempson, too, was excellent – and a great improvement in the part Emmy Sonnemann had played.

There was a lot of praise for Ruth Draper who'd been at St Martin's earlier in the year. It was this particular edition of the celebrated one-woman show, in which the American actress toured the world, which tempted Annie to the same enterprise some years later.

For the present, though, there seemed little hope. Annie had been back in England for three years and the work wasn't coming. There had been a film for J. Arthur Rank. That was what brought her back. Then there was a West End revival of *The School For Scandal* – opposite Ralph Richardson. That had been an unhappy experience. Richardson preferred his leading ladies sweet, docile and *well* downstage of him. Even before the first night, all they were saying to each other were the lines they were obliged to speak on the stage. Of course, it's the

273

man's play, so perhaps he had every right to behave like an under-rehearsed and erratic god. 'The hell of it is,' Annie remarked, 'every play being done in London seems to be the man's play.'

The Canadian revue star, Beatrice Lillie, was another of Betsy's guests. 'Sweetheart,' she privately advised Annie, 'what you need is a work permit.' Her eyes goggled to signal taking this ludicrous suggestion to greater length. 'Like a title, or the DBE. That's the only way I could get by in London,' said Lady Peel. She was over from New York preparing for her show *An Evening With Beatrice Lillie*.

Annie said, 'I haven't a hope in hell of getting a DBE.'

'Then marry a title.'

Annie laughed. 'That's quite a sacrifice, just to get work.' But the idea was planted, and had a great deal to do with Annie's further involvement with Sir Austen Frysor and the scandal at the Dorchester.

'Surely you could get work?' I suggested to Annie. She had been released from hospital and sent home to convalesce in Dumbarton. We were back in the huge reception room where she really did feel most comfortable. Barbara had thought of a reason for that. The floor space was the same as that of a good-sized stage. Being used to 'room' sets which stretched the whole breadth of the proscenium, Annie could not really feel at ease in ordinary 'room-sized' rooms.

Six weeks had passed since my overnight visit to London. Annie did not know I'd been to see her daughter. In fact, she had no clear recollection of Rosemary's calling at the hospital, either. The immediate past seemed much more remote than events of thirty years earlier. So I taxed her on the assertion that she could not get work in London of the 1950s.

She sighed. 'Bill, I have explained this to you before.'

'Please explain it again.'

'Well . . . there was I, a famous Hollywood film star. Also, a stage actress of some European repute. When I say I couldn't get work, I mean I couldn't get the *sort* of work which was appropriate. That is leading roles in well-mounted productions.

274

God knows, I could have had scores of character parts, cameos or even straight supporting roles as somebody's mother.'

'What's wrong with that?'

'Nothing. If you are going *up*. Remember I told you? It's like a moving stairway. The part doesn't matter – if you are going in the right direction. For me, appearing in those parts would have looked as though I was tumbling down a rising escalator. My reputation . . .' She raised a cautionary finger and gave me a faint smile, '. . . my *artistic* reputation would be shot to hell. My moral reputation never did hold much water – but that doesn't matter in the theatre if you are very good where it counts.'

'I'm sure you would have been marvellous, even in supporting parts.'

'Bill, there is no point in being marvellous if you are on your way *out*. The wrong kind of work is worse than no work at all. During that spell when I did nothing, everyone assumed I was turning down trunkloads of star material.' Her eyes crinkled with recalled mischief. 'I even sent scripts to myself at the Dorchester.'

I laughed. 'Who did you send them *back* to?'

'No need. Actors never return scripts. I also invited various producers and directors to drop in for tea. That sort of thing gets around. The people I did not invite could assume I was being pestered with offers.'

'And all of this made it more likely that whatever was offered to you would be star material?'

'Exactly.' She snuggled down into the chair and tucked the car rug more securely around her. 'There would be no lost ground to make up.'

Her saying that struck me as odd, because now she was not making up the ground she'd lost during her illness. I wondered if she ever would. When I went to Glasgow to collect her, the doctor warned me, 'Don't expect her to get back to the same level as she was before. A person of that age never does, no matter how fit they were to start with.' So maybe, at last, Annie Jeynor had started the descent which she'd tricked fate to avoid so many times in the past. And she still thought she could do it.

It was then the idea occurred to me that perhaps she intended this book as her last starring role. And as Barbara had recently pointed out to me, she'd chosen her stage, author and supporting cast with some care.

My reflection was interrupted by the leading lady. 'Austen,' she said. 'He wasn't responsible, you know?'

'Responsible for what?'

'For being such a . . . clown!' She sat up a bit straighter and reached for her glass of neat whisky. 'He was brought up, and trained, and educated to be exactly what he was. By the time he'd got through all that, *and* a marriage of convenience, there was practically nothing of him*self* left.'

'I'm not sure I understand that.'

She chuckled. 'That doesn't surprise me. You probably came through the same system.'

'Yes. I did. But I rebelled against it.'

'Good for you! Austen never realised he was a zombie.'

'Perhaps because the English political zombies enjoy such a pleasant life.'

'And so they *should*,' Annie said firmly. 'God knows, there's nothing *else* they can do.'

It was in this vein she told me about her venture into politics. Frequently, I tried to get her to deal with the episode in a sober manner. She tried, but she couldn't keep it up. Her second marriage was just ridiculous. And it reached a breaking point in the downright farce of Eden's Suez adventure.

After their first meeting it seemed unlikely that Sir Austen Frysor and Annie would meet again. She made him feel uncomfortable and he made her feel sorry for him. In fact she regretted having exposed the fatuity of his argument. It really was not fair to treat politicians like grown-up, responsible people. But however incompatible they might have seemed – and, in fact, were – each had something the other thought very useful. He had the title. She had the popular appeal.

Although she couldn't get the right sort of work in the London theatre, Annie had millions of film-fans all over the country. Even the propaganda pap she'd made for Twentieth Century-Fox

276

had been popular in Britain, and the good films had won her the admiration of a large part of the female population. She was a Hollywood film star, and in Britain of the 1950s that was a rare and magical thing to be.

Even so, nothing would have come of it without the stories in the American press. Professor Ira Dilke, an historian at Johns Hopkins University in Baltimore, had been wading through Nazi archives for years. Now he published his findings in a book, *Totenkopf*, which dealt with Gestapo enforcement of the German security services before and during the war. Amid much else, he'd discovered the records pertaining to Frau von Bohlen, whose code name was Cesario. She was, he claimed, an English-born agent who worked for Goebbels' ministry. In the tradition of academic research he assumed that the limit of his available material was the limit of all knowledge. Quaintly, he wrote, 'Evidently Frau von Bohlen (Cesario) posed as an actress in her missions between Germany and the United Kingdom.'

He further traced this obscure lady's file and discovered – as the Nazis had discovered – that Cesario was a double agent. The Gestapo had picked up a lead from an MI9 agent who'd been captured in the Harz mountains. Then there were details of a case being built up against her with examples of the misinformation she'd persuaded German Intelligence to accept as true. Finally, there was an order to arrest Frau von Bohlen – but she had somehow escaped from Perpignan on the Mediterranean coast.

It was the popular press which gleefully seized on these nuggets. They informed Professor Dilke, and reminded their readers, of the sensation about ten years earlier when it was discovered that Annie Jeynor was Frau von Bohlen. Also, the woman who 'posed as an actress' had quite a bit going for her in that direction. They referred the professor to such august journals as *Screen, Photoplay* and the *Los Angeles Examiner*, not to mention the Academy Award nominations for best actress in 1944 and 1946.

None of this information was published in England. But the people who mattered knew about it. Sir Austen heard the subject discussed at his club. Of course it was not a focus of attention in Whitehall, but the tag 'unsung heroine' had become discreetly attached to the actress. And a remarkable gaffe by Churchill's son-in-law was recalled. Sarah Churchill had married the entertainer, Vic Oliver. He'd faced some press carping about his lightweight contribution to the war effort. Anxious to point out that many theatre people had used their peculiar status to the nation's advantage, he gave examples – 'Like Noël in Paris, and Annie in Berlin.' He wouldn't say more than that. The 'Noël' could only be Noël Coward, but now it was known which 'Annie' he'd meant.

So Austen's perception of the actress changed. Once he'd had it confirmed she was the sort of woman one wanted to know, he was astonished to discover how popular she was with the ordinary people. Pretty soon he felt free to mention that he'd met Miss Jeynor; then that they had mutual acquaintances; finally, that she was a close friend. By that time Annie had begun to fit an already established priority. Central Office had as much as demanded that he remarry if he expected to be nominated for a remotely winnable seat.

Meanwhile, Annie's grasp on a long-held dream was loosened. It had been her hope when she returned to England that she would somehow meet Rolf Templar again. There seemed no way in which she could contact him, but she felt sure the publicity surrounding her arrival and subsequent work would give him the opportunity to get in touch with her. Assuming, of course, that he had managed to get home. And that he still wanted to see her.

The hope had faded quite a bit in those three years. There had been no message from Rolf, and now she knew why. It was really the only fact she saw in the cuttings which were sent to her from America. Professor Dilke's research had mentioned that the Gestapo reported the capture of an MI9 agent in the Harz mountains. She wrote to the professor asking if there was any further information about that agent.

After several weeks' delay she received confirmation of what she'd feared. Rolf Templar was the agent who'd been captured. He had been taken to Nordhausen and identified there as former cultural attaché at the British embassy in Berlin. From Nordhausen he was taken north to the capital. It seemed he held out against interrogation for some time but finally his name was linked to that of Frau von Bohlen. There was also, the professor informed her, clear reference to a warehouse by the Landwehr-kanal. Did she know anything about that?

Annie knew all about that, and remembered it with a kind of guilty joy. It was possible, she told herself, she'd left some incriminating evidence of her frequent visits there. But from what the American professor had discovered, there was no proof that Rolf had been tortured into betraying her.

And if there was proof, she did not want to hear it. Even the inconclusive report sharply increased her feelings of loneliness. She was determined that no man would ever matter as much to her again. There had been too much loss. From now on, she decided, the only safe way was to play it for laughs.

Austen Frysor gave her the perfect opportunity to test this resolution. For, at his behest, she was asked to dine by a woman she hardly knew. The hostess mentioned several of the guests who wanted to meet the actress, adding, 'And Austen, of course. He asked me to promise you he has quite reformed.'

Annie smiled. 'He has left it late.'

'Never *too* late,' the woman confided. 'Poor man. He's been quite lost since Mary died. Did you know Mary?'

'No,' Annie said, and thought of adding that she didn't know Austen either. 'Are there any children?'

'Alas, no. That would have been some comfort.'

'Perhaps.'

'Oh, surely!' The woman seemed put out that Annie had not made the proper response to the cue.

'It depends on what sort of persons the children are,' Annie said. She was thinking about Gerda and about the curious change which had occurred in her own relationship with Rosemary. That had been another hope which had lighted her return to England. But Rosemary had been evasive and curiously unenthusiastic in greeting her old friend. She seemed determined that Annie should not see Gerda, or Gertrude, and gave the excuse that the girl was away on an extended tour of Europe.

The dinner party was a great success, but only because Annie

279

behaved herself. That is, she did not behave *as* herself. She behaved in the manner which she privately thought hilarious but which had served Greer Garson so well in *Mrs Miniver*. To it she added the well-drilled humility of Anna Neagle's heroine roles. This combination of good breeding, gallantry and womanly virtue quite enchanted Austen Frysor. Himself a consummate hypocrite, he was a connoisseur of the quality in others. And there were plenty of others who had it.

Suddenly Annie had a rapidly expanding circle of friends. The trick was absurdly simple and she cursed herself for not having used it before. The trick was to pretend. To pretend that London was the centre of the civilised world; to pretend she liked people she couldn't stand; to pretend she was amused by jokes which weren't funny, and spellbound by bores; to pretend that Britain was a democracy; that there really was no class system any more; that opera was a serious art form; that it mattered a damn where she bought her clothes; that she was even remotely interested in who was sleeping with whom (if she wasn't one of them) and that she was falling in love with Austen Frysor.

This last was the easiest to manage because he himself thought it so likely. Many quiet little meetings were arranged as that autumn slipped into winter. Then he suggested they might hop over to Davos together for a week, but Annie couldn't ski (though she pretended she could) and opted instead for the sun on the Caribbean, where, she understood, Austen had business interests in any case.

'Bauxite,' he said.

'I beg your pardon?'

'It's aluminium ore. That's what we mine in Jamaica.'

'Would you mind awfully if we went there instead?' Annie asked. She'd altered her speech pattern to suit her new persona.

'You don't want to watch them actually *digging* for it, do you?'

'My dear, not in the least. It's just that I thought you might have a little place out there where we could stay.'

'I have a residence there. One of the legal requirements, you see. But I've let that.'

Annie nodded sympathetically. 'Yes, naturally.' She sighed. 'I do so love the Caribbean.'

He leaned closer and said in a mock whisper, 'There's the Cayman Islands, of course.'

'I've never been there.'

'No. Somewhat off the beaten track as far as our friends are concerned.' He smiled. 'Maybe just the place, in the circumstances.'

Annie said nothing and tried her hardest to look demure. But she really did want to have a holiday in the sun. Her years in California had quite spoiled her for the English climate. And besides, if she was going to make a fool of herself with Austen Frysor she wanted the location for his seduction to be well away from any theatre folk.

In the 1950s the Cayman Islands were not yet a tax haven. However, they were already barren reefs. Annie and Austen flew first to Jamaica, then took the small island-hopper to Georgetown. As the plane circled above the landing strip, the island looked so bare it did not seem possible that anyone could live there. But the sun was shining and the sea glittered in wide bands of green and blue.

At ground level things seemed better. There were people and they looked happy. There was, too, a very relaxed, lazy attitude which disarmed criticism. The hotel was a ramshackle structure in flaking white paint. In the tiled lobby the dusty air was slowly agitated by a huge rotating punka. Everyone seemed to be dressed in worn pyjamas. The bedroom was dominated by a huge brass bedstead. Annie wondered if she'd be able to resist the urge to black up and sprawl around like Tondelaya in *White Cargo*.

But really the holiday turned out to be very pleasant indeed. Austen was charming and attentive. Against her better judgment, Annie found herself liking him. And that was just as well because, at the end of the first week, he proposed to her. He chose to do so just before dinner. The dining room of the hotel was at its best in candlelight and there were only two other couples isolated in remote corners of the room.

Having ordered and watched the waiter vanish into shadows from which he might never return, there followed a long stretch of desultory chit-chat about the condition of the water that day, and the sand, and the heat. Then Austen felt he must make sure of his ground. 'Annie, you are having a good time, aren't you?'

'Oh, yes. It's very restful.'

'And we do get on together quite well, don't we?' He was not a man to claim more than the minimum where women were concerned.

'Of course we do.' She touched his hand. 'You've been very sweet.'

In Austen's language that meant he was satisfactory as a lover. 'Thank you.'

Annie smiled encouragingly. 'Why do you ask?'

'Well . . . er . . . I've been thinking we might make a go of it.'

The actress simulated the pleased surprise that was expected of her. Then, after a pause, 'My dear, I'm not at all sure I'd fit in.'

'Nonsense! Of course you would.'

The exchange was taking on a kind of ritual unreality. Annie had to concentrate quite hard to make sure she delivered the predictable lines with just enough conviction. Too much conviction would have ruined everything. What it came down to was that this man was willling to do her a favour by marrying her. Thus the burden of proving that it would be a suitable match fell to the woman.

She summoned modest doubt. 'I'm afraid I wouldn't be terribly useful in your career.'

Since his career was the only area of his life where she *would* be terribly useful, Austen felt free to be definite. 'Oh, I suppose you'd soon get the hang of if,' he said. 'Do say you will.'

'Will what?'

'Marry me.'

Final pause, then, 'Yes, Austen. I'd be very, very happy to be your wife.'

Rather awkwardly, he got up, came round the table and kissed her. Then he resumed his seat. But there was nothing more to say and it would be ages before the waiter came back. He lit a cigarette.

As though to do no more than bridge the growing silence, Annie remarked, 'Do you suppose it will be all right if I still act occasionally?' She added quickly, 'In suitable material, of course.'

'In London, you mean?'

'Well, *yes*.'

'Because I don't know where I'll get a seat, you see.'

Annie waited for the point of this caveat to surface.

He went on, 'I'm sure you'll appreciate that it would be jolly awkward if you wanted to act with people in my constituency – wherever that might be.'

Her overall concentration wavered and focused only on the word 'jolly'. She wondered who taught people like him – and *only* people like him – to say 'jolly' in that context. No other group in the English-speaking world used 'jolly' in that way. Her mind siezed on this unique identifying mark and repeated it over and over.

But Austen interpreted her increasingly glazed look as a persisting urge to act with his future constituents. He tried to reason with her. 'You do see that, Annie. Spoil the image, you know.' He sighed. 'Awkward.'

'Oh, yes! Jolly awkward,' Annie said.

Then she went on to assure him that it would be only in prestige London theatres that she'd consent to act. And, further to safeguard his reputation, she mentioned, it might be a good thing if her own standing in the profession could be assured.

'How can that be done?' he asked.

She gave a self-deprecatory little laugh. 'Well, if I should ever merit such an honour, a DBE would transform my work into a public service.'

'Hmm,' he nodded. 'When is it due?'

'Austen, the theatre is not like Whitehall. You don't get an honour just because you've been there long enough.'

'Oh? Yes. Well . . . I'll look into it.'

At that point the waiter hove out of the shadows to announce that the dish they'd been awaiting for half an hour was, regrettably, off.

*   *   *

When they got back to London at the beginning of January, Austen was shaken by the privately circulated news that the Prime Minister was in a bad way. This indicated that there might be some urgency in settling his own marriage plans and prospects of selection. He immediately consulted the Chief Whip, Edward Heath, privately at his chambers in Albany. Heath said that Churchill seemed determined to hang on, though frequently comatose and in no condition to make lucid decisions.

There was better news, though, about possible opportunities for Austen. Two sitting members had given notice that they would not stand at the next election. The seats were Perth Central and Sibley. Austen asked how the majorities compared in the last poll. Heath told him that Perth was by far the safer seat.

Austen considered. 'It is in Scotland, of course.'

'Always has been,' Heath said.

'Is there any trouble in Scotland at the moment?'

'What sort of trouble?'

'Well . . . any home rule nonsense?'

'Not in Perthshire,' the Chief Whip assured him.

Of course, it could not be decided there and then that Sir Austen would be selected for the Perth Central constituency, but at least he knew where he should direct his energies. And first, he had to get married. His own Parish church was St Mary, Bryanston Square. But Annie was firmly against a church wedding. The reason she gave was that it surely would be 'rather vulgar' if Austen married her in the same church where he'd married his first wife. Austen saw at once that this was entirely valid and rather sweet. In fact, her real reason was that she could not provide the documents required by a church.

So they settled for a civil ceremony at Marylebone registry office. And, again at Annie's insistence, they kept it very quiet. She explained to her mature fiancé, 'Darling, I don't want you to be fussed by all the showbusiness nonsense my marriage is likely to attract from the press.' Austen was stunned by this affront to his most deeply held conviction. All his adult life had been dedicated to the view that personal publicity is the lifeblood of democracy. Annie could see she would have to invent a better reason.

'Besides,' she said, 'it would be a pity to give the wrong impression.'

'How do you mean?'

'Well, it would be such a shame if the public got the idea you were marrying again just to improve your chances of a safe seat.'

He was horrified. 'Good heavens! How could they possibly think that?'

Annie shook her head dolefully. 'The gutter press has a lurid imagination.'

Austen abandoned his principles at once. 'Very well. We'll keep it quiet.'

'In fact,' the actress said, 'it might be best to give the impression we've been married for some time.' She smiled. 'Which is true – in a way.'

He smiled approvingly. He was all for things that were true – in a way.

The question of where they should live was next on the agenda. Austen's first wife had been a rich woman (too) but he had sold her house in Eaton Place when he lost her. Then, when he lost his seat as well, he'd taken a small flat in Marylebone. He asked Annie if she'd ever thought of buying a house in London. She said no, she hadn't because London had never seemed a very permanent place to her.

'How about Perth, then?'

'Scotland or Australia?'

And now she learned for the first time that there was a good chance of his being Conservative (or Unionist) candidate for Perth Central. Annie's only recollection of the town was as a touring date for summer shows in the 'twenties. There had been no time then to explore the rich farming country of Tayside. She said, 'I know the west coast of Scotland much better.'

Austen's eyes gleamed. 'Really? And have you any Scottish connections at all?'

'Yes. I was born there.'

'My dear,' Austen gloated, 'why haven't you told me this before?'

'Because you never wanted to be a Scottish MP before.'

He ignored this. 'So it wouldn't seem at all strange if you bought a house on your native heath.'

Annie smiled with secret amusement and quoted, '"There's the wind on the heath, brother; if I could only feel that."'

He ignored this too. 'If the Chief Whip points me at Perth, you can be sure I'm the fellow they have in mind.'

'But Austen, I've just told you I'm from the west, near Glasgow.'

'All the more reason why you'd *want* to settle on Tayside. Besides, there are no winnable seats for us anywhere near Glasgow.'

That seemed a conclusive argument and Annie was persuaded to buy a house for them in the ancient Scottish capital. It was a rather square villa on the North Inch. The property had been on the market for a considerable time – and with good reason. Placed as it was, on the low, broad meadow of the river bank, the house was notoriously prone to flooding. The estate agent made no mention of this regular inconvenience. As soon as he received an enquiry he just sent a boy out with a bucket of whitewash to cover the most recent high water mark.

When they'd seen the house and Annie had decided to buy it, she made only one condition. It was agreed that if ever she was working in London she would stay at the Dorchester and not at Austen's pokey little flat in Salisbury Street.

All this was accomplished by the end of March 1955. By then, too, Austen had been assured that he was the chosen candidate as far as Central Office was concerned. But he persuaded the Party organisation to keep quiet about it until he had gained the approval of the constituency officials. For, as he told Annie, 'Things go much more smoothly if the locals think it was their own decision.'

But there really wasn't much time for Sir Austen and Lady Frysor to settle in. Early in April, Churchill at last stepped down. Eden became Prime Minister and, after a couple of weeks, announced that there would be a general election at the end of May. 'My dear,' Austen told his wife, 'you chose to put down your Scottish roots not a moment too soon.'

And so they were plunged immediately into an election campaign.

Annie wanted me to name the Labour candidate. Considering what happened later, that seemed unwise. 'He's still alive, you know.'

She was indignant. 'So am *I*!'

'But he might sue.'

'Let him. The publishers can stand a law suit. It will do their sales the world of good.'

'Not if they lose and the book has to be withdrawn.' I added: 'He would also be suing me.'

She struggled out of her chair, annoyed with me and angry that sudden movement was becoming so difficult for her. 'Damn, damn, damn.' Having fought her way out of the entangling rug, she threw it on the floor and kicked it out of her way. 'You're perfectly happy to name Austen, aren't you? But just because some mud might stick to a Labour man, you want him protected.' She made for the drinks cupboard under the window seat. 'God! You middle-class socialists give me the pip!'

I tried to reason with her. 'I name Austen because he was your second husband and the fact is fairly well known. Also, he is dead.'

She held up a bottle inviting me to have a drink. 'There are too few people in this book who are *not* dead. Has that thought occurred to you? Where's the proof that I was *ever* an attractive woman?' She slammed the bottle down on the window seat. 'I'd like some evidence from my last surviving lover – even if it *is* a law suit.'

I joined her at the window. 'But you are not the one he might sue.'

She shook her head. 'I don't think he would. In fact, he might be flattered.'

'I'm sure he would not be flattered.'

'Shall I call him and find out?'

'No, Annie!'

As she was now sitting at the window where the draught was keen, I fetched her rug and wrapped it round her. She watched with some amusement as I performed this service. 'Thank you, Bill.'

'It would be much better if we just gave him another name.'

'What name?'

'Anything you like.'

'How about Wilson?' she asked sweetly.

'No.'

'Foot?'

'No.'

'You said anything I like.'

'That was a mistake,' I conceded. 'Think of a suitable character in a play.'

This seemed to please her. She sipped her whisky. 'Well, at the time, he was about thirty-five and behaved like Hotspur in a cloth cap.'

I groaned. '"Hot spur". That's far too suggestive. And it's a nickname. What is Hotspur's real name?'

'Henry Percy.'

'Surely not?'

Annie nodded. 'Can you wonder he preferred a nickname?' I decided. 'We will call the Labour candidate Harry Bellamy. Is that all right?'

'As in "Bel ami"?'

'At the very least, I gather.'

'And young! He was twenty years younger. That's a great attraction in itself. But his main virtue was that he didn't take himself seriously.'

I asked her, 'What was your main virtue?'

She seemed to give it a lot of thought, then replied with endearing candour, 'Generosity.'

The first time Annie saw Harry Bellamy was at an open air meeting. She saw him from the window of her sitting room. For it was another hazard of the house in Perth that the flat ground it overlooked was also common ground and the traditional gathering place for public harangues. Naturally, in the run-up to an election, the religious freaks and other fanatics were replaced by political shysters. It was particularly favoured by the Labour Party because they resented the cost of hiring a hall.

Annie watched the stocky young zealot in the cloth cap prancing about on the back of a lorry. He waved his arms about a good deal and, though she couldn't hear what he was saying, she could see that he was drawing a good audience. She put on her coat and went out to join them.

Of course, she was recognised at once by the crowd around the lorry. They drew back a little to let her through to the front row. Bellamy was aware of this surprising addition to his listeners, but did not at first acknowledge it. He was too busy castigating the good citizens of Perth for letting the Tories in last time.

During his pause for breath Annie shouted, 'They always do!'

Bellamy turned slowly and looked down at her in surprise. 'What was that, *Lady* Frysor?'

'I said, Perth always returns a Tory.'

'And why is that, do you think?'

'Because the Labour Party doesn't like farmers.'

There was such authority and candour in her voice – and the logic was so inescapable – that the crowd began to mutter agreement.

Bellamy sensed rebellion in his hard-won crowd. He turned his back on Annie and made to resume his set speech.

Annie interrupted. 'Why does the Labour Party hate farmers?'

He spun round and shouted, 'The Labour Party does not hate farmers!'

'Then why don't they vote for you?' Annie invited the men on either side to lift her onto the back of the lorry. They hoisted her up with a cheer. 'Why don't the farm workers vote for you?'

He drew back as she alighted, smiling, beside him. 'You have not read our agriculture policy,' he said.

'Printed words won't raise crops!' she declaimed. It was one of Austen's pithier slogans.

But now everyone could see who was up there on the lorry. It was Annie Jeynor, the film star – *in person*! That realisation prompted the first few demands for autographs. Most of the people who asked were women. They had no pens or paper.

Annie glanced around and spotted a pile of leaflets among other Party propaganda handouts stacked behind Bellamy. She snatched up a wad of the leaflets on which was printed 'Come with Labour'. She merely crossed out the word 'Labour' and wrote her signature under it.

Bellamy was amused. He was also impressed. For, looking around, he could see people streaming towards the lorry from all directions. Annie kept scribbling away and handing out the leaflets without pause. And all the time she maintained an unvarying litany, 'Lovely to see you; Please give us your support; Your help is all we need . . .' These were the same words she'd used at her War Bond rallies in California. The routine was identical – autograph, smile, personal remark.

The other Party officials were less tolerant than Bellamy. They decided to get out of a situation where they could not win. A signal was given and, without warning, the lorry lurched forward. Annie was hunkered down at the very edge of the platform. Had it not been for Bellamy she would have pitched head-first onto the grass. He grabbed her with such force she fell backwards on top of him. They continued to lie like that as the lorry gathered speed over the rough ground. When she got over the shock, Annie squeezed one of the arms which still held her. 'Just as it should be,' she said. 'Conservative on top.'

'We'll soon change that,' he told her.

'Mr Bellamy, I *do* admire your blind optimism.'

In fact Harry Bellamy knew very well that he had no chance whatever of winning Perth Central for Labour. This was his first contest, and his only obligation was, if possible, to increase his Party's share of the vote. If that could be managed – together with a display of energy and dedication – he stood a good chance for a winnable seat at a by-election elsewhere.

As the present contest ground on, his amusement at Lady Frysor's shameless tactics increased. He also came to admire the way she was able to mix with the ordinary folk and exchange banter. In the section of the public which he hoped to claim for himself, it was clear that Annie Jeynor might steal them away. The men admired her and the women found her admirable. It seemed ironic that whereas he had been selected chiefly for his ability to attract the female vote, the women preferred a woman.

They met again at the count. In fact, Annie made sure they spent quite a lot of time together at the count. If she had been tempted to break her life-long resolution never to use her vote she would, this once, have cast it in favour of Harry Bellamy. She found him very attractive. And she was aware that, now Austen was in with a big majority, she'd be spending a lot of time in Perth. It seemed sensible, if not prudent, to make this virile young man aware of her interest.

He was, she learned, a native of Perth and a miller by trade. He was not married 'or anything' because he thought such trivialities would stunt his career. 'That is,' he said wryly, 'unless I was lucky enough to marry a film star.'

'You should have thought of that sooner,' Annie told him.

In fact, things did not work out as she'd anticipated. For Beatrice Lillie's advice worked. In the space of a few weeks towards the end of the summer, Annie was offered three excellent opportunities for her return to the stage. All of the scripts, she noted, were addressed to 'Lady Frysor'.

Austen seemed to be doing less well at his end of the bargain. He'd expected to get a ministerial post in the new government, but Eden had merely hinted vaguely at something being sure to turn up in the future. Macmillan had the Foreign Office and insisted on having junior ministers he'd worked with in the past. Selwyn Lloyd got Defence. Maudling got Supply and Butler kept the Treasury. A much more extensive reshuffle was promised for later in the year.

'Darling, you're sure to get something then,' Annie said. Austen was gloomy. 'I wish that seemed likely.'

His wife brought logic to bear on the matter. 'Eden must be pretty sure the ministers he's appointed now will make a mess of things or he would not be promising to re-shuffle in a few months time.'

'But what if they all do a marvellous job?'

'Be serious, Austen! Have you ever known an entire Cabinet to do a marvellous job?'

He brightened. 'Never. No. Not even for a few months.'

'Besides which, Eden's sure to quarrel with the Foreign Secretary.'

'Macmillan? Why?'

'Because Anthony was Foreign Secretary for *so* long, he'll think nobody else can do the job.'

'Very true,' Austen said, and went out for a walk, much comforted.

Annie turned to consider her scripts. Two of the plays were historical costume pieces. And whereas the leading role offered in each case was excellent, she felt she had to get out of the period stuff. The modern play, offered by Henry Sherek, was called *Encore, Mrs Dalby*. Sherek's management had a suitable up-market image, but the play was very entertaining. The comedy was sharp and there was an opportunity to sing.

She made arrangements to discuss the project in London.

It was not until the spring of the following year that Annie met Harry Bellamy again. She was in London for rehearsals of the play but had gone up to the Memorial Theatre at Stratford to see the new production of *Twelfth Night* which had just come into the repertory. Advance gossip had it that Vivien Leigh was an adorable Viola but Laurence Olivier a rather muted Malvolio.

A gala opening night was laid on. That meant a full attendance of all the local dignitaries – and some from further afield as well. One of these was Harry Bellamy. Annie was astonished to see him there. There were three reasons for this. First, he was not in Perth; second, he was in a theatre; third, he was wearing a dinner jacket.

He smiled broadly at her through the hectic bustle of people in the foyer. A few moments later he was at her side and offering to buy her a drink. As they waited their turn he explained. 'I'm fighting a by-election in Worcester.'

That certainly was near enough for a jaunt to Stratford. 'Have you come with a party?' she asked.

'No. I've come *for* the Party,' he muttered *sotto voce* and fingered the lapel of his dinner jacket. 'This is my Gaitskell gear.'

He looked around cautiously. 'Old Clem never demanded such a sacrifice.'

Annie laughed.

A few months earlier Clement Attlee had retired from the leadership of the Labour Party. His place had been taken by suave Wykehamist, Hugh Gaitskell – who certainly was more used to dinner jackets than cloth caps.

'Do you have a chance of winning this seat, Mr Bellamy?'

'Call me Harry, Lady Frysor.' He handed her a drink. 'Yes. I have a very good chance of winning – as long as I cheat a bit.'

'How will you manage that?'

'By pretending I care as much for this lot . . .' he indicated the well-dressed playgoers '. . . as I do for the workers.'

'I wasn't aware that you cared for the workers, either.'

'Why else would I be standing for Labour?'

'I imagine because you're fed up *being* a worker.'

His laugh seemed to acknowledge the truth of that. 'You're a very cynical woman, Lady Frysor.'

'Call me Annie.' She looked around the affluent gathering. 'I'm sure you'll manage to get in without difficulty. As long as Gaitskell comes up to support you.'

'He's promised,' Harry said.

'Get it in writing,' Annie suggested. 'You know what they're like at Winchester.'

'No I don't. It's a hell of a bind when you have to think like a Tory to keep the red flag flying.'

Annie pretended alarm. 'For God's sake, don't show Gaitskell the red flag. It makes him very queasy.'

When the bell rang for the start of the performance, Annie suggested that he sit with her. She'd been sent two complimentary tickets and had come alone. As they went in together she mentioned that this was the play in which she'd made her first big success. 'I've never seen it before,' Harry said.

Nor did he enjoy it very much, though Vivien Leigh's figure and beauty made a stunning impact when she was dressed as the boy Cesario. As Malvolio, Olivier was much more human than that gargoyle is normally played. Annie thought the audience felt sorrier for him than was wise in a comic part. But neither they, nor she, could feel sorry for a girl who looked as cool and lovely as Vivien Leigh. *Her* Viola was so evidently slumming in Illyria.

After the performance there was a party. Harry declined the invitation to join in the celebration. But he did promise that if he got to Westminster he would make a point of repaying Annie for a very pleasant evening. She told him she would hold him to that promise.

At the opening of *Encore, Mrs Dalby*, Annie had a surprising backstage visitor. One of the first people to congratulate her was Jamie Northcott. It was twenty years since they'd last met and Annie had difficulty recognising him. His face was so much thinner and his hair had completely retreated, to leave only a sun-bleached fringe. Of course, he was well into his sixties now, but his expression had the same, almost boyish, charm. And his voice, though overlaid with an Australian accent, had lost nothing of its warmth. He asked her to have supper with him and, as soon as she'd spent enough time with a crowd of enthusiastic well-wishers, they left the theatre arm-in-arm.

As she'd already guessed, he'd been living in Australia. In fact, he'd recently retired from a post as shipping controller at Sydney harbour.

He said, 'I went out there immediately after the war.'

'Did you marry?'

'No.' He smiled. 'You remember I promised you I wouldn't at that party in Marlow.'

It seemed he'd forgotten his proposal on the Hamburg bridge. She shrugged. 'We don't always keep our promises.' But the recalled event prompted her to ask what she should have asked before. 'And your sister? How is she?'

'Celia's fine. I saw her earlier this evening.'

'Does she still have that house in Bayswater?'

'No, no. She has a bungalow out by Chiswick. Once the children were all married off there was no point keeping a house in town.'

There was a pause and Annie's mind raced to try and think

of other suitable questions she might ask. It vexed her that she could not think of anything. Celia, and Marlow, even Jamie seemed so far away. The words to deal with them were like the lines of a play she'd once learned, then forgotten because she did not expect to play the part again. For this intimate supper to be a success they really should have had some time to rehearse.

Jamie asked, 'How is Gertrude?'

'Very well, I gather. Rosemary tells me she's living in Germany.'

'Really? After all the trouble we had getting her out of there.'

'Yes.' Annie did not pursue that either. She rallied. 'And what will you do now you're back in England?'

'I shall enjoy a quiet life. I've taken a little house in Chelsea. You must drop in whenever you feel like it.'

'Oh, yes! I shall,' she said heartily. But she knew she would not.

In Dumbarton, Annie was feeling much better. And I was anxious to pursue the information she'd let slip to Austen about her birthplace. As I drove up the loch shore towards Luss one afternoon with her at my side, it seemed as good a time as any to get that cleared up.

'Was it the truth you told Austen about being born here?' Her reply was sharp and forbidding. 'I didn't say *here*.'

'Annie, you haven't said *any*where. Why do you want to hide that?'

'Because I'm not sure I can afford it – yet.'

'I don't understand.'

She snorted. 'Indeed you do not.'

I drove in silence for a bit, hoping she would enlighten me. But she seemed content to let it pass, so I was obliged to insist. 'Tell me what you mean by being able to "afford" it. Afford what?'

'Afford . . .' She sighed. 'Afford to be completely honest. You see, it could spoil everything I've done. It could undermine everything.' I was about to speak but she went on. And her voice was more regretful than I'd heard before. Wistful, almost.

She said, 'It depends really on how good I have been at my job. I've discovered that people will forgive a lot if the result is excellence.'

'Surely you know how good an actress you were.'

She gave a soft bark of a laugh that turned into a cough. 'No, I . . . I know how good I *thought* I was. And I spent my life trying to be better. But excellence? I don't know. I never saw me as they saw me. And there are damn few people you can trust on excellence. They have to have it themselves before they can see it.'

Having negotiated several hairpin bends in silence, I resumed, 'Now, let me get this clear . . .'

'No,' Annie said. 'It's not something you can help with, Bill. You never saw me. You never saw me when I was at my best.' She seemed to relax with a kind of comforted pride. 'Though it lasted a long time.'

I knew there was no point in pursuing the matter during that outing. Nor could I think of any argument which might later persuade her she could 'afford' to let go of a secret she'd defended all her life. Probably it was something which was important only to Annie herself. But, since her self was the whole object of my book, that just made it more crucial. Certainly, this must have been a major obstacle to the biography Dr Sleavin embarked upon. And no doubt a source of conflict. I'd no intention of providing Annie with grounds for an injunction against my book – now that it was nearly complete.

I turned to the much safer subject of adultery. 'When did you and Harry Bellamy become lovers?'

'At the earliest opportunity.'

'Yes, Annie,' I smiled. 'But when did the opportunity occur?'

'When he got into parliament.'

'Did he make the first approach, or did you?'

'Oh, the first approach was made long before that. In fact, the first time we met I think we both knew it was only a matter of time.'

'But you were the one who decided now was the time?'

'I suppose so. But he had promised to take me out if he got to Westminster. I naturally accepted his invitation.'

'Naturally.'

'Austen was kept very busy, you see. He was often doing constituency work in Perth. And then he got involved with some sort of trade commission which took him over to Europe a lot.'

'So he didn't get a ministerial post in the re-shuffle?'

'No. If only he had! It would have kept him well out of the mess.'

'I thought it was you who got him into the mess.'

'Certainly not. It was all Eden's fault.'

Later, she explained the Suez crisis to me in terms which enabled me to understand it for the first time.

In July 1956 Britain and America decided they would not finance Egypt's long-promised dam on the Nile at Aswan. Colonel Nasser was not best pleased. To make up the deficit on the money required for the project he, very properly, realised an asset he should have realised before. He claimed Egypt's Suez canal as Egyptian territory. He also claimed its considerable revenues for his own country. The concessionaires and their shareholders would be paid compensation. The canal was nationalised and would be run by Egyptians.

It was this last proposal which troubled Western users most. The bulk of Britain's oil supply came through the canal. How could we possibly entrust our valuable shipping to a bunch of ignorant wogs? The complex operation of the canal had always been managed by highly-paid Europeans. It was the only way to get things done right.

In fact, the Egyptians soon proved themselves perfectly capable of operating the vital waterway – and at a much lower cost than the Universal Company had managed. The endless passage of ships to and fro continued unimpeded, keeping better time than had been common since the days of the efficient Victorians. There was absolutely no reason to suppose that Egypt would jeopardise such a fruitful source of income. The better the canal worked, the greater was the national profit.

But the British government had already determined that this efficient re-organisation in the hands of the wrong people could not be allowed to continue. Eden wanted British control or nothing – even if it meant going to war. Gaitskell, whose party had nationalised half of British industry into waste and penury, declared that nationalisation was evil. It was, he said, like Hitler claiming *Lebensraum*. But he did *not* want to go to war about it.

This constituted a slight conflict of ideas. To begin with, the Suez canal was already *in* Egypt, so there was no territorial expansion. And even if there had been, that was exactly what Britain *had* gone to war about with Hitler. In fact, there wasn't much to choose between the Labour and Conservative parties on the issue. What drove Eden to disaster was much stronger than global politics. It was his personal spite against Abdul Nasser.

During that summer, Annie 'arrived' on the London scene. She was interviewed on all manner of subjects. Lady Frysor attended a host of charity functions. The glossy magazines took her up and plastered photographs of her all over their society and fashion pages. For a time she eclipsed Norah Docker, and that redoubtable lady had to engage in a series of vulgar stunts in order to reclaim the initiative.

On Annie the 'Princess' look looked good. Fashion photographer John French was engaged to do a double-page spread and even Barbara Goalen had to concede that Lady Frysor was the epitome of good taste allied with flair. This impression was fostered by the evidence of the actress being seen only in the very best of company. But journalists even pursued her to Perth one weekend to show how well she got on with the natives.

Considering the result of all these endeavours, Annie was reminded of the days when she'd first settled in London. Some of the magazines which now craved her 'co-operation' were the same magazines she'd studied then, in an effort to learn how to be a lady. She smiled to herself and at herself. Really, there was less to it than she had anticipated. It was like any other role – but performed more slowly. However, she was well aware that she would never have got the part had it not been for dear muddled Sir Austen. And he would not have been *Sir* Austen if his father had not shown such rapacious skill in dealing with the City, then generosity in courting Lloyd George. This explained her rather gnomic response when questioned on her popularity in society. She merely sang a snatch of song and the words, 'Lloyd George knew *his* father.'

As to her secret of looking so young and beautiful, she would not say. At least, not in public. Often, though, she was tempted to paraphrase a more recent popular song as 'I'm being screwed by a wonderful guy'. That would be no more than an accurate explanation. And it was a method long-hallowed by theatrical tradition, in the teaching of Elsie Fogerty at the Central School. There were many great ladies of the English stage who took Elsie's advice and never looked back once they started *lying* back and giving vent to their vowels.

Harry Bellamy proved an eager lover. Soon he knew more ways in and out of the Dorchester than its architects had ever envisaged. The new extension on Deanery Street proved particularly useful. Often he was waiting in her suite when she got back from the theatre. He had a key which was never left at the reception desk, where Annie collected hers. Sometimes he was there between matinée and evening performance.

This sometimes led to complications when Austen brought visiting politicians round to see her for tea at the hotel. Once or twice Annie had to get dressed very hurriedly to play hostess, and Harry had to escape in broad daylight. Normally, though, they managed things very well indeed.

Parliament was recalled early in September to debate the Suez crisis. And Austen got promoted. In a mood of great elation while they were dining at the House, he told Annie, 'I've been seconded to a Cabinet committee.'

'Darling, how nice! Does that mean you're a minister again?'

'Well, not officially. You see, I'm under Thorneycroft.'

'And what is he over?'

'He's the president of the Board of Trade. But the committee isn't about trade really.'

Annie had no interest in what it was really about. She was merely pleased that her husband was pleased. 'So you're a sort of *secret* minister?'

'Yes. My contacts in Europe have turned up trumps. It's to do with "Musketeer", you see.'

Annie smiled her most encouraging smile. 'Oh, really?'

Later, when she was lying in Harry's arms, she happened to mention her husband's good fortune. 'He's become a secret musketeer.'

She felt Harry's arm stiffen around her waist. '"Musketeer"?'

'Yes. At his age! Isn't that sweet?'

'No, Annie, it is not sweet. It's mad. "Musketeer" is the Anglo-French plan to invade Egypt.'

Annie laughed. 'I just cannot imagine Austen invading Egypt.'

Harry withdrew his arm and got out of bed. It was in the late afternoon and for a moment his naked body was boldly silhouetted against the drawn curtains of the bedroom window. He started searching for his underpants. 'I don't think they'll send Austen in person,' he said. Then in casual conversational tone, 'So, he's on the Suez Committee, is he?'

Annie raised herself on one elbow to admire his lean, muscular back as he pulled on the briefs. 'Apparently. Something to do with the Board of Trade.'

'Balls!'

'Under *Thorney*croft?' Annie asked incredulously.

'I mean, that's just a cover.'

As Harry completed dressing, he managed to pursue the subject and Austen's new job without displaying too much interest. But Annie got the firm impression that he'd welcome more information on what the enemy was up to.

She noticed, during the following weeks, that the official guests Austen invited to have tea with her were merely using her as a decoy. And now they were almost exclusively French. Then French and Israeli. It was odd. The French were Britain's chief adversaries in Europe. And Britain had been Israel's chief adversary in the Middle East.

Annie was enjoying herself so much recounting this bizarre tale that I felt reluctant to question what seemed to me the oddest part of it so far. 'Why did Eden bring Austen into it? Surely this business was too rich for his blood?'

'He was convenient,' Annie said. 'You see, he had established cover. For some time he'd been shuttling back and forth on boring trade talks. That made him an ideal contact when the plot was laid.'

'Even so, I don't get the impression your husband would be at ease dealing with international affairs.'

'Oh, he loved it!'

'But was he any good at it?'

'Whether he was good at it or not wasn't Eden's priority. The Prime Minister was rather short of blind followers. But he knew Austen was intensely loyal. That counted for much more than intelligence – or scruples.'

'What about your own scruples?' I asked.

She seemed puzzled. 'With regard to what?'

'With regard to passing confidential information to an unauthorised person.'

Annie laughed. 'Bill, they were *politicians*. There's no point in anyone like me having scruples about politicians.'

I still found it difficult to accept her effortless contempt. 'How long was it before you realised that Harry was just using you for his own ends?'

The sparkle in her eyes signalled that she'd located a double entendre in the question. However, she tried to answer solemnly, just to please me. 'Harry didn't try to conceal how he was using me,' she said. 'I understood what he was doing. If I hadn't understood, I wouldn't have been able to find out what he wanted me to find out.'

And it was the man from Israel who chiefly interested Harry. 'Annie, you'd be doing me a great favour if you could find out more on this.'

'I don't see how I can. They're all going to Paris next week.'

'Are they really? Did they say why?'

'No. They all seemed to *know* why.'

'Or *where* exactly?'

Annie shook her head. 'I don't think they mentioned that either.'

'Get Austen to tell you, when he comes back.'

'I don't know if we'll be having a tea party when he comes back.'

Harry embraced her and spoke with great seriousness. 'Annie, it doesn't have to be at a tea party. What I mean is, for my sake, it might be a good idea if you slept with your husband.'

She bit her lip to suppress a giggle. 'Is it really important to you?'

'My career could depend on it.'

Probably Harry did not know exactly how the crisis could be used for his own personal advancement. As a new MP, in the opposition party, there were few opportunities to shine. And there was the further limitation that, even in his own party, he was on the wrong side. Gaitskell had beaten Bevan for the party leadership, and although the contest was still going on beneath the surface, Harry was a Bevanite at a time when that blazing Welsh star was in decline.

Gaitskell had already fumbled a few times in dealing with Suez. Of course, he was a man who seemed to be fumbling even when he had a firm grip. But if a situation could be arranged where he not only fumbled but loudly dropped a clanger, Bevan might yet be called to save the day before another election. So Harry's primary aim was not to discomfit Eden but to humiliate his own leader. Eden, after all, was in no position to give Harry preferment. But with Gaitskell out of the way, Bevan certainly might.

When Austen got back from his Paris trip, Annie made plain how much she had missed him. She was there in his flat to welcome him when he arrived, and she suggested that she might return there after the performance. Austen was touched by her solicitude. He thought it a good idea that they should spend some time together. Events *were* becoming rather hectic, and on top of the foreign business, he had the party conference at Llandudno all the following week.

Harry had just returned from *his* party conference where Gaitskell had got a roasting in their Suez debate. Overwhelmingly, the Labour delegates were in favour of Nasser. Their leader seemed to be telling them to side with the Tories. So now was a perfect time for some elegant backstabbing.

Having seen Austen off to Llandudno, Annie took a taxi back to the Dorchester. Harry was waiting for her. But he was not waiting in her bed. He was fully dressed and interested only in what she'd learned from her husband about the secret meetings near Paris. Annie had made a note of the address and she gave it to him. That made him happy. By the time she had finished her report on Austen's Paris jaunt, Harry was ecstatic. This was better than he'd ever dreamed of.

Of course, it was already public knowledge that Britain and France had made plans to invade the canal zone. That had been decided soon after Nasser seized it. Since then, however, three months had passed in which the combined weight of American policy, world opinion and various resolutions at the United Nations had dulled the impetus of the combined operation.

What the Anglo-French force needed was an excuse for invasion. Everything was quiet along the canal. The world's shipping continued to use it without hindrance or delay by the Egyptians. Eden realised that soon even British public opinion would be willing to let things go. But that would mean he personally had been humiliated by Nasser and done nothing about it.

Annie now reported the insane scheme which was meant to save Eden's face. She told Harry, 'They're planning an *Israeli* invasion.'

'Christ! Why?'

'Israel will invade Egypt. That's meant to put the canal in great danger. Then, it seems, France and Britain will launch a "policing" manoeuvre. It is our duty to separate the belligerents.'

'So Eden will have his excuse to get in there.'

'The way Austen tells it, we'd have no choice.'

'But how do they know Israel plans to invade Egypt?'

Annie laughed. 'Oh, Israel has *agreed* to invade. As a favour to Anthony. That's all part of the deal. Of course we'll pretend we knew nothing about it.'

'And all this has already been discussed?'

'In detail. They had a strategy conference at that house outside Paris.'

Harry rubbed his hands. 'Great! Now, if only we can get

people to believe that Gaitskell knows about this – he'll be lucky to get his old job back in the civil service.'

'Gaitskell *doesn't* know,' Annie protested. 'For that matter, very few people in the *Cabinet* know.'

Harry smiled. 'I'm sure that's true. But the public is going to find it very hard to believe.'

He went on to exult over the marvellous timing of this bombshell. In a week when the papers were full of the Conservative conference here was an item which would send them all running for cover. It was just a matter of getting Bevan to write to Eden asking him if he could confirm the Israeli role in operation 'Musketeer'.

Bevan, however, was far too wily a politician to put such an inflammatory suggestion in writing. He telephoned Eden at Llandudno and mentioned 'a rumour'. That, he felt, would be enough to halt the charade. But he completely misjudged the strength of Eden's paranoia, as Annie, Harry and Austen were to discover.

The Prime Minister at once set MI5 to work. The source of the rumour must be found and silenced. It had to be someone directly connected with the Suez Committee. Nobody else knew about the secret collusion with Israel. Naturally, MI5 started on the lowest rung and prepared to work their way up to full Cabinet members like Selwyn Lloyd, Macmillan and Lord Salisbury. Our secret service is always at its best when pursuing clerks and typists.

But the search could be narrowed much more readily on this occasion. It was a matter of the time at which the rumour had surfaced, and the particular details which Bevan had mentioned. The words, based on what Harry had passed on, were 'strategy being planned at a house outside Paris'. Unknown to Harry, and thus Bevan, was the fact that the planning headquarters had recently been moved from the Hotel Matignon to the secluded villa in Sèvres outside Paris. So, since the left hand didn't know what the right hand was doing in the Musketeer conspiracy, it followed that the traitor must be among those at the most recent meeting. The service chiefs were absolved without question, as always. And that left Sir Austen Frysor.

He was interviewed and proved very willing to co-operate. It was possible, he told the officers, that he had mentioned 'the beauty of the woods' at Sèvres to his wife. Surely there was no harm in that? It would have given a jolly rum impression if he'd refused to answer her perfectly innocent question about where he'd been spending his time. They asked him exactly *when* he had told his wife these things. And, with the answer to that, they also learned that the sleeping arrangements of the Frysors made the occasion memorable for Sir Austen. He was able to give the precise date, and could, if pressed, have given the precise hour.

Sleeping arrangements are very important to MI5. It is an item of faith with them (and with the British press) that suspected parties are incapable of passing information while on their feet and fully dressed. It is only in bed that secrets which could imperil the State can be imparted. This ludicrous contention gained the full support of the Macmillan government a few years later, during the Profumo scandal. If John Profumo had met Christine Keeler only at vicarage tea parties, or in the privacy of his constituency surgery, it would have been quite impossible for him to mention NATO secrets. As soon as they went to bed, however, they talked about nothing else.

In the Suez sex case, the matter was not so clear cut. MI5 had never had to deal with a member of the Tory government who actually talked to his wife in bed. This could set a dangerous precedent.

A round-the-clock surveillance operation was mounted. The plain blue van in Deanery Street was the centre of activity, but there were watchers in Park Lane as well. And Lady Frysor was tailed wherever she went. Her telephone was bugged with the full co-operation of the Dorchester management. There were complications when she phoned the House of Commons because the high-frequency gadget in her phone jammed the permanent bugging apparatus in the Commons phones.

All this bustling, secret activity produced little result. In fact, it was an ordinary constable on his beat who broke the conspiracy. He happened to see a man behaving in a very suspicious manner at the back of the Dorchester. He saw the man gain unauthorised entry and hurried round to alert the hotel's security staff. However, one of the secret agents was loitering nearby and joined in searching for the intruder. That was when they found Lady Frysor and Harry Bellamy in bed together.

Annie laughed at recalling that most hackneyed and embarrassing of moments.

'So there were no photographs,' I said.

'No. In fact the whole thing was conducted quite decorously, under the circumstances. When Harry had put on his clothes the constable was able to identify him as the intruder. Then the agent asked for identification. I mean, he knew who I was, but he smiled fit to bust when he found out Harry was a Labour Member of Parliament.'

'What happened then?'

Annie continued her stroll around the reception room. 'Then there was the great cover-up. Eden was told. Then he told Gaitskell.'

'Not about the Israeli collusion?'

'Certainly not! He played the record in reverse; making out that *I* was the danger.'

This was puzzling. 'How could that possibly be?'

'Well, think of it! One of Labour's men could have been passing Labour secrets to the *Tories*. That made Harry a security risk to Gaitskell.'

'But surely Harry was able to tell Gaitskell the real story.'

Annie gave me a delighted smile and shook her head. 'Oh, no! You see, Harry still had it mind that "the real story" was all he needed to plunge Gaitskell in the shit. He was determined to keep it to himself, until the right opportunity.'

'What about Austen?'

'Austen lied as well. He swore he hadn't told me about the Israeli collusion. He'd just happened to mention the place where they'd been discussing farm produce in France. Everything else, he implied, was ferreted out by me from other sources. He hinted that the French were notoriously susceptible to a woman's

to put him up in Perth again,' he hazarded. 'It would be awkward if you were there.' This was much nearer his fear and, having discovered it, he pressed on quickly. 'And even if Bellamy isn't there in person, he'll certainly *know* the man they put up against me next time.'

'That does seem likely. These socialists tend to know each other.'

'And *tell* each other anything which might be useful to their party.'

Annie was both amazed and amused. 'Oh, I see! There could be a whispering campaign which would dent your image.'

'Well . . . you must admit, it would be . . .'

'Jolly awkward,' Annie said.

She reported this conversation to Harry when she was spending the night at his flat. He thought it very amusing. He also thought it might prove useful. He was going to need all the help he could get in his career.

His involvement with the Suez fiasco was less fruitful than Austen's. Gaitskell strengthened his grip on the party. And he still believed what Eden had told him about the Dorchester scandal – that Lady Frysor had wheedled secrets from a fallible Brother. That meant Harry would have to wait quite a while before there was any hope of promotion.

'Why don't you become a Gaitskellite?' Annie suggested.

'I intend to,' her lover said. 'But there's got to be a decent lapse of time during which I have re-thought our priorities.'

'Humbug!'

'Yes. But it's got to be convincing humbug.'

'Couldn't you be struck by a blinding light on the road to Wigan Pier?'

'No. That's been done too often. The Party wouldn't believe it.'

'What does that matter? The voters will believe it. They'll believe anything.'

Harry rolled over and lay on his back. He also changed the subject. 'Annie, I don't think we should see each other any more.'

'Oh! Why?'

'Well, there just doesn't seem much future in it.'

'There never was any future in it. We have always been just for the day and the hour.'

'Mmmm,' he said.

But it was very clear how this decision fitted. Harry could scarcely start his rapprochement with the Gaitskell camp until he was demonstrably free of his entanglement with her. She got up and got dressed without another word.

Harry called from the bed. 'Where are you going?'

'Back to the stage,' she told him. 'I'm suddenly tired of all this pretence.'

And that was how the whole imbroglio ended. Austen and Annie were divorced to avoid future threat *by* unscrupulous socialists. Annie and Harry parted company to avoid embarrassment *to* unscrupulous socialists. She made a gift of the Perth house to Austen – which he thought was jolly decent – and they bade each other goodbye amicably enough.

But it meant that towards the end of the 'fifties, Annie was without: a husband, a lover, a title, the DBE – or work. Of these, work was the most important thing. She started making plans for a return to America.

TIMOTHY GILCHRIST

During the time Annie was in hospital she had surprisingly few visitors. No doubt that was the penalty, or the blessing, of merely being so old. She'd already outlived most of the people who knew her well. But, of course, there was a lot of publicity and the Glasgow hospital had to deploy considerable skill, and blank-faced rudeness, in order to protect their patient from media attention. There were only three visitors apart from her staff, Barbara and myself. They were Rosemary Straven, Peggy Ashcroft and Timothy Gilchrist.

In fact, it was due to my presence that they let Tim Gilchrist in. At various times during my earlier conversations with Annie she'd referred to him with admiration and affection. He'd been her long-suffering stage director for the world tours of the one-woman show. She'd always referred to him as 'young Tim'.

When he was shown into her room by the nurse he still looked fairly youthful, for a man who was then about fifty. He was rather plump but held himself well. His face had an open, ingenuous expression and was healthily tanned. His abundant hair showed no trace of grey. I stepped back to let him get close to the bed. The nurse hovered protectively. Annie was conscious, but very confused. Tim leaned over her and smiled. She tried to focus on his face.

He spoke softly. 'What's all this nonsense, you ridiculous old whore?' The nurse was startled. But the visitor was still smiling, willing the patient to respond. 'Mm? What's your excuse this time?' He waited for a reply, then said firmly, 'I'm damned if I'll give them their money back tonight, darling. *Look* at me! You've done this once too often and it's got to stop. Do you hear?'

311

But Annie did not respond. We could see she was making a great effort to connect the voice and the face but it was no use. Her eyelids fluttered and she started to doze. Tim held his position for a few moments then straightened up. 'Poor old sweetheart. She must be very tired,' he said.

The nurse urged us out of the room and I discovered how tired he must be himself. As soon as he heard the news at his home in Florida he'd set out for New York where he caught a transatlantic flight. From Heathrow he took the shuttle to Abbotsinch and came directly from the airport to the hospital. That meant he'd been travelling steadily for almost twenty-four hours.

I said, 'You must be dead on your feet.'

'Sure. It's worth it, though, to see Annie's still alive.'

On Annie's behalf I invited him to come back to Dumbarton to sleep for as long as he needed.

When Barbara got back from the theatre that night I told her of our surprise guest – already in bed for some hours. She was very impressed at the trouble Tim Gilchrist had taken so that he could be at Annie's bedside. I asked, 'Do you know anything about him?'

'Not much. She used to talk about him when I first worked with her. I believe he was at Birmingham Rep when he applied for the job as Annie's stage director. She took him with her to Broadway in the early sixties; then on the international tours. There are quite a few stories about that.' Barbara shook her head admiringly. 'That's a man with stamina.'

'He must be very fond of her.'

My wife gave me a quizzical glance. 'Fond?' She helped herself to more stew. Barbara was always very hungry after the performance and, since she didn't like to eat alone, we were seated at a bare table in the kitchen. Everyone else had gone to bed and the house was very quiet.

'Don't you think so? He must be fond of her, to come all this way just to see her?'

Barbara said, 'Long stage partnerships develop a peculiar intensity, Bill. I don't think *fond* is the word for it. Selfish, is better. Annie is part of him*self*. After all the years they worked together . . . as closely as they did . . . there must be a big slice of his life that will never be his own.'

That seemed to me an odd way of expressing it. 'Not very flattering.'

Barbara shrugged apologetically and continued eating. But she knew her instinct was right. 'I don't think Tim Gilchrist can choose. And when he found out Annie might be dying it must have seemed as if he was facing major amputation.'

Next morning, Tim's attitude seemed to confirm that assessment. He was not merely sad at Annie's illness – he was *angry*. It was as though she had led the way into a dangerous situation and obliged him to follow, while giving no thought for his safety. He immediately phoned the hospital and seemed only slightly mollified to learn that the patient's condition had not worsened during the night. He wanted to go to Glasgow immediately but was told there could be no visitors that day.

Thus it was that I had the opportunity to hear at first hand of Annie Jeynor's career following her divorce from Sir Austen Frysor. Tim Gilchrist was very anxious to talk about it. I remembered what Barbara had said and now was able to identify his peculiar eagerness to reclaim his own past. Sitting in the other armchair of the reception room I had a man who'd contracted a wonderful disease which he delights in, and defies anyone to cure.

'I was twenty-eight when I first met Annie. She's exactly thirty years older than I am. We have the same birthday . . . the eleventh of March. I'd done some good stuff in Birmingham and one of the shows had transferred to the West End.'

'Did she see that?'

'No! No, she didn't.' He chuckled. 'Oh, she pretended she had, when I went for the interview. But she really hadn't seen anything of mine.'

'Then why do you think you got the job?'

He unbuttoned his jacket and leaned back. 'Two reasons. First – she liked me. Second – all the other umpteen applications were from directors who'd done fine work in the *London* theatre. Mine was the only application from outside London. You've got to understand that, for years, Annie had been snubbed at every

313

turn in the West End. She didn't want to give the job to anybody who'd refused *her* work.'

'It seems odd that so many people should apply.'

'Bill, directors weren't God's only articulate mouthpiece in those days. Also, she was offering great money. And the interview was at the *Dorchester*. That was real class. She was wearing blue, which should have clashed with her auburn hair but didn't. Maybe because her eyes are so blue. And I remember that room. Her sitting room. Silvery grey with spindly embroidered chairs. She got up in a kind of eager way and came to meet me. Relax, I told myself, she's probably done the same thing for all the others. We shook hands and she held on to my hand and led me to a sofa that felt hard. Not uncomfortable, but hard.'

I fidgeted in my own chair. It was going to be a long day if he insisted on such detail. But this, I realised, had been a big moment in his life. It would be churlish to interrupt.

He seemed to be aware of my uneasiness for he increased the pace of his recollections. 'Before I left that room I had the job. No shit about "I'll consider" or "I'll let you know". "Right, Mr Gilchrist," she said, "how soon can we start working on the programme?" Now I am twenty-eight, remember. A *young* director. I still have my contract in Birmingham, and lucky to have it. What do I tell her? That I can start with her at the end of the season . . . the beginning of next season? Something like that? No! If she can hire me at that fee in twenty-three minutes flat, then I'm her man. So – "Tomorrow," I tell her. Let Birmingham fend for itself.'

'That must have impressed her.'

'No. She *expected* people to jump when she said boo. No, what impressed her – or so she said later – was that I didn't ask for any particulars on what my duties would be.' He shook his head ruefully. 'Christ! Did I live to regret that. Time came when I was on call night and day.'

'But what was it you were supposed to do?'

'Her one-woman show. I staged that.'

'Forgive me, Mr Gilchrist . . .'

'Call me Tim.'

'Tim, I really don't know what is involved.'

314

The first sign of incredulity showed on his face. 'But you've seen the show. Haven't you?'

'No. I'm afraid not. In fact I've never seen Annie on the stage at all.'

He was shocked. *'Never?* Then why, in God's name, did she want *you* to write her book?'

'Perhaps she liked me.'

He took the point, but still seemed bewildered. 'I just don't see how it's possible to write a book about Annie Jeynor when you've never seen her.'

'I've been living here for nearly five months. And I've seen her every day.'

'That's not her,' Tim assured me. 'That's not even what she's *for.*'

The image came back to me of how I'd felt when I first saw her ill. Not herself. It had occurred to me then that this was not Annie Jeynor. Now I was being told, by an authority on the subject, that I'd never really seen her at all. 'Tell me about the show,' I said. 'Describe her performance.'

He offered me a choice. 'Drunk or sober?'

This immediately diverted me to the more worrying topic. 'Was she really an alcoholic?'

'No. But for a long time she was one hell of a drunk.'

'What's the difference?'

Again there was that incredulous expression. Evidently Tim thought he was dealing with a curiously limited intelligence. He spelled out the difference. 'It's a matter of cause,' he said. 'An alcoholic is disgusted with his sober self. There's no cure for that. A drunk just wants the world to be rosier – too often.'

'What was wrong with the world . . . as Annie saw it then?'

Tim shrugged and settled himself again in the armchair.

'She was getting old. And she couldn't pick and choose among the guys any more. Let's face it, she scared them rigid . . .' He grinned. 'Or flaccid might be more accurate. Except in the Latin American countries. But there they were too respectful. *However*, we did tour Latin America a lot.'

I was beginning to see the difficulty. In her sixties, Annie's intimidating presence and authority, together with the fierce reputation she'd earned, must have made her seem quite un-approachable. And on the occasions when she approached them, they probably took fright.

Tim assured me, 'Of course they loved her onstage. She still looked beautiful there – and young. Or a lot younger, anyway. The lighting man she hired had once worked with Marlene Dietrich.' He raised his eyebrows. 'More flattering than that you cannot get.

'She realised the stage was where everything had to happen. There the lovers lurked not single spies but in battalions. Very little could stand in the way of keeping that date, wherever it was, no matter what condition she was in. Of course, sometimes it just was not possible, and sometimes she was off in the woods somewhere keeping another kind of date. Those times, we had to give them the money back. Rarely, though. Usually she was there. Once she got out on the stage she was adorable.' He leaned forward suddenly. 'Believe it!' He repeated the word softly, but as though there was no other. 'Adorable.'

'I'm quite willing to believe it.'

He threw up his hands in despair. 'But you've never seen her! Bill, I pity you. Annie Jeynor in front of a live audience could raise you to a higher state than you ever thought possible. It happened for me every time. And I'm the man who often had to carry her into the wings; then steady and *aim* her at that warm lighted space. But once she was out there, and the band playing "Lorelei", and the audience cheering there wasn't the hint of a stagger. In fact, she seemed to be lazily flying a few inches above the stage. Then she reached the centre spot and landed, light as thistledown. The audience was suddenly quiet. Holding its breath. Waiting for her opening line. They knew it as well as she did. She learned that line in six languages but it was always the same lost girl asking, "What country, friends, is this?"'

'But she didn't perform the play, did she?'

'No, no. The only other thing she did from *Twelfth Night* was the "Damask cheek" piece. She learned that in several languages too.'

'Oh, yes! I heard her recite that on television. But what did she do in this show?'

'She sang. She did mime characters. She danced. And she *listened.*'

This was totally mystifying. 'Listened?'

Tim nodded with great enthusiasm. 'That was a brilliant piece of stagecraft she made her own. She could break your heart just watching her listen. So simple, but marvellous when she did it. Some of the best acting I have ever seen was Annie, just listening.' His eyes shone when he thought about it, but he could see I needed a lot more information. 'Annie realised when she was working with other actors in plays that, no matter how big a part it is, you spend more than half your time on the stage listening, reacting, being affected by other people.'

'Yes. I suppose that's true.'

'Of course it's true! And it's very important. Think of *The Stronger.*'

'Is that a play? I don't know it,' I confessed. Again it struck me that Tim Gilchrist would have been much happier talking to somebody who knew those things which, clearly, every acceptable adult should know.

'It's a play,' he said. 'It's a short play by Strindberg for two women. One is a wife and the other may be a mistress – and the subject is a man. The thing is, one of the women does all the talking and the other does not say anything at all. She just listens. And *she*'s the one who makes the biggest impression. It's a fascinating play. So when I was arranging an engagement in, say, Rio, I'd contact the resident theatre company and have them put up their top actress to play the talker. She would do it in Portuguese . . .'

'Spanish,' I corrected.

'No. In Brazil it's Portuguese,' he said. 'Then Annie, who knows the play backwards in English, comes along and *listens* – in Portuguese – or Spanish, or any damn language you care to mention. The local actress is flattered to be sharing the stage with Annie Jeynor – and may even do her stint for nothing. The local audience is delighted. And if they didn't know the play they come away convinced that Jeynor is fluent in their language. But she isn't. It's just that the listener is the *best part*.' He beamed triumphantly. 'We had a whole repertoire of scenes that could be adapted and played that way. She was brilliant at it. Nobody had ever done it before . . . and nobody has dared to do it since.'

I got up to tend the fire. It was unnerving to realise that this man probably knew Annie better than any other. And yet it seemed to be his firmly held belief that the real woman was the actress. It bothered me that I had not questioned Annie very closely on her stage or screen performances. I'd noted the titles she'd mentioned, well aware that these were only a few names plucked from hundreds. Even then, I had not asked her about the roles or how she had played them. But what if that was where the whole truth lay? What if the thing which was rare about Annie Jeynor did not exist except in performance? That may have been why Dr Sleavin's biography had annoyed her so much. With sudden insight, it seemed to me quite possible that, perversely, I'd chosen the method which would tell me *least* about my subject.

And maybe that's why stage biographies are full of plays and performances. Maybe it's not a matter of vanity. Maybe it's a matter of going where the truth is. And what looks like the lightest confection of stage memorabilia could be simple realism.

While I was preoccupied with the fire, Tim took the opportunity to get in some questions of his own. 'What sort of book are you writing about Annie?'

'The story of her life, really. In terms of the men in it.'

He gasped. 'What, *all* of them?'

'No. Just the main ones.'

'Am I in there?'

I replaced the poker and smiled at him. 'You will be now.'

'So I'd better make a good impression, eh?'

'You already have,' I said and sat down again, notebook at the ready and recorder spinning.

'Good. Because the 'sixties were not the best of times for Annie.'

'Were you in love with her?'

He gave me a startled look. 'Not in the way I'm sure you mean. Of course I loved her, still do. But I never went to bed

318

with her, though many times I had to *put* her to bed.' Tim smiled knowingly. 'You see, she sussed me out at that first interview.'

'About what?'

He shifted uneasily in his chair. 'Well, let's say she put it to me the way Bobby Helpmann's landlady put it to him.'

(Later that day I asked Barbara for clarification of this puzzling allusion. Apparently, when Robert Helpmann was a young dancer on tour there were some high jinks at the respectable digs which scandalised the landlady. But she kept her dignity when she confronted the chief offender next morning. With commendable understatement she observed, 'Mr Helpmann, I understand you are a gentleman who prefers gentlemen.')

Tim Gilchrist made no further comment on that aspect of his life. 'There's no doubt that the remarkable Miss Jeynor hit a sticky patch in the 'sixties. But it all started well enough in New York. The idea was to open the show at the Music Box and run it there for three months before we took it on tour. Do you know the house?'

'No. The theatre, you mean?'

'Yeah. A gem of a theatre on 45th Street, jointly owned by the Shuberts and Irving Berlin. He wrote a song for her, you know – Berlin. That was after he saw the show. Because she was such a riot as Annie.'

'I'm sorry, I don't . . .' Tim Gilchrist's reporting method made bewildering jumps which I could not follow. Also, he tended to make assumptions about my limited knowledge of theatre. 'I don't quite follow the connection there.'

He gave me a worried glance then took a deep breath and started speaking slowly. 'Irving Berlin is the greatest popular song writer in the history of American showbusiness.'

'Yes, I know that.'

'Ah. He also partly owns a theatre on Broadway called the Music Box.'

This was too slow. 'Yes, Tim. I do understand that. What I don't see is how he's connected with the musical *Annie* – who is a little girl.'

He laughed. 'No, no, no. Not that Annie. In her opening show in New York, *our* Annie sang the song – brought the house down singing the song – "You Can't Get A Man With A Gun", which is from *Annie Get Your Gun*, which was written by Irving Berlin. He said, on the strength of that performance, that our-Annie was the best his-Annie he had ever seen. A lot of people agreed with him – though Ethel Merman wasn't very pleased. Anyway, plans were started to mount a revival of *Annie Get Your Gun* as soon as the tour was over. Meanwhile, Berlin wrote a special song for our show.'

'Thank you. I've got that now.'

Tim relaxed again and resumed his erratic recital. 'It really was a great night, that opening night in New York. As far as the public was concerned, here was a famous movie star appearing live for the first time. And not only that. Here was a glamorous, real-life spy who'd bluffed the Nazis. The hype was overpowering. And *everybody* was there to see it happen. Dietrich with Coward and Kit Cornell, Helen Hayes, Danny Kaye and Sylvia, Irving Berlin himself, Irene Selznick, Jessica Tandy and Hume Cronyn, Cary Grant . . . oh, you could have a cast a hundred blockbusters from the stalls alone. But the guest of honour was Mrs Kennedy – not the wife, you understand – the president's mother, Mrs Rose Kennedy. That made it the equivalent of a *royal* occasion in New York.'

'What year was this?'

'In 1961. The fall of '61. That was a year I thought would never *end*. We'd been working on the show from February, then all through the summer without a break. The heat was incredible. That's why we were so glad to get invited to Cape Cod for four or five weeks before total exhaustion set in. Actually, it was just Annie that Mrs Kennedy invited to Hyannis Port, but there was work still to be done and she couldn't leave me in Manhattan to melt.'

'How did Annie come to know Mrs Kennedy?'

'I've no idea. Seemed to go back a long way, though.'

As soon as the patient had recovered sufficiently I challenged her on this long-term friendship which was news to me.

'Didn't I tell you about Rose?'

'No, you didn't.'

320

Annie sniffed. 'She was friendly with Frau Mosen in Hamburg. That's where I first met her. Rose Fitzgerald and Frau Mosen had attended the same finishing school in Prussia. Later, I met her several times in Berlin. She spent a lot of time in Europe in the mid-'thirties. And she stayed with me once or twice at Ziegelstrasse – once Frederik moved out.'

'Why didn't you mention this before?'

Annie subsided again with a great show of weariness. 'Bill, I cannot possibly tell you absolutely everything that happened. *And* remember everyone I knew, or met.'

It was difficult to suppress my irritation. 'I don't expect you to remember *every*one. But the parents of a president of the United States are of passing interest.'

There was a pause, then she happened to recall another detail that might be of interest to me. 'Old Joe Kennedy got me out of Lisbon.'

'Really?'

'It was an American ship, you see. Joe Kennedy arranged the passage.' She raised her head helpfully. 'He was in London then.'

'Yes, I know. The first Catholic ambassador to the Court of St James.'

'*No!*' Annie levered herself almost upright in her irritation. 'For God's sake don't get that wrong.' She corrected me. 'It's ambassador "to the Court *at* St *James's*."'

'Okay.' I made a note of it. 'And the next time you met Rose Kennedy was at Hyannis Port in the early 'sixties?'

She nodded eagerly. 'Yes. I remember . . .'

'Yes?'

'It was a very hot summer.'

The inadequancy of this addition made me smile. 'The temperature is immaterial!'

Annie closed her eyes and sighed. 'That sounds like Lady Bracknell.'

I asked Tim Gilchrist, 'How did Annie and Mrs Kennedy get on together?'

'Great. They were about the same size, about ten years'

difference in age, and they had the same sense of humour. But Mrs Kennedy treated Annie as though she was a scatter-brained girl. "A hoyden" was what she called her. Seemed they knew each other quite well. But Mrs Kennedy frightened me a bit. She was so *right*, in a very sweet, reasonable way, of course. Also, she tended to treat me as a friend's aberration, which had to be borne with good grace. Still, the working conditions were great, if only you could get away from the noise. That compound at Hyannis Port was alive with the sound of yelling kids from dawn to long after dusk. Quite a few yelling adults, too. They were a very large, noisy family.'

'But they were happy.'

'I suppose so. But does happiness need all that *proof*? To be honest, I got on better with old Joe Kennedy. He knew what made everything happen. And he had a caustic tongue.'

'Wasn't he very ill at the time?'

'No. This was before he had his stroke. That happened right at the end of the year in Palm Beach. No, he was in fine, bitter form that summer.'

'Why was he bitter?'

'From what I heard at the dinner table and around the pool, Jack wasn't taking his advice. "Goddam it! Why else would I make him president except to get things done *right*?" Annie told him, "Ambassador, there's more than one way of doing things right." Old Joe wouldn't have that. "Sure! But he's not doing *any* of them."'

'Did you meet the president at Hyannis Port?'

'He came once while we were there. It seemed within seconds the whole place was packed with bodyguards, agents and marines. Then all the women were herded out.'

I gasped. 'What?'

'Sure. All the women moved across the yard to one house – family guests and children. All the men of the family and guards and advisors crowded into another house.'

'Which house were you in?'

He raised an eyebrow. 'With the women, naturally. But the only woman who objected to the harem mentality of the Kennedy men was Annie. She was furious. Rose Kennedy tried to calm

322

her down, but she was all for leaving right away. Rose told her, "You'd never get through the security cordon." Annie said, "Maybe not, but it would give them one hell of a fright that somebody's trying to break *out*." '

I smiled. 'It was a curious way to treat a guest.'

Tim nodded grimly, 'I tell you, they treated the servants better than the guests. That is, if you didn't like swimming. They loved swimmers at Hyannis.'

There was a pause while he contemplated the injustice of this and I took the opportunity to move him on. 'Did Annie do that revival for Irving Berlin when she came back from the tour?'

'No. They couldn't get the backing. And the music scene was changing. And Annie really was too old to play a romantic lead – even on the stage. Oh sure, Berlin thought she would be great. But then *he* was over seventy.'

'And there was no romantic lead for her off stage either?'

'None,' Tim said. 'So we waited around for a while then started planning another tour. Months of rehearsal on new material. A back-breaking, nail-biting slog. I don't know how she did it. The amount of time and work she put into it would have worn out a full cast of characters. But Annie had to master all of it on her own. Then, when the preparation was done, came the travelling. Trains and planes and ships. The second tour was even more gruelling than the first.

'This time Nederlander was the production company. We did the United States up the west coast.' He recited the names like a mantra. 'Los Angeles, San Francisco, Sacramento, Eureka, Salem, Portland, Tacoma, Seattle. Then on into Canada.' He took a quick breath. 'Vancouver, Calgary, Regina, Winnipeg, Ottawa, Montreal, Quebec. Now – across the Atlantic. France, Spain, Portugal, Spain again, France, West Germany, Italy, Portugal. Back across the Atlantic. Down the *east* coast of the States and right on overland into South America.' He took another breath. 'Venezuela, Brazil, Paraguay, Argentina, Bolivia, Colombia.' He shook his head. 'She might well ask, "What country, friends, *is* this?"'

'It took over three years from start to finish and long before the end we'd no idea where we were. The tour manager did all the booking and handled transport. And it was a tight schedule. The whole object was to get the merchandise from one earning location to another. It didn't matter a damn to them that the whole of the earning merchandise was wrapped up in one tiny woman already over the age when most people retire.

'For Annie and me it got so that nothing existed except movement, then a dark alley, then a lighted stage. Then more movement and another stage. On, and on, and on. After a while we didn't even notice the movement. There was just the houselights going down, the band playing "Lorelei", then two and a half hours in which every word, every gesture and every look was the same as the last time we'd come alive. It seemed as though we were the only two human beings who existed in the whole uncaring, foreign-speaking, fouled-up world. And we clung to that. We wouldn't budge, one without the other.'

Tim gave a long sigh. 'But, come the end of the second tour in 1967, I'd had more than enough. When she got on the plane for New York, I cut out for Florida.' Even at this remove the consequence gave him pause. 'I'm sure it wouldn't have happened if I'd stayed with her. You see, Nederlander had arranged to put her into the Palace, "Just to round things off."' He slapped the arm of the chair angrily. 'Just to round things *off*? Christ, they nearly rounded *her* off. Later I heard. It seems she arrived at the theatre all right. Well, not all right, but *there*. Like she was in a trance, they said. But when the boy went round to call the half, he found her dresser in hysterics. Annie was sitting stark naked and cataleptic. They couldn't bend her limbs. They had to carry her out strapped to the chair and covered with a blanket. So – one more dark alley but this time only a short journey . . . then, nothing. It took her six months in hospital to recover. That was the last time I saw her in hospital. In fact, that was the last time I saw her at all – until yesterday.'

There was a long silence. I stopped the recorder and asked him, 'What did you do after Annie came back to England?'

'Oh, I did some radio work. Directed a few plays in Tampa. Then I got into television. That's what I do now. I'm a T.V.

presenter for a talent show.' He got up and stretched his arms, standing in front of the fire. 'It's a living. And it doesn't take very much out of me – which is just as well because I don't have that much . . . now.'

This seemed rather worrying. 'You are in good health, aren't you?'

'Sure! Oh, sure. My health is fine. It's just that whatever I gave Annie in those years with her, she kept. It wasn't long after I left her I realised that. She kept part of me.' He grinned. 'And knowing her, it was probably the best part.' His expression sobered. 'In fact I *know* it was the best part.'

'And what do you think you have kept of her?'

He looked down at me for a moment then shrugged. 'Good question.' He strolled away from the fire, towards the window, thinking about it. 'I suppose what I've kept . . . what she wanted me to keep was her uncertainty. Fear, sometimes. Many times when she was low she'd tell me how unsure of herself she was. Being who I was, she could confess things to me she wouldn't tell any other man. Personal things, mainly. Weaknesses that nobody else was allowed a hint of. And when she'd told me, I could see it made her feel better.' He chuckled. 'Let somebody else carry the albatross for a while.'

I joined him at the window and we both looked out across the Clyde under a strong westerly which dotted the surface with white wave caps. 'Since you were so close,' I said, 'why didn't you come back to London with her?'

'She didn't need me in London. Not then. They'd finally let her in, you see. The National Theatre, West End transfers, then a Dame. When you think how hard it was for her to get in on her own, there was no way she could have made a place for me.'

'I don't believe that was the reason.'

He turned to look at me squarely. 'Don't you, Bill?'

'No. I think you were afraid to take any more responsibility for her.'

'Maybe so.' He grinned. 'Anyway, I sure as hell wanted to get on with my own life while the going was still fairly good.'

*   *   *

The following day I drove Tim up to the hospital and we went in to see Annie together. But really it wouldn't have made any difference if I had not been there. Though still very weak, she was wide awake and extended her arms to welcome Tim. He went to the bed and practically lifted her out of it with the all-enveloping strength of his embrace. When, after much kissing, he laid her back, she cried, 'Tim! Tim dear, why are you *here*? I'm not dying am I?'

'Apparently not. But I thought you were.'

She smiled and shook her head. 'Poor lamb. All this way for nothing.' She gripped his hand. 'And you can't even claim for expenses!'

'Lousy management,' Tim said. 'God's even more tight-fisted than the Shuberts used to be.'

'I *am* sorry.'

Tim straightened up. 'Of course . . .' He gave a sly look at the nurse then me. 'If you want to make it worth my while . . .' He turned a full and ingratiating smile on the patient. 'How about a quick *relapse*?'

Annie gave a hearty laugh which ended in a cough. She tried to speak before she had the breath for it. 'In . . . in *this* . . . costume?'

Tim gave her a hostile assessing stare, then turned up his nose at the costume. 'A touch of the Motleys on a bad night.'

He went on to tell her about the T.V. talent show he hosted – and even gave some impressions of some inept contestants.

I could see Annie was delighted in his company. He made her laugh so much the nurse grew worried. But the patient waved her away. 'This,' she said, 'is the best medicine I've had since I came here.'

As I watched them together I persuaded myself that I was just irritated that Tim was òvertiring Annie. But that wasn't really it. In fact, I was jealous. Weak though she was, I'd never seen her so unguarded and happy. She'd never been like that with me – even during our closest conversations.

And now I could see in her a kind of childlike willingness to please – which was totally at odds with everything I'd heard about her. Was that always there? Was that really what the audience saw and loved? If so, I could never recapture it. I'd never seen her on the stage. The incongruous idea occurred to me that perhaps it was her personality *off*stage which was acted. That daunting, implacable performance as the egocentric monster might well be the illusion. It could well be no more than the armour she put on to protect the girl locked inside her.'

I turned away from the real, vulnerable and happy old woman and went out into the corridor to wait for Tim. It was another half-hour before he came out – and then only because the nurse had summoned the Sister to get rid of him. I rose from a deep armchair as he came down the thickly carpeted corridor. He seemed startled that I should be there. 'Bill! I didn't know . . .' Then he remembered that I had been with him when he arrived and changed the remark. 'I'm sorry to keep you waiting.'

As arranged, I drove him to the airport. Several times he tried to start a conversation, but got no encouragement from me. And yet there were so many things I wanted to ask him. Or, at least, many things I *should* have asked him. What stopped me was the fear of finding yet more evidence that I was a hopeless outsider. During the drive my resentment was still keen.

I dropped him at the Abbotsinch forecourt. We exchanged a few formal observations. But he must have realised exactly what was bothering me. When I was about to pull away he tapped on the window and I wound it down.

'Bill,' he said. 'I lived and worked with Annie for seven years. We're partners.'

'Yes. I realise that.'

'Sure. But you don't realise what it means.'

'And what does it mean?'

'We're part *owners*. Of each other.'

He gave me an encouraging smile, then shook my hand and strode in to the building.

As I drove back over the Erskine Bridge my feeling of despair lifted a little. There really was no point in my regretting my exclusion from the very close, mutually dependent life which Tim had described. Those journeys, hotels, dark alleys and lighted stages all over the world were lost. And there was no point in trying to imagine what it felt like to be either of those individuals bound together by professional necessity and love. 'As the Americans say,' I told myself, 'you'd have to have been there.'

That night I discussed the question with Barbara. It was something she knew all about. She said, 'In the theatre, we have a very strong cast system. For example, take the last few days of any rehearsal period. That's when *esprit de corps* goes into overdrive. The cast of the play – whether they like each other or not – becomes an indivisible unit. Anybody who is not in that cast is an alien – that includes husbands, wives, lovers and family. That grip does not relax until several weeks after the opening, or when the production closes.'

'I haven't noticed that with you.'

'Only because I make a conscious effort to conceal it.'

'Do you?'

'Yes, of course. I often have to pretend you are real.'

I laughed. But that did connect with everything else I'd noted about the relationship with Annie and Tim Gilchrist. 'Do you think Annie is convinced I'm real?'

Barbara suddenly appreciated how deeply I'd been affected. Instead of lying to me, she tried evasion. 'What does it matter?'

'I'm worried that the book might not be accurate.'

'Bill, the book is for people who never *met* Annie Jeynor. They won't know the difference – and they won't care, either way.'

WILLIAM URQUHART, JP

At the beginning of March there were several fine and fairly warm days. Annie felt well enough to go out of doors for the first time since she'd come back from hospital. It was no more than a walk around the garden, but it was a start. Elspeth and I kept pace on either side of her, each of us resisting the temptation to take her arm and give support. The exercise lasted some twenty minutes and then, with every sign of irritation, she had to turn back towards the house.

It seemed to me I had already collected all the material that could be used in the book. After all, the period from her seventies to the present was free of significant male relationships. The following day, when we were seated on the porch after lunch, I asked her to confirm that I had dealt in some way with all the men in her life.

'All except the first,' she said.

I thought she'd forgotten. 'Albert Lane? We've covered him.'

'I know *that*,' she retorted sharply. 'At the time when I met Albert I was over twenty.'

'Yes. Was there someone before that?'

She gave me an impatient look. 'Of course. William Urquhart.' She tapped the boards of the porch with her walking stick. 'This is his house. Hmmm! A lot warmer now than it was in *his* day.'

I was astonished. 'Who was William Urquhart?'

It now got through to her that it was not oversight on my part which had left the man out. Nowadays she had to be careful about blaming things on people, because often it turned out to be her own fault. The illness had affected more than her mobility. Her clarity of mind was not as it had been and her speech was slower. She said, 'I'll be eighty-five or eighty-six. In a few days.'

'Eighty-one,' I corrected. 'On the eleventh.'

'Did I tell you that?'

'No. Tim Gilchrist told me.'

She smiled. 'Ah, yes. Young Tim. It's *his* birthday.' Leaning carefully towards me she added, 'And it is his *proper* birthday. He'll be fifty-one. I must send him a present.'

'I think you already have sent him a present.'

She didn't argue. 'Oh, good!'

I returned to the puzzling assertion before she might forget she'd made it. 'Isn't the eleventh of March *your* proper birthday?'

'No. That's when I came here. To this house.'

I took it slowly. 'You mean, you came here, on your birthday, a few years ago?'

Annie gave me an incredulous look. 'A *few* years? No! About . . . *eighty* years ago. Early in March. And Mr Urquhart decided we would count that as my birthday. Later on, I counted it from that year as well as that day. As though I'd been born in this house.'

This seemed to me rather fanciful. I smiled. 'What did your parents think about it?'

'My parents?' Annie seemed to recall them with some difficulty. 'Mrs Jeynor said I must have nothing more to do with my parents.' She turned to me helpfully. 'Mrs Jeynor was the cook.'

'Mr Urquhart's cook?'

'That's right.'

Every statement she made seemed more bewildering than the previous one. 'So the cook was a relation of yours?'

'No. Why do you say that?'

'It's just the name. She had the same name as you.'

Annie laughed. And the laughter brought on her cough. 'No! I . . . had . . . *her* name. They gave me her name.' She composed herself and took a deep breath. 'After all, if I was living in a house, I had to have *two* names – like everybody else. Just being called "Annie" wasn't enough.'

'Annie,' I said, 'I'm very confused. Let's start at the beginning.'

'The beginning.' She nodded. 'All right.' She placed her walking stick carefully and, using that and the arm of the chair, she

330

levered herself to her feet. When the manoeuvre was fully accomplished she looked at me triumphantly. 'Would you like to see where I was born?'

'Yes! Oh, yes, I would!' I got to my feet. 'I'll bring the car round.'

'No need,' she said. 'Just come this way.'

She led me slowly down through the garden and onto the track which led to the shore. It was a narrow track which sloped quite steeply in some places. I was as close behind as possible, so that I could steady her if she faltered. It was a sunny afternoon and though there was a cold breeze off the Clyde the conditions were quite pleasant. When we reached the paved esplanade along the high water mark, Annie sat on a bench and beckoned me to join her.

She gestured with her stick. 'This is all new, of course. There used to be nothing but rough pasture between the tide and the hill.'

I looked along the deserted stretch between the headland upriver to the widening estuary. 'This is called Havoc, isn't it?'

'That's right. Between Dumbarton there, and Cardross further down. You can't see it today, but the sand is a reddish colour, and very fine. Too fine. You can't build sandcastles with Havoc sand.' She glanced away from it and up at the house, where the upper windows could be seen. Annie pointed with her stick and then described a sloping movement – as though siting the trajectory of a shell to a spot about a hundred yards from the bench. 'Over by that bridge,' she said. 'There used to be a clump of gorse bushes at the mouth of the burn.' Again she got to her feet and I followed.

From the line of wintry trees which straggled up the sloping ground I reckoned that probably there had been a stream. It was covered over now.

Annie stopped. Once more she lined up her position with the upper corner of the house. 'Here,' she said, 'I was born under a tarpaulin.'

In 1906, William Urquhart was forty-two, still unmarried, and settled in the large, gloomy house above the Clyde shore. His

331

family were import merchants across the river in Greenock. Their principal trade was sugar. William, the second son, had no interest in the business. As soon as his income was assured, he was glad to grant full responsibility to his elder brother and escape from the bustling, reeking, dock office. Soon afterwards, he became a JP.

He was a tall, quiet, bookish man with some artistic talent. Frequently he was able to sell his watercolours to dealers in Glasgow. He travelled a great deal and developed a passionate interest in the performing arts. His neighbours, who were mainly in shipping or shipbuilding, considered Urquhart a rather pretentious fellow; unsociable and too much of a dreamer. Certainly, there was some feminine interest when he first moved to the area. He was still in his early thirties then and handsome, in a rather distant way. A rich, eligible bachelor had been added to the pool. Their optimism was soon doused by his constant refusal to involve himself with his neighbours – and particularly with girls of marriageable age.

Urquhart didn't mind his unpopularity. Life was full enough with his own solitary pursuits. Nor did he need a wife. His house was well staffed with servants and efficiently run by his housekeeper-cook, Emily Jeynor. She was a respectable widow, devoted member of the Kirk, and widely regarded as a shrewd and sensible woman.

Urquhart's study was upstairs, in the corner of the building with a good clear view over the river. It pleased him to watch the endless succession of ships on their way to or from the Glasgow docks. He had a telescope so that he could identify the name and registry port of any vessel which was not familiar. Then he would consult his reference tables to discover where it had come from, so that he could imagine the voyage now ending before him. He was pleased, too, by the changing face of the river under different conditions and by the progression of the seasons.

In particular he noted that every spring the vagrant tinkers set up camp on that part of the shore he could see from his window. They always came in March. Usually it was about the middle of the month, but sometimes earlier, sometimes later.

Apparently they moved on long-established paths from the south of England to the north of Scotland – keeping pace with the gradual warming of the country. Urquhart entered the date they arrived in his journal, together with any other observations which occurred to him.

Sometimes, when the tinkers were there, he went down to walk along the shore. He was fascinated by their skill. They mended iron pots and pans, they mended and sharpened garden implements and they made baskets. They also made weird little ornaments of ancient design. All their abilities seemed to be bred in them, requiring no learning and little effort. This particular group, he learned, was part of an Irish clan. They spoke Irish gaelic among themselves with great vivacity. Their English was halting, heavily accented and servile. All of them had thick, tightly crinkled orange-coloured hair, high cheek bones, short noses and long upper lips. There seemed to be at least three separate families in the camp, but they lived and traded as one large family.

There were always several children, and on one occasion Urquhart's attention was claimed by a very pretty little girl. She was no more than four or five years old. Her hair was a darker shade than that of the other children, but equally thick and frizzy. Thinking she was unobserved, the child was dancing on the wet sand just at the water line. And dancing with an invisible partner to whom she extended her arms, and curtseyed and smiled. Urquhart stood watching for some minutes. The little creature was so tiny and neat and graceful. Barefoot, she left a whirling, looping track on the wet sand as she danced to her own imagined music.

But there were chores to be done. A woman emerged from the tent and shouted, 'Annie!' The child immediately froze, then turned and started to run back to the camp. As she passed Urquhart she paused, aware that he must have been watching her. She looked boldly up at him and smiled.

After a week or two on the Havoc shore, the Irish tinkers moved on to the north. And Urquhart resumed his summer hobby of driving out into the country with pony and trap on sketching and painting excursions. But he did not forget the little dancing figure on the sand. He painted a watercolour of the scene and hung it in his study.

It became his favourite, though only the latest of several paintings he'd done of little girls. Urquhart was very fond of little girls. He told Mrs Jeynor that they brightened his life with their chatter. And she, of course, always needed help in the kitchen. Actually, she would have preferred older girls for the work, but the master seemed to have little patience with these small casual labourers once they reached puberty.

The next year, the same families came back again. And the dainty girl was still with them, a year older and grown a bit. She came with her mother to the back door selling the ornaments painted with archaic design. Mrs Jeynor sent them away. But Urquhart was out walking and met them on their way back to the camp. He bought several pieces and thus gained the confidence of the girl's mother. She asked if there was any mending the gentleman wanted done. He felt sure there must be and asked them to go back with him to the house.

During the two weeks of the camp there was a regular exchange between the big house and the shore. Usually Annie was the messenger. She'd never been *inside* a house before and was amazed by the grandeur of this one. At first she only got as far as the kitchen. After a few visits, though, the gentleman asked if she'd like to see the other rooms. He also showed her the painting of herself. She laughed with delight. Then the gentleman played the piano and she danced for him again. He seemed very pleased and told her he wanted to speak to her mother.

When the camp was being dismantled that year, her mother asked her if she would like to live in the big house with the kind gentleman and work in the kitchen? Annie could think of nothing she would like more.

'How could that possibly happen?' I asked Annie.

'What could prevent it happening?' she challenged me. 'My mother knew that after a year she would be back again – and would see if I was all right. It meant one less mouth to feed. And Mr Urquhart gave her my wages in advance.'

'Did your father not object?'

'I don't think my father was there at the time.'

'Surely you remember?'

Annie smiled at my naïveté. 'I mean, there was no way of knowing which of the men was my father. I don't suppose my mother knew that, either. There were four or five men in the camp.'

'Oh. I see.' But suddenly a void had opened before me. 'Well, which man was your mother living with at the time?'

'We were all living together,' Annie said. 'But in our tent there was . . . my grandmother, my mother, my three sisters, my two brothers – and my mother's brother.' She shook her head. 'Is it any wonder I preferred a bed raised off the ground and an attic room to myself?'

'No. I suppose not.'

The first few months passed very quickly for Mrs Jeynor's new little helper. Everything about life in the house was so new. And the work was not hard, though the hours were long. She had no trouble getting up at dawn to clear out the ashes and set the fires. She took some pleasure in cleaning and scouring the pots until they shone. Soon she was trusted to run errands – carrying notes from Mrs Jeynor to the shopkeepers in the town. They asked her what her name was and she said, 'Annie.' To her surprise they then asked, 'Annie who?' She didn't know the answer to that. But the tradesmen and shopkeepers connected the name on the notes with the only name the girl would give. So they called her Annie Jeynor.

Whereas her duties in the kitchen seemed straightforward enough, the things Mr Urquhart wanted her to do were puzzling. He wanted her to look at little pictures which all had different sounds. Mr Urquhart made the sounds over and over and pointed at the picture. Then Annie must make the sound. This, he told her, was called 'reading'. And, apparently, it was very important to breathe properly when making the sounds. To help in this, Mr Urquhart placed his hands around her waist or over her ribs and squeezed. For other sounds he ran his hand up and down her back or pressed it between her legs. Even so, he was often disappointed that she wasn't making the right sound. He said that this was because her clothes were restricting her breathing. On difficult days she had to take all her clothes off. Mr Urquhart was usually pleased with the sounds she made then.

Mrs Jeynor seemed more worried about her hair than her breathing. The housekeeper had a strong aversion to the girl's tangled, frizzy, glaringly red hair. It didn't matter when the child wasn't seen in public, but frequently she accompanied Mrs Jeynor shopping in the town. The good lady was mortified to be seen with a creature who was so obviously a tinker. Something would have to be done about it. To begin with, it was just a matter of cutting, thinning and constantly washing. But still the tight frizzy waves held firm, and the colour of the hair when it was clean seemed even worse. Mrs Jeynor decided it would have to be dyed. It was dyed black. But still the indestructible kinks remained.

During Annie's first winter in the big house she found her tiny attic bedroom warm and cosy. She could read now and Mr Urquhart allowed her to borrow books from his library. Usually she chose books with large print and lots of pictures. The books with the prettiest pictures, in colour, were those about the stage and the music hall. Often Mr Urquhart would help her with her reading. And often he read to her. He read her fairy tales which held her spellbound in the telling and whose characters peopled her imagination long after the reading was done.

He also told her about her own people. There was one book which dealt with nothing else. The book was called *Lavengro*. Young Annie took that beautiful word to be her very own and joyfully repeated it to herself. Lavengro. It had the scent of wild lavender and the promise of growing. Mr Urquhart read to her from the growing lavender book:

> '*There's night and day, brother, both sweet things;*
> *Sun, moon, and stars, brother, all sweet things;*
> *There's likewise a wind on the heath.*
> *Life is very sweet, brother;*
> *Who would wish to die?*'

336

That was so beautiful she learned it by heart. It was Mr Urquhart who called it 'learning by heart'. And it was amazing how quickly her heart learned to do it. How marvellous it was, she thought, that she could carry a bit of the book about in her heart. And yet when she looked in the book, it was still there as well.

But Annie liked it just as much when he talked to her about the wonderful plays he had seen and about the great actresses, singers, dancers who always included Glasgow on their tours. He also talked about the marvellous buildings and theatres he'd visited abroad. The girl soaked up all this information.

Indeed, she found Mr Urquhart a very gentle, kind man who often rejected the complaints which Mrs Jeynor made about her. But it seemed he was a man who suffered a great deal from cold. It was during that first winter he asked Annie, 'Are you warm enough in your room up there?'

'Yes, sir. Thank you.'

'I am glad to hear that. It must be warmer than *my* bedroom.' He smiled at her. 'Of course, my bed is much larger than yours.'

Annie nodded. 'Oh yes, sir. For you are so larger than me.'

'Much larger,' he corrected. 'And much colder. It seems nothing can be done to improve matters. Blankets, hot water bottles are no help. The water gets cold, you see.'

Annie nodded brightly.

'What I really need,' he said softly, 'is somebody to keep me warm. To fill up that large bed.'

The girl saw the sense in that. When she'd been with her family in the tent they often had to lie all together with the youngest on the inside to keep warm. She mentioned this to Mr Urquhart and he agreed it was very sensible. 'Young people are much warmer than older people,' he said.

And that was how it was arranged. On cold nights, Annie went first to her own room to change, then she went down to Mr Urquhart's bedroom. He was always in bed by then and threw back the clothes so that she could lie beside him. At first she was surprised by how he looked in a nightshirt but she got used to that. She also got used to his body when he asked her to lie on top of him. Of course she had seen naked men before

337

– there is little privacy in a tent – but she had not realised how delightful it was to be held in a man's arms. Only her mother had held her before, and not very often.

The old woman smiled at the recollection of the tousle-haired girl in the big bed. 'That,' she said, 'awoke a need in me which was never really satisfied.'

I was shocked. 'How could such things go on? Didn't Mrs Jeynor know? Or the maids?'

'If they did, it didn't bother them. Probably they didn't know. The maids were at the top of the house. Mrs Jeynor was down in her room next to the kitchen. There was nobody on Mr Urquhart's floor at all. And I went back to my room before anyone else was stirring.'

'But surely *you* knew it was wrong?'

'No. I was six or seven years old that first winter. Nobody had told me it was wrong. In fact, I found it very pleasant to be caressed and hugged. He never did me any harm, you see. There was no question of rape or intercourse.'

'But he must have been aroused – having you in bed with him.'

'Oh yes! But at the time I thought that's what always happened to men as soon as they went to bed.' Annie shook her head wryly. 'You can imagine how disillusioned I was later on in life.'

'Really, Annie, I don't think this is anything to joke about.'

'Then or later?' She laughed.

'It could have caused serious psychological damage.'

'Rubbish! Children are much tougher and more resilient than they're given credit for. It's all the wishy-washy do-gooders who cause the trouble later.'

'That is unfair.'

'It's true! All these experts are expert adults. They don't see it from the child's point of view. And they pass their sense of guilt onto the child. But the child never thought there was anything to be guilty about.'

'Annie, they go out of their way to avoid that.'

'Well, they don't succeed. Thank God there were no social workers when I was a child. For, it wasn't Mr Urquhart who

338

scarred me for life. It was Mrs Jeynor. If not for life, a long miserable part of it.'

Mrs Jeynor continued with her obsession of straightening Annie's hair. For several weeks one potion was tried every night. When that did not produce any obvious result, another concoction was tried. All the while, Annie's scalp was absorbing punishment. But still the search went on for a method which would straighten the stubborn hair. That method was never found. Then, after two years, the hair started falling out.

The tinkers came back each spring. Some years Annie's mother was with them, some years she wasn't. But she never made any enquiries about the daughter who had been so favourably placed. Meanwhile, the child's education was advanced by Mr Urquhart. Having taught her to read he taught her to write – and then to count. All of these lessons were ingeniously arranged so that the teacher gained as much benefit from them as the pupil.

And it wasn't all work. There were always a few hours each day which Annie had to herself. In this free time she explored the town and the surrounding countryside. She traced the River Leven from where it enters the Clyde at Dumbarton, back five miles up the valley to its source in Loch Lomond.

The banks of the river were bustling with activity. The whole Leven valley was given over to textiles. Bleaching, dyeing and printing works all required an abundance of fresh, clean water and the Leven supplied it. Huge steaming, gurgling factories were strung out along its banks on both sides. Their chimneys towered into the sky. But, even a little way back from this industry, the hillsides were gently sloping and green.

By the time she was twelve years old, Annie Jeynor was better educated than most girls of her age. But she was also completely bald. That distressed her very much. Mrs Jeynor realised that her dedicated treatment had gone too far and provided the girl with little lace bonnets which tied under the chin. The effect was not satisfactory. For, since there was no bulk of hair under the bonnets, they clung to Annie's scalp and made her look emaciated. Mr Urquhart was not pleased with the effect. And besides, she was getting rather bigger now than suited his needs. He told her that next spring it might be better if she went back to live with her own folk. Annie accepted the decision but privately doubted if the clan would have her back.

And they would not. As soon as the tinkers' camp was pitched she was sent down to them. Before she got to the tents, several boys set upon her, jeering and plucking at her clothes. They also snatched off her cap and shrieked with laughter at her bald head. The girl wanted to turn and run but doggedly walked forward to the group around the camp fire. Her own family was not there. Nor did she recognise any of those who were there. And they refused to believe she could be one of them. They sent her back to the house, mudspattered and weeping.

Annie knew she was no longer wanted in the house. She had the money Mr Urquhart had given her as a parting gift. She was now old enough to work at a proper job. It seemed as good a time as any to start out on her own. She walked away from the house and took the road into the town. On the way, there was time to consider which shopkeeper would be most likely to employ her.

As Annie recalled her early youth, I got the impression that she was recovering much of her former vigour. Perhaps it was merely time and a lot of rest which improved her condition but I was sure she also derived strength from the relief of telling these things she'd kept secret for so long. And I took it as a rare compliment that she should tell it to me.

I asked her, 'Have you decided you can "afford" this honesty?'

She remembered our earlier conversation and nodded firmly. 'Yes.'

'Why have you changed your mind?'

'I almost died in the hospital. That made me realise there's nothing I can't afford now. There's no use saving what you'll never be able to spend.'

This sounded rather gloomy. 'Nonsense. There's no telling what you'll get up to next.'

'Bill,' she said briskly, 'I'm eighty-six. What do you have in mind?'

There was nothing I could think of, offhand.

She went on, 'Besides, I don't want people like that Sleavin woman digging about when I'm dead and blackening Mr Urquhart's name. I don't want you doing it either.'

I was astonished. 'He deserves to have his name blackened.'

Her voice was suddenly very strong again and charged with energy. 'No he does not!'

'Annie! A child molester.'

'Is a damn sight better than a man who'd starve a child, or beat it to death the way so many *fathers* do.'

My patience was running out. 'You cannot honestly condone child molesting.'

'No. I don't. But I want it known that William Urquhart was kind. Also, that I was grateful to him for the rest of my life for the knowledge, and wonder, and beauty he gave me.'

'Only because of the pleasure you gave to him.'

'I still got the best of the bargain,' Annie said. 'If it hadn't been for him I'd be dead years ago from hard winters, poor food and constant child bearing.' She challenged me, 'Suppose he had not plucked me off the shore? What would have become of me? A tinker wife to the very end. Nothing accomplished.'

It was very difficult to contest that argument. And it did not lessen my astonishment. Even with Mr Urquhart's help, it seemed quite remarkable that a child with such disadvantages could have achieved so much. There was no justice in it. For I shared the modern view that socially deprived children can expect nothing but failure. The fact is held sacred by psychologists, psychiatrists, sociologists, social workers, doctors and academics. They have all the statistics to prove it so. They lack only one essential factor. None of them was ever a deprived child; far less a nomadic tinker.

I made this point to Annie. We had resumed our afternoon walks. They were shorter, slower walks and now she always used a stick – but they were as lively as before. On the question of her poverty and social deprivation she was concise. 'I had talent,' she said. 'The real deprivation is lack of talent. Or congenital stupidity.'

'That seems a bit harsh.'

341

'It's a harsh world. Anybody who tries to disguise *that* fact is courting despair.'

On the question of her secrecy she was less direct. But she claimed she had not really hidden anything from me. The clues were there. And, when I considered it, I did find several. For example, there was Ma Duggan claiming that Annie was 'one of ours'; the playwright, J. M. Barrie, remarking on how convincing was her Irish accent; what she'd told Jamie about the Wandervögel camping on the banks of the Rhine. Also, what she'd said about watching women giving birth in open fields. Indeed, there were all kinds of remarks and allusions I'd glossed over which now fell into place.

I asked Annie why she had wanted to settle there, in that house.

'It was a dream of mine,' she said. 'And because I dreamed it when I was very young, nothing was ever strong enough to replace it.' She bent her head suddenly, as though embarrassed with what she was about to say. 'And I thought I might repay a little.'

'In what way?'

'Well, I was sure the tinkers must still camp down there on the shore – and I thought that one day there might be a little girl dancing.' She tried to dismiss this fanciful suggestion with a gesture of her hand. But the idea would not go away. 'Oh, not necessarily a little girl. But a child, anyway, who could be offered a new world as I was.'

'Annie! That would be marvellous.'

'Yes, it would be. But, after a couple of years, I found out. The tinkers don't come this way any more.'

When she left the big house, the fishmonger on Dumbarton quay was willing to give her a job. She spent a couple of years gutting and cleaning fish before she was promoted to serving in the shop. Neither job paid very well, but it was enough to keep her in a garret down the Vennel.

The first major change in her fortunes came with the war. The Argyle motor works in nearby Alexandria was taken over as a munitions factory, locally known as 'the Gunwork'. They wanted girls to fill shells and they were offering good wages. Annie jumped at the chance for there was another advantage to the job. The employees had to wear protective headscarves *all* the time. Thus nobody need find out that her hair was still pitifully thin and patchy.

The Gunwork was a very cheerful place and soon Annie was one of the most popular girls there. Dancing was already the craze and she could dance. Better, she could teach her new friends how to dance. Lunch hour was devoted to little else, with Annie at the centre of attention. She enjoyed that. She also enjoyed the independence which her increasing wage allowed.

She started to save. As the war dragged on her savings grew. She bought new clothes and stored them with great care. And all the time her hair was growing back. Straight hair now. Straight, glossy auburn hair. Mrs Jeynor had done her a favour after all.

When the war ended she went to the dyeworks for nearly two years. But all the time she was planning the great change that would soon be possible. She was going to be a professional dancer. There was a place in Glasgow where she went for lessons, but really she did not need them. She was ready. And, being ready, she set out for London.

Barbara was due back in London to start rehearsals for a new play. I'd worked hard at the book so that I'd be free to go back with her. But a few days before we were due to leave Dumbarton, Annie fell ill again. At first it seemed just tiredness.

Barbara said, 'You must stay with her.'

'It's not necessary. A few days in bed, she'll be all right again.'

'Maybe. But you can't desert her when she might need you.'

'My book's finished. We've got to get back to London.'

'*I've* got to get back. Why do you have to?'

I was bewildered by the edginess of her tone. 'Well . . . to be with you. I mean, the arrangement was that we'd both stay here for your season in Glasgow, then go back to London.'

Barbara, seated at the dressing table, continued to brush her hair, not looking at me. Then, as though clarifying something in her own mind, she said, 'You really don't have your own life.'

'What was that?'

She spoke louder, still looking into her own eyes in the mirror. 'I said, you don't have a life of you own.'

'Barbara! Don't be ridiculous. *We* have *our* life.'

With a sudden movement she turned completely round. 'No, Bill. *We* have *my* life.'

Early the following morning Mrs MacKenzie roused us to go at once to Annie's bedroom. The old woman was much worse. She was awake but did not seem to recognise us. She lay on her back with her arms stretched out and her hands making curious, quick, darting gestures. There was a pallor on her skin and her eyes seemed incapable of focusing.

Barbara asked the housekeeper, 'Have you called the doctor?'

'No. Not yet.'

'Call him now.'

Mrs MacKenzie hurried from the room.

I went close to the bed. The old woman looked up at me, as though fearing some threat. 'Annie. What's wrong?'

With evident effort she tried to reply. Her mouth worked convulsively and the muscles of her jaw strained. But there was no sound.

We could hear Mrs MacKenzie's voice from the landing as she spoke to the doctor's receptionist. She came back and told us the doctor had had an urgent call and had gone off early.

Annie's movements became more frantic. Her hands searched the bed on each side of her and her body was trembling. Mrs MacKenzie said, 'I think she's cold. Shall I get another blanket?'

Barbara shook her head. 'I don't think that would help. It's more than cold.' Then, with quick decisive movements she took off her dressing gown, kicked off her slippers and got into Annie's bed. Immediately, the old woman's frantic searching stopped. Barbara moved closer to her. Slowly, gently she placed Annie's thin arms around her neck. The arms tightened and gripped hard behind my wife's head. Barbara pulled the frail little body against her and held Annie in a tight embrace.

Mrs MacKenzie and I looked on in amazement. The trembling stopped. Annie seemed to relax. Her eyes lost their wild staring

344

look and, after a moment, her mouth creased in a faint smile. But there were tears running down Barbara's cheeks.

The housekeeper went back to the landing telephone to call an ambulance.

It was a while before the ambulance or the doctor arrived. And, by then, Annie was dead. It was difficult to tell exactly when it happened though I was watching all the time. Barbara continued to stroke Annie's hair as they lay locked together in that bedroom overlooking the Clyde shore. The little tinker girl had taken a very long way home. She'd also become someone else. Finally, though, she was in the arms of her own kind. She died warm, and comforted, and knowing she was loved.

TOM GALLACHER

JOURNEYMAN

'For reasons I'm ashamed of now, I was living in Montreal in the spring of 1967.'

Bill Thompson is hiding out in scruffy digs on the city's lower east side, a refugee from his own father and his father's ambitions for him. He meets Glaswegian Hugh Gillespie. From completely different backgrounds, yet they grow close. Hugh, pursuer rather than pursued, is seeking out a long vanished childhood friend.

Both sense that their lives are at a turning point. Against the blare and glare of Montreal's Expo 67 – the World Fair – optimism, idealism and wishful thinking are shown up and reduced down in the harsh light of reality.

'A perfect command of dialogue and of pace'
Norman Shrapnel in The Guardian

'Depth and complexity of viewpoint . . . I hope he will give us more'
The Scotsman

'A fast-paced novel with some of the elements of a thriller . . . It is an excellent read'
British Book News

TOM GALLACHER

SURVIVOR

When the tanker *Niome* goes down with the loss of five lives, Bill Thompson's relief at surviving is short lived. The cause of the explosion lay in the engine room and Bill is Chief Engineer.

As the accusations of negligence start, he in turn begins to suspect a deliberate sinking for the insurance payout. His careful detachment is under threat, his life suddenly full of complications. Then, as he falls in love, complexity is piled upon complexity. Yet it is through Barbara – an actress – that a way forward begins to open up and the trilogy begun with *Apprentice* comes full circle.

'Satisfying, honest, well-written work. I hope that those who haven't read the two accounts of Bill Thompson's earlier years will now feel prompted to do so'
Martin Seymour-Smith in the Financial Times

'I would put my money as a potential best-seller on the final volume of Tom Gallacher's trilogy about Bill Thompson'
Philip Thody in the Yorkshire Post

sceptre

TOM GALLACHER

THE JEWEL MAKER

Five fine short stories, each unravelled by the inquisitive mind of Howard Murray, playwright and would-be detective.

'Crisply stylish and often incisively witty, THE JEWEL MAKER is an absorbing sequence of tales . . . [Howard Murray's] fascinations are instantly infectious and his detective work provides a compelling element of suspense'
The Times Literary Supplement

'Convincingly set in Dublin, London and Lewes, a Highland cottage, New York and Copenhagen, as ever Gallacher has a fine ear for dialogue and creates dramatic encounters between characters. [Howard Murray's] deductions are often worthy of Sherlock Holmes'
The Scotsman

'His craftmanship is clever and inventive, his thinking original and the matter of fact and fiction that links together the stories will prove irresistible to the curious reader'
The Irish Times

'His are theatrical stories in every sense of the word and the dialogue is particularly strong'
Glasgow Herald

'Gallacher is a superb storyteller – inventive, amusing and a master of dialogue'
British Book News

Current and forthcoming titles from Sceptre

TOM GALLACHER

APPRENTICE
JOURNEYMAN
SURVIVOR
THE JEWEL MAKER

WILLIAM McILVANNEY

THE BIG MAN
DOCHERTY
WALKING WOUNDED

GUY VANDERHAEGHE

MY PRESENT AGE
MAN DESCENDING

BOOKS OF DISTINCTION